VANISHING

GERARD WOODWARD is the author of a number of novels, including *Nourishment* and an acclaimed trilogy comprising *August* (shortlisted for the 2001 Whitbread First Novel Award), *I'll Go to Bed at Noon* (shortlisted for the 2004 Man Booker Prize) and *A Curious Earth*. He was born in London in 1961, and published several prize-winning collections of poetry before turning to fiction. His collection of poetry *We Were Pedestrians* was shortlisted for the 2005 T. S. Eliot Prize. His most recent poetry collection, *The Seacunny*, was published in 2012. He is Professor of Creative Writing at Bath Spa University.

GERARD WOODWARD

VANISHING

PICADOR

First published 2014 by Picador

First published in paperback 2014 by Picador

This edition first published 2015 by Picador
an imprint of Pan Macmillan, a division of Macmillan Publishers Limited
Pan Macmillan, 20 New Wharf Road, London N1 9RR
Basingstoke and Oxford
Associated companies throughout the world
www.panmacmillan.com

ISBN 978-0-330-51865-9

1 3 5 7 9 8 6 4 2

A CIP catalogue record for this book is available from the British Library.

Printed and bound by CPI Group (UK) Ltd, Croydon, CR0 4YY

Visit www.picador.com to read more about all our books
and to buy them. You will also find features, author interviews and
news of any author events, and you can sign up for e-newsletters
so that you're always first to hear about our new releases.

To Suzanne,

For *Vanishing*, and for not vanishing

PART ONE

I

He came into my cell this morning. No knock, no announcement, just the approaching beat of nailed boots on a concrete floor, the oiled fuss of several keys in several locks, then the door swinging open, and Davies entering with a casual, off-hand saunter that contrasted with the military stiffness of the armed guards who preceded him. I was still in bed at this point, even though it was several hours after breakfast, and out of a sort of panic I decided to feign sleep, and lay there with my face half turned into the pillow, allowing a little dribble of saliva to roll off my lolling tongue.

'Lieutenant Brill,' he said, in quietly amused officer tones, making it obvious that he recognized my fakery, 'your snoring is most convincing, but I could see that your eye was open as I entered the room.'

The problem of pretending to be asleep is having to carry through the whole charade of waking up, which is somewhat harder to fake. How should one play it – the sudden startled bolt into the vertical, or the long, slow dredging of the self from the depths of dreamlessness? I went for the slower option, gradually lifting my head from the pillow, sucking in my remaining spit and blinking in the glare of Davies's uniform.

He was in full officer dress – Sam Browne, Brassoed buttons, a strip of medals, pips. He held his peaked cap beneath his left arm, along with a cardboard folder of documents. He smelt of snuffed candles.

'So sorry if I've disturbed your sleep, but I thought you would be up and about by now. I would call back later but I'm rather rushed. Would you mind getting up and dressed, so that we can talk properly?'

I looked around for my clothes. I had rather carelessly left them in a heap on the floor by the bottom of the bed. I had nothing on beneath my blanket. It had been a stiflingly hot night. Davies followed my gaze and recognized my concern. Wordlessly I hinted that he might do me the favour of picking up my clothes and passing them to me. He in turn gestured for one of the guards to do the deed, and the fellow promptly shouldered his tommy gun and bent down to pick up my things, handling them with arm's-length distaste, and depositing them on my bed. Seeming to think that this was sufficient, all three stood in a row and watched me, like an audience at a late-night cabaret.

'Am I allowed no privacy?' I said.

Davies smiled. 'After all these years in the army, you expect privacy?' He indicated with a wave of the fingertips that the guards could wait outside, and when they had gone he turned half away, so that he was facing the little window, high in the wall, which revealed nothing but sky. I struggled to dress while concealed beneath my blanket. Davies spoke without looking at me: 'This obstinate modesty of yours is rather touching. It's not something I would have expected of you. Not with your record.'

'I don't know what you mean.'

Davies went over to the small, bare table and placed his folder there. 'Though, on the other hand, perhaps your work in the Camouflage Corps has given you an instinctive urge for concealment. I imagine to be a successful camoufleur one must have a predilection for privacy. To be obsessive about it, even. It seems to go against the natural instincts of display and advertisement, the urge to announce one's existence to the world. Did you ever struggle with that contradiction?'

By now I had pulled on my trousers and the dirty pullover that was too hot for the room (but they would supply me with nothing else). Davies's remarks about concealment had put me half in mind of presenting my naked self to him, dropping the blanket and standing to attention by my bed, everything on display. How would he have liked that? I wondered.

'The only contradiction I've struggled with is that of a soldier who has served his country with distinction in one of the cruellest theatres of war and now finds himself incarcerated in a dirty little cell for no good reason at all. That's not just a contradiction, but a damned affront. An insult.'

'Sit,' Davies said, pointing to the bed. I had taken some steps forward and had raised my voice. I must have looked as if I was about to lose my temper. He reminded me that the guards were outside, and I sat meekly on the bed while he leafed through some of the documents he had extracted from his folder.

'By the way,' I said, 'I think it's quite ridiculous that you should think it necessary to have an armed escort when you come to my cell. What sort of person do you think I am?'

Davies smiled again. 'That is precisely what I'm here to find out. In the meantime, you mustn't mind the guards. This is a high-security establishment. Armed guards are the norm.'

'And what have I done that is so dangerous that I need to be locked up twenty-four hours a day, with a guard outside my door?'

'The charges have been explained to you, have they not?'

'They are absurd charges. And what do you think I'm going to do? Escape? You think I'll just disappear?'

'Well,' Davies laughed, 'that is your job, as you put it yourself.

You make things disappear. Whole armies, so you claim. What leads a man into a profession like that – to be so dedicated to the arts of deception? Was it anything to do with your father, perhaps?'

'My father? What has he got to do with it?'

'One of the increasing number of things we know about you is that you are the son of a man who spent some of his working life as a stage conjuror.'

I was momentarily stumped by this turn in the conversation. Very few people knew about my father's remote past; I myself had only learnt of his music-hall career a few years previously; that Davies should know about it was the first indication of the thoroughness with which they intended to conduct their investigation. Had they been to my father's house? Had they interrogated my innocent parents in their own home? Or, more worryingly, had they been arrested as well, to be held in some similarly bleak cell? I tried changing the subject.

'Do you have any idea what would have happened if we had lost at El Alamein? There was no other defendable line west of Suez. If we had failed, Egypt would have fallen, and without our foothold there, we might well have lost the whole of the Middle East. The Nazis would have taken control of the oil supplies, and could have marched eastwards to India, just as Napoleon had once dreamed, to capture the pride of our empire and meet the Japanese coming the other way. The Axis could have taken the whole land mass from Calais to the Bering Straits. And I heard that from the lips of General Auchinleck himself, outside an officer's tent on the edge of Benghazi.'

'Ah, yes, the battle of El Alamein in which you, as a camouflage officer, played such a vital role.'

It was always hard to tell when Davies was being sarcastic.

'Churchill himself praised our contribution . . .' I was going to go on to quote his speech, which I had off by heart: 'The Xth Corps, which the enemy had seen from the air exercising fifty miles in the rear, moved silently away in the night, but leaving an exact simulacrum of its tanks where it had been, and proceeded to its point of attack . . .'

'I just want to know how long I'm going to be kept here.'

Davies seemed not to hear and looked about the cell again, squinting closely at the walls. He touched the painted plaster with his fingertips and looked to see if it left a mark on his skin. Then he sat on the cell's only chair.

'You will be kept here for as long as it's deemed necessary.'

'But this is so damned ridiculous,' I said, raising my voice again. 'All I was doing was painting a picture. I've told you I'm an artist. Imprisoning an artist is a crime! It is murdering life in the bud!'

'Even if that artist is a spy?'

I was exasperated, and made no reply other than a moan of disbelief. I felt confused, unfocused. Since my arrest I had been cut off from all contact with the outside world and could only tell if it was day or night from the colour of the window.

'As I've said before, I don't see how the innocent act of painting a landscape can be construed as a form of spying.'

'And as I've said to you before, that landscape you happened to be painting is an area of extreme strategic sensitivity.' Davies said this with the patience of a Sunday-school teacher explaining Heaven to a little boy. 'Those few dirty fields you were painting in such detail are shortly to become one of the biggest military air bases in Europe. That land has all been requisitioned by the Air Ministry. There are notices to the effect all around the site. It has been said that you were earlier seen painting a view which included a squad of sappers digging a tank trap. I fail to understand how any artist could, on the one hand, find anything of artistic value in such a subject, and on the other, not realize they were doing something that could be construed as spying.'

I could tell that Davies was not a bully or a man without a sense of humour. He seemed to be roughly my age, perhaps even younger. He had the rosy knuckles and slender fingers of someone raised in a soft, comfortable household. His Adam's apple bobbed awkwardly in periods of silence. Whatever he was doing, whatever his role in this ridiculous affair, I suspected it was his first time. I began laughing.

'What are you laughing at?'

'I'm just trying to imagine myself posting one of my four-foot-by-three-foot oils on canvas to my accomplice in Germany, then a German bomber crew using it as they fly over to bomb the fields of cabbages. Would they have it mounted on an easel at the back of the cockpit, do you think?'

Davies appeared to ignore my musings, or at least to hear them only with his ears.

'You would be surprised, or perhaps not, at the lengths to which people go to convey secrets to the enemy. I've seen coded messages in the flecks of paint on a ceramic vase. I've seen map co-ordinates carved in mother-of-pearl on an inlaid vanity case. You would not be the first artist to put his skills to the service of espionage. And, I can assure you, your paintings are at this moment being examined in microscopic detail for any additional coded information. Perhaps you need reminding of the consequences if any such information is found.'

'No, I don't. And I can guarantee you that there is nothing in those paintings that could be of any use to the enemy.'

Our eyes met each other's and locked themselves in a stare for several seconds. Davies's Adam's apple bobbed. So did mine, I expect.

'So tell me again why you were out there in the middle of those godforsaken fields. In my humble opinion as someone who has had no artistic training, the landscape you were painting has no aesthetic value whatsoever. Is there an antonym for "picturesque"? If so, then those fields exemplify it perfectly.'

His provocative dismissal of the landscape of my childhood couldn't help but arouse a passion of indignation in me. 'Those godforsaken fields, as you call them, happen to be very important to me. I have known them since childhood. I have played in them, worked in them, wandered in them . . .' I paused, remembering to keep my voice down. I continued in a more conversational tone. Davies could be reached, I believed, if one trod the path of reason and common sense. He didn't respond well to outbursts of passionate rage. 'When I returned from Egypt I was quite horrified and heartbroken to discover that they are shortly to be destroyed by your Air Ministry, and that my father's house and all his land are to be swept away – you have ruined my father's fortune. But how can you comprehend the pain and struggle he has gone through to acquire it? Fighting all his life to claim his right to the land that has now been so callously and heartlessly taken from him. Not just that but our house as well – the whole village, the whole district. All those pretty cottages. That is why I was out in those godforsaken fields. I was trying to make a record of them before they are gone. Oh, you are such fools. You claim to be fighting for the English way of life while behind the scenes you are casually destroying that way of life.'

I had not managed to keep my voice under control. One of the guards opened the cell door and looked in. He glanced at Davies, who gave him a reassuring nod, and the guard resumed his post outside.

'Yes, very moving. But I'm glad you mentioned your father again. Tell me some more about his time as a stage magician. Did he teach you any of his tricks? I'm sure he must have entertained you in the evenings with some card magic when you were little. Or the rabbit from the hat, perhaps.'

'I'll tell you the biggest trick,' I carried on as before, assured, since the exchange of glances between Davies and the guard, that I was permitted to shout as much as I liked. 'The Air Ministry said it wouldn't pay him anything for his land because he didn't have any receipts. Receipts! Who do they think he is? The postmaster-general? The land came to him through his stepbrother, Tiberius Joy. Old enemies for many years, it was their final act of reconciliation. There were no documents, of course not. It was a gentlemen's agreement. But what would people like you know about that? He's ruined. Completely ruined, and taken away from the land he has loved all his life, and his ancestors before him . . .'

I stopped, realizing I was not doing myself any good at all. I was coming across as someone who had a deep grudge against the British government. Davies saw how I checked myself and read my mind perfectly. He gave a half-smile as he always did at such moments.

'So perhaps you would prefer it if that land and all the land that surrounds it were to be swept away instead by a tide of Nazi jackboots?'

I sighed. The war had become a religion. To question its strategy was like questioning the tenets of a faith, and no matter from which angle you examined it, no matter which argument you followed, it always came back to the same question: are you a believer or a non-believer? As such, it allowed for no argument, no discussion.

The folder Davies was leafing through looked alarmingly thick. I could glimpse densely typed pages, reports, charts, stamped documents. Davies continued, 'I would find your story easier to believe if your record hadn't thrown up so many surprises. I am assuming you are the same Kenneth Brill who was arrested in London in 1937 and charged with giving false information to the police. And again in 1939 – for an act of trespass in a royal household. The Palace, no less. Apart from that, your record shows that you seem to have an unstickable quality. You cannot stay in one place for very long before you are either dismissed or you disappear.'

This put me in mind of my father's little magic shows. Davies was correct – there were *ad hoc* performances at the dinner table after one of Mrs Rossiter's heavy puddings. He did the usual things a father will do to try to amaze a child. The difference was that he had skill. He had legerdemain. He was practised in the arts of misdirection. He could juggle five objects. He made coins appear from behind my ears, cut a string into little worms that miraculously became whole again. Then one day, with a wave of his magic fingers and a whispered *shazam*, he made me disappear. I looked at myself and declared that he had failed. 'Who said that?' he replied, looking right through me. 'Of course you can still see yourself, but no one else can. Where are you?' And he looked about the room for me, waving his hand, like a man in the dark, in the space just beside me.

'Your vanishings have been a noticeable theme in your life, wouldn't you say? Expelled from your primary school, St Saviour's, in Sipson. Expelled from the Slade School of Art. Dismissed from Berryman's Academy. Invalided home from the army.'

'Now look here, you can't try to bring my army career into this catalogue of "vanishings", as you call them. I was wounded during active service. My war record is exemplary. Just because you have so little regard for the importance of camouflage.'

'I have the highest regard.'

'Then why do you have that smirk on your face?'

'Well, it's probably unfair of me, but I can't help being amused at the thought of a camouflage officer getting shot at. The last person you would expect to become a target.'

'Have you ever been shot?'

Davies didn't answer, though his smirk slowly left his face. He perused my notes again. 'Can you recall the circumstances of your injury?'

'No. I wasn't even aware I'd been shot until someone noticed the blood on my trousers. Would you like to see the scar?'

To my surprise Davies said that, yes, he would like to see the scar, so I stood up and unbuttoned my trousers, lowering them to within a half-inch of decency. 'The bullet went in here, missing my pride and joy by a matter of inches.' The wound was now hardly visible, a little circle of slightly brighter, shinier skin, just above the pubic area. I turned round to show Davies the exit wound, in the lower portion of my right buttock. It made rather a mockery of my previous shyness about getting dressed, and I looked at him over my shoulder, wondering what he would make of such proximity to my nakedness. But, then, what was I expecting – that he should become nervous and breathless, hot under the collar? That he should begin panting, salivating? He did nothing of the sort, but examined my wounds with the detached curiosity of a doctor.

'Nasty,' he said. 'I should think sitting down was rather painful for a while.'

'The bullet missed my bladder by a quarter of an inch, but perforated my lower bowel. This was what caused the blood poisoning that nearly killed me.'

'Yes, I see. How long were you in hospital for?'

'Doesn't it say in your notes? After being patched up in a dressing station I was in the British Military Hospital in Alexandria for nine months. Then, for reasons I was never quite clear about, I was moved to a sanatorium in Palestine. For a while I could identify all the songbirds of Galilee. By that time I was considered fit enough to make the journey back. The Med was safe, so I sailed home the short way. Convalesced for another six months in Ashleigh, a little place in the Oxfordshire Cotswolds. From there I went home.'

'What are those other scars? The ones higher up?'. Davies appeared not to have listened to a word of my medical history.

'Childhood injury.'

'Pretty nasty injury. Turn around again. I'm not a medical man but it looks like another bullet passed right through. There's a wound on both sides.'

'No,' I said, 'not a bullet wound. I was impaled on a sword. Missed my vital organs by a hair's breadth again.'

'Quite incredible,' said Davies. 'To survive one such injury is lucky enough, but to be run through twice and live to tell the tale.'

'But I haven't told the tale. Not yet.'

'No. Well, there's plenty of time for that, I suppose. But there is one thing that puzzles me about your desert injury.'

'What's that?'

'Well, according to all the records and reports, your squad wasn't under fire at the time. Nor was it engaged in any action with the enemy.'

'That's ridiculous.'

'Well, that's just according to the reports. In fact, your injury was sustained a full two days before battle commenced.'

'Like I said, that's ridiculous. There were all sorts of skirmishes before the main battle began. Little raiding parties, reconnaissance parties – the dunes were crawling with enemy patrols.'

'And one of them opened fire on you?'

'Yes. Several of us were ambushed by a raiding party in some dunes south of Martello. Bullets were flying everywhere. Bloody good camouflage – it was as though the sand had suddenly turned against us. As I said, I didn't even realize I'd been shot until it was all over.'

'Was anyone else injured?'

'No.'

'Was a Mr Arturo Somarco among your group?'

I hadn't heard that name mentioned for a very long time. I tried not to wince too visibly. 'Somarco. Yes, Somarco was there. He wasn't injured. Somarco could never be injured.'

'A friend from your art-student days, I believe.'

'Correct.'

'In fact, your tutor.'

'Yes.'

'Along with most of the others in your squad. Alfred Knell. Captain Learmouth. Quite a pals' regiment.'

'Well, when Learmouth was asked to assemble a team, naturally he turned to people he knew. We weren't all from the Slade, at least not later.'

'"Arturo Somarco" doesn't exactly sound like a full-blooded English name, does it?'

'Neither does "Davies".'

'You know what I mean.'

'Somarco's ancestors span the Mediterranean – he is half Italian, half Spanish. But he was born and raised in England.'

'And you and he worked closely together?'

'Yes. In the beginning there were just four of us in charge of camouflage for the whole of the Middle East. It was madness. Once, when we were recceing the region, we divided the map into three and took a kingdom each, like Lear's children. Somarco and I were given the whole of Libya to survey, which we did while trying to catch up with the Army of the Nile. Knell took Egypt down as far as the Sudan while Learmouth had Sinai, Palestine and Syria. We had to kidnap people to become our assistants, borrow planes and pilots. Oddly enough, Somarco could fly – he'd been trained in the RAF before recruitment to the Camouflage Corps. That gives you an indication of how highly camouflage came to be regarded. They sacrificed a trained pilot for the sake of it.'

*

I wonder if Davies is a musical man. From his whistle, I would think not. But, then, why must he insist on whistling? He whistles like my father, flat and tunelessly. That was my father's weak spot – a lack of musical ability. He had the dancing, the patter, the jokes, the tricks, but not the songs.

> *Oh it's easy to be gay*
> *If you but try,*
> *And here's a simple way*
> *Just do the same as I*
>
> *I love to whistle*
> *Because it makes me merry,*
> *Makes me feel so very . . .*
> *Da da da da daaaaaah*

II

They have refused, so far, to tell me where I am. If I stand on the chair I can see out of the window. I appear to be in one of those new, cheaply built army bases, all low-roofed anonymity, half-cylinders of corrugated iron that have somehow been thickened and coated so that they resemble permanent buildings. In the distance there are low, bald hills, which strongly suggest chalk downland. I imagine we are somewhere in Wiltshire.

I have become very attentive to noise, and the sounds produced by the base. It is mostly very quiet, but certain noises recur regularly. The grind and growl of a heavy vehicle. A sudden burst of dogs barking in the distance. A gramophone playing an aria from *The Gondoliers*. Always the same aria.

*

The next time I saw Davies it was in the small interview room that was our usual place for meetings. It was still thought necessary to handcuff me when out of my cell, and the two armed guards were their familiar silent selves. The corridors reeked of iodine. I was told to sit at a table. It was about forty minutes before Davies arrived.

'So sorry to keep you,' he said, focusing on me more closely than before, as he took his seat opposite me. I felt bashful under the intensity of his gaze. Then, seeming to realize the oddness of his behaviour, he said, 'Pardon my curiosity. I'm just wondering if there's anything in your face that betrays your ancestry.'

'Oh, really?'

'Yes. Certain anthropologists say the individual races of mankind can be identified by cranial and facial bone structure, but I always wonder if Jewishness counts as a race or a religion, or both.'

'You think I'm Jewish?'

'Are you saying you're not?'

'Why on earth would you think I am? And what has it got to do with anything anyway?'

'Well, actually I didn't think you were, until I looked into your school records.' He opened the folder he had brought with him again, took out a document and held it up at close enough range for me to read the large lettering on the heading.

'Jacob College,' he said, 'your school report, where it says you excelled at art, drama, ballroom dancing and Hebrew. Well done, Lieutenant Brill. This is an exceptionally good report. Dr Merryman writes at the bottom, "Young Kenneth is a dedicated and studious young man, popular with his classmates. Well done, Kenny."'

'Merryman wrote that on every report, word for word. No one ever called me Kenny at school.'

Davies readjusted himself on the chair, sat up straight and smart, like a good schoolboy, then raised a hand to his chin and tapped his lips with an index finger, in a carefully practised portrait of thoughtfulness. 'So why do you deny that you are Jewish?'

'Because I'm not. Jacob College was a Jewish school in name and curriculum only. The school was set up by a foundation in the nineteenth century to serve a local Jewish community that has since moved away. Places were filled by gentiles until, by the time I got there, there was hardly a Jew in the place, either among the pupils or the staff.'

'That sounds very odd. A whole school devoted to teaching a faith in which no one in the school believed. Can it really be the case?'

'Well, that's how it seemed. To be honest, I paid no attention to whether teachers or pupils were Jewish or not. It wasn't something that entered my thoughts. All I know is that no one seemed much bothered about teaching religious subjects. If that report says I did well in Hebrew, it's a lie. I never had a lesson in Hebrew in my life. The success of the subject was a fabrication to keep the foundation happy.'

'We've spoken to Dr Merryman. He says there were and are Jewish children at Jacob College. He said the Jewish children were often targets of bullying. I asked him if he knew who the bullies were, and your name was mentioned.'

I could hardly speak for a few moments. 'What on earth are you talking about?'

'It's all on record, Lieutenant Brill.'

'I've never bullied anyone. This is outrageous. Dr Merryman must be an old man by now – he's getting me mixed up with other people. If you are trying to fit me up with anti-Semitic sympathies, you will fail, I can assure you. The situation was quite the opposite – I was as much bullied as those others you speak of, when out of school and wearing my yarmulke, by local boys on my way home. Spat at in the marketplace, mud thrown at me on the Heath. It got so bad I had to stop wearing it. I have much sympathy for the suffering of the Jews under the Nazi regime, having been given the merest hint of what life for them might be like.'

'And were you happy at Jacob College? Was it a good school?'

'Of course I was happy there. After the brutal philistinism of St Saviour's, it was a paradise. I came under the spell of a truly wonderful art teacher, Mr Toynbee.'

'Dr Merryman says he always had misgivings about admitting you to the school because you and your mother had lied about your reasons for leaving your first school. You told him you had been expelled for fighting, whereas he learnt that you had stabbed a boy, had stripped him and locked him in the school toilets.'

Quite a picture, I could now see, was beginning to emerge from Davies's preliminary investigations. Over the next few days more details were gleaned. He had people running up and down the country conducting interviews with my old teachers, work colleagues, former friends. They were going through records, looking up articles.

'At the Slade you were expelled because, among other things, you and your mentor Mr Somarco were running a brothel for students in Old Compton Street. At Berryman's School in

Somerset, where you were art master, you were dismissed after an act of immoral conduct. In 1939 you were found near the King's apartments in Buckingham Palace. For this offence you served a term in prison, didn't you, Lieutenant Brill? If we combine this catalogue of delinquencies with your affiliations and associations with known anti-Semites and pro-Fascist movements – for instance you spent a spell as what you called artist-in-residence at Hillmead Manor, run by the self-acknowledged Fascist sympathizer Rufus Quayle, and your friend Mr Somarco, we believe, has or had strong links with the Hitler Youth movement in Germany. I could go on, Lieutenant Brill. How about Mr Kuratowski? Remember him? Your first art master at Jacob College. He and his family died when their house burnt down in 1931. You say there were no Jews in Jacob College. Well, Mr Kuratowski was one.'

The climax of this tirade had Davies at his most animated. I had not heard him raise his voice before, and though he wasn't exactly shouting, he was voluble enough to send a shiver through me, banging certain supposedly incriminating documents down on the table as he spoke (then taking them up again before I could get a look at them). My heart was drained, my throat clogged with dust. He had presented to me a version of my life so different from the one I'd experienced that I hardly knew if I had existed as a person at all in the years I'd been alive. Yet nothing he had described was incorrect: it was simply that without the context it appeared incriminating. In truth each point had a mostly innocent explanation. It was like stripping a man down to nothing but his teeth and his fingernails and saying, 'Here is a creature who is designed to kill.'

After a prolonged pause, in which Davies refused to take his eyes off me, I could only try to explain.

'Apart from the death of Mr Kuratowski, about which I know nothing, everything else can be explained, though without the proper context, the explanation will seem ridiculous. I have never stabbed anyone in my life, and I certainly did not run a brothel for students of the Slade. Those are both hideous distortions of the truth. As for Mr Somarco, I'm sure you have concocted some ghastly account of our friendship. I will confess that our relationship overstepped the bounds of respectability, but that is not why you have arrested me, is it? The man is a hopeless romantic, as were many who regarded Herr Schicklgruber with any sort of admiration in those days. He was trained as a botanical illustrator, and seemed to think a political solution to mankind's troubles could be found in the lives of plants. You cannot take seriously the politics of a man like that. I can't tell you how angry I was when I found out what was happening at Hillmead. It broke my heart, and Somarco assured me he was as deceived as I. It made me abandon my vocation as an artist. It is only the war and the work of the Camouflage Corps that has restored its meaning for me. I can assure you, sir, that Somarco is wholly on our side. He is a good man at heart – he doesn't even really care about politics.'

'And do you care about politics, Lieutenant Brill?'

III

I begged Davies for painting materials. He was reluctant at first: 'What on earth is there to draw?'

I asked if I could have a mirror and draw myself. The answer to this was an emphatic no. Mirrors can be broken, the fragments used like daggers. Did Davies really think I might slit his throat? I tried reasoning with the man.

'I can't think unless I can draw. You're asking me all these questions, asking me about my life, and all I have to think with is this empty cell. I'm losing all sense of who I am. If this carries on long enough you may as well interrogate the table. It will know as much. I don't expect you can understand that, can you? You don't even know what I'm talking about. What did you read at Oxford?'

'Cambridge. I read law.'

Learmouth had read law. When I'd said I thought it was a strange transition, from lawyer to artist, he'd said that reading law was the perfect way of getting to grips with the labyrinthine channels of the human imagination. *The law is nothing less than the social imagination exposed and codified. Every aspect of the human experience has, at some point, found definition and expression in the law. Though, of course, it is the most pared-down and minimal expression one can think of.* I put this to Davies, who smiled in a patronizing way and said, no, law is simply the expression and definition of crime.

Oh, how he could flatten a feeling, Davies. How he could banish all love with a simple glance.

But he did bring me some painting things. A little water-colour box, well used, the colours worn down like the steps of a medieval chapter house, some dirty paintbrushes stiff with colour, an old fruit tin to wash them in and a single pencil. He refused to give me anything to sharpen the pencil. If I needed to sharpen it I was to call the guard. I laughed. The first time I tried to get my pencil sharpened, I had to wait two hours after the guard, with solemn ceremony, took away my blunt HB. When he returned it to me, I was surprised to find it had been meticulously sharpened to a very fine point.

The world came into focus as soon as I applied brush to paper, not only the world of my immediate surroundings, which I rendered in several layers of brown wash, but the world in its temporal dimensions. Long-forgotten juxtapositions reasserted themselves; the dead emerged from their gritty resting places; the trivial moments of a life lived on several translucent strata became statuesque and heroic.

*

The first thing I saw was my father, bow-tie at his silky throat, hair smooth as Bakelite, shouldering his way into the house after a long road trip, his hands weighed down with suitcases, merchandise stuffed under each arm, the front door swinging open to its full extent so that it nearly knocked the porcelain ballerina off the hall table. His arms, in fact, were many, for he had recently invested heavily in prosthetic limbs. The peg-leg business, he called it, a branching out from the more easily portable medical hardware he usually dealt in – stethoscopes, tongue depressors, sphygmomanometers. He saw it as a shrewd move with Europe drifting, as he saw it, towards a new war.

He was very proud of his merchandise. He would lay the ingenious little limbs – all hidden pulleys, springs and vacuum cups – carefully on the back parlour's chairs, so that it seemed like a waiting room of the damned: tan-coloured legs lined up politely on the settee, with arms beside them.

But the war, of course, was late. My father had overstocked himself, and the house was overflowing with prosthetics. He tried to maintain an optimistic outlook, but he could see that it put him in a horrible dilemma, for he greeted every headline that talked of peace in our time with a pain in his heart. Without a good war, he was finished.

So the rituals of his return from another sales tour, heavily laden with arms and legs piled beneath his real arms and hanging by their straps round his neck so that he look like an almighty spider or some updated version of a Hindu god, were tinged with a little bitterness, and he would curse the amputees of England, for their fussiness and impatience.

On the particular evening that sticks in my mind I can see him standing in the doorway, concealing the despair on his face with his reliable and long-serving music-hall comedian's perky and comical front. The limbs fall from under his arms and land in a shocking heap on the floor. He holds out tired arms to embrace me (real ones, I had to look twice). Unsure of his mood, I approach cautiously.

He then begins speaking in his music-hall patter, a tightened, Munchkin voice, which he produces by sinking his head as far as he can into his body.

'Come here, son, come here, little Kenny,' he says, 'come and hug your old man, who's been on the road for nearly a week in a car that has cost me more in repairs than a fleet of Hispano-Suizas, who's flogged fewer artificial legs than Long John Silver's brother-in-law, who's sold fewer artificial arms than Horatio Nelson's right-hand man. Do you know what happened to me yesterday? I was accosted by a client, the poor chap only had one leg, he said he was hopping mad, I said why, he said that artificial leg you sold me, it's given me blisters on my knees, I said blisters on your knees, what do you want me to do about it, he said I'm going to take you to court that's what I'm going to do, I said take me to court, you won't have a leg to stand on. It's cost me an arm and a leg it has, an arm and a leg I tell you . . .'

My mother was less able to see the comical side of my father's predicament – but, then, she hadn't been schooled in the music-hall tradition. How could a classical pianist ever appreciate my father's outlook? She had become exasperated by his speculative venture.

– You care more for these artificial limbs than you do for your flesh-and-blood wife. I'd like to see one of your plastic arms do this (a slap around the face), or one of your artificial legs do this (a stamp on the toe).

– If I wasn't a gentleman I'd let you know what it feels like to be smacked in the chops by an artificial hand. Think yourself lucky, my girl. As soon as the Germans cross the Rhine and start shelling our boys in the new trenches, the government will pay me a fortune for these beauties.

– Oh, don't be so stupid. If there's a war they'll be requisitioned – you won't get a penny. Face up to the facts. You're stuck with this lot for the rest of your life, while we have to rot away in this hell-hole.

– My mother's resentment overspilt into the ongoing resentment she felt at their general way of life. These arguments erupted with such frequency they passed almost unnoticed by me and my sisters.

– How can you complain when we have one of the best houses for miles around?

– When you look at the competition, that isn't saying much.

– So you'd rather live in a bow-walled hovel with rot in the thatch, like the Morrises?

– I'd rather live anywhere so long as it's in a proper town with proper shops, where there isn't the stench of manure coming in through the windows every hour of the day, where people don't give you strange looks when you try to dress decently. I'd like to live somewhere where there is a good hat shop, a nice tearoom, a proper concert hall. I haven't been to a recital for over ten years.

– Well, London is just down the road. I've heard they have many concert halls there.

– And how do you propose I get there? Walk? Hitch a ride on one of Mr Morris's vegetable carts? Perhaps you think I should ride a horse into town, like some fancy-dress John Gilpin.

I have a picture in my mind of my mother and father gesticulating wildly, the gestures multiplying, augmented as they were by the threatful waving of prosthetics, so that they looked like a painting by Boccioni.

*

In those days I still believed my father was a doctor, because of all the medical supplies we had at Swan's Rest, and because he often dispensed medical advice to his family and others, if needed. Neighbours would sometimes call and offer a blotchy tongue or speckled midriff for diagnosis, and my father would use impressive medical terms instead of the traditional country names for ailments. Thus he would diagnose a case of peritonitis or influenza rather than cow colic or spinnywort ague. He could advise a neighbour on what to take for a migraine, and would even provide a few tablets or powders to cure what the yokel would have called 'thunder fever'.

On his own children he was always keen to act the doctor. If we were sick he would take our temperatures with a real thermometer, look inside our mouths using a wooden tongue depressor, listen to our hearts with a stethoscope, test our knee reflexes with a little ebony hammer, and finally (his party piece, as it were), he would take our blood pressure using a most impressive piece of apparatus that resembled, to my young eyes, a miniature, folding grandfather clock. He would then pronounce us clinically dead. 'Sorry, Alicia, but there's nothing we can do with these kids but sell them to Harrison-Barbers, should get a good price . . .'

My sisters and I were better prepared than most children for games of doctors and nurses. The back parlour was stocked with brown cardboard boxes, each one of which presented an intoxicating mystery to us children, who never knew quite what we would find inside them. Then we would discover an inexplicable piece of instrumentation wrapped in creamy tissue paper, items that needed slotting and screwing together, gadgets of chrome metal and black, fragrant rubber, things of mirror, of Bakelite and polished teak. My father's medical equipment had exactly the same allure as toys.

Sphygmomanometer. Stethoscope. Hypodermic. Speculum. Haemostat. As a five-year-old I had developed an unusual vocabulary. The words were bandied about in our house in much the way that 'bread knife' and 'teapot' are bandied about in others. 'Alicia, who's been playing with my sphygmomanometers?'; 'Kenneth, please don't eat your food with your father's lancets. We have perfectly good knives . . .' There was always a surplus of medical equipment at Swan's Rest – damaged goods, out-of-date instruments that somehow found their way into other parts of the house, and I did enjoy dissecting my food with a scalpel, imagining myself a gowned and gloved surgeon at the dining table.

By the age of five I was as familiar with the sound of blood flowing through an artery as I was with the chanting of nursery rhymes or the chiming of musical boxes (which my mother collected). Countless times I had put a stethoscope to my sister Pru's pale chest and listened to the slamming doors of her heart, or the sudden blasts of turbulence, the vortices and hurricanoes of her breath, or the belfry and breaking-glass clatter of her laughter.

But it was the sphygmomanometer that took up most of our time, since it seemed to combine many different 'toys' in one – thermometer, stethoscope, pump. It was our mother who showed us how to work it. I think she might have harboured hopes that such educative playing might inspire us to become real doctors. So it was that we strapped the cuff to each other's arms and inflated it with the rubber bulb, and watched the mercury rising and falling in the U-shaped tube. Then, through the stethoscope, listening to the pulse becoming fainter and fainter until – what a shock it was at first – it stopped. The blood in little Pru's body fell silent. I looked at my mother in alarm, and repeated my father's oft-repeated joke, but this time as a serious statement – 'Pru's clinically dead!'

But my mother laughed. 'No, not dead, Kenny, you've just blocked her veins with the tightened cuff. Read the level in the mercury. What is it? Now release a little bit of air at a time and listen carefully for the pulse to start again.' I listened. I looked at Pru. She seemed a little bit worried. But then I heard it. The return of her heartbeat, like a butterfly walking downstairs on the other side of the world. I was told to take the new reading from the mercury.

'She's come back to life,' I said, and Pru looked as relieved as any Lazarus or Lazarene.

*

'And what became of your father's peg-leg business – has the war made him a rich man?'

I looked at Davies, wondering if he was joking. 'I imagine you, or one of your minions, have been to Swan's Rest. You'll have seen the shambles my father's life has become. Does he look like a rich man? In 1936 his business went up in flames. He took all his arms and legs out into the orchard, arranged them in a heap and set fire to them. Odd, when war seemed more likely than ever. His business had been limping along for years – my father's joke – and he must have just grown sick of the sight of them. One of our neighbours glimpsed the fire through a hedge, saw feet and hands reaching out of the flames and raised the alarm, thinking that my father was purging the products of some hellish human abattoir.'

Davies was silent, though he had a thoughtful smile on his face. I was waiting for him to say something about my father.

When I saw that he wasn't going to, I continued: 'He never wanted to stay in the medical-supplies business. His very purpose in coming back to the Heath was to get away from that game. He wanted to get back to the land. The land was important to him. More important than anything.'

*

Back in my cell I was shocked, after a long day of gentle interrogation, to experience a sense of homecoming. I was glad to be back in the brown, four-walled space. And then I was ashamed of the feeling, as though I'd betrayed Swan's Rest. It was true that the land around the house was important to my father, and yet it was a disastrous inability to understand the nature of that land that had nearly done for him, in the early days.

He had grown up on the Heath – its hedges and drains were the lines that enclosed his nature – yet he cared nothing for it until it was a distant memory. Then, living a life of walled-in drudgery in the shabby terraces of north London, he had leapt at the chance to return to the rural life when his father died and left him the house, along with a small parcel of land.

Yet something in that scuffed, unschooled upbringing had sharpened his mind, given him a silver tongue and a quick wit. As a child he had always shied away from doing the manual work in the fields and eventually his father relented and confined him to administrative chores. He was given the paperwork to do. At the age of seven he was responsible for keeping the accounts, making deposits in the local bank, dealing with seed merchants and market officials, and of course he excelled on the market stalls, where he had worked for almost as long as he could talk.

When he was eight years old his mother died, a tragedy that must have affected him profoundly. I know nothing about her. She died long before anyone with a camera visited the Heath, and I never met anyone, apart from my father, who had known her. And he never spoke about her. Though he did speak, often and with great vitriol, about her successor. My grandfather remarried with unseemly haste, a widow who already had a son, a little older than my father. A contemptible clog-wearing muck-dweller, my father called him, though he went by the name of Tiberius Joy, and retained that name, even after his mother's marriage to my grandfather.

Even as a boy Tiberius was an excellent spademan, a valued skill on the Heath where the earth was mostly turned over by hand. Some of the bigger farms used horse and plough, but most of the gardeners were bent-backed shovellers, hoers and rakers. In any family the boy who could cut the most soil would rise to the top of the pecking order, and Tiberius, in competition with my pencil-wielding father, had an easy journey into his step-father's affections.

My father became so unhappy in the new set-up that, at thirteen years old, he ran away from home. His experience with handling money and dealing with businessmen, and his skills of salesmanship on the market stalls of Covent Garden and else-where, had equipped him with the basic tools for survival in the adult world, but he had a strongly romantic and adventurous streak and somehow managed to spirit himself out of England altogether. He spent a while as a wandering minstrel, troubadour or scholar gypsy (depending on his mood when recounting his exploits), playing a penny whistle in the dusty village squares of southern Europe. His wanderings took him from the fishing villages of the Algarve as far as the olive groves of Thrace. This was the beginning of his career as an itinerant performer.

At some point around the turn of the century he found him-self in Marseille, and expanded his romantic ambitions by going to sea, apprenticing himself as an assistant to a ship's surgeon on an American vessel, whose normal run was the transportation of sugar and beans from the Isthmus of Tehuantepec to New

Orleans, and various manufactured goods in the opposite direction. After less than a year he jumped ship and tried to make his own way in the United States.

I don't know much about my father's time in America, or what curious career he followed that caused him eventually to be arrested for impersonating a doctor in Newark, New Jersey, though not before he had successfully delivered a baby, and performed an appendectomy. After a short spell in a penitentiary, he was deported.

He landed in Liverpool and settled in that city for a while, fascinated by the culture of the variety theatres and music halls. It seemed that in a sudden revelation he believed his life thus far had been nothing more than intensive training for a career on the stage. He was by now a pushy, self-confident, ambitious young man who thought nothing of blustering his way into the offices of theatre managers and theatrical agents and pestering them for a turn on the stage. Proudly he showed me one of the letters of recommendation he was given by an agent he'd hounded for weeks. He was to hand the letter, sealed, to the manager of the Liverpool Empire, a portly but stonily solid man called Joe Graves, who read it while my father stood expectantly before him. Mr Graves exploded with laughter (not a good thing, my father said, for a man of those proportions) and handed him the letter. It read:

Dear Joe

Pay no attention to the bearer – he is troublesome. I am only writing this to get rid of him.

Yours ever
Terry (Sharp)

Graves was so amused by the letter that he gave my father a five-minute slot on a Saturday night, without even so much as an audition. My father said, once he was on the stage and in the spotlight, all he could think to do was to tell the story of his life. Somehow, by compressing his already considerable achievements into five minutes, he delivered a narrative that had the unexpected effect of producing uncontrollable laughter in the audience.

It had not occurred to my father that his talents lay in comedy, but he embarked on a career in that direction with some moderate success. Then he teamed up with the person my mother called 'the Little Fellow' and formed the double-act Brill and Miller. Miller was a dwarf, and was only known by that single name. Like Harpo Marx, he performed mute. He vocalized only once on stage, and that was during his death throes. Miller died when their comedy knife-throwing act went wrong.

My mother told me the story when I was older.

'They'd never quite found their niche, you know, Kenneth. That was the problem. They tried things before they'd properly acquired the skills. It takes a great deal of skill to be a knife-thrower. And, of course, they always tried to make something of the Little Fellow's tiny frame, so instead of knives they used darts, and Miller was tied to a dartboard, slowly revolving. And he didn't realize that a dart, if it hits a particular spot, can do a lot of damage. And Miller, the poor little chap – he was such a small fellow – it didn't take much to kill him. The coroner said that Miller's skull was hardly thicker than an eggshell at the point where the dart entered, like a baby's soft spot.'

My father suffered from the clown's affliction, the terrible consequence of dedicating oneself to making others laugh – he could not be taken seriously. I could only laugh at the picture my mother had painted.

'Kenneth, what do you find so funny about poor Miller? He was only a little thing.'

Every decision my father made in his life after that point was shaped by the death of Miller. It was the reason that he abandoned his stage career, it was the reason he was a conscientious objector during the Great War. It was why he became a travelling salesman in medical supplies (which he believed was as close to being a doctor as he would ever get), and the reason why, when the business began failing, he took the chance of returning to the Heath and working on the land.

Swan's Rest was an important house on the Heath, standing at the end of a curving gravel drive that cut the lawn in half. Its front porch rested on two tusk-like Doric columns that gave the Georgian frontage the appearance of a sad walrus. Bay windows on either side of the porch gave light to the front parlour and the morning room, and above, three windows belonged to the bedrooms of myself and my two sisters, mine being on the right as you approached the house. Downstairs there were three more rooms – the back parlour (at various times used by my father as an office and warehouse), and an L-shaped dining room with flock wallpaper and grand-looking oil paintings of local views by artists whose signatures (W. H. Riley, Stanton Hope) always struck me as too legible. Finally there was an enormous kitchen, the domain of our housekeeper, Mrs Rossiter.

After their two-up-two-down Holloway terrace it must have seemed like a mansion to my parents. I was six years old, and can still remember the shock of so much space, both inside and out. The long lawn at the front with its curving drive, the walnut tree (the reason for the curve) and the shrubberies that bordered it either side. Then at the back, an orchard of twenty-six ancient apple trees, most of which were beyond their fruiting days.

There were other houses like ours scattered about the district, some bigger and grander – stately farmhouses and old halls, some newly built suburban villas grotesquely out of place – but Swan's Rest was reputed to be the oldest, and was certainly the most beautiful.

It was, of course, my father's childhood home but he hadn't lived in it for nearly thirty years, and had only visited the Heath on a handful of occasions in all that time. It was a shock to many that his father had left him anything, let alone this enormous house. That was certainly the opinion, so it transpired, of his stepbrother Tiberius Joy, who'd stayed on the Heath but now owned his own house some way down the lane. No one really understood the peculiar disbursements of my grandfather's will. Tiberius was left the majority of the land, but my father got the big house. Tiberius was deeply aggrieved.

IV

We called it the Heath, but apart from a small gorsy tract near Feltham, the last scrap of heathland had vanished in the previous century. Now it was fields all over, divided by willowy hedges and screens of shimmering poplars, run through with streams and ditches, and pocked with ponds and pools. A silty, alluvial district reclaimed from the great rivers that looped through its parishes, it looked as though it had been pressed down on by a great weight. Emphatically flat. Apart from some Bronze Age burial mounds there was not the slightest undulation, the littlest hill. Some may have called it drab, but I found it to have a haunting, two-dimensional beauty. Even the modest perch of my bedroom window seemed giddyingly aloft in such a level land, and I could lean on the sill and feel my viewpoint extend into infinity. It was a chessboard world, but one in which the squares had been stretched and pulled into a sweeping tessellation of rectangles and rhomboids. And within the fields, rigid lines of planting – furrows and trenches that resembled the vigorous scoring of a giant pencil. It was a land of shacks and roofless outhouses, of broken gates and mossy forcing sheds. But it had a sweeping grandeur to it, reminding me of the paintings of the Dutch masters. When I first encountered these in the National Gallery many years later, I was instantly transported to the flatlands of my childhood. I, too, had scampered in those scrappy fields of Hobbema and van Ruisdael, I had climbed Jan Wijnants' lurching poplars, and had trailed a finger in one of van der Hagen's sparkling dikes.

And the figures in those paintings were little removed from the people I observed in the fields when standing at my window, from a distance at least. Up close you could see they were in modern dress – they tended to wear cast-off versions of their Sunday best, blue serge trousers belted with string, stained and torn pinstripe waistcoats with watch and chain, shirts with no collar, sleeves rolled up to the elbow, and dusty, crumpled fedoras on their heads – but from a distance they were indistinguishable from the peasantry of the feudal age, working the land inch by inch with no mechanical assistance, bent double at the backbreaking task of raising crops from a reluctant, sulky soil.

The soil was called brick earth, a light brown silty clay that in the past had been more commonly used as a building material. Some of the older houses on the Heath, including parts of our own, were made of it, and a little brickworks in Cain Lane still survived, though it had all but ceased production. If properly treated with fertilizer, brick earth could be made into a very productive soil. It formed a porous, fertile loam in which almost anything could grow: raspberries, blackcurrants, strawberries, damsons, gooseberries, kale, cauliflowers, leeks, lettuces, spinach, beetroot, peas, artichokes, rhubarb, radishes, onions – they could all be brought to a perfect ripeness in our soil, but only as long as there was a constant and ready supply of manure.

VANISHING

Manure was a scarce resource on the Heath, and since such large quantities were needed, it would have been unprofitable to buy from farms or merchants. Besides, being mostly arable country for miles about, there was little to be found on the surrounding farms. Instead, most of our neighbours looked to London and its vast population of horses for a supply. There were still some coaching inns with stabling in those days, and many of the factories used horses for delivery, and the general traffic of the capital was predominantly animal-hauled. In fact, the city was drowning in manure, its streets paved with the beige gold for which none of the inhabitants had any use, unless they grew roses. And since the farmers and gardeners of the Heath visited the city nearly every day to sell their fruit and vegetables at the markets, it made sense to use the very same carts to bring fresh manure back to the Heath.

A secure manure supply was therefore vital. Without it, the nutrients in the soil were quickly depleted and the loam would close up and become airless. Fresh manure had to be dug in with each planting and continually mulched in thereafter. An acre of land could use up to forty tons a year. Manure was the foundation of our local economy. Those with the best suppliers grew the best produce, and they guarded those suppliers jealously. And they would lend it, at a price, to those without such ready supplies. Manure was, for our neighbours, a currency. It was something they traded and something they saved. They accumulated it, invested it, put some by for a rainy day, and when they weren't actually using it, they spent their time counting it, turning over the droppings with a fork as though they were gold sovereigns, reckoning up their heaps and comparing them with other men's. And they never squandered it. Every last spadeful was spent wisely, applied with an eye on future returns, the dividends of blackcurrants, carrots and cauliflowers.

Tiberius Joy took all his manure from a brewery in Uxbridge where a team of bell-bottomed drays, fed on a diet of cobs, stale mash and oat husks, could produce enough of their shiny, smooth, olive-green, cabbage-sized, nitrogenous boluses to fill Mr Joy's high-sider twice a week. (Had his own little mare known what work it was doing in hauling that steaming load down Cain Lane, would it have trotted so proudly, I often wondered.) The Joys, it was reluctantly acknowledged, were the richest of families in manure. Its quality couldn't have been bettered, and it was produced in such quantities (think of those drays, almost elephantine: a single bowel movement could fill a whole wheelbarrow) that the Joys had far more manure than their land could swallow. Mr Joy's heap was like a replica of the Malvern Hills, and ran all down one side of his long field. There were others with good suppliers but the unluckier families had to go far away for their manure, or worse: parade up and down the main roads with a shovel, scraping horse droppings up off the dust. (Road manure was always thought of as the poorest quality, for no good reason, as far as I could see.)

My father was slow to understand the importance of manure. He was paying the price for all those childhood years when he'd refused to help in the fields and had done the paperwork instead. His knowledge of market gardening was limited to costs and numbers. He didn't realize that the ground needed opening up first, that it needed to be fed a constant supply of nutrients. Not until the first crops came – shrivelled and stillborn, spongy and bitter-tasting – did he wonder what was wrong. When he finally grasped his error, and that he needed forty tons of festering horse dung a year just for his two little fields, there was no one to turn to for help. The gardeners – our neighbours – were not going to share their supplies, least of all to an outsider, a city boy like my father. They offered to sell him some from their own heaps, but always at an inflated price. As a moneyman he knew when he was being diddled. If he'd paid them to fertilize his land he would have had to sell Swan's Rest.

I imagine my father put his skills as a commercial traveller to best use when he scouted around for a supplier, but everyone locally was already partnered with a gardener. It was considered the poorest form on the Heath to try to muscle in on another man's supplier, and when rumours reached our neighbours that he had been sniffing around the stables of local hotels and factories, there were angry deputations to our front door and growly altercations in its porch. I remember one argument that went on for what seemed like hours and ended with an angry gardener yelling, 'That's what we don't do round here, Larry Brill – may the Lord rain dung upon my head. We never take from another man's heap!'

Well, my father hadn't gone as far as that, not by then, at least. But he began to feel that the whole community was against him. He even began to feel that the legacy of Swan's Rest was nothing more than a cruel joke played on him by his father, who was taking posthumous revenge on a son who'd strayed. Swan's Rest, though grand by our Holloway Road standards, was worth very little. It was the land that had value on the Heath. You had only to sneeze, my father once said, and something would grow from the spot where it fell. The soil had become something independent of the land beneath it: enriched and charged with human labour, it was as artificial as a layer of tarmacadam. Houses were cheap in our hamlet, but fields were precious.

My mother later said she recalled the day we arrived at Swan's Rest, my father's Morris Cowley filled to the brim, towing a rickety trailer and bearing, Atlas-like, a burden of belongings on its roof. We were greeted with what she said was real warmth by the locals – Mrs Rossiter, the housekeeper, had put up a little string of bunting, left over from King Edward's coronation, on the walnut tree, and others came out of their cottages to see us, buttoning their collars and adjusting bright bonnets as they walked up the lane – fascinated to see how the wayward son had turned out, and because no one could remember ever seeing a motor-car on the Heath before. Within minutes of our arrival, Tiberius had come over with his family, equipped with a trestle table, chairs, a baked ham, a dish of creamed kale (a speciality crop in the area), pickled radishes, potato salad, cucumber and cheese sandwiches, and we were served a feast on the lawn, toasted with the Joys' potent blackberry wine. Tiberius gave my father many a hug, handshake and slap on the back.

Afterwards, when the struggles with the land had taken their toll, my father spoke bitterly about that moment, about how the whole village might have come out to celebrate his return, but in reality they were carefully plotting his downfall, conspiring with all the suppliers of manure in the area to cut him out of any deal, leave him to scrape the muck off the Great West Road (which he tried, for a while, before realizing it was a hopeless task, providing no more than a crumb of the total needed).

After two years of breaking his back over that sticky, clogged stretch of unyielding earth, he found he would have to go back to selling medical supplies if he was to have any chance of feeding his family.

It can't have helped matters that I had become friendly with some of Tiberius's family. I enjoyed working the fields, but by now we had all but given up on ours, and there was little work to do. Instead I wandered down the lane to the Joys' vast furrowed tracts and made myself useful there.

I tried to keep secret the fact that I was working for my step-uncle. Mr Joy would sometimes press a farthing or ha'penny into my palm, so firmly it left a circular indentation there, but even without the money I was happy to be working out in the fields, sometimes alone, sometimes with others. Mr Joy had a large family, and I became friendly with the tall, gangly, hollow-chested second son everyone called Three Cylinders, who drifted about the fields like a wandering question mark but who could perform, with that light bent body, feats of incredible strength, after which he would grin at you with overhanging, buttercup-yellow teeth. Three Cylinders was like an older brother to me, who had only two sisters, and I aspired to be like him in every way, apart from physically. Like his father, he was a very good spademan, and could singlehandedly turn over a field in an afternoon. He claimed to owe his skills to the digging of trenches in the Great War, and it was many years before I realized he was far too young to have taken part in that conflict.

His older brother Roddy, on the other hand, had been in the trenches, and had suffered such disfiguring injuries that he never came out of the house. My mother claimed she'd had nightmares for months after first seeing him face to face. Such remarks turned Roddy Joy into a mythical Heath creature for us, a kind of anti-unicorn with Medusa-like powers, someone to be avoided at all costs. Since no one would describe him, he grew in our minds into a highly elaborate form of monster, so that when I did finally see him, pushing a bent-wheeled bicycle along Cain Lane, he was rather disappointing. Poor Roddy Joy had simply lost the lower half of his face. With no discernible jaws his visage seemed to end at the nose, below which there was a puzzling nothingness – no mouth, no chin, no jowls. The absence was so abrupt, the cut-off so clean, it was more as though part of his face had become invisible. It was a shocking thing to see, but the shock was a shock of absence – Roddy was in every other respect an ordinary, rather good-looking man.

At certain times the fields were very busy, and would be as crowded with people as a marketplace. With no machinery used, nor any animals, it took a great many hands to sow or plant seedlings, to pick or pull the fruit and vegetables from the soil, and most of the shelling, peeling, popping and pricking was done in the fields, usually by the womenfolk, who would sit on milking stools with big hessian aprons spread on their knees, wicker baskets by their sides and heaps of pods or peel or roots or leaves at their feet, which later they would hurl onto the manure heaps, adding to their bulk and goodness.

I was never allowed anywhere near the furrow-digging, but I was permitted to shovel the manure into the barrows and carts. The soft, yielding excremental mounds were as malleable as warm butter. I spent most of my time at the Joys' tending their vast heap, shovelling it into barrows for others to wheel away. Sometimes I was in charge when a neighbour would call, saying they had come for their load. Three Cylinders would bound over, his straw hair flying, to make sure their claim on the manure was genuine or, if he already knew, he would give me the nod from the far end, and I would load the customer's barrow, while they waited patiently for my young limbs to do the work.

At other times the fields were empty, or near enough, and I would have little to do but stir and prod the smouldering mounds, an unnecessary task, but one that gave me a great sense of importance. Or I would chat with Three Cylinders, and sometimes Mr Joy himself came by and would talk for a while. He was a man full of advice and warnings and homespun philoso-phizing. 'So, you're Larry Brill's little lad, are you?' he would say, with menacing thoughtfulness. No matter how many times we spoke he always began by confirming this fact, as if not quite able to believe his stepbrother's offspring could take human form. 'Larry Brill the cheeky chappie's little boy / Has come to work for Tiberius Joy.' He would chuckle. I understood I shouldn't be there, but now that my father was often away for days at a time it didn't really seem to matter.

V

When, after the events I'm about to describe, my mother said to me, 'Kenneth – how could you? How could you work on Tiberius Joy's dunghills when you knew what he was doing to your father?' I was unable to answer except with a plea for ignorance. I was a little boy who liked clambering about on slopes of excremental waste. When my father was around he was like a man from another world, slick and shiny in his salesman's suits, polished shoes without a speck of mud on them and, of course, his medical man's bow-tie. As far as I knew he had abandoned all hope of growing anything on our two little fields. I had heard the shouting and the slandering, and sometimes I would catch my father's door-slamming return home after an evening in the Plough and Harrow where he must have had another set-to with Tiberius, or other gardeners who, behind their smiles and laughter, were enjoying his rapid decline.

'Won't be long before he sells up and moves out. That's what they're thinking, Alicia,' I once heard him say, as I leant over the landing rail in my pyjamas to hear him. 'Then we'll have his land and we can dig in all the manure we want and have his house and the whole bloody lot.'

'Well, Larry, darling, is it really worth the effort . . . ?'

'But this is my land. This is the house I grew up in. Tiberius is nothing but a thief. He can have this house if he'll let me have a look in on his manure and a share of all those acres . . .'

When my father was at home he liked to take me for walks, with the girls as well sometimes, but more usually just myself. If it was possible for someone to walk angrily, then he did it, striding through the mud with a small cigar in his mouth and his coat collar, even in the warm weather, turned defensively up. I would hurry along behind him as we trod the margins of empty fields or the nettle-bordered drift roads that criss-crossed the Heath, until suddenly he would stop and stand silently, looking out across a view of soft fruit, or an ocean of kale, or the ranks of beetroot plumes, like old ladies seated for a matinée.

If there was a gardener in the fields he would often stop and exchange pleasantries in such a friendly way you would not have suspected there was any enmity between my father and our neighbours. That was why I was somewhat baffled by his actions one Sunday evening when we found ourselves alone on a distant corner of one of Tiberius Joy's fields: my father took off his coat and jacket, rolled up his sleeves and began yanking a row of young parsnips out of the ground.

I knew a little about growing crops by this time, and from my months spent watching Three Cylinders and his family working on the land, I knew that these vegetables were far too young to be harvested. My father laid them in a neat row along the side of the field – pale, naked embryos that, had they been animal rather than vegetable, would have been too weak even to cry out. Then, having recovered from his exertions, he completed the job by stamping and trampling the frail white bodies beneath his heels. The process was carried out in a very thorough and energetic manner, my father lifting his knee high to bring his foot down heavily on the vegetables, grunting with effort each time he did so. Then he would carefully look up and down the row of what must have been two hundred parsnips, shifting them carefully with the toe of his shoe, checking for any he'd missed, then finishing off those. I must have looked shocked because afterwards he turned to me and said, 'Don't worry, little Kenny – they can't feel anything.'

My older sister Prudence told me, some years later, that she had seen him massacre a field of ripe raspberries when she was walking with him. She said he had simply gone through all the rows, pinching the fruit between finger and thumb and crushing them on their stems, leaving the smashed heads hanging and dripping on the canes. His fingers, she said, were running with red; it made her feel quite sick to see it.

Nothing was ever said to me about the dispute between Tiberius Joy and my father. He had become passionate about the land and the gardens of the Heath in a way that surprised everyone who'd known him before he left London for Swan's Rest. The sad parsnips lined up on the verge, taken before their time, vegetable abortions stinging in the cold air, were but one of many such acts of sabotage my father committed.

'I don't want you working on Mr Joy's fields any more,' he said to me one day, while he was doing his accounts. He'd called me into his back parlour office; there were ledgers and folders on a shelf above the small oak desk on which he worked in the soft light of a gas jet. The room was thick with pipe smoke. My father's manner was always different when he was in this room, as though it were a little theatre of professional restraint and formality. Meeting him there was like going to see a doctor.

'Why not?' I had long given up on the idea that my father didn't know about my working for the other side. I had hoped he'd been turning a blind eye to the fact, and perhaps he had, until now.

'Now just don't ask. I don't want you going to help on the Joys' land any more, and that's enough of it.'

He could be frightening when in such a mood, and I didn't ask him any more questions.

And then, a few days later, I heard the same thing from the opposite direction. It was Three Cylinders who came up to me while I was atop of one of their heaps, stirring the straw into the dung: 'My dad says he don't want you in our fields no more.

You got to clear off.' Three Cylinders was wearing his straw hat that day, the one we called the sombrero, though it wasn't. Lord Freddy, his pet magpie, was in attendance, winking at me with little flashes of inner eyelid. When I asked why, Three Cylinders shrugged, as if he thought it was a lot of nonsense, what was going on. 'I don't know. He'll probably calm down in a day or two, change his mind. He says your dad's trying to rob him, and he thinks he shouldn't pay you money while he's doing that. So I said, "You don't pay him nothing anyway, do you?" Come back in a few days – he'll have forgotten all about it . . .'

So I stopped going to Mr Joy's long field after school and at weekends.

And then one Saturday morning there came a colossal noise from downstairs, a soft thud, but of an immense and prolonged volume, as if an elephant had fainted in the hallway. It seemed to cause a rush of air to run up through the house and set every-thing a-rattle. And in the silence that followed I could do nothing but make the memory of the noise grow in the mind. Shortly the silence was interrupted by my mother's voice, loud and forceful, though at the same time perfectly calm and controlled, calling up the stairs. 'Kenneth! Kenneth! Could you come down here a moment?'

Father was away on his travels and I was the only male in the house.

I climbed out of bed and went straight out onto the landing in my pyjamas. My sisters were at their bedroom doors, looking scared.

As I descended the stairs I could see what had happened, though I could not at first properly explain it. There was a mountain in the hall. A heap of mud filled the open portal of the front door and sloped downwards into the house, almost filling the space. For a moment I wondered where my mother was, even when she called to me.

'Kenneth, could you be a good boy and get a spade? I appear to have fallen victim to a terrible prank. There's a good boy.'

The voice came from what I at first took to be the tasselled and rucked corner of a Persian rug poking out of the muck, but which turned out to be my mother, lying flat on her back on the hall floor, covered up to her shoulders in mud, only it wasn't mud, as I could now see, but manure. It seemed that a pile of the stuff had been placed against the front door during the night, piled as high as the porch would allow. When my mother had opened the door that morning, she had unlocked a small avalanche, which had knocked her flat on her back and consumed her up to the chest. She had been three-quarters buried alive.

'Tell the girls not to come down. I would rather they didn't see me like this.'

But it was too late: Prudence and Angelica were already descending the stairs and peering over the banisters in wonder. Their reaction was unexpected: they began tittering at the sight of their mother beneath a pile of dung. By the time I had returned with a spade they were sitting on the floor next to my mother's head and conducting a very mundane conversation about a book they had been made to read at school.

'But it's so boring and Mr Bowling doesn't know the first thing about cannibals . . .' Prudence was saying, in a deeply disaffected tone.

'Well, I'm sure it's all for the best, Prudence, and your reading has come along so splendidly in this last year. Ah, now here's Kenneth with the shovel. Kenneth, did you go all the way to Sipson for it? You have been gone for ever.'

'I couldn't get the door of the outhouse open.'

'Oh, well. You may begin digging your mother out of her earthy predicament. But just be gentle, Kenneth. No, don't start near my head, start at the bottom, where the heap is highest, to take some of the weight off my legs. This stuff is so very heavy. I think one of my ankles may be broken.'

The manure was giving off gentle drifts of steam. Tiny creatures of all kinds were moving around – millipedes, slugs, worms, woodlice, those busy inhabitants of the heaps whose home had been so unexpectedly destroyed. I began attacking the mound from the summit, just below the lintel, and redistributing the muck on the floor, where Prudence and Angelica were instructed to put down newspapers, though they wouldn't touch the manure itself. I was doing precisely the work I had done in Mr Joy's fields, from which I had so recently been dismissed, but indoors. Mr Joy's fields had actually invaded the house.

'Oh, I can breathe again,' my mother said, as the muck was cast aside and the pressure on her body eased. By this time a little external scream had announced the arrival of Mrs Rossiter, who had approached, as usual, up the curve of the gravel drive, puzzled all the way by what appeared to be brown excrement vomiting from the walrus mouth of Swan's Rest. By the time she had reached the entrance, the pile was low enough for her to look over and see my mother, hence the scream. Once she'd collected herself she went about summoning further assistance, and soon a small squad of neighbours was bending to the task of harvesting my mother, using all their skills as farmers and gardeners to work the dung aside, to redistribute and turn it over. Wheelbarrows were brought, and one could tell there was a covert conversation going on about who should take possession of the manure. Deals were being made, more wheelbarrows fetched. Eventually my mother's form emerged from beneath the festering heap and, with the aid of two people either side, she was able to stand. Mrs Rossiter made her a cup of tea. 'I should think you've grown at least a couple of inches, after all that time under the manure,' she said.

I was never to find out what happened about this incident. Since I no longer worked for Mr Joy, I could not pick up from Three Cylinders anything about his side of the event. It was never openly acknowledged by anyone that Mr Joy was responsible, though he was the only one with enough manure to spare, and if I had gone to his field I might have been able to tell (had I still been its custodian) if an equivalent quantity was missing from his heap. Apart from that, I could tell by the smell that it had come from those great Uxbridge drays: their cob and mash dung was distinctly beery. But, then, you could argue that just because it was Mr Joy's manure it didn't mean Mr Joy had done the deed: someone else with a grudge might have decided to appropriate a portion of the biggest shit-heap in the district.

When my father came back a few days later, the manure had been so thoroughly removed that there was not the slightest trace of anything untoward. Mrs Rossiter had spent a day and a half scrubbing with bleach and carbolic to remove the stains and odours, recruiting her daughters to help in the task. I don't know what he was told about the event, but I do not believe he ever tampered with Mr Joy's crops again.

VI

My father was powerless to take any form of revenge against his stepbrother – he had to wait for the course of history to do that for him. Things were changing rapidly in the world beyond the Heath. The motor-car was coming of age. What had begun as a trickle of automobiles on the distant A-roads had turned into a steady flow. There were traffic jams on the Great West Road;

petrol stations and garages were springing up in lonely spots outside the towns.

And horses were disappearing.

One day I heard from Three Cylinders that he and his father had gone to the Uxbridge brewery for their weekly pick-up, only to find that their team of proud, thoughtful drays had been transformed into a fleet of brightly painted lorries with blankly staring headlights and nothing in their heads but engine oil and timing chains. Three Cylinders said his father was actually sick with shock. In a single night his supply of manure, which I believe had first been established by my grandfather as a young man, had gone. The brewery hadn't even mentioned the fact to him. He was just the man who came every week to clear the shit out of their stables.

I watched the magnificent heap, which had stood, continually replenished, at the edge of Mr Joy's two-acre field for perhaps a hundred years or more, vanish. It took a few seasons, but its shrinkage was steady and unstoppable. There was nowhere else the Joys could obtain a supply of manure in such quantities. And the decline of the Joys' mound affected the whole of the Heath. For years it had been acting rather like a currency reserve. Smaller gardeners had come to rely on it when their own assets ran low, but the collapse of the Uxbridge supply had suddenly made borrowing from the Joys very expensive. Whereas before they had lent often, with the expectation of nothing in return but repayment in kind, now they expected substantial interest, a share in the crop, or even financial settlement. The Heath was thrown into turmoil. As the seasons progressed and the heap continued to dwindle, passing from Himalayan to Alpine to Pyrenean and finally to Chiltern, and as smaller farmers – their own supplies having succumbed to the spread of mechanical traction – went under, there were some angry scenes on the Heath. Gardeners would turn up with a cart to take a load, and

Three Cylinders would tell them no, or that the price had gone up to a level they couldn't afford. Fists were raised. More than once I witnessed someone being knocked backwards into the heap.

I once saw Three Cylinders out in the field, just standing there, resting his hands on a pitchfork and looking out across the land, as though it was the last time he would see it. And when he saw me he came over, forgetting we weren't supposed to be friends or associates any more. And he said something like, 'We're done for, Kenny. Not just me and Father, but everyone on the Heath. If we have to start buying fertilizer we'll all be going out of business. Either that, or we'll have to throw in our lot together, sell up and let one of those big amalgamated farms take us over, like they have north of Sipson, with the fruit farms and the jam factories. They've got farms up there covering forty acres or more. People like us, our time's gone.'

*

'This really is most moving, Lieutenant Brill. It's like something out of a Thomas Hardy novel, wouldn't you say? I would never have guessed at your earthy origins. A son of the soil. A tiller and toiler. *Of good peasant stock.* Though, of course, those grim predictions can't have come true. The land around what you call the Heath seems to be farmed still, and to be growing crops in abundance.'

'It is, and would continue to do so, if you didn't have it in mind to destroy the entire area with your blasted aerodrome.'

'I find it interesting that you keep referring to "our" aerodrome, and "our" Air Ministry. One would almost believe you didn't feel it was also your Air Ministry.'

'You know what I mean. I don't mean "you" as in *English*, I mean "you" as in *interfering busybodies who make great plans without taking the needs and rights of ordinary people into account*.'

'And in your mind such needs outweigh the needs of the country as a whole and the fight against Fascism?'

'Like I said earlier, if we destroy what we're fighting for, what's the point of fighting?'

'And in your view we're fighting for a few piles of horse manure?'

'Take that back. After what I've just described, how can you speak of it so deridingly?'

'What if I suggest that we're fighting for a world in which we don't have to depend on the shovelling of manure for our food source, where we can produce food cleanly and efficiently?'

I refused to rise to Davies's ridiculous suggestions. Only a man brought up in the pruned and trellised suburbs of an English city could believe in the possibility of food without dirt. In truth I had no idea where Davies had been raised, but a glance at his pink, silky hands was all the background knowledge I needed. A boy raised on the warm milk and sunny smiles of a well-run household.

I wondered if I should tell Davies about how my father was able to capitalize on the loss Tiberius had suffered. Perhaps it was my father's comic imagination, or his years as a stage performer of magic illusions, that enabled him to see what others on the Heath had missed: the answer to all our problems had been in our midst for many years.

The Perry Oaks Sludgeworks, about a mile from our house, appeared a few years after our arrival on the Heath. It was not a welcome development, particularly for the Twelvetrees family, a large portion of whose land was requisitioned by the government for the purpose, though many thought Mr Twelvetrees had done very well out of the deal. Perry Oaks was on the edge of the Heath, so the presence of the new works could be conveniently ignored. Once the traffic of manpower and machinery had finished clogging up the lanes between Twelvetrees Farm and the

Great West Road, the site fell into an ominous silence, invisible behind high-turfed embankments. There were no engines to disturb the peace of the Perry Oaks orchards; no industry seemed to operate behind the grass ramparts. All that could be seen, if one took the trouble to climb the low picket fence that cordoned it off and clamber up the steep slopes, was a series of lagoons that, but for their regular shape, could have been natural lakes.

When I first saw these, as a little boy, I was impressed by what seemed to me their almost infinite vastness. The rectangular lagoons, like fields composed of liquid, seemed to stretch to the horizon, and existed with a rather awe-inspiring sense of purpose. Although the familiar rectangles of the fields were man-made, the lagoons were of a different order of artificiality. They were scientifically constructed. They were concrete-lined, neat-edged, right-angled and accurate.

Inaccessible in the distance could be seen some industrial paraphernalia – low, windowless buildings, inexplicable towers, turrets, cranes, a conveyor system of some sort. But it seemed, although brand new, uninhabited and desolate, like a ghost town, similar to those abandoned prospectors' settlements I sometimes read about in my child's papers.

I knew nothing at the time about the processes of water treatment. I didn't know how the invitingly calm waters of the lagoons were fed a constant stream of human sewage, that several tons of night soil were poured into them every day. That London, the vast city I had yet to visit but whose near presence haunted my childhood, was dribbling its waste into the heart of our land. Well, the capital's horses had for a long time been feeding our soil while the products of that soil went to feed the capital. It made me think of the city as a type of animal itself, a great flat beast that existed beyond the horizon, that brooded and spawned and digested.

My father was far-sighted and sharp enough as a negotiator

to spot the potential of the sludgeworks as a source of organic fertilizer. The lagoons worked by a simple process of sedimentation. Each in turn was slowly filled with sewage and then, when full, left alone for gravity to do its work. The particles of sewage slowly accumulated on the floor of the lagoon, until the water itself was almost pure. Then the lagoon was drained, the water discharged into the Duke of Northumberland's river, and thence into the Thames. What remained in the lagoons after the water had gone was the sludge. This was moved by mostly automated processes onto drying beds where it set into a substance that was hard and compact, a pallid, coarse mud called sludgecake.

Sludgecake was of no use to the people who ran the sludgeworks. In fact it was a profound nuisance for them – they had to pay to have it taken away and disposed of. When my father offered to pay them for the privilege instead, they were, of course, very interested. A deal was struck. I imagine it was somewhat to their bemusement that my father presented them with a contract to sign, granting him sole rights to the purchase of sludgecake for twelve months. They could hardly have known what it meant to him. Almost overnight my father became the most powerful man on the Heath.

It took a while to convince the others, of course. He was ridiculed when it became known what he was doing. My father had no transport of his own, apart from the car. He had to borrow one of Mr Morris's high-siders, drawn by a very clumsy mare, to transport his first load of sludgecake. Then I was called to help him in the field. By this time I had grown up a little and could do the same work as most men. But it was a backbreaking fortnight we spent working our two little fields, turning over ground that had been fallow for several seasons. The sludgecake was in rectangular blocks and, from a distance, looked little different from the type of breezeblocks you'd build an army bathhouse with. We carried them over singly to our digging, and under a spade they'd break up like stale bread. There was very little odour; they were much less pungent than the manure of the more usual dung heaps, and I, along with almost everyone else on the Heath, thought the sickly looking lumps of pallid matter could be of little use to a gardener. Apart from that, most people were disapproving of the very idea of using fertilizer derived from human waste, especially for the growing of food crops.

I met Three Cylinders one day when I was walking back to the house after a long afternoon's digging, and he had a crooked smile on his face, his overbite hanging a dismal yellow above his chin. 'So what's this I hear? Your dad's been up to the sludge-works for his fertilizer? What are you hoping to grow? Little men?'

'I dunno,' I said. 'My dad's just got some crazy idea.'

'You can't grow crops using that stuff – it's just not right. For one thing it won't work, and for the other, if it does work, it won't be moral. That's what my dad says. You'll be feeding people their own selves, and that can't be allowed. He said he'll report you to the council, and to the police and everyone. He told me to tell you that, and your old man.'

That season my father planted as much sea kale as he could, an added insult to Tiberius, as this was regarded as his best crop. He also planted leeks, parsnips, new potatoes and celery, and several rows of soft fruit bushes, a heavy investment: he had to buy all the seeds from the Feltham seed merchants.

Well, you should have seen the crops that came up that summer, and all the way through winter. The little fields that had been scrub for two years, and before that had never given much more than mildewed and wilting dwarf versions of their strains, gave forth greenery in such abundance it was as though the soil had found a voice and was singing. The early crops of carrots and new potatoes were the first indication of the soil's new strength, then the summer fruits that arrived a month early with no great sun, the sea kale and cabbages, the leeks and parsnips that made the fields green all winter. Meanwhile my father continued to stockpile his sludgecake. Every time a lagoon was drained and the sludge dried off on the drying beds, my father would go over with Mr Morris's high-sider and, making several journeys, add to his stockpile. The other farmers and gardeners could do nothing but watch in dismay. The rectangular blocks of cake accumulated until my father had built a miniature windowless Manhattan in his first field. He managed to secure his own stall in Covent Garden and bought a motorized van to transport his goods there, at a time when the Joys were still using horses and making an overnight journey. He began employing extra labour, both on the fields and for the stall. And before long he was selling his sludgecake on to other farmers on the Heath. They had no choice, once they'd witnessed the success of his first crops and with their own manure supplies having almost dried up, but to try and strike a deal. You might have supposed my father looked with glee upon such an opportunity for vengeance but he behaved with great magnanimity, even to those who had gone out of their way to make life difficult for him. That is not to say that he didn't profit from his exclusive rights over sludgecake, and he would sometimes teasingly delay and prevaricate over the terms of a deal, but anyone who wanted sludgecake for their land could come to my father and eventually get a price.

Tiberius Joy, having failed to undermine my father's contract with the sludgeworks by legal or devious means, at first steadfastly refused to strike a deal with him. If he needed to buy fertilizer he would buy proper fertilizer from outside, rather than pay for the human compost my father dealt in. But even he could keep up such a protest only for so long. My father's sludgecake was a fraction of the price of outside fertilizer, and was many times as powerful. Tiberius had put a lot of effort into discrediting sludgecake. As a lay preacher in the local Baptist church he wasted no opportunity in putting forth a vision of purity and cleanliness to his congregation. I never attended these, of course, but sometimes Three Cylinders would impart to me the gist of his sermon. 'The Lord sayeth come not to me for a clean heart unless thy hands be clean,' or something like that. It was a half-hearted campaign against a notion of my father as an agent of impurity in the Heath, but gardeners tend to be dispassionate about the metabolism of growth, and have always known that the jewels of flowers and fruits are usually presented on a cushion of the most putrid filth.

An uneasy truce was eventually negotiated between Tiberius Joy and my father, which resulted in a share of the land my father had always believed to be his. You could say a new harmony had been restored to the Heath, now that a scarce resource had been replaced with one of endless and abundant supply. Thanks to the continued appetites of the people of west London, there will never be a shortage of sludgecake. The territorial rivalries of the manure economy have been replaced by the commonwealth of sedimented dried sewage.

And this brings us almost to the present day. My father has become modestly wealthy through his control of sludgecake. He is now one of the most prosperous gardeners on the Heath, and has been out of the medical-supplies business for some years. He has found reconciliation with Tiberius Joy, and I probably can't get through to you what an extraordinary achievement that was for the two men, who now share pre-eminence on the Heath. My father has won true respect from his neighbours.

And now, just as he is beginning to enjoy the fruits of those long years of struggle, the first compulsory purchase orders arrive. They are paying him a pittance for Swan's Rest, and nothing for the land he struggled for so long to nourish. Land that has been in his family for generations. The land you and I are expected to die for in fighting for our country. They say he has no proof of ownership.

I am saying all this not because I want your sympathy for my father and his family – you clearly couldn't care less about our fate – but because I want you to understand why the destruction of our land is so important to me personally, so that you may understand why I was out on the fields when your men found me, and why I was painting what you describe as a strategically sensitive area.

*

Davies gave one of his donnish smiles. 'What you have told me only provides you with a strong motive for seeking redress against the British government for taking away the land your family struggled so hard to "nourish" as you put it. Perhaps that means you would like to supply our enemies with useful information on the precise locations of the main runways, fuel dumps, ammunition caches and bomb-loading areas that will eventually be built here.'

'But don't you understand? Of what I have painted, nothing will remain. It is all going. It would be of no use to a German spy – he will simply have a painting of the remote past, the moment he takes it home.'

'You know it is not all going, Lieutenant Brill. This utter devastation – why do you imagine it? We are simply planning something a little larger than what is already there.'

'I imagine it because I have seen the surveyors out on the fields as far as Perry Oaks. I've seen them south as far as Three Trees Ford. I've seen them with their tripods on their shoulders trampling Mr Morris's redcurrants as they go to measure the fields south of Hope Bridge, Fear Bridge, Lord Northwick's Drain. I am quite certain that within a year every last pond will have been sucked up, the top soil sheared off and your hideous bulldozers with their caterpillar tracks – tanks in all but name, the armoured divisions of the civil engineer and the busybody parish councillor – will come along and fell every last blasted building and tree. Swan's Rest has been in my family for two hundred years, but what is that to the likes of you?'

VII

The vicar of Harmondsworth must take some of the blame. How appropriate for a man of the cloth to sell a plot of land to the men in the leather flying helmets and Biggles jackets. Perhaps he mistook them for a squadron of angels who had come to lift him by his rancid cassock into the realms celestial. He persuaded the church commissioners to sell some of their land at the southern end of Cain Lane, about a mile from our house, to an aviation company owned by a man called Sir Richard Fairey. They built an aircraft hangar and a small grass landing strip. One would hardly have been aware of its existence but for the afternoon buzz and drone of small aircraft, as lazy and unobtrusive as bees. Apart from my father's car, the aerodrome was the only evidence of the modern world in the whole area of the Heath. I could see it from my bedroom window, the hangar raising its black brow above distant trees, such a straight-edged structure it seemed that someone had cut a hole in the landscape with a scalpel.

When my father and I went for our walks I would always urge him to take the route that led closest to the aerodrome. It was in his reluctance to do this that I began to understand his feelings about modern civilization, and his loathing of it. He would far sooner walk along the festering banks of the Perry

Oaks lagoons than by the perimeter fence of the Fairey aero-drome. It was used mainly as a place where aircraft were tested, and the little planes, their engines straining as they were put through their paces five thousand feet above us, seemed to him to represent everything that was vulgar, incongruous and unnatural about the modern world. Sometimes we would pause in our ramblings among the cabbages to watch a Jupiter or a Spartan go into a perilous dive, only pulling up when it seemed its nose was nearly in the trees.

My father would shake his head. 'How long before one of those machines crashes into our village and kills a dozen people?' In fact, the planes were always a distant spectacle, no bigger than mayflies from our viewpoint, but that didn't seem to stop him fretting about them.

'Only birds and the angels have wings,' he said one day. 'We are fools to think we have any business being up there. One of those planes will come up against the face of God Himself. And what'll they do then?'

I, on the other hand, loved the aerodrome, and had a fascination with planes. My father could overcome his distaste for aviation long enough to acknowledge my obsession, and provided me with gifts at Christmas that were the finest treasures I could imagine – model aeroplanes, correct in every detail, perfect miniatures of those that frequented the aerodrome. I cannot describe the thrill when the first of these arrived in my pillow-case one Christmas morning: a de Havilland Hercules complete with a propeller that revolved, and a brave, begoggled detachable pilot and passengers. Others followed at later Christmases and birthdays, and were supplemented by the frequent arrival of the cheaper versions, little diecast pocket-sized models that could be bought for a few pennies from newsagents, and which my father would bring back from his travels. Soon my bedroom was as crowded with planes as the aerodrome itself, arranged carefully along a shelf or windowsill, some suspended from the ceiling as though frozen in mid-flight.

On rare occasions I could persuade him to take our walk right up to the perimeter fence of the aerodrome. If we were lucky we would see a plane take off or land. I was fascinated by how the world seemed to change on the other side of the fence. The muddy industry of the fields gave way immediately to grass, in clipped swathes of level greenness. There was no hard runway in those days: the planes landed on treated lawns, which seemed appropriate given their daintiness and delicacy. Occasionally social events were held in the airfield – a marquee would be erected and posh cars would line up beside the planes. In the remote distance we would watch modishly dressed women step from their earwiggy cars and sip cocktails while watching a Vickers Vulcan sweep gracefully into the air. My father would continue to mumble about the folly of flight, but to me the vision of the world beyond the chain-link fence seemed tantalizingly bright and sophisticated. Dainty little aircraft landing on croquet lawns.

Then we would turn and have to walk home through the long furlongs of cabbages.

It was on one of these walks, though in the opposite direction to the aerodrome, that we found the fallen aviator. He was in one of Tom Edwards's fields. Even before we climbed the stile we could see something odd in there. A grey shape, a small heap of something, in a patch of beetroot. Being taller and having a longer perspective, my father was first to realize what we were looking at. As if to make light, he said, 'Oh dear, dear, dear. Oh dear, dear, *dear*, dear, dear.' As if he had come across a child who'd grazed his knee. 'Oh, dearie, dearie me, what have we here?' We were approaching the figure in the beetroot leaves slowly, until my father suddenly stopped.

'You wait here, Kenny.'

'What is it, Daddy? Is it an animal?' I had thought it might be a pig or a sheep that had collapsed and died, except no such animals were kept in the fields.

'Just you stay there, Kenny.' And so I stayed where I was while my father walked over the rough, furrowed soil towards the figure. I inched forward while he had his back to me. I must have been thirty feet distant from the figure in the leaves. Suddenly what had seemed confused and indistinct took on a recognizable form. A hand and a bare forearm among the green and crimson leaves, the fingers lightly curled, and as white as china. It was a man lying down in Mr Edwards's crop.

I could see now that my father was crouching beside him, and inspecting him in a thoughtful way. Shortly he stood up and walked towards me in a calm and nonchalant manner, casually glancing at the view around him, as if still on his peaceful after-noon walk.

'Looks like Biggles has come down to earth with a bump,' he said, when he arrived at the spot where I'd remained.

'Is it a man?'

'Yes. A pilot. The poor chap must have fallen out of his plane when they were doing one of their loop-the-loops. Look over there.' He pointed. Following his finger I could see, on the hori-zon, a plume of black smoke. 'I wouldn't be surprised if that's where his plane crashed. It could have flown on for miles without its pilot . . .' I detected a tremor in his voice. He was trying very hard to sound calm, to make it seem that this was just an ordi-nary occurrence, that pilots fell out of the sky every other day. 'Listen, Kenny, I need you to run home as fast as you can, and get Mummy to raise the alarm. The best thing would be for her to take the bike and cycle to Sipson police station. I'd better stay here with Biggles – there might be something I can do. OK?'

I hesitated. 'Is he dead?'

'If you run it'll only take you ten minutes. Go on now, shoo!'

'But is he dead?'

'I'm not sure, Kenny. That's why I need to stay here. But tell Mummy we need the police here, and the police will be able to help him. You must run.'

How old was I? Seven or eight years old. I hesitated because I didn't want to be alone, even if I was going away from the body in the beetroot. As I quickly made my way back across the fields and over the stiles, I felt a growing sense of terror. It was peculiar, but the more distance there was between the pilot and myself, the more terrified I became. There wasn't anyone else out in the fields that day. The landscape was an empty vista of ripening fruit and vegetables. I stumbled several times, nearly falling headlong into a dung heap, cutting my legs on some barbed wire, and bruising my knee as I climbed a gate.

My mother was in the front parlour, giving a piano lesson to a little girl with brown ringlets, when I arrived sweaty, tearful, bruised and bleeding. She shrieked when she saw me. 'Kenny, what's happened to you? You're all bloody.'

'There's a dead man in Mr Thomas's field. You've got to go to Sipson on the bike and get the police . . .'

It all seemed to come out as a single word.

'Kenny, what are you saying? I can't understand you. Where's Daddy?'

'He's with the dead man.' I took several breaths to calm my voice, taking bites of air as though it was sandwiches. 'Out in the field. He fell out of a plane. You've got to get the police.'

The girl with brown ringlets was looking at my mother and me with horrified eyes.

'I'm in the middle of a lesson, Kenny. What are you talking about? A dead man? Marjorie, please go into the hall for a moment. Or, better still, why don't you sit at the piano and practise those three bars, and I'll take little Kenny into the lounge . . .'

'You're wasting time. You've got to get on the bike.'

'Don't be silly, Kenny. I can't cycle now – I'm not dressed for it.'

She was wearing one of her long wispy gowns that reached down to the floor. She always put on her best clothes for teaching.

'And, besides, I need to attend to your cuts before I start thinking about going to the police station. Let's go to the bathroom.'

I screamed. My mother was shocked. For the first time she actually seemed to listen to what I was trying to say. 'There's a dead man in the field. Daddy's trying to help him.'

'But if he's dead . . .'

'He might not be completely dead. Dad said he might be a little bit alive. He's trying to help him.'

My mother gathered her thoughts. It seemed that I had managed to convey something of the sincerity of my plea, and that my fear appeared genuine.

'Very well. Now listen to me, Kenny. You stay here and don't move. I'll go to Billy Listbury's and see if he can ride over on his horse. Do you promise me you're telling the truth?' I nodded vigorously. Now my mother was beginning to panic. 'Why didn't your father come back? He could have driven. Oh, the car's in the garage, isn't it? This is ridiculous. Are you sure it was a man? What? He just fell out of a plane? People don't just fall out of planes. Where's my coat? Oh, well, I suppose it's sunny enough. What about my shoes? And Marjorie. What'll I do about Marjorie? I can't just leave her. Oh, if only the girls were here. Oh, Lord, I could have run to Sipson by now. Stay here, Kenny, don't move. And, Marjorie, keep practising those bars. And then do some scales . . .'

These last instructions were shouted through the door as my mother left, wrapping a shawl around herself as she ran as quickly as her cumbersome garments would allow down the gravel drive and onto the lane.

The awful silence of the house was broken by the clumsy and terribly slow opening chords of the Moonlight Sonata, played by the little ringleted girl at the piano. My mother always had her students learning this piece. I knew every bar of the first movement (beyond which the students never seemed to progress), from the cautious, clumsy first attempts of the beginner to the slightly more polished clumsiness of the more practised student. I crept towards the open door of the front parlour to glimpse the little girl, Marjorie, at the Bechstein. All I could see of her were her eyes, frowning with concentration above the music rest. The sonata stopped and started, went back, started again, hesitated. Her presence meant I couldn't leave the house. But there was a dying man out in the fields, and there was nothing I could do. My lateness in getting back to the house might have cost him his life.

And then I thought about all the medical equipment that was stacked in the back parlour. Daddy was out there with the dead or dying man and nothing about his person to help him, not even a tongue depressor.

I darted to the back parlour and thought frantically for the best thing to take. There was a doctor's bag, but it was empty. There wasn't much other stock – Daddy must have been running things down. I grabbed what I could and thrust it into the bag, closed it with an efficient snap of its brass catch, then lugged it quietly past the front parlour, from where Beethoven continued to stumble, and slipped quietly out of the front door. The little girl at the piano would be safe enough for a while.

I ran back the way I had come, the journey made much more difficult by the weight I had to carry. The medical bag continually banged against my legs. As I climbed the gate into Mr Thomas's field I was dismayed to find that my father wasn't there. The fallen aviator, however, was just as he'd been. I couldn't think how this had happened. Surely if my father had left we would have passed each other. I looked all around me, in case he was sitting down, or taking a nap in long grass. There was no one within sight. Just beetroot, cabbages, swedes, celery, blackcurrants pruned down to the ground, all sitting in their silent rows, like an audience. And in the far corner, one of Mr Edwards's dung heaps. The aviator was still just visible as a grey shape in the middle of the beetroot leaves. I found myself drawn towards him. My blood was rushing, my breath was short. I took pigeon steps, but I was relentlessly drawn to the figure of the fallen man. I put my hand over my eyes and peeped through the crack between my fingers, in case what I saw was too terrible. As I came nearer, and the form of the fallen man became clearer, I was relieved to see that he didn't appear too damaged. There was bruising, a few gashes. He was lying on his back, his limbs flung out in a rather odd way, the joints bent at right angles.

I turned my attention to the man's face. The eyes were invisible behind cracked flying goggles. The nostrils were stuffed with a black substance that I didn't immediately recognize as dried blood. The mouth was slightly open and solid with the same stuff. Despite this and the other signs indicating long-deadness, I went back to my medical bag. Perhaps more for show than anything else – whenever the rescuing parties arrived, they would find me valiantly struggling to save a life just gone – I began to administer medical treatment to the dead man.

I took his left arm and rolled up his sleeve. The exposed limb was as cold and hard as stone. I concentrated on avoiding the man's face as I performed this intimate task, wrapping the cuff of the sphygmomanometer around his arm, inserting the stethoscope beneath the cuff and pumping the little rubber ball. I listened. Nothing but silence from the dead man's body. But then, with the cuff fully inflated, silence would be all there was, just as there had been in Pru's body. Surprise came when I began the process of deflation because there was suddenly a sound in my ears, a vibration. A moth bumping against a windowpane. In the remotest distance of the airman's body, a pulse was making itself known. I looked at the man's face. The blood-caked grin was still there. Nothing had changed. The nostrils were still plugged. But now there was a distinct pulse. I took a reading from the mercury. Then I let some of the air out. I listened. And there it was, the heartbeat, just as I'd heard it in my sister's arm, the faintest coming-back-to-life kind of heartbeat. I let out a little more air, just a tiny bit, and the heartbeat grew stronger. Lub-lub, lub-lub, lub-lub, all four chambers of the heart now doing their work, all those valves and portals opening and closing, and all those veins and arteries flowing with crimson. He was alive, and I had brought him back to life, the fallen airman.

I felt elated. And I was, literally. Two powerful hands in my armpits pulled me up into the sky, the ear buds of the stethoscope popped out and fell back into the mud. I was spun in the air and found myself face to face with a policeman in full uniform; he had a cross, red face.

There was another policeman behind him, other people I didn't recognize, someone dressed as a nurse, people in white coats, and there, in the middle of them all, my mother and father.

It wasn't the heartbeat of the fallen man I'd been hearing but the pounding footfalls of this posse as they'd raced over the field towards me.

I thought at first they were angry with me, but they weren't: they were just in a panic, and shocked that I'd spent so much time alone with a corpse. It turned out that Daddy hadn't after all trusted me to get home and rouse the police: he had gone himself to Billy's house using a shortcut, and Billy had gone long before my mother got there. So everything was sorted out. The airman, quite dead beyond any hope of recovery, was stretchered back across the fields.

VIII

It was a world stripped bare. The earth was stark – unclothed, indecent. A world of immodesty. I, personally, had never felt so at home. But, as a camoufleur, I could see there were going to be problems.

We had first caught sight of the Army of the Nile from the steamer, having taken the long way round, entering the Red Sea via the Cape of Good Hope. The six-week voyage had filled us with a great sense of anticipation, at the same time as weakening our bodies and sapping our strength of will. To be so long sea-bound had had a mesmerizing effect on our brains. We passed our time in games of chess, stretched out on the deck, propped up on an elbow or pillowed against a bulkhead, a chess board between us, on which our battles concluded with interminable endgames – two kings and two knights playing tig across the board. Later in the voyage someone organized boxing bouts, roping off a section of the well-deck, aft of the fo'c'sle, around which, on every rail, board and rope that could be used as a viewing point, nearly the whole passengerload could watch. Sergeants, corporals and other ranks fought without gloves in the most undisciplined way. Even I, who knew nothing about the sport, could see they were lunging and swinging like barroom drunks. The practice was eventually banned when a thin little sapper with the fragile features of an Oxford aesthete removed eight front teeth from his opponent's jaws.

We were travelling in convoy, escorted by up to six destroyers that weaved a course in and out of our own, continually changing tack and position, swinging about in the waves for some strategic purpose I was never to understand. Our white wakes were plaited like ropes to the horizon. Our own vessel was the *Lima*, a rather splendid ocean liner, just a few years old, that had hardly done any civilian work before she was converted for troop transport. Apart from four anti-aircraft gun placements, she was little different from her peacetime self – a clean white vessel with a buff funnel that produced an inky black plume to mirror her white wake.

We were three to a cabin. I shared with Knell and Learmouth. Somarco was billeted on another deck, and I was very pleased about that. It is a difficult thing, even on a twenty-five-thousand-ton ship, to avoid speaking to someone for six weeks, but I managed it with Somarco. Learmouth was exasperated with us. He wanted to use the six weeks profitably, to plan and research and formulate what we were going to do when we got out there. He arranged meetings and conferences we were compelled to attend, and Somarco and I would sit as far apart as possible and refuse to meet each other's eyes. 'Damn you, why don't you speak?' Learmouth once burst out. 'We should be fighting the enemy, not each other!' It only set us more firmly in our avoidance, and we turned our chairs to face different ways.

Learmouth wanted us to do as much as we could to promote the use of camouflage among our fellow soldiers, passing on our recently acquired skills whenever we had the opportunity. It had surprised us how much camouflage had been neglected since the Great War. It had been left to individual regiments to manage their own arrangements for concealment, and much specialist knowledge had been lost. Learmouth had played a key role in reviving the practice, and had persuaded the authorities to form a specialized corps. We had undergone six months of training at various locations in England and Wales (none of which, of course, had borne the least resemblance to desert terrain), where retired majors lectured us on trench warfare, and emeritus professors of entomology and botany were delighted to give lectures on leaf mimicry.

Now we were sailing towards our first opportunity to use our skills in the field, and Learmouth was desperate to convince the fighting soldiers that our knowledge could be useful to them. In short, we needed customers. So we would approach groups of squaddies as they sat playing cards, or were simply sunning themselves on the deck, and offer them tips on how to disguise a machine-gun battery. I had thought we might be cold-shouldered by the regular fighting soldiers, derided as namby-pamby artistic types who'd secured non-combatant work, while everyone else had to take their chances on the battlefield, but mostly they were interested, particularly when we spoke in detail about the technical craft.

Learmouth, of course, had no trouble fitting into military life. In fact it seemed, during the war, that he had found his ideal role. He had risen through the ranks as effortlessly as he had previously scaled the hierarchies of the London artistic establishment. Apart from Somarco, whose stock had fallen in the last few years, he was the only one of us to have made any reputation as an artist since leaving the Slade. And Somarco had had a head start on us anyway, as he had been one of our lecturers there.

On the other hand, there was something different about us to anyone who looked closely enough. It was amazing that someone like Knell, with his fondness for religions of his own devising, had even survived this far. The shock of seeing him shorn of the tangled beard that had clung to his face for as long as I'd known him was a jolt in itself. And you would not suppose that he could ever be made to wear a uniform – the ragged cricket pullover and the tatty Oxford bags of his student days had seemed a second skin. Now, clad in homogenous khaki, he could pass for any other soldier, but for the haunted look in his eyes.

VANISHING

Our voyage was one of interminable boredom and frustration. We had hardly seen land since we passed the Isle of Wight (I heard Somarco lamenting to someone that we might never see such vegetation again), and by the time we put in at a port on the west African coast for replenishment, we had been so used to uninterrupted blue in all directions that the sight of red earth, trees and buildings seemed an aberration. We heard on crackly radio broadcasts that General Wavell had launched an offensive in the western desert, and that the Army of the Nile was already up to the Libyan border. Twenty-six thousand prisoners had been taken, and hardly any of our own blood spilt. This news had an unsettling effect on us. If they could manage such swift and bloodless victories without camouflage, how could we persuade anyone of our usefulness? Apart from that, the war in the desert might be over before we even arrived.

Somarco came up to me one night while I was trying to find some moments of solitude among the davits of the boat deck, when the blackness of the sea seemed to glow with its own invisible light, and when the lines of our own ship, like a city in blackout, were visible only as a different type of darkness, its rails and derricks scored black against a universe of stars. I suddenly became aware that he had been standing close to me for some time, just another of the dark shapes on a moonless night.

'You are depressing me with your romanticism,' he said.

I said nothing. He continued, 'You have committed an act of inhuman cruelty, marrying that woman. She can only be brought into a state of deep unhappiness through a marriage to someone whose heart lies elsewhere.'

'I have nothing to say to you, Somarco,' I said, and moved away, managing to lose him in the darkness. Those were the only words that passed between us for the whole voyage.

*

It was when we were steaming slowly up the canal from Suez towards Ismailia and Port Said that we saw the task that had been set for us. I thought at first that we were looking at a sprawling city, perhaps a suburban outpost of Cairo (I had little grasp of the geography of the region at that time), but as we came nearer we saw that this spreading structure was mostly made of canvas – one of the main bases of the Allied armies – workshops, depots, cookhouses, store dumps, munitions dumps, vehicle-repair bays, hutted and tented camps, anti-aircraft batteries and defence works, herds of men and vehicles moving in all directions and raising great clouds of dust. Here it was in all its untidy glory, the incredible mess of an army on the move, and all this just a fraction of the Allied presence in Egypt. Somewhere else, beyond the beige horizon, a regiment of tanks and all their back-up and supply vehicles was trundling through an even starker terrain. The thought that we, who had trained by draping scrim over the odd armoured car in forgotten corners of Wiltshire, could render this straggling mass invisible seemed like a poor joke. We were expected to conceal an army the size of a city in a landscape that offered no cover.

'I don't think I have ever seen anything quite so visible,' I remarked to Learmouth, after we had passed the enormous base in silence.

*

At Port Said we negotiated a sea of paperwork, and packs of children offering us pictures of busty women in frilly lingerie, then took the great white train to Cairo. I should have been thrilled, as someone who had never been abroad before, to be travelling in such exotic realms, but I could think only of the problems that lay ahead of us, and how difficult our task was going to be. From the train, after following the canal for a while, we came upon more of the desert, the parched ground like nothing I had seen before, and I noticed how Somarco, a man who had trained as a botanical illustrator, was horrified by the absence of plant life. The only vegetation was the great spreading palm trees that seemed to grow out of nothing, as if all the greenery of a landscape had been pushed through the eye of a needle, to erupt in plumes of vegetative energy.

It was hilarious for Somarco to accuse me of romanticism, because – oh – he could talk. And I could hear him all through the train journey, even though we were sitting at opposite ends of the carriage. At all the little stations we passed, when people would clamber on, their luggage passed through the window after them, Somarco would chat happily to his new travelling companions, whether they spoke English or not. And it was not just the dragomen he talked to, but families with restless children, officials and holy men in venerable beards, stout businessmen in fezzes. I suppose he was doing good work for the British Army, charming the locals with his conviviality. After all, we had all but taken over an entire train. The handsome white express had become a khaki snake winding on its belly through an arid land.

Learmouth was more the reserved Englishman. He had his sketchbook out and was drawing Egypt as it glided past our windows – palm trees, low-storeyed little towns, scrubby plantations. When I looked at what he'd drawn I couldn't help but laugh: he had reduced all that flow and movement into resolutely motionless images in pastel. And I realized that was Learmouth's special ability: he could freeze the living world of movement at a glance.

I had Knell for company. He had been quiet for some weeks now. I wondered if he had found the privations of travel inhibiting. It was curious for he, more than any of us, had previously glorified the notion of travel. It was he who had proposed that English life and English culture were too small and stifling to

allow the human spirit to fully emerge. He had spoken enthusiastically about the religion of Islam as being one that was free
from the petty restraints of Protestant Christianity. But now that
he was free of those restraints, his spirit seemed to have with-
drawn. But one could never tell with Knell whether it was the
army, or the war, or the foreign land or some as yet unexpressed
inner turmoil that was working on him to suppress his spirit.
Whatever it was, he said hardly a word on the four-hour journey
to Cairo.

In the city itself we were amazed by preposterous Parisian
boulevards of the *belle époque*, town houses that looked hewn from
the Isle of Portland rising out of the desert, squares filled with
lemon trees and statues of squat bronze dignitaries on plinths of
white marble. The continual jostle of Arabs in their long shirts
against the bourgeois plumpness of women in the European style
of dress, with cloches and bonnets and tight-buttoned frocks,
brooched and beaded as if fresh from Schiaparelli's: the latter
stepped from Bentleys and Daimlers, then sailed with the smooth
unstoppability of ocean liners through the crowds and into the
vestibules of grand hotels. Every action in the street seemed to
attract a crowd, everything was spectacle. Then down a corner
from a stately plaza, you would be lost in a bazaar, among the
fakirs and the snake-charmers and the carpet salesmen with the
clouds of burning betel nut, the pungent scent of turmeric and
clove oil.

We put up temporarily in a hotel almost next door to Grey
Pillars, the home of GHQ, Middle East Command. I shared a
shabby, shuttered room with Knell and, with Learmouth and
Somarco, we spent a couple of days in orientation and recupera-
tion. Naturally much of this was spent in contemplation of the
works of the ancient dynasties. Somewhere in the world there
may be a little black-and-white photograph that shows four
tired-looking British officers standing in a row beneath the

noseless face of the Sphinx. One vast head of wind-smoothed sandstone towering above four tiny little human heads – frail, eggshell thin, almost empty. Knell was the most moved by the sights of Giza. He had long dwelt in the galleries of the British Museum, and claimed to have become so well acquainted with the smiling head of Rameses II that a trip to Egypt felt rather like visiting the relations of an old friend.

At Grey Pillars we were dismayed to find that our arrival was entirely unexpected. The man who had sent for us had, while we were at sea, himself been sent elsewhere, and it took an afternoon of delving through more paperwork before the file was found. Luckily a lieutenant colonel, sympathetic to the cause of camouflage, took us under his wing and managed to find a corner of a labyrinthine basement we could use as an office. I believe we were, at that time, the only trained camouflage officers in the whole of the Middle East. Learmouth rose to the occasion, as the senior officer among us. At the lieutenant colonel's suggestion he made preparations for reconnaissance expeditions. There was little point in spending our time in the middle of the city, he said. Our immediate task should be to acquaint ourselves with as much of the terrain as we could. This was when he had the idea of dividing the world into three, granting Knell dominion over southern Egypt and the Sudan, while he would reconnoitre Sinai, Transjordan and Palestine. Somarco and I were to take northern Egypt and Libya.

It was perfectly reasonable of Learmouth to place Somarco and me together. The stand-off between us needed resolution somehow, but at the time I certainly didn't see things like that. I was furious with him, and expressed my feelings at the earliest opportunity.

'What you are doing is grossly unfair,' I said. 'Don't make me spend time with that man. Let me come with you to Palestine.'

'There would be little point in two of us going to Palestine,' he said. 'Libya is far more important at the present time.'

'Then you go with Somarco to Libya. Let me go to Palestine on my own.'

'Brill, you seem to forget that I am your commanding officer, and that you are under an obligation to follow my orders.'

Learmouth gave me an all-knowing look over the rim of his beer glass, for we were drinking in a green-walled bar near the hotel. He was right in what he was thinking, that I had no real desire to go east when the push westwards still had momentum. If Somarco and I were to survey the western desert we might catch up with the Army of the Nile itself. An assault on Bardia seemed likely soon and it was generally thought that a war of movement could develop at any time. So why didn't Learmouth want Libya? I was never quite sure, though I suspect there were people he wanted to meet up with in Jerusalem, old friends of some sort.

'And I'm damned sick of this sulking. How can you sustain such pettiness when we've travelled halfway around the world? I'm putting an end to it, that's what I'm doing. You can live or die by your quarrelling, but you will at least do so while serving the front line.'

It was quite a tirade from Learmouth. He had finally lost patience with us, and he certainly wasn't going to be dissuaded from his plan.

Knell departed almost immediately. We saw him off in a jeep with two specially recruited sappers and an engineer. He had a pencilled itinerary that included all the great sights of the ancient kingdom that existed on the banks of the Nile. I was glad that Knell had company: I wasn't sure about the wisdom of letting him wander alone through southern Egypt but it seemed that he was in good hands.

Learmouth set off the next day in a truck groaning beneath

its load, with another small crew in attendance. Then it was left to Somarco and me to prepare for our journey.

We were given a fifteen-hundredweight truck with desert tyres and we filled it with enough rations for three weeks – mostly potatoes and onions in hemp sacks – and two fifteen-gallon fantasies of fresh water. We also packed bivouac tents; Primus stoves; tobacco and matches; bedrolls and blankets; maps, rolls of canvas cleated with wood to help us out of soft sand; picks and shovels; cord and wire; camouflage nets; rolls of garnish, paints and other camouflage materials; and countless tins of petrol tucked in wherever space could be found.

All of this preparation was undertaken in near silence. We had our lists and we each ticked off those items we intended to procure. But Somarco is a talkative man. Until the present moment he had always had people to talk to, but now there was only me. As we set off, I realized it would be just a matter of time before he felt compelled to break the bitter silence. I had a little bet with myself as to how many miles it would take.

Our route out of Cairo took us past the Pyramids, the camps, Half Way House. We were silent as we passed all of these. It takes a special form of reticence to be silent when passing the Pyramids, but perhaps 'silence' is not quite the right word, for we were travelling in a great caravan of noise – from the roaring of the engine to the street noise that came in through our open windows, to the continual hum and bump of our tyres on the rough roads. Any conversation would have had to be conducted at full volume.

When we finally came to leave the main Alexandria Road and head west, things became a little quieter. In the world around us, too, the cultivation of the basin was becoming sparser, the fields emptier. Ragged fig-tree plantations seemed shrivelled against the immensity of the sand. The sombre camels that aided the white-robed farmers were the only creatures that belonged in such a place. The grand boulevards of Cairo were now a long way behind us, and still we had not spoken. Were we going to spend three weeks in such Trappism?

Finally, the cultivation gave way to the desert proper. It was as though the colours of the world were being removed, one by one; the variousness of things was being edited and simplified until we were travelling in a world of just one hue – an infinite beige, marked here and there by flecks of sage green, or the red rust of an underlying geology. We were nearing the coast now, and northwards the sand was rising to dunes. We looked out hungrily for any glimpse of the sea.

We had set off from Cairo early and were making rapid progress. In the mid-afternoon we were nearing Sidi Barrani, on a small road parallel to the main coast road. We had plans to make Sidi Barrani by nightfall and the next day press on towards Tobruk, where we hoped to catch up with the army. We had heard they were pressing in closely upon the city.

And then we came across a sign – hand-painted and set into an oil drum that was packed with stones. It pointed into the heart of the empty desert, and on its arrow-shaped face it said, in English, '*Aero*'. Somarco brought our truck to a halt beside the sign and stared at it for a few moments. Then he looked at me.

Well, we had discussed with Learmouth how important it was that we find some means of getting into the air and viewing the terrain from above. In nearly seven hours of driving we had not come across a single airfield. Now, it seemed, one was waiting for us, though the sign seemed to point across empty desert, with no discernible track. Somarco gave me a look that said, 'Shall we?' I nodded. He swung the vehicle off the road and followed the direction of the arrow. If the airfield existed, it must be hidden behind the low, rocky crest about two miles ahead of us.

Sure enough, after twenty minutes' difficult driving on loose terrain, we made the crest and the airfield was revealed to us: a few low buildings of badly pointed breezeblocks, a scaffolding tower and three or four ancient aeroplanes lined up beside a flat stretch of sand. At first it appeared to be deserted, but as we approached, figures emerged from some of the buildings. Local people in traditional clothes, they seemed pleased to see us, smiling and waving. There were children among them. We didn't know if these were the staff of the airfield, or Bedouins who were using the buildings as a temporary home. No one spoke any English.

We tried to ask about the planes – were we able to use any of them? The people instead tried to offer us eggs, which they displayed for us in little wooden boxes lined with a sort of grey cotton wool. They swarmed around us with these boxes, holding them up for our inspection, and it was clear we wouldn't get anywhere near the planes until we'd bought some eggs. They weren't interested in money, however: they wanted to barter. After some lengthy negotiations we bought five eggs for a half-cup of sugar, and they seemed very pleased with the deal. It was odd that there weren't any chickens around.

The airfield had the feeling of a place abandoned by both the Italians and the British. Inside one of the buildings we found a picture of Mussolini hanging on one wall, and King George VI on the other. There then emerged an authoritative-seeming figure, a tall, dignified man in a green turban who greeted us with more smiling and, to our relief, some scraps of English.

We made clear our intentions to borrow a plane for a short flight, and the gentleman explained, mostly by use of sign language, that none of the planes had any fuel, except one, which had only a small amount in its tank. We explained that we didn't want to go very far, just a short reconnoitre. Eventually he led us out to the planes. The one with some fuel in its tank was, as we might have predicted, the oldest and most dilapidated of the four available, an open-topped biplane with several struts missing. A museum piece.

'Are you really sure you can fly one of these things, Somarco?' I said, a little nervously.

'Why do you look so worried? You have only begun to fear death since you became a married man, is that it?'

'No, I have only begun to fear death since I learnt that you became a pilot.'

He laughed, and the tension between us eased a little.

'We should offer these people some training in camouflage,' said Somarco. 'Those buildings stand out like boils, with nothing surrounding them but sand.' We were still being followed, as we inspected the planes, by a curious crowd, attentive to our every move. The gentleman did his best, in broken English, to explain their situation. He said they had been forgotten. No one had flown anything from here for months. Yet he said they kept getting told to prepare for the arrival of new squadrons, and for the enlargement of the base. So they stayed here, keeping the place ready.

We began making preparations for a flight in the old Handley Page. Somarco seemed to have fallen in love with the plane, and I was impressed with the thoroughness with which he went about his pre-flight checks. I still couldn't believe he was a pilot. Somarco was such an impractical man, in so many ways. He was not the sort of person you would think of calling for any household repairs, for instance. He surely could not mend a puncture on a bicycle. Yet here he was kicking the tyres of the plane's undercarriage as though he knew exactly what to expect from the dainty little wheels. He checked the remaining struts of the wings, and he inspected the inner workings of the magnificent engine, once he'd thrown open the hood.

I was left to wonder if I'd ever allowed one of these machines, in a near infinitely shrunken form, to land on my carpet-aerodrome back at home. I had had many biplanes – authentic replicas of real machines – that had landed and taken off from there. And when it came to our moment of take-off, I felt as though I was being lifted into the air by the careless fingers of a giant boy.

I had climbed into the cockpit with no more concern than if I was climbing into the back seat of an army jeep, but once Somarco started the prop and was doing all the things a pilot does, the things that suggest a certain degree of technical, indeed scientific, skill, much more than is required for the driving of a land-based vehicle, I was thrown into terrible anxiety. The sheer volume of noise generated by the machine, the uneasiness of the conveyance, the fact that in taxiing onto the desert runway I was lurching about as though I was on a funfair ride – all these sensations filled me with a rising panic, made worse, once we were moving, by the knowledge that there was nothing I could do to stop the progress of the machine into the air.

Then came the sudden surge of speed: in a few seconds I was travelling at a velocity far greater than I or anyone in my family had ever travelled, faster than an express train, and even in the featureless sand of the airport I had a sense of the landscape racing past me, the shake and buzz of speed-vibration coming up through the undercarriage and into the delicate framework of the fuselage. Then the buzzing, rattling ground was neatly unspliced from the wheels, and a sensation of floating replaced it, of riding on the smooth, silky currents of desert air. It is astonishing how quickly the world falls away – in two or three seconds you have reached the top of a cathedral, another few seconds and you are the height of the North Downs, then before you know it you are on a mountain peak and the world is tiny beneath you, except you are, in fact, on nothing. As we ascended, the size and scale of our aeroplane seemed to diminish accordingly, and my cockpit felt like a tiny basket, with nothing but a thin sheet of metal separating me from the immensities of the troposphere. To the north the curtain of the dunes dropped instantly to reveal the blue expanses of the Mediterranean. How could all that seawater have been so near, yet invisible? Suddenly it seemed to fill half the world, and the sky filled the other; the land seemed to exist as a supposition between the two. When we had reached a certain altitude one could only see the ground by leaning over the side and looking directly down. At such moments I felt my life slipping through my tightly clenching hands.

In front of me was the back of Somarco's head, and beyond that the furious whirr of the propeller, and a sense of the universe exploding out of a pinpoint and rushing past us. Somarco signalled something to me without turning, which on reflection I think was an imploration to 'hold on tight', for he then made a couple of sweeping turns that, had I not been strapped in, would have thrown me into the wild air. But this brought the landscape into sudden, sweeping view. The sea was removed, as if someone had pulled a blue cloth to reveal a fantastically intricate piece of wood carving, for that was how the land revealed itself to me – something notched and carved and planed, as though a great carpenter had tried to fill an afternoon by practising his techniques: was that a row of badly hammered nails down there, crooked, some bent? Had someone sawn that piece of headland out? And down there, some careful sandpapering had smoothed those dunes to an incredible fineness.

Somarco gesticulated again, pointing down, making a scribble gesture. I remembered my sketchbook and took it out. I was terrified: to do this I had to let go of the handles. I felt as though I was walking on a high wire with no support, no safety net. But so absorbed was I by the textures and patterns I could see in the world below that I couldn't help but start to make drawings, rapid sketches of curious patterns, the delicate feathering of the dunes, the marbling, pokerwork and stippling. The impasto of a series of beige foothills, the polka-dotting of a little tract of coastline, the crushed velvet of some screes. I saw a plain washed with spilt coffee, in which sugar lumps were dissolving. I saw a thousand broken eggshells. I saw what looked like a deck of playing cards scattered over twenty miles of desert. Wadis, like passion flowers, pressed into the sand. Far more than I could draw. I was producing sketches in a matter of seconds, turning the page, desperately trying to control the paper in the excited air, and labelling the various and many patterns I was seeing, naming them sometimes after artists – Pissarro, Van Gogh, Turner – all the while half conscious of Somarco in front, wielding the controls of the plane.

And then I looked down and the patterns had changed. The beige and brown and yellow of the desert had become the green quadrilaterals of the English countryside. I could see ditches and meres, lonely farmsteads, drift roads, lanes like lengths of wet string, and I could see the elbow of lane on which Swan's Rest stood, I could see the stipple of the old orchard at the back, even the curve of the gravel drive and the circle of the walnut tree. I could see the lagoons of the sludgeworks, like sheets of brushed steel, the underscored plantings of the fruit fields. I could see the drifting smoke from the late bonfires, and I could see myself and my father walking one of the margins, myself following with difficulty my father's big, pacy strides.

And that was when the fallen aviator came to my mind, for he must have seen this view as well – if he had been conscious during the brief journey he made downwards; he would have seen those little fields, the meandering lanes, the straight rivers approaching him with, at first, an imperceptible velocity, which, at a certain moment, gathered itself into an overwhelming preposition – above, below, into . . . Did he have time, I wondered, to take in the landscape that was about to consume him, to take note of those intricately tended fields, the sculpting of crops, the rake marks, the hoe dibbling, before the world had taken him to its bosom? I suppose, as he landed on his back, he might have seen nothing but the sky all the way down, with perhaps his pilotless aircraft sailing away, and shrinking to nothing in the blueness.

Then, quite without warning, Somarco threw the plane into a nose-dive.

I had removed my straps in order to get a better view while I sketched, and was only saved from being ejected into the air by my knees coming up against the bulkhead of my cockpit, the force of which nearly tore them both open. You cannot imagine the sensation – I was effectively weightless for a minute, the plane was dropping away beneath me, we were falling together; my balls, the poor little things, seemed to have travelled up through my body and to be pressing against the base of my heart. The stippled and scalloped desert I had been so absorbed in sketching a few seconds before was now filling all of my forward vision, and seemed to be unfolding and opening like a vastly intricate and complicated flower. Then Somarco pulled us out of our dive, and my weight became that of several elephants. Crushed into the cockpit, all the matter in the universe seemed to be travelling downwards through my body and compressing my bowels. I feared I would soil myself, but by this time we were ascending and it was the bright sky in front of me now, the surface of the Earth had been whisked away and we were soaring vertically. The wings of the plane were shaking so much they seemed to be flapping like the wings of a bird. Struts broke with loud reports. Somarco, either through some blazing recklessness or furious, suicidal indignation, continued his arcing progress and was performing an inside loop, inverting the aeroplane through another ninety degrees until we were upside down. Now, with the ground above my head, the sky beneath me, I fell out of the cockpit, still unstrapped and my knees too weak to hold me. I managed to grab the handle, my legs dangling in the void of the open air. By now, hanging by my hands, I was oriented with head skywards, though the plane was inverted, and it was a strange thing but, even in the utmost startling terror, my life depending entirely on the muscular strength of my fingers, my thoughts were with the fallen airman and how I didn't want to be discovered in the same way, and I imagined that if I did fall, I would plummet the thousands of feet of desert air to land with a thump in Tiberius Joy's dung heap, and be back on the Heath and be filthy, to be taken to the school where the headmaster separated those boys from the Heath into a different line from those who'd come from the suburbs north of the Great West Road, barking at anyone from our demesne for the mud on their shoes, though everyone said it was not mud but shit, which was literally true in my case, as chief teller at the Joys' Bank of Shit, and thinking, all those thousands of feet in the air, how I would like to see that headmaster, Mr Locke, head down in a great heap of horse manure. And now we were in a dive again, as Somarco continued his inside loop – had he noticed that I was now outside the plane? I think that even if he had he wouldn't have cared; in fact, I thought the whole manoeuvre might be some sort of attempt to eject me from the plane and deposit me in the sands of my death. I was now riding the plane like a bareback bronco buster, my hands still clinging, flying as near-freely as it is possible for a man to fly without falling to his certain death, and by now this manoeuvre had been going on long enough for me to experience the true fear of my predicament, to understand that I was suspended between being and non-being, the universe around me winking in and out of existence, and for a moment I felt borne upon unseen hands, of he who covers himself with light like a garment, who stretches out the heavens like a curtain, who walketh upon the wings of the wind, who maketh the clouds his chariot (except there were no clouds out here), and as we approached the Earth once more, I felt myself guided back into the cockpit, and the thought that I might fall receded. By now we had levelled out, and Somarco was beginning a more conventional descent. Though I had fallen into a state of shock, I managed to strap myself in, and was silent and barely conscious for the rest of the journey back to the airfield.

To add to the peculiarity of that day, the staff at the airfield had, while we were in the air, organized a little reception party for our return, thinking us to be distinguished air aces, and being particularly proud that this little-used airfield should suddenly be taken seriously. Being ardently opposed to the Italian imperialism this region had seen in recent years (and overlooking Somarco's phenotypical resemblance to that race), they had thought the occasion worthy of waking the local village chiefs and dignitaries, along with their wives and families. A table had been put out and a samovar of tea prepared, parasols and a rather ornate arbour erected, and as we landed, light applause sprinkled itself across the desert air.

'*Bastardo*,' I said, in barely a whisper, seeing all this as though in a dream, '*Bastardo, bastardo*,' getting gradually louder. Somarco calmly taxied the plane towards the reception party. '*Bastardo*,' I cried.

IX

He appeared at our house one Saturday morning. I was alone in my bedroom when my mother called me downstairs. I found her standing in the hall with a boy who looked a little older than me. He was squat and squarish with a squashy face set in a conical head tipped with orange hair. He was wearing an expression of puzzled affront. His bottom lip protruded. He was holding a briefcase in one hand; the other hung limply by his side. He gave the appearance of having just been delivered, and that he was waiting for someone to sign for him.

'This little fellow,' my mother patted the cold flame of his head lightly, 'is called Marcus Boone. Marcus doesn't have any friends. He has just moved to the village with his mummy and daddy, and he doesn't know anyone, do you?' My mother bent down and delivered this question directly into the boy's cross face. He recoiled slightly, but remained silent. 'Poor thing, it must be so frightening. But he's been told that there's a very special little boy – a very friendly little boy – who lives here. And I've just told Marcus that we have been waiting for years for someone like him to come along. All the times you've complained that there aren't any little boys of your own age to play with. Well, now our prayers have been answered.' She gently pushed the boy towards me. He faltered, as though he had been pushed into a pane of glass. 'Kenneth, why don't you take Marcus to play in the back parlour, and I'll go and make us all some tea?'

And she left us, just like that, left me alone with this terrifying, orange-headed stranger. I had never seen anyone like him. He was wearing a tweed suit, buttoned tightly over his slightly tubby torso. At his neck there was a pale green bow-tie. He was wearing knee breeches and long dark green socks, and polished brown brogues. His cuffs were fastened with emerald cufflinks (from a Christmas cracker, I later learnt). Every inch of his appearance seemed to have been thought about with careful deliberation, every inch of him scrubbed and polished. He seemed to have been fashioned into an awful parody of an adult countryman. I detected a fussy, overbearing mother behind it.

When we entered the back parlour, Marcus stood in the centre of the room, and looked about him rather in the manner

(I imagine now) that a bailiff looks about a room – summing up the value of its contents with a few brief glances and mental calculations. I looked around too, wondering what on earth we were going to do. Then suddenly he spoke.

'I'm not frightened,' he said.

'Pardon?'

'I'm not frightened. Your mummy said I was frightened, but I'm not. I'm not frightened of anything.'

'Oh. Good.'

'I've got lots of friends. I don't know why I'm here, really. I'm not lonely.'

'No. Well, neither am I.'

'But you are. Your mummy said you didn't have any friends.'

'No, she said *you* didn't have any friends.'

'No, she said *you* didn't have any friends.'

'Well I've got two sisters, and some friends as well.'

This brought the argument to a conclusion. It seemed that Marcus didn't have any sisters. He looked around the room again. 'This is a strange room. It looks like a shop.'

He had noticed my father's boxes of merchandise. I was wondering how to reply when he spoke again. 'What are we going to play?'

His voice was distinctly urban. He wasn't a twangy-voiced country boy, like most of the children I knew.

'I could take your blood pressure,' I said.

'Is that a game?'

I tried my best to produce a shrug of indifference. 'Don't know.'

I walked over to where the sphygmomanometers were stacked. Marcus watched with puzzlement, now seeming rather like a customer in the shop he had seen, where I was the obedient proprietor. I was conscious of him watching me as I walked across the room. He was watching me with his whole head, so that, instead of just his eyes following me, his whole head turned, and seemed to echo my movements: when I dipped, so did his head; when I sprang up suddenly, Marcus's head sprang up. I felt inexplicably attuned to Marcus Boone.

I unpacked a sphygmomanometer and assembled it. 'I'll need you to roll up your sleeve.'

'What are you going to do?'

'Just take your blood pressure.'

'I'm not sure I like the sound of that. And what's that you're putting in your ears? That's one of those things doctors wear.'

'It's a stethoscope,' I said.

'Well, what do you think I am? Some sort of girl, who'd want to play doctors and nurses with you?'

'No, I—'

'I'm not going to be the patient, if that's what you're thinking. I'm always the doctor when we play doctors and nurses. But I don't suppose you'd want to be the patient either, would you? So we might as well forget it.'

I dreaded the thought that I would have to take Marcus Boone up to my bedroom and show him my aeroplanes, my only real toys.

'Anyway,' Marcus went on, 'these don't look like toys. Where did you get them from? Why have you got so many of them?'

'My daddy's a doctor,' I said.

'Is he?'

Marcus weighed up the value of being a doctor, just as he had weighed up the value of the objects in the room. Unable to complete the task, he decided to change the subject.

'We can play with what I brought with me,' he said, lifting up his black briefcase. I wondered, for a moment, what wonderful game he had brought with him. Marcus set the case down on a chair, turning it carefully on its side as though it contained something fragile and precious. He snapped open the brass catches, and raised the lid. Then, from behind the lid, he lifted two objects that shocked me with their dangerous beauty. Marcus was holding a full-size silver revolver in each hand, ornately scrolled along the shaft and around the stock in the old West style, with long slender barrels and handles of whorled wood.

'I ain't got any caps,' said Marcus, 'but they make a mighty good click anyway. They're my dad's, and he played with them when he was little like us. Now he's a proper soldier and he don't need them any more because he's got real guns.'

He handed me one of the weapons, proffering it by the barrel. I took it and we began playing instantly. We shot each other, ducked for cover behind settees and armchairs, wriggled on our tummies across the floor, rolled and tumbled, burst out with silent gunfire from behind a curtain, swivelled ourselves on piano stools and other furniture, all the while firing our empty pistols at each other.

When my mother called us into the dining room for tea she looked at us in some alarm. 'Well, you certainly seem to have been using up some energy, haven't you?' Marcus's face was now as red as his hair. His little bow-tie was cocked at an angle. His shirt had come untucked. We each holstered our pistols in our pockets, and as we ate our cake and drank our lemonade, we couldn't resist taking the odd, quiet shot at each other across the dining-room table. Then, when tea was over, it was straight back for another hour of duelling, battling and sniping.

When it was time for Marcus Boone to leave, he suddenly reverted to his former stiff, miniature-adult self. He placed the guns carefully back in his briefcase and clicked it shut. 'I won that game,' he said briskly, holding out his hand to shake.

'What? I didn't think it was a game you could win.'

'You died seventy-six times. I died three times.'

'But that was only because I liked dying,' I said. 'I didn't know you were counting.' It was true: I had found a great thrill in dying theatrically, in the manner of the cowboy films I'd seen in my very rare visits to the cinema in Hatton. I considered myself something of an expert at the heart-clutching, tumbling-downstairs, rolling-on-the-floor, half-sitting-up-and-gasping-for-life-before-collapsing-again kind of death, and had performed it enthusiastically all afternoon.

'Well, you died seventy-six times to my three. I think that makes me the winner fair and square. Don't worry, you just don't have enough experience yet. When you're a little bit older, you might get quite good. Cheerio.'

And he walked briskly out of the house to where a tall, angular woman in a fur coat was waiting for him. I ran to the front door and, as if on a sudden impulse, shouted goodbye to Marcus Boone, who was walking down the drive towards the lane, his podgy legs skipping along a little hurriedly to keep up with his mother. His orange head was inclined towards hers, busily telling her something. Neither of them heard me.

*

There was no school in our hamlet. For my education I attended St Saviour's in Sipson, which provided for all the children of the Heath. Most of them travelled there in the back of a horse-drawn truck driven, usually, by Three Cylinders, and provided voluntarily, but we were not allowed that privilege, my mother insisting that it was not a safe way to travel, although I think she was more concerned about the girls soiling their dresses. Instead she would walk us there, Prudence, Angelica and me, wheeling her bicycle all the way for the solitary return journey. A quiet, slow meander along the lane, deep in the hedgerows, usually with Prudence perched in regal side-saddle on the seat of the bicycle, her legs too short to reach the pedals, Angelica alongside holding one of the handlebars. I usually walked a little apart, either ahead or behind, because I didn't want to be seen with the girls and my mother when the farm truck overtook us, as it usually did shortly before we reached the main road.

It was a mile to the Three Magpies, where the lane took a sharp double turn, as if shaking itself in preparation for what was to follow – its emergence onto the Great West Road and the modern world. To my young eyes this thoroughfare seemed like something handed down from the distant future – broad and recently tarmacadamed, it carried what seemed a continuous flow of motorized traffic, a rattling, chugging, burping cavalcade of cars and lorries that thrilled me. All this machinery with somewhere to go, and somewhere to come from. Tired horses would stand defeated by the roadside with their faces in nose-bags, but in truth the traffic was a fraction of the volume that would be flowing in a few years' time. The wide carriageways seemed generous provision for what was in fact still just a trickle of motorized vehicles.

My mother would carefully shepherd us across this vast stretch of tarmac, after waiting anxiously by the side of the road for a long enough gap (which to her meant no car visible in either direction). Even so, we never had to wait very long to cross.

The school itself was small, squat and chapel-like. Three classrooms were built around an assembly hall with a polished wooden floor, an expanse that, like the A4, seemed vast to my undeveloped sense of proportion. That floor was a treasured asset of the school, constantly polished and buffed by our menacing caretaker, Mr Egford, who would stand at the entrance to the hall with his broom held forth like a lance; he used it to divide the children as they entered, according to the muddiness of their shoes. Only those with clean feet were allowed passage across his precious floor; everyone else had to take the long way round, and that usually meant anyone from the Heath, since it was assumed that their feet were permanently mud-caked.

It was the petty little discriminations like these that made me aware of the divisions in the district. On the north side of the Bath road, new avenues were being constructed that connected Sipson with the suburbs of London itself. Dainty, clean, dapper little streets with gabled and pebble-dashed houses that sat as smugly as cats in their topiaried cul-de-sacs. Sipson was beginning to regard itself as part of the great metropolis, while the people of the Heath, on the south side of the Bath road, were regarded as backward country folk, grubby earth people, knee deep in manure, backs permanently bent from pulling root vegetables out of the ground.

The three classes were large, overcrowded and widely ranging in age. Lessons were conducted briskly and impersonally. Punishments were severe. The infants cavorted in a tiny playground that bordered the Bath road; the juniors had a larger area at the back, on the far side of which were the toilets, in a wooden, roofless hut.

After a day of readings from scripture, the recitation of tables and practising our copperplate on slates, and after a lunch of boiled cabbage and salty rissoles, we would be released back into the world where our mothers were waiting. Then the much more joyful journey back to our secluded land, exchanging the stink of petrol exhaust for that of animal manure.

Prudence, Angelica and I would often act as each other's playmates, when we were away from school. Games involving medical equipment were always our favourites, though when I became bored of these I would retreat to my bedroom and lavish my attention on my collection of model aircraft, which grew by the week. Soon I was assembling my own models from kits. Even my father, when he dared venture into the hated world of aeroplane simulacra that my bedroom had become, was impressed by my aptitude in this direction. Regular little craftsman, he called me.

Sometimes our playing was an attempt to reproduce the world we saw going on around us. We would play gardening games and farming games, and manure games. At other times we would play school games with Angelica, the cleverest, in the role of teacher.

*

'Who was that orange boy?'

We were at the dining table. Angelica and Prudence had been out all afternoon playing in the orchards, but had seen the coming and going of Marcus and his fox-furred mother.

'What orange boy?' said my mother, distracted as usual by thoughts too intricate and troubling to allow her much time in the present moment.

'That little boy who came to the house today.'

'He wasn't little,' I said, performing my very first act of Marcus Boone advocacy.

'Oh, that nice young man,' said my mother, her memory recovered. 'He is a new boy in the village – what was his name? Martin something.'

'Marcus,' I said, too loudly. 'Marcus Boone.'

'That's a stupid name,' said Prudence.

'It's not,' I said. Already I had decided Marcus was one of the best Christian names I had ever heard.

'Why couldn't his parents just call him Mark and have done with it?'

'I should think his parents had very noble intentions in giving their son the Roman form of that name, Angelica. Mark Antony, of whom I am sure you have heard, is really Marcus Antonius.'

'Well, I think it's silly going round the Heath with a Roman name.'

'He's not from the Heath,' I snapped. 'He comes from the

city. And anyway, if it comes to stupid names, I think we could start with Angelica.'

'Kenneth, I will not have that name insulted. It is a perfectly wonderful and suitable name for my elder daughter.'

'It would suit her if she was angelic, but she isn't.'

My mother smiled, and I couldn't help feeling that when she smiled something incredibly precious was wasted. A smile like that deserved a wide and sophisticated audience. It was not in the least bit tainted by the manure incident. I was surprised, in some ways, that it wasn't. I had a dread that her drenching in dung would mark her permanently, that it would leave an indelible stain or an odour that would never budge, but she'd emerged from the shit-heap like a figure in gold, untarnished and resplendent. I hadn't noticed her beauty before then. It had taken the dung to point it out to me.

'Oh, Kenny, I'm sure you know all about angels . . . But tell us about your new friend, Marcus Aurelius, whatever his name is.'

And so I told them, and from that moment onwards I would talk about little else. Marcus Boone – always his full name – Marcus Boone was the son of a rear admiral. Marcus Boone was the grandson of a duke. He was the second cousin of a Knight of the Garter. Marcus Boone's father owned a restaurant in the Place Vendôme. His mother was a Parisienne, a dancer at the Folies-Bergère, star of a little-known French film called *La Petite Pute*. At the same dinner table, a few weeks later, I was scolded for talking excessive, incessant nonsense about Marcus Boone, and for believing everything he said. 'Kenny, we do not want to hear any more about the magnificent Marcus Boone. If he really is a descendant of Viscount Palmerston, then why isn't he called Temple? Oh, you say it's on his mother's side that he's descended. Well, I've never heard such nonsense. And what about his father's private army? Do you really think there are such things as private armies in this day and age? You say he just has to light a beacon in his back garden and a hundred dragoons will converge from far and wide, ready to do his bidding?'

'Well, I like his stories,' said Prudence. 'I think they're funny.'

'They're not funny,' I said. 'Marcus Boone's father has a private army . . .'

'Oh, Kenny, why do you believe anything anyone tells you? Would you believe me if I said I'd been to the moon?'

It was true that I was smitten with Marcus Boone. He was so un-Heath-like, his bearing and manner so urban and urbane. In comparison to people like Three Cylinders, he had all the glamour of an aristocrat, a political doer, a future prime minister. I had never met anyone like him before: he could pronounce with such ease the names of sophisticates; he knew the calibre of every bullet fired by every gun in the British Army. The thought of him astride a shit-heap with spade in hand, his feet in cut-down gum boots, shovelling the droppings – the image was impossible to conjure, and my own past shrank in his light. It became a source of embarrassment, because Marcus and I, in our many confabulations, had become near equals, as I saw it, in our opposition to the ways of the Heath.

We walked to school together along the lane and made a point of chuckling at anyone we saw working in the fields. At school we couldn't sit alongside each other because Marcus was a year older than I, but at playtimes we stood apart from our muddy cohort and mixed, if we mixed at all, with the sons of townspeople. Marcus was careful not to practise his storytelling there, knowing (I now realize) that his absurd claims would be scoffed at. He swore me to secrecy on matters such as his father's private army – 'I don't want people to know how important we are, otherwise I might have to be taken away to a private school.

Or boarding school. Normally the males in our family go to Eton, but they were full up when I was born.'

Marcus Boone very quickly picked up on the divisions that followed the route of the Great West Road, and we were able to place ourselves in the northern camp by pointing out that we both came from grand dwellings to which no land was attached. That fact somehow placed us squarely with the town children and their accountant fathers. Marcus would flick farthings into the air for anyone to catch, and was soon holding court in the playground, at which times he could hardly resist telling something of his family's noble standing and glorious achievements. Why didn't I understand, when it was made so plain, that Marcus Boone was making it all up? Even when there were glaring contradictions in his claims. I should have known it was impossible for a military man to achieve distinction in all branches of the armed forces, and that Marcus's claim that his father was a rear admiral, a general-in-chief and a wing commander was impossible. Others were convinced along with myself – there was something about Marcus Boone's credibility that was undeniable: perhaps his brandy-snap hair or his teddy-bear eyes, his Argyle socks or his countryman's tweeds, perhaps his exquisite elocution, the way his tongue brought out the complicated words that the rest of us could only pretend we knew. Though he couldn't say sphygmomanometer, and didn't know what it meant.

I was never invited to Marcus's home, even though he became a frequent visitor to my own. Marcus would have had it otherwise: 'I do wish you could come to my house, but my mother is not accepting visitors at the moment.'

'Why not?'

'She says the house is unstable.'

I knew the house very well, as we passed it every day on the way to school. Old Hall, at the eastern end of the village, a grand farmhouse that had been empty for as long as I could remember.

It was not easy to see from the road, except in the winter when the hedges became transparent. Dusty, ancient curtains had hung in the windows, slowly rotting in the sunlight. Now they were gone and pretty new ones put in their place. The drive had been re-gravelled, the gardens tidied and the rambling ivy cut back from the walls. Marcus was usually waiting for us at the gate when we passed in the morning, and we would walk together, a little ahead of my mother and sisters. Then the same on the way back, during which we had long conversations, usually on military matters, such as the specifications of certain items of military hardware. Marcus seemed to know everything about every gun that had ever been made. He knew about tanks, bombs, shells, planes. 'What size shell would you need to bomb Mr Evans's farmhouse from here? Thirty-five-millimetre? Fifty-millimetre. Brill, you don't know your calibres. The thirty-five-millimetre could reach from here to Charing Cross station. Oh, I despair of you sometimes, Kenneth Brill.' Then, as we passed the entrance to the driveway of Old Hall, he would suddenly, without any goodbyes or valedictions, scuttle in through the gate and up to the half-hidden house.

Marcus was better than me at almost everything. Not only did he have better parents (I had exaggerated my father into the doctor I knew by now he wasn't – but that didn't work: Marcus had an uncle who was a surgeon), a better house, better toys, he could read ahead of me, count ahead of me, he could run one mile per hour faster, jump an inch or two higher. He exceeded me in everything. Everything, that is, except drawing. I could draw better than him, but that cut no ice with Marcus Boone, because he didn't think drawing was particularly clever. In fact, he thought it was the opposite of clever, and that it was a token of being 'not very bright'. Not that he recognized his inferiority in drawing. As with everything else, he took it for granted that his drawings were better than mine, and became quietly infuriated whenever a teacher praised mine over his (think of that runny-eyed clown you daubed, Marcus Boone, and how blurred and crooked he was compared to my steadfast colour-fixed pierrot – you lost the clown-painting contest, didn't you? Admit it!).

We had long arguments about who was better, a soldier or a doctor.

'Of course a soldier is more important,' he said. 'Who are you going to call upon the next time the Hun tries to invade our island? A doctor?'

'Well, who are you going to call next time you feel sick? A soldier would just shoot you.'

'Don't be a fool, Brill. Anyway, if it wasn't for soldiers, we'd all be speaking German by now.'

'I'd rather be speaking German than speaking dead.'

'Oh, Brill, you've gone and done it now. That's treachery that is.'

'Who cares? My daddy says the King is German anyway.'

'Ooh, Brill, you've gone and done it now – saying the King is German, by Jiminy! My daddy would have you shot for talk like that . . .'

My sisters got out of the way whenever Marcus called because our playing could get quite rough. It was the physical games we played so well, shooting games, chasing games, wrestling games. For variety we sometimes played something quieter, a board game or cards or something else that Marcus had brought with him in his little black briefcase. Marcus was still not tempted by any of the medical equipment, though by now I longed to have a listen to his heart. I was sure it would be a big strong one, a big thumping ginger heart in the middle of that solid chest.

I had even allowed Marcus upstairs to my bedroom for an inspection of my model aeroplanes. He couldn't quite conceal the fact that he was impressed, but was soon telling me about his own models, how much bigger they were. We had many happy hours on the carpet of my bedroom, taxiing de Havillands and Sopwith Camels onto the runway (the Turkish pattern provided perfect runways and holding areas, just like a real airfield), launching them with appropriate vocal sound effects, occasionally crashing them.

Then one day Marcus said, 'I know – why don't we have a sword fight?'

'Because we don't have any swords.'

Marcus rested his elbow in the palm of his other hand, and made as if to stroke a beard on his chin thoughtfully. 'What about knives?'

'Knives? I don't think my mother would like us to play with knives.'

'I don't mean sharp knives. I don't mean daggers or carving knives. I mean those knives you eat your dinner with. They ain't sharp at all. You got any of those?'

Of course, we had a whole drawer full of knives to eat our dinners with, bone-handled, round-tipped instruments of Sheffield steel, blunt as hell. We stole down to the kitchen that very minute, knowing that Mother was in the garden and that Mrs Rossiter wasn't at home. We shuffled in nonchalantly and made for the large oak dresser, pulled open one of the slightly stiff drawers and, with a little jangle, they appeared. Marcus picked one up and examined it in an expert manner, holding it close to his eye and looking down the length of the blade, as if to check its straightness. He brushed the pad of his thumb over the leading edge several times.

'It's as blunt as buggery,' he said. 'No one could cut themselves on one of these.'

'And there's so many, no one's going to miss them.'

We took two of the knives upstairs to my bedroom, believing the sound of metal against metal would be inaudible from there.

It was gingerly (an apt word) at first that we applied our weapons. In the kitchen drawer the knives had seemed commonplace and unremarkable, but in my bedroom they seemed to acquire a new density and shine. They were no longer those everyday things you eat with, rather, they had become what we intended them to be – swords, just as if they had lengthened and sharpened in our hands. We were scared. I could see it in Marcus's eyes, and in the slight tremor in his hand as he held forth his blade. So our first touches were gentle, tentative, speculative. But we soon got used to the knives. We never dreamt we could harm ourselves with such lame weaponry.

We tried the same thing again the next time Marcus visited. More confident now, Marcus was waving his knife around almost as soon as the door was closed. 'On guard!' I held up my knife: the blades touched and gave what seemed like an electrical spark of light. Then instantly we were parrying and counter-parrying, chopping the air back and forth, the blades flashing. I would chase Marcus onto the bed, and we would have a quick sequence of blade clashes. Then, leaping onto the chair (the turret of a Spanish castle), I would flash my blade against his, clash, clash, clash . . .

And then it happened.

Marcus stood on my bed and, with some hurried struggling, freed himself of the smart blue shirt he'd been wearing. Beneath it was a white vest. He pulled this over his head and stood before me, naked to the waist, and all the more fierce and magnificent for it. The podgy flesh was shining with sweat. The lumpy ginger nipples glared at me. I laughed. This, of course, was what real sword-fighters did. I was thrilled, and took my own shirt and vest off. Two warriors, like the mighty captains of Achaea standing on a promontory of Troy, our little bodies seemed transformed by this act of disclosure, and as if stunned by the manliness we had revealed to each other – for beneath the podginess could be discerned the contours of iron-hard muscle – we began unbuckling our belts.

It was as though I had simply invented a new rule of the game, which had to be followed. Within a few moments we had stripped down to our skins. Then, with swords aloft and ready to do battle, we fell into fits of giggles. We were both naked in my bedroom, with knives in our hands. My sisters were somewhere downstairs. My mother was in the back parlour giving a piano lesson (the plodding octaves of the Moonlight Sonata drifted up the stairs) and Mrs Rossiter was washing pots in the kitchen.

Suddenly our nakedness became much more interesting, more exciting, than our sword fight. We ran around the room, bounced on the bed, jumped up at the window, all the time listening carefully for any approaching footsteps. Then I went to the door and opened it a little. Beyond was the world of the fully clothed. It suddenly seemed like an alien place. Dare we enter it?

From then on and for many weeks, our favourite game was 'stripping', as we called it. As far as I can remember, there was nothing sexual about it. It was the transgression that thrilled us, the fact that we were doing something very wrong. And our game of stripping always involved dares of some sort. We would dare each other to venture out of the bedroom and into the house, just a little way at first. I dared Marcus to go out on the landing and stand there for three seconds. As I remember, it seemed to take him hours to summon the courage to do this. Then, after painstakingly checking that there was no one in the upstairs parts of the house, he dashed out, stood there pale and trembling for three very short seconds, then was immediately back in the bedroom, door slammed behind him, and we would again fall into giggling. Then it was my turn. By small increments we increased our dares. Soon we were dashing down the length of the landing to the bathroom and back. Our ambitions grew with each session. Our ultimate goal was to dash down the stairs and into the kitchen without being seen. What would happen if we achieved that? To go even further, to venture outside? To run through the village, over the fields?

Before long we had taken our new game to school. The boys' toilets had large wooden cubicles that could easily fit two people. We would go into one of these during break and, trembling with nervous excitement, strip down to our skins, racing each other into the land of nudity. But that was as far as we dared go at school. There was no question of trying to take our nakedness beyond the privacy of the toilet stall, the risk of being seen was too great. To be naked in the locked cubicle, while all around the fully clothed world of the school was carrying on as normal, felt quite daring enough. The excitement was exquisite.

At home there was the added thrill of the near sightings – to be on the third step down when Mother emerges from the back parlour, and you dash back to the bedroom wondering if she caught a flash of bare boy-ankle at the top of the stairs. Marcus and I would hotly debate the likelihood that we'd been seen during one of our excursions. Then the beautiful terror of hearing footsteps coming up the stairs. How quickly could we get our clothes back on? Like lovers in the third act of some antique farce, we stumbled into our trousers and shirts. It happened once that my mother came into the room just as we were getting the last of our togs back on, and we could act all calm and serene as she came in. Was there the slightest puzzlement as she gazed at us? Of course there was. Looking back on it from all these years in the future, how else could we have seemed but profoundly guilty, standing there in my bedroom, doing absolutely nothing? She must have known that we'd been up to no good, but she could hardly have guessed how.

It was as though, in stripping, we had constructed a kingdom of our own – the land of the naked, which was governed by strict rules and a rather rigid dress code. It was a release from the adult world that had, since we were born, clad us in these peculiar things called clothes. By entering the land of the naked we had defied the oldest and strictest rules of all. It was a simple procedure to get there, if one had the opportunity. One simply had to strip. Any enclosed, secluded space would do, though for the moment the school toilets and my bedroom were the only portals to this land.

Who knows where we might have taken things, how far we might have dared tread naked into the world of the clothed, had not this game come to an abrupt end one evening when, for reasons of overexcitement and a growing sense of invincibility, I took a lunge at Marcus Boone during one of our naked sword fights. Shocked, he grabbed hold of my blade.

'No stabbing, Brill. That's very bad of you.'

He had a firm grip on my knife. He wasn't going to let go until I apologized. His whole body was quivering with tension.

Tapping into a store of indignant energy, I pulled the knife out of his grip.

I should hardly have been surprised (though I was) that, along with the blade of the knife, a spurt of dark liquid came from Marcus's fist and fell on the floor. Marcus was left holding a bulb of his own blood. When he opened his hand it dropped in variously sized spheres onto the Turkish-patterned carpet, which, being already patterned intricately in a shade of wine red, assimilated the new redness instantly (my little aviators ran for cover as a shower of blood fell from the sky). What was less easily ignored was the thing that remained on the palm of Marcus's hand: a deep wound following almost exactly the furrow that palmists call the line of the head. Marcus peered at this gash, then looked at me, then back at the gash with wonder-filled eyes, which soon produced (I swear it) orange tears. Marcus's freckled face glistened like marmalade, then creased in all the usual places as the wounded boy went into a rapture of agony. He looked like an opera singer about to embark on an intense aria. For several minutes (it seemed to me) Marcus's agony was silent. He opened his mouth as wide as the muscles and bones of his face would allow, screwed his eyes as tightly shut as if he had opened a door onto a furnace, but no sound came from the gaping mouth. He was holding his sliced hand by the wrist, unconsciously doing just the right thing to stem the blood flow. Then, eventually, sound came from the depths of Marcus Boone's crimson gullet. An orchestra consisting entirely of bassoons might have made a similar sound. And then he began dancing, if dancing is a good enough word. I don't mean a waltz or a foxtrot: Marcus was performing something more like a morris dance, hopping from foot to foot and spinning round on one leg, kicking the other as high as it would go, then giving double-foot frog-hops. I tried shushing my friend, beseeching him to stifle his deafening yelps, because the last thing I wanted was for my mother to be alerted, since she was only downstairs at the piano with a pupil. Above the basso lamentations of the Moonlight Sonata, I feared she would hear Marcus's cries very clearly.

'I'm bleeding,' said Marcus, though again, it wasn't his voice that spoke the words, but a sort of mouse or rat that must have been concealed in his larynx, because it came out like a dreadful, grating, fork-against-enamel-plate kind of squeak. 'I'm bleeding. I got to have a bandage . . .'

'Your pants,' I said, thinking quickly. Marcus's pants were lying on the floor nearby.

The boy's howling must have been audible downstairs, for the piano had fallen silent mid-Moonlight. I heard my mother calling, 'Is everything all right up there?' In a frenzy I got dressed, urging Marcus to do the same. 'We're OK, Mummy,' I called back, but not very loudly. Marcus was still hopping in pain. I picked up his pants and put them into his hands. 'Get dressed, Marcus – quick! My mummy's coming upstairs.'

Marcus clutched the pants and wrapped them round his torn hand. I yanked my shorts up, buttoned the fly, didn't bother with my own pants, kicked them under the bed, then straight on with the shirt – no vest: I threw that under the bedclothes. I was doing well, nearly dressed. I could hear my mother's footsteps nearing the top of the stairs. She called out again: 'Anything wrong up here? Kenneth, have you been silly?' Only now was Marcus becoming conscious of his nudity above his pain. Through tear-washed eyes he began looking around for his clothes. I threw him a pair of shorts, but too late, the door was opening. There was nothing Marcus could do. My mother was standing there.

From then on I became merely a distant observer of the situation. My mother acted with extreme calmness. You would think she came upon such scenes regularly, a nude boy covered with blood (it had splashed him all over, looking far worse than it was). She took him in hand. There was no scolding, no requests for explanations. Not once during the process of treating Marcus's cut, or shortly afterwards, did she ask any questions at all. She must have seen the two knives on the floor and guessed what had happened. Or perhaps she thought we were in the middle of some sort of blood rite. She got snivelling Marcus his clothes, cleaned and dressed his hand (there was enough first-aid equipment in the house to treat an army), made him decent, and prepared to take him back to his home. All the while I lingered by my model aeroplanes. Marcus and I had been thrust apart. I was very disappointed by his behaviour – to screech so, to howl and snivel so. It was just a cut on the hand. You would think he had lost an arm the way he went on.

I am not sure now what I thought we might be in more trouble for – playing with knives or doing so in the nude. I fully expected, when my mother returned, for her to tell me off – but what about? Knives or nudity? Or both? But I was sure one was worse than the other. The injury could be explained as an accident, but the nudity was self-evidently deliberate. Of course we shouldn't have been playing with knives, but it was never our intention to inflict injury on each other. But we had taken our clothes off with cold intentionality.

Kenneth, would you care to explain why little Marcus had no clothes on just now?

Oh, we were just playing.

That's not really an explanation.

It is, actually.

Kenneth, to an outside observer it looked as though you'd forced little Marcus to strip at knife point.

What? Why would I want to do that?

I don't know. Perhaps you wanted to humiliate him . . .

This was the conversation (re-imagined by my older self) I expected to take place on my mother's return from Old Hall, or something like it. The girls had gathered in the hallway to watch Marcus being led out by my mother, dishevelled, still snivelling, and with an enormous bandage on his hand, through which redness was seeping. They were too shocked by this sight to say anything to me about it. They had been given charge of the student whose lesson had been interrupted, and she stood between them in the hall. It was the same ringleted girl who'd been there on the evening of the fallen aviator. Surely she was not still pounding away at the Moonlight after all this time? Had she made no progress at all? She was half smiling at me as I came down the stairs with the two knives, which I carefully and nervously placed back in the kitchen. Eventually Prudence spoke.

'Kenneth, what did you do to the poor orange boy?'

I decided to act the tough, dangerous knifeman. 'What's it to you? You never liked him anyway.'

'Did you cut him, Kenneth? Because I don't think that's a very clever thing to have done.'

'Well, just you watch your step or I'll cut you up as well.'

The girls gave shrill screams, half fearful, half thrilled, and ran away into the safety of the orchard.

When my mother came back from taking Marcus home, she looked at me with a troubled face – but said nothing.

Later, there were visitors. Marcus Boone's mother and a policeman were at the front door. I listened from the top of the stairs, my mother's soft voice all but drowned by the harsh tones of her accusers. I wondered if they would come for me there and then, and take me away to a cell. The voices continued. I heard the word 'blood' mentioned several times. The policeman spoke with the deep reverberation of a cello – and I recognized the voice: it was the same policeman who had lifted me up to his chest a few months earlier when I had been found beside the body in the fields. The female voice, quieter but with a sharpness to it – the sort of voice a knife might have – spoke with an accent that had a little Cockney in it, not the upper-class tones I'd heard from Marcus's mother before. In times of stress, it seemed, she reverted to her working-class roots.

And then nothing. No reprimand or scolding. No punishment of any kind. Soothed, I presumed, by my mother's unshakeable calmness and her quiet, even tones, the posse of accusers made their way back into the night from which they had come. I heard nothing more about it, although I was asked to stay in my room and sent to bed early that night.

*

My father had been away during this incident. The days of his sludgecake empire were yet to come and several years of commercial travelling lay before him. His return to Swan's Rest after one of his long sales trips was achingly anticipated and rapturously celebrated. I would spend all my time at my bedroom window attentive for a sign of his approach, like a watchman of

Mycenae waiting for the fires that signalled the return of the heroes of Troy. From my window I had a clear view of the drive, and of the lane beyond, and if I leant out I could follow the hedges almost as far as Old Hall. The black roof of my father's Morris would protrude a little above the foliage, like the slick back of a narwhal breaking the green foam of the hedge tops, gliding effortlessly where for days only tired horses and rickety carts had travelled. Then the sad headlamps and slightly dismayed mouth of the car would swing in at the opened gate and crunch through the gravel, flicking stones left and right, showing what I thought to be such a wonderful disregard for the carefully put-together world of Swan's Rest.

And then I loved to see him emerge. He was so unlike the other men one saw around the place: he looked so damn smart in his lounge suit and mackintosh, his feet tiny and pointed in a world where everyone wore wellingtons and mud-caked working boots; his bow-tie – he always wore a bow-tie for work, believing it to be an essential fashion item of the medical classes – the brushed Homburg hat, the sheaf of cardboard folders and account books under one arm, and some medical equipment under the other, leaving the car door wide open as he stepped towards the house, usually to be greeted, before he got that far, by myself and my sisters, when he would drop everything and pick us all up in fond fatherly greeting. I saw him do this now, to my two sisters, the same routine as ever, the account books spilling, invoices and receipts, pink triplicate order forms and carbon paper fluttering across the drive while he picked up Angelica and Prudence.

But on this occasion I couldn't bring myself to run downstairs and join the others. I could only look down from the casement. I watched my mother go out to the car and embrace her husband, and I noted the pureness of contact between them – not so much a ritual of greeting but a moment of fulfilled longing. Then, after a brief conversation between them, he swung a glance up to my window, too quickly for me to hide, and I realized he had been told about the goings-on with Marcus Boone.

*

At dinner I sat quietly at the table, but was pleased to see that I seemed to be under no spell of punishment, and that Father was telling his stories as happily as ever. The room was full of cigar smoke. My father was rarely without a cigar in his mouth when at home. Even during meals it would be smouldering away in the ashtray beside him while he ate for him to take a sip of smoke between mouthfuls. And along with the smoke, there came stories, hugely exaggerated and elaborated but told in the most amusing voice.

'Do you know there's a doctor in Luton who drinks so much he buys two of everything, because he sees double? He even thinks there's two of me. I only know this because I went into his surgery one day when he was sober, and he said to me, where's your twin brother? My twin brother, what are you talking about? – You know, that fellow who looks like you, always stands right next to you. Come to think of it, he says everything you say, at the same time. Oh, my word . . . That's not my twin brother, you're seeing double, that's what. Seeing double? Don't be so silly. It's true, that's why I always have to shake hands with you twice when I leave. Don't be so silly, I'm not seeing double, am I? Tell your twin brother I'm not seeing double. There you are, you're doing it now, there's only one of me, one of me, I tell you. I had to take hold of his head like this,' he grabbed hold of the teapot in its cosy, and shook it, speaking into its blank, knitted face, 'look me in the eye, how many of me are there now? It was no use . . . But why should I complain. Having a client who sees double is good for business. Like I said, he buys two of everything.'

'But why would he buy two of everything, just because he sees two of everything?'

'Oh, now, little Miss Spoil-my-joke, you behave yourself. Behave! Behave!' A raised index finger was thrust before little Prudence's lips every time she began to speak, and she could only giggle instead.

Did the Joys have such entertaining mealtimes, or did they sit in a solemn Baptist silence and think of God? Everything for them seemed to happen in a spirit of eternal thankfulness. They had prayer meetings out in the fields sometimes, Mr Joy and the family gathered around an itinerant pastor standing on an upturned vegetable crate. But we had no need of such pieties in our family, not with my father in full music-hall blast.

There was nothing said about the incident with Marcus Boone, and after dinner Daddy had his customary bath, wallowing loudly in the echoey bathroom. To wash all the money off, he said.

*

For three days I wondered if Marcus Boone had died.

On Monday morning his absence created a sizeable hole in the classroom. Fifth row back and fourth along, there was the vacant desk of Marcus Boone. Like the desks of most absent children, it possessed a strange power – the scratched and scraped varnish, the inky splashes around the inkwell, traces of a presence inexplicably lost. Some children were mysteriously absent for long periods, whole terms sometimes, and their desks remained untouched in all that time. It was almost as if people were consciously avoiding them. It was as though they were haunted.

His absence quickly became a cause of great speculation. Being recognized as Marcus's closest friend, I was continually asked if I knew the cause of his absence. Here I was put in an awkward position. If I claimed ignorance, I would lose the respect I had recently attained as the closest of Marcus's inner circle, but if I admitted the truth, I would be accruing witnesses to testify against me if my actions were ever to be brought before a court. Moreover, if Marcus Boone was dead, the possibility of which now and then crossed my mind, I would have as good as admitted to being his murderer.

'He had an accident with his hand,' I finally said, after a day of intense interrogation.

'What sort of accident?'

'He cut himself.'

'Must have been a jolly bad cut.'

Having given this little morsel of truth to my colleagues, it was taken by them and lovingly fed and nurtured until it had grown into a full-bodied myth. By the following day it was widely accepted that Marcus Boone had cut his entire hand off.

'How'd he do that?'

'Well – 'is da were chopping down a tree an' – whoops-a-daisy – he chopped his little 'un's mitt off instead.'

By the afternoon this had developed into: 'Marcus – he got both his hands cut off. He were feeding apples into the cider press, an' 'is 'ands got caught in the blades.'

'My da says it'll make the cider extra strong.'

A few hours later: 'Marcus Boone – they've given him hooks for where his hands was.'

'How's he going to play cricket now?'

'How's he going to do Spuds?'

'Oh, no, he'll be standing there – one potato, two potato, three potato, four. But he'll win very time. Oh, no – he'll win every time at Spuds . . .'

The following day: 'Marcus Hook – his wrists got infected before they could get the hooks on him. They had to amputate his arm off.'

'Both arms, they said.'

'He'll find swimming a proper struggle now. That's a darn sight harder without any arms.'

'How's he going to hold his slate?'

'How's he going to write?'

'He'll lose all his intelligence.'

'He'll have to go to an orphanage.'

Later that afternoon: 'Marcus has been taken very poorly.'

'Cos he ain't got no arms he can't clean himself, so he caught a disease.'

'Marcus Boone has got yellow fever.'

'Scarlet fever.'

'Black death.'

'Smallpox.'

'Cow colic.'

'Spinnywort ague.'

Finally, on the third day of speculation, the history of Marcus Boone came to its sad and inevitable conclusion.

'Marcus Boone – he's dead.'

On the fourth day Marcus Boone returned to school.

X

So powerful had been the rumours of Marcus's death, so richly had that myth been embroidered, that his return did seem like a resurrection. I first became aware of his materialization as I waited for the opening of the blue doors to the junior corridor. I was leaning against the dirty brickwork, a little weary after the long walk from Swan's Rest, when I heard a commotion in a corner of the playground. A crowd had formed around the miraculous figure of Marcus Boone, who not only appeared to be vigorously alive but to have grown substantially in the meantime. He returned to us twice the boy he was, thrice even. He seemed to have been enhanced, given a growth spurt; he had been magnified, recalibrated. It was as though his magnificent boasting had become physical as well as verbal. From afar I could see how his hair had changed, the ginger biscuit crown, glossier and stiffer and redder than ever. He was a walking exaggeration.

I wanted to approach him and strike up a conversation about guns, but he was in the middle of a fascinated throng, upon whose surface he seemed to float. I was happy to let him hold court. I would soon have my opportunity, once the excitement had died down, of speaking to Marcus again. I relished the prospect. But Marcus remained out of reach all morning. Through the playground and down the corridors the throng persisted, an entourage that could not be penetrated. Never mind, I could wait.

The bandage was still there on his hand. A small white dressing wrapped around the palm and held in place by a safety pin on the back. It looked clean and fresh. As it was on his left hand, it posed no problem for his writing.

In the classroom I could not catch Marcus's attention. My desk was three rows back from his, which meant I had no choice but to wait for him to turn around, but for most of the morning he remained with his back to me. There was one chilling moment when I glanced up from my slate, suddenly aware that I hadn't looked at Marcus for some time, and caught sight of his face fully turned in my direction. I could feel my lips widen, but my smile met with no response. Instead Marcus slowly and coldly withdrew his gaze and returned to his work.

By lunchtime I sensed that something was wrong, and that an unbridgeable divide had opened between us. I hung back and watched him from afar. He took his lunch with new-found friends and in the playground continued to entertain his flock of disciples. He was spinning wonderful stories about the cause of his injury – I heard *knife-fight* mentioned several times. I got the gist of his story – that he had been ambushed by a group of toughs from another village, another school, and that he had fought them off with a branch, knocked the knife out of one of their hands, which he picked up – by the blade at first, hence the cut – then fended them off with valiant thrusts. At the back of this group, on the very edge of earshot, even I found myself moved by this exemplary tale of chivalry and heroism. By the afternoon, indeed, a maiden was involved in the scenario: he had found the toughs bullying a young and very pretty girl. I was stirred to admiration for the boy and his manliness. There was no doubt in anyone's mind that Marcus Boone had become a man in the aftermath of his injury.

We didn't exchange a single word that day until its end, when the school bell had rung for the final time and I was finding my coat in the cloakroom. A little portion of the day seemed to have been set aside for us alone.

'You'll be hearing from my solicitor,' was all he said.

And it was such a manly, grown-up thing to say that I had no reason to doubt that I would, and that once I'd found out what a solicitor was, I would appreciate the full seriousness of the situation.

*

Marcus Boone had manly powers and manly opinions. His favourite subject was the future of the British Empire and the Sudanese question. What should we do about the Boers and the Blacks in South Africa? The Zulus? Never afraid to give his opinion on Bismarck and the Reparations Act, he was at least correct, even then, back in the dark days of the 1920s, to predict another war with the Hun. Then he would pick me out from the crowd that surrounded him, and subject me to ridicule for something I'd said in our previous life – 'Apart from Brill, who, he has confided in me very closely, is a supporter of the Hun in all his protean forms. Why – his father believes the King of England himself is no more than a brother of the Hun. If there will be another war with Germany, it will be the likes of Kenneth Brill we shall send into the breach.'

The taunting at the hands of Manly Marcus was distressing. He persisted, whenever he could, with his stories about my imminent arrest and trial at the hand of one of the fiercest hanging judges in Britain – a close friend of his father's. The chain of connections possessed by Marcus Boone up the hierarchies of power knew no end. Only a residual sense of excess stopped him claiming he had the ear of the prime minister himself. Yet everyone seemed to believe him, including myself, at times.

'Won't be long now, Brill, before you get a knock at the door and there'll be a policeman standing there, and a judge alongside him, and a hangman as well. They'll probably do the deed in your own back garden, from the pear tree, tie a rope over one of the branches, yank you up . . .' He performed a grotesque mime of a lynched man, pulling up his school tie, his tongue sticking out, his eyes popping.

It wasn't in my mind to question Marcus's authority on the matter, though I should have wondered why, given that Marcus was alive and well, I should be executed, a fate I knew to be held in reserve for murderers.

The bandage disappeared after a few weeks.

*

By some means or other we found ourselves in the netherworld behind the hall, an out-of-bounds area whose lord was our boiler-suited janitor, who, Cronus-like with his trident-broom (an object of fascination in itself, so wide and thickly bristled), would sometimes sweep us out of his domain if we strayed in there. But Marcus and I were in a fierce argument that meant we had no care for boundaries, and neither did the little audience we'd garnered, who'd followed in expectation of a display of childish boxing, though mostly our conflict was at the stag-rutting stage, in that we were locked forehead to forehead in a duel of staring. Marcus was the first to strike, though it was more of a rough push than a blow, but it was enough to knock me off my balance. Unaware that I had been slowly moving backwards to the very edge of the big coke heap by the boiler house, I slipped on some loose pieces and fell backwards onto the heap. It was like being cast upon a sea of ball bearings. If I tried to upright myself I slid further into the coke, and all the time every piece was scribbling its dirtiness on me. Dirtiness was very much disapproved of at St Saviour's – Heath boys were regularly caned for muddiness; I had seen children chastised for as little as a grey cuff. To make matters worse, Marcus Boone began throwing pieces of coke at me. The crowd were laughing and cheering. I was, for a few moments, a clown in a slapstick routine who falls over the moment he rights himself, who slips back two steps for every one step forward. Why did I think climbing the coke heap might save me? I did my best to scramble to the top of the thing. Perhaps I thought by attaining the summit I would be out of range of the black missiles that several boys were now hurling at me, or that I would have a better vantage point from which to return their fire. But the coke was like quicksand: it gave way under my feet, and the more I tried to climb the deeper I sank. By the time Mr Egford arrived, with his all-sweeping broom, I was wedged up to my waist in coke, a stump of a boy, all torso and arms, left alone on the black slope.

Mr Egford was more furious, at first, for the way in which his carefully tended heap had been broken and scattered, and ignored my stuck self while he rounded up the dispersed coke with a few strokes of that broad broom. I wiggled half-heartedly while he did this, the sole inhabitant of a scorched island who watches the approaching armada and knows there is nothing he can do. But Mr Egford had wasted his time in tending his heap, for when it came to extracting me, the coke was everywhere again. This made the janitor all the angrier, and he pulled me hard by the wrist so that I nearly cried out.

I begged to be taken to the washroom before I was returned to my class, but Mr Egford would have none of it so I was robbed of the chance of redeeming the situation by washing what I could from my face, hands and clothes. Instead I was shoved into my classroom, where everyone was already settled at their desks, and the whole class erupted with laughter at the sight of me. I had not realized just how black I'd become, until I glimpsed my reflection in the classroom windows, and saw in there a figure I didn't recognize, with spiky hair and darkened skin and filthy clothes, a piccaninny, a blackamoor, a dishevelled little Othello.

I received two strokes for being late, and another four for being dirty. They were delivered with bored efficiency by Mr Thomas, who administered the cane without raising his eyes from the poetry he was reading aloud, synchronizing his strokes to the metre. It was Milton's iambic pentameter that day – 'Is this the Region, this the Soil, the Clime, said then the lost Arch-Angel . . .' It did at least instil an understanding of poetic rhythm in me, but it is hardly surprising that I have despised poetry ever since.

I'd never had six before. It was as though I'd been given gloves of fire.

I was told to go straight to the washroom, which I was glad to do, and managed to hold back my tears until I was out of the classroom, though I glimpsed Marcus Boone's face on the way, bigger and rounder than all the others, and filled with a satisfied grin.

*

'Have you ever had your palm read, Davies?'

'I don't think so.'

'Would you like me to read yours now?'

'I don't think that would be appropriate.'

'Well, then, would you like to read mine?'

'And what do you think I will find there?'

'Perhaps evidence of my innocence.'

I held my hand up, palm facing him. He refused to look at it directly.

'The military courts tend to look for stronger forms of evidence.'

'You're quite right.'

I turned my hand to face me and examined the palm. I was surprised the caning hadn't left a permanent mark. There should have been a red gash to match that which now marked Marcus Boone's. That was the reason for the grin – he had managed to contrive the return of his wound.

'It seems such a cruel thing, to punish by inflicting pain on the hands. They are sense organs, after all, as sensitive to touch as the eyes are to light or the ears to sound. Imagine that teachers began caning children on the eyes or ears: they would be regarded as inhuman. Yet to cane the hands is just as bad.'

'The hand is a very resilient thing,' said Davies, 'whereas the eyes and ears are delicate instruments, easily broken beyond repair. And there would be little point in caning someone on a part of the body that is insensitive to pain.'

'A lawyer's brain is such a wonderful thing. Did you know I once took up palm reading? No, don't reach for your notes, there won't be anything about it in there. It was on a purely amateur level. My father claimed to be a palm reader. Well, with all the people he must have met in his early days, it would have been more surprising if he hadn't picked up that knowledge some- where along the way. He used to read our palms, but in a very jokey way, never saying anything serious. *This is your heart line, which says you'll live to a hundred, this is your head line that says you're a genius, and this is your washing line, which says you need a bath.*

'The wonderful thing about palm reading is that you can read anything you like into the lines of the hand. I once found a book on the subject in a second-hand shop in the Charing Cross Road. This was while I was at the Slade, and one evening, for amusement, I read Alfred Knell's palm, in the saloon bar of the Flag. I had never seen such a cracked and crazed hand, so riddled with lines, so furiously and chaotically mapped. The sur- prising thing was that, once I had started reading Knell's palm, a queue instantly formed of customers who'd seen what I was doing and wanted their own reading. They had no evidence of my abilities, they had simply assumed I knew what I was doing. If they had known that my entire knowledge consisted of an afternoon spent languidly browsing a cheap guide to palmistry, and that I was making most of it up . . .'

'And what did that experience teach you, Lieutenant Brill?'

'Well, it taught me that people are jolly gullible, and will believe anything you tell them, so long as there is the slightest air of authority about you. For me, in the pub, it was simply the fact of my apparent confidence in doing what I was doing that gave me the authority. In other cases, a peaked cap, a bit of ribbon on the shoulder, that's all it takes.'

'Because these are recognized ways of real authority signal- ling itself.'

'Of course, but how do you know there is anything behind

the signal, that the signal isn't an empty sign and that there is nothing behind it?'

'You don't, of course.'

'Even if you could see the authenticity of someone's uniform, you have to take it on trust that the uniform isn't an elaborate and painstaking forgery. So no matter, really, how elaborate the signs, one has to take it on trust at some level. I mean, for all I know, this whole set-up could be a hoax and you and your colleagues could be a bunch of actors, and you've conjured all this out of nowhere, borrowed an abandoned army base . . .'

'For what possible purpose?'

'Who knows? It's not for me to understand the purpose. Rather like God, the con man has his own designs of which the victim can have no inkling. My father, as you say, had some training in the arts of deception. He said that the most valuable thing for a magician was the trust of an audience. It is something you very soon come to understand. Even when they are expecting to be tricked, they do not expect you to go to such elaborate lengths to deceive them.'

'Well, Lieutenant Brill, before long you will be appearing before a court, complete with judges, officers of the judiciary and many others. You will have to stretch your imagination very far indeed to suppose such a situation could be faked. You are taking your interest in camouflage too far, aren't you? I suppose a man who has been dedicated to the arts of deception for so long must have difficulty in the end in distinguishing what is fake from what is real.' Davies sat back in his chair and looked, for a moment, outrageously relaxed. 'Like the famous Camoufleur O'Hara. No doubt you've heard of him?'

'No, I don't think I have.'

'Oh, well, an apocryphal story, no doubt. The Camoufleur O'Hara was a private in the Camouflage Corps operating in Northern Ireland, and was given the task of disguising a tractor factory. He decided the most cunning thing would be to disguise the factory as a cathedral – the chimneys could be easily converted into spires – and so on. It worked and the bombs never fell. This was fine, except for the fact that work had to stop every Sunday when the entire population of the town arrived for mass. You must have heard of the Camoufleur O'Hara.'

*

For some time I had been taking a different route to and from school, to avoid passing Old Hall, Marcus Boone's house, walking instead along Pease Path, which ran in a straight line across the fields connecting the Bath road with Swan's Rest. After my caning that day I ran along Pease Path as fast as I could, to avoid the few other children who took that route because I didn't want them to see the tears I'd been saving all day to dispense in solitude. I've never cried so much, not even when I was a baby (and I didn't cry much then, so my mother told me). When I got to Swan's Rest I still hadn't finished, so I took the path opposite and almost lost myself in the fields and their maze of paths south of the lane.

The world had changed in ways I couldn't understand. Marcus Boone had taken a leap into adulthood and had left me stranded in the mucky leagues of my childishness. And yet it was I who had facilitated this transition, because it seemed to me that something extraordinary had happened during Marcus Boone's brief convalescence. A metamorphosis had occurred, which had enabled the red-haired boy to soar on wings of manly proficiencies. That is why I felt it so necessary to contain my tears until I was out of his sight.

I walked past Mr Horton's Brussels-sprout field, then a narrow quarter-acre of cabbage. Crows poured upwards as I approached. The cabbagy stench of the air, undercut by the foul reek of manure – so much more natural than the schoolroom smells of disinfectant and pencil shavings. I didn't care if anyone said we were a dirty people, I loved those shit-heaps, the rotten, stunted Alps of my childhood.

I crossed the crumbling stile that led into the beetroot field, though by now another crop had taken its place. There were neat rows of carrots with their fluffy green plumes. The Fairey aerodrome was just visible in the distance. I heard the purr of a de Havilland making its final approach, and could see the machine as a silhouette in the last of the day's light. I suddenly felt a sense of terror that the thing would crash, and listened carefully for the familiar change of tone as the plane touched down, then the dying away of the engine altogether. Another human soul delivered back to the surface of the Earth, where it belonged.

I realized I was near the spot where my father and I had found the fallen aviator. I suddenly felt as though I was approaching sacred ground. With a new pattern to the soil, it was difficult to locate the spot where the poor man had landed. Even so, when I thought I had found that spot, I couldn't help but look for some trace of him there, the imprint of a human form that might have survived the spade and the hoe. There was none, of course, but that didn't stop the image re-forming in my mind, of the dead man lying folded in the leaves.

There was a noise behind me and I turned to see the figure of Roddy, Mr Joy's eldest son. I was so shocked I could do nothing but stare at him stupidly. I don't think I had ever seen him so close before – to see how the top half of his face was rather handsome, with sensitive eyes, delicately curved eyebrows – far more handsome than that of Three Cylinders or any of the other Joys. But the lower half of the face was a horrible counterweight, reminding me, a few years later when he first appeared, of Popeye the Sailorman, for his mouth seemed to have been relocated to the side of his nose, and the rest of his face sewn together with a round puffiness. Of the mouth itself there was nothing recognizably mouth-like – no lips or teeth, no mouth-shaped hole. Instead there was a kite-shaped orifice, whose skewedness gave it a permanent smirk. He was wearing a rather elegant and incongruous lounge suit with wellingtons, and was balancing a bundle of tools on his shoulder. He looked as though he had been ordered out into the fields by a well-meaning parent who thought he needed some fresh air. His eyes were expressionless as he gazed at me – no surprise, no curiosity or embarrassment. He was standing by the stile, which was the only exit from the field. I could either stay where I was or walk towards him and leave the field, because Roddy had settled himself at the stile, and had taken out a packet of cigarettes. I hesitated, curious to see how he was going to smoke them with that broken mouth.

He made a noise. A vocalization that couldn't quite be called a word, though the tone suggested some sort of greeting. Then he gestured for me to come closer to him.

'Hello,' I said, as calmly as I could.

He said something else, a sentence. The struggle to produce it made a strand of saliva drop from his mouth. But I couldn't understand. He tried again. I listened carefully and this time realized I could comprehend. 'Have you been crying?'

'Yes,' I said, aware that I felt no shame in admitting this fact to Roddy. I didn't mind him knowing I'd been crying.

'Why?' he said. Still no emotion in the eyes, just an intensity of focus.

'I got the cane.' I thought how feeble that must sound to a man who'd suffered like he had, though Roddy didn't seem to think so. For the first time an emotion flickered in the beautiful eyes, a sense of concern. I felt that Roddy shared my grievance. I sensed he regarded the caning of boys to be wrong under any circumstances.

He held out his pack of cigarettes to me. I thought it would be rude to refuse, so I took one. I had never smoked before, or even touched a cigarette. There was something exquisite about the way it yielded to my little tug, and unslotted itself from its nineteen companions. Roddy held out a flame from a silver lighter, and I had to perform the whole task of smoking, for the first time, in front of him. It was a disastrous event: the smoke burnt my throat, and I bent double with coughing, then heaving, the tears pouring from my eyes in a continuous river. When I stood up, Roddy was laughing, which meant that his non-mouth gave a curious, pink pulsation. I thought it a little unkind of him to find amusement in my suffering, but then again I realized the very idea of suffering became small and obscure in the shadow of the mountain of suffering Roddy had experienced.

'You should have said you don't smoke,' he said.

'I didn't know,' I replied.

When it came to Roddy's turn to smoke, he did so through his nose, taking the smoke in through a nostril, exhaling through his mouth. Without lips he couldn't direct the smoke as it exited, and it just drifted out, which made it seem as if his head was on fire.

'Took me months to learn how to do this,' he said. 'At first it makes you sneeze, but then your nose gets used to it.'

He had come out into the fields to repair some fencing and asked me if I would like to help. So I spent the rest of the afternoon working with Roddy in the field where I'd found the fallen aviator, feeling in a curious way as though the weight of that fallen man had been lifted from me. There was something touching about the spirit of Roddy, the man who had come so close to death, about his cheerful demeanour, his honesty and concern for me. We hammered in loose posts with a mallet, nailed broken postlings together, slowly repaired the boundaries of the field.

We would stop for breaks now and then, and Roddy would let me drink from the flagon he had with him, which contained a very weak cider. Like the cigarette, I was determined to find this pleasurable, and drank as much as I felt able, though I found the sharp yeasty taste revolting. We spoke a little more. I was desperate to ask him about the war, and how he had sustained his injuries. I almost wished he had lost a leg or an arm, so that I could tell him about my father's prosthetic business, but below the neck, Roddy appeared disappointingly complete.

I was conscious by now that I had missed my dinner at home, and that my mother would be wondering where I was. She would have heard from my sisters about my punishment, but I didn't care. It felt good to be doing something useful with my wounded hands, and I couldn't leave Roddy: he was too interesting.

Afterwards he asked me if I would like a reward. I was expecting him to produce some other revolting comestible of the adult world from one of his pockets, perhaps a pipe stuffed with rancid tobacco, or a hip flask full of overpowering brandy, but, no, this reward was stored somewhere else. I found myself following Roddy back towards the Joys' land, where I hadn't been for some time. I helped carry some of the equipment he had brought with him. The fencing mallet in one hand, and a canvas bag strapped over my shoulder, I rolled along behind Roddy's tall strides, too afraid to refuse, even though I knew I would be in trouble if I went anywhere too close to the Joys' farmhouse.

In the end Roddy took me not to his family's farm but to a stone barn close by. He dropped his things by the large door and unbolted it, then swung it open with a little shriek from the rusted hinges.

'In here,' he said, motioning me to go first. I felt great apprehension, wondering if I had been foolish to trust Roddy. By stepping into the barn I was suddenly aware that I could be entering some sort of trap. The interior, glimpsed through the open door, seemed impenetrably black. Nevertheless I put all my trust in the person of the disfigured war veteran, and stepped through. My eyes adjusted slowly to the gloom and I saw that it was indeed an Aladdin's cave. Things of silver glinted in the dim light from slit windows, jewelled clusters, beaten and polished surfaces, enamelled scrolls, like a workshop of heraldry, or a dressing room for medieval knights.

'You can have one of these,' Roddy said.

The barn was full of bicycles, some complete, some in pieces, some in a terrible state of decrepitude, having been hauled, so it looked, from rivers and ditches, others of pristine brightness, with not a mark on their paintwork, their manufacturer's badges shining proudly. From a beam, dozens of tyreless bicycle wheels hung; the bare frames of others were laid against the wall; handlebars, headlamps, brakes, leather saddles, tyres, inner tubes, they were all neatly piled around the barn.

'I'm going into business, soon as I can get myself up and running. All these bicycles here, I've just put them together from old machines people have left in ditches. As long as the frame's solid enough you can find all the spare parts from other bikes, or even buy them new for a few bob. I don't know why people throw away perfectly good bikes just because the brakes don't work or one wheel's bent. I went out with my old man and we found ten bikes in one day, fishing them out of drains we were, and they came out all dripping with weeds. Then when you clean it up and retouch the paintwork and polish the chrome, you've got a bike almost as good as new, just needs a tyre or two. And people will pay good money for a bike like this.' He pulled out a sleek black machine from a row of identical siblings. The wonderful thing about this bike was the love that had gone into its restoration, apparent in the imperfections of the machine; the fact that the retouched paint didn't quite match, that there were still rust spots on the chrome, worn down with polishing until they were as charming as freckles. It was apparent in the black insulating tape that had been used to bind the brake cables to the crossbar, as tender as bandage, and in the silver bracket heads that peeped periscope-like above the lamp holders. Then the chevroned blood of the mudguard reflector, pert and proud on the bicycle's rump, bringing the body to a beautiful stop.

'Have a feel of it,' said Roddy, offering me the horned head of the beast to hold. The handlebars were sheathed in suede. I had never seen or felt anything like it. On curling my fingers round the grips I seemed connected to every spoke and ball bearing in the machine.

'A good, heavy bike,' said Roddy, a long string of spittle falling from the diamond-shaped mouth. There was a permanent damp patch on his shirt where this spittle landed. I had no trouble understanding his talk now. 'Made of tubular pig iron, same stuff they made cannons from. Unbreakable.'

Roddy gestured that I should try the saddle. 'Proper leather, seasoned and waterproofed. And properly sprung.'

It seemed that Roddy considered his bicycles as proof of something, or as an answer to a question no one had asked. It was as though someone had said, 'What has become of the world's bicycles, Roddy? Why are they such sad, flimsy, abandoned things?'

'This will last you a lifetime,' he said. 'If you need any repairs just come back to me, or leave it outside if I'm not here. I'll fix it for you.'

I didn't immediately comprehend that he was saying I could have the bicycle. Bicycles were not easy to come by, in our world. At school, Bobby Turner was always telling us how he was saving up for a bicycle, and that he estimated it would take him another three years, with some help from his dad, before he could afford one.

'I haven't got any money,' I said at last.

Roddy frowned with shock and wagged his head at me, as if to say, 'Don't be silly, just take the bike.'

'Thank you, Roddy,' I said, a little overcome.

'And when you have children of your own you bring them to my shop, and you can pay me back by buying them their bicycles from me.'

I wheeled my new bike down to the lane, watched by Roddy all the way, and waved to him when I pedalled, a little shakily, away.

*

When I got home I remember being surprised by the completeness of my mother's face. In the short time I had spent with Roddy, his half-face had become normal. My mother, for her part, was shocked by the state of my hands. Having heard I'd been caned, she inspected them and was aghast at their state, for they were covered with weals and proto-blisters and were scarlet from my fencing and my cycling. Moreover, my face had been thoroughly rinsed with sweat, which she took for the wash of tears. 'Barbarians,' my mother exclaimed. 'That school is quite barbaric . . .'

Much as I wanted to let her think that the cane was solely responsible for my state, I had to explain my bicycle so had to tell her also about working in the fields with Roddy Joy. The experience had almost entirely cancelled out the pain of corporal punishment.

'Kenneth, how can you have anything to do with the Joys after what they did to me?'

'But Roddy had nothing to do with that. He's different.'

'He certainly is.' I was shocked by my mother's lack of understanding. 'Now, listen, you must wash and change. You look absolutely awful. And I don't want you talking to the Joys any more, and certainly not helping them. I don't care if Roddy is a war hero, you cannot bury people under piles of manure and think the world will carry on as if nothing has happened.'

'But he didn't bury you—'

'Bath!'

I had a bath, grateful that Roddy and my work in the field had almost completely erased the anger and humiliation I had felt that day, first at the hands of manly Marcus, then at the indifferent hands of Mr Thomas and his iambic cane. Roddy had shown me what it really meant to be manly, and I also felt that there was a redemptive energy in the physical labour of farm work. I had missed working in the fields with the Joys. I had missed Three Cylinders and the shit-heaps. In the months that I had scorned them in the company of Marcus Boone, I had stupidly rejected and denied a vital part of my own self.

XI

Now that I had my own bicycle, my world was changing. It was a far bigger world, and a faster one – it rushed by and filled my eyes with light, my ears with breezes; the hedgerows loosened into green rivers either side of me, and the lanes had kinks and corners I'd never noticed before that needed steering around. My favourite route was along High Tree Lane to the ford, where sometimes I would splash toddlers fishing for tiddlers. Then on as far as Stanwell where they had dug the enormous reservoirs, so big that flocks of little yachts could sail on them, and which were the much bigger brothers of our baby lagoons at Perry Oaks, which I would pass on my way back up Tithe Barn Lane. It was here that I was thrown backwards off my bicycle one afternoon by a string tied across the lane between a gatepost and a tree. I had seen this obstacle too late for me to stop and I lay flat on my back in the middle of the lane while my bicycle wonkily journeyed on alone, before tipping into a hedge. Girlish laughter came from behind the hedge and, looking through a wall of hornbeam, I could see something pink, moving.

'I can see you!' I shouted, annoyed that my voice had a tremble in it. No reply but for more tittering. I realized I was next to a gateway in the hedge that led to a driveway and a large house. 'You could kill someone like that, you know.' I was growing a little braver each time I heard the tittering that came in reply, convinced that it was only a little girl behind the hedge. I walked through the gateway and saw the girl sitting on the grass beside a doll's house that was lying on its side, the dolls and furniture having tumbled out onto the neatly cut grass. On seeing me she instantly turned her attention to her dolls, as though she couldn't be less interested in what she'd just seen through the hedge. It was then that I recognized her as the girl from the music lesson, the innocent-seeming, disdainful, boy-hating ringleted girl with her Beethoven sonata. 'I said – you could have killed someone like that.'

'Well, when it comes to killing people, Kenneth Brill, you have a head start on all of us.'

'What do you mean by that?'

'I heard what you did to Marcus Boone. You tried to kill him.'

'No, I didn't. It was an accident.'

I was surprised that she knew about this, as she wasn't a pupil at St Saviour's. Had my fame and notoriety extended beyond Sipson as far as Perry Oaks?

'An accident?'

'Yes. We were having a pretend knife-fight.'

'A pretend knife-fight? But with real knives?'

'Yes. But not very sharp . . .'

'Well, what do you expect?'

'Did you tie that string across the road?' I couldn't at first believe the little girl had done something so boyishly malevolent by herself. Surely she was just the last remaining one of a gang that had fled.

'It's my road. I can do what I like with it.'

'It's not your road. It's the King's highway.'

'When did you last see a king using it?'

I had no answer. Some years later, when we talked about these times, Marjorie confessed she had tied the rope across the lane specifically to catch me. It was like setting a trap for fish, she said, like catching something in a river. She had seen me cycling past her house several times and knew the time of day I was likely to pass. I was very regular in my cycling habits. There was barely any other traffic on Tithe Barn Lane. And she was interested in me because of what she perceived as my badness. The first time we met I had just discovered a dead man in a field. She had been in the house for a piano lesson on the day I came home after being caned for fighting in school. And in the meantime she had learnt of the deep gash I had inflicted on the palm of Marcus Boone's hand. But what moved her was not so much a sexual thrill as a promise of escape. Little Marjorie Twelvetrees felt trapped at Twelvetrees Hall, the red-brick-and-ivy former farmhouse that backed onto the sludgeworks. Her yearnings and complaints were like those of my mother – a detestation of the Heath and its muddy lore, spurred by a dream of wonderful things beyond its boundaries.

'Where did you get that bicycle?'

'A friend.'

'How far have you ridden it?'

'All over. I've ridden up to Sipson, Stanwell, down to Feltham, West Drayton.'

I went out into the lane to retrieve my bike from the hedge. Marjorie came with me. It was deep in a bed of nettles and I had to reach my hand between them, but I was stung anyway.

'I saw you go past the other day – you were going so fast I thought you must be on a motorbike.'

'You can get a good speed up once you get going,' I said.

'Can you fit another person on the back?'

It was then that Marjorie's mother called to her from the house, and Marjorie, suddenly looking scared, ran back through the gateway without a word to me. I was left in the lane with my bike. The rope was still tied across the road. I wondered if I should untie it or just leave it. If anyone ever came up this lane they would get a nasty shock, I thought, and Marjorie could end up in trouble. But, then, she would have only herself to blame. She had tied it there, after all. Why should I have to untie it? So I left it there and cycled home.

The next time Marjorie came for her piano lesson she was back to her old, disdainful self, and pretended not to know me. I listened at the door as she stumbled through her Beethoven. If there is a piece of music that defines my childhood, it is that mournful first movement of Opus 21 or, rather, the sound of a little girl straining her fragile hands at those great octaves, my mother vocalizing the melodic line with a mournful wail – 'It's all in the weight of the little finger, my darling, imagine a ball and chain hanging on your little finger, give it some power . . .'

Marjorie was silent. Then the music would come through beautifully, but it was only my mother giving a demonstration. In reply, Marjorie's trembling, faltering rendition was a crippled echo of my mother's fluency. For the first time I felt disappointed by the shortcomings of one of my mother's pupils. Usually I rejoiced in their cack-handedness, their nothing-but-thumbs clumsiness at the keyboard, but this time I wanted Marjorie to be skilled and deft, I wanted pure, sweet music to come from her hands, not the lumpy, muddy substance they seemed to give. I could hear my mother's voice praising her pupil's efforts. I wanted to hammer on the door, and tell her to buck up her ideas about teaching. *Make little Marjorie into a proper musician! For God's sake, make her into a proper musician so that I can love her! How can I love a girl who flattens the music of the great masters?* But no, Marjorie continued to plink and plonk at our Bechstein, and my mother continued to coo words of encouragement and praise.

'Do you think my mother is a good teacher?' I asked Marjorie, when I next had a chance to speak to her.

'I don't know,' she replied, 'but she enjoys hearing me play for her.'

We spent the next few weeks in each other's company as far as we could. I would cycle over to Twelvetrees Hall whenever the weather was good, and she managed to convince me that she had her mother's blessing for us to go out together on my bike. It was an awkward manoeuvre at first and took a bit of practice. In the end Marjorie would sit on the saddle and I would stand forward on the pedals. She would lightly grip my waist to steady herself. I was thrilled by this invisible touch. It seemed to work as part of one great complex of connectedness – the road vibrating up through the wheels and pedals into my legs, then through the saddle and into Marjorie's susceptible body, through her heart and shoulders and into mine, then back in the opposite directions, echoes and re-echoes of vibration and contact. And somewhere behind it all, though I was far too young to think it at the time, there was another vibration – the shell-bursts of a European battlefield, and a soldier, mute and incomplete, shivering in a Flanders hospice.

Our first journeys were short, wobbly rides to the end of the lane and back. As we gained confidence we cycled further. Soon we were roaming all over the Heath, up to its boundaries. We particularly enjoyed exploring the north side and the Bath road, though with its thunderous traffic we tended to stay on the pavement or else to get off and push. We would stop at the Old

Magpie and watch the drinkers sitting on the benches outside, under the thatch. Once a driver pulled up, his horse towing a low, flat cart on which something large was covered with tarpaulin. When the driver went inside for his ale, we peeked under the tarpaulin to discover a dead horse with green angelica eyes and saxophone nostrils runny with gold. The driver was on his way to the knackers at Colnbrook and always stopped at the Old Magpie, we later learnt. 'Poor old horse,' said Marjorie, then, 'Why don't we trap some rabbits? They say he buys them for their skins.' But Marjorie and I didn't belong to the world of rabbit-catchers. I had noticed, by now, that since the falling out between the Brills and the Joys, I had only associated with outsiders on the Heath.

We saw the motor-bus go past, which had the word 'Bristol' on the front. I knew where that was because a fingerpost near Mad Bridge said 'Bristol 104 miles', pointing resolutely to the west. In the other direction it pointed to London and said '21 miles'. Marjorie said, 'Do you think we could cycle that far?' I considered the possibility. It was roughly two miles from my house to the signpost via Twelvetrees Hall, and it took us a quarter of an hour to cycle there (there was a clock in the butcher's at Longford). This meant, I explained to Marjorie, that it would take us about two days to cycle to Bristol, allowing for rest periods.

'We could sleep under a haystack, or in a barn somewhere, and take sandwiches with us.'

'I don't think I could sit on this thing for two days. And, anyway, what is Bristol? It's probably only a little place, like Feltham. What about London? How long would it take to cycle there?'

I looked at the signpost again and made a quick calculation. 'Three hours,' I said.

Marjorie was thrilled to think of London so close. 'Shall we do it, Kenny? Shall we cycle to London?'

We might have done it had it not been for the sword incident, which put an end to our days of cycling together.

*

It was a frighteningly blue day in late spring or early summer. Marjorie and I had been friends for about a month and had been cycling all over the Heath from Sipson to Stanwell to Longford to Hatton, but never beyond. North, we had not gone further than Harmondsworth; towards the east, Cranford was as far as we'd managed. We had thought about going further but a nasty incident, when we were thrown from the bike by a belligerent motorcyclist, meant that we did our best to stay clear of the busy roads for the time being. And Marjorie, on this brilliantly bright and hot day, took me to her playhouse and showed me what she had. Which was a sword. A real sword, grey, glinting and heavy.

'If we were still young and stupid,' Marjorie said, 'we could play Kings and Queens and I could knight you.'

'Where did you get it?'

'I told you, there are crossed swords on the wall. My mother likes to think she lives in a baronial hall' (I'm using Marjorie's grown-up voice again, if that's OK with you) 'rather than a run-down farmhouse.'

'What'll we do with it? We can't have a sword fight. Not with one sword.' I spoke, of course, as something of an authority in sword-fighting, as Marjorie was quick to acknowledge.

'But if you could fight with it – do you think it would be an adequate weapon?'

I brought its shaft to my eye and looked down its length. I held it crossways by hilt and tip, and worked it up and down to test its flexibility. I made some practice strokes, slicing the air. 'It is a very good sword. But look here, you see? The tip has been blunted. Filed down.'

'Well, how about we chop some apples out of the trees, see how sharp it is?'

Marjorie said her parents were away: there was no one in the house apart from her governess, who never paid any attention to her. We were dangerously free.

There were only small apples on the trees at that time of year, and in Marjorie's orchard the apples were never used, because the trees were old and the apples had turned crabby, so it was OK to use them for sword practice. And this venture led me into a terribly dangerous position, halfway up an apple tree, swinging my sword about to bring down the apples, urged on and guided by Marjorie below. I managed to fall out of the tree and land on the sword, impaling myself. It passed right through my body from front to back, entering at the tummy level.

I felt no pain. In fact, I picked myself up from the grass and was looking about on the ground for the sword when Marjorie pointed out its true location, and gave a delicate little scream. I can recall looking down and wondering why there was an ornate, jewelled sword handle fastened to my pullover, and then I believe I passed out.

My survival was a miracle. The sword passed through my abdomen without puncturing a single organ or severing an artery, thanks to its blunted tip. It was as though a bee had flown through a thunderstorm and not been touched by a single drop of rain. My kidneys were untouched. My liver, so the surgeon said, had been kissed by the cutting edge; my renal and aortic arteries had also been caressed by the blade, but not severed. I was in the operating theatre for three hours while they removed the blade. I'd been fed analgesics through a mesh and I crunched on colourful sweets, and all I could feel was the pricking of a thousand pins and needles, which, being such a minor pain, was all the more frightening.

I call it an impaling, but that is somewhat disrespectful to the memory of anyone who has been truly impaled. During my time in Egypt I heard many stories about the practice, from those elders whose great-grandfathers remembered the time of the Ottomans and the impaling of Suleiman al-Halabi, and how he bore his punishment without expressing a breath of fear or pain. The procedure is a type of vertical and infinite sodomizing, where the anal penetration of the stake is aided by the weight of the victim's own body, until eventually the point emerges through the mouth. Some people claimed the victims were still alive even then. The point of the stake was often rounded, so that it didn't penetrate the internal organs but pushed them aside, thus prolonging the agony of life for as long as possible.

But I was given paints in the hospital. I had never had such things at home. I had never had a sketchbook before. It amazed me when I first saw it – a book of entirely blank pages. As someone who has a fear and loathing of books, to find one with no words in it was a special treat. And I could fill it, not with words, but with pictures. And to my delight I found this an easy thing to do.

My parents had brought my toys to hospital, and my bedside table was filled with all the model aeroplanes it could hold. I was astonished that I could get a convincing representation of those little objects onto the paper. In fact, because I was drawing things that were already representations, my drawings were more like the real thing than the things I was drawing. I came to love the world of objects, the more self-contained the better. A chair, a table, a bed. When I drew these I again had the strong sense that what I had rendered in pencil on paper was even more real than the thing it represented. In the real world a chair is unstable and indistinct, but in a drawing it is there in every detail, complete and perfect, in shape, volume, texture. All the information is there distilled and compressed, whereas in the real world, these qualities can be only fleetingly discerned.

I was so enthralled by my new-found abilities that my convalescence passed almost without my noticing. I only recently
remembered the suffering and anxiety on my mother's face
when she came to visit me. Only later did she recall the shock at
having the policeman call to inform her that her son had been
'run through with a rapier', 'and I imagined that you had been in
some eighteenth-century duel. But how that sword managed to
pass through your body without puncturing a single element of
your vitals, I don't know. You must be immortal.'

It was a long time before my mother noticed my drawings.
She was so concerned with my healing that she was unaware of
how I'd passed my time. But one day on the ward she finally
turned her attention to my sketchbooks, and after turning a few
pages she said, with genuine puzzlement, 'Who did all these
marvellous drawings?'

When I returned home after two months in hospital (I had
suffered various infections and complications), my drawing
mania continued and I was given a stack of paper by my father
who had picked it up on his travels – thick, smooth, almost
card-like, and dazzling in its whiteness. There must have been
hundreds of sheets in the stack, and every day I would take
another, and it was like being given a kingdom to populate, a land
of unblemished snow in which I could make my mark. My father
was also able to procure some good-quality pencils – sleek black
instruments from which the shiny greyness poured like liquid,
soft and yielding. I became aware of the pencil's range, how
similar it was to the piano downstairs, with low registers and
high registers. If you pressed down hard you got something that
was almost pure black, and then, as you released the pressure, an
almost infinite range of tones ending in a trill of near-white.

My mother continued to be baffled by the sudden intrusion
of talent upon her previously unadept son. 'You didn't do these
yourself, Kenneth?'

'I did.'

'But – these are marvellous. They have such – maturity of vision.'

I didn't know what that meant. (I still don't.)

'I like drawing.'

Even my father was impressed, and he was not a man easily given to praise of his children. 'Not bad little sketches. Better than I could do myself, I have to say, much as it hurts me to admit it. You're smarter than your old man – with a pencil, mind. I could still outdo you at everything else – so watch it!'

The world was more complicated and interesting than I had ever thought possible. I could not free myself of the need to represent it with my pencils.

*

When I returned to school, it was I who had grown.

There was only one art lesson a week. It provided little opportunity for relishing the world of objects and usually consisted of the meticulous copying of pictures from books about the British Empire. The lesson usually began with squabbling over the limited supplies of pencils and paints, and we sometimes had to share one paintbrush between four people. But I enjoyed the copying exercises. It seemed that, by accident, our philistine teacher, who had devised an art lesson that required the least teacherly input, had stumbled on the perfect way to instil the skills of the illustrative artist. My talents were suddenly noted, though not so much by our teacher as by my fellow pupils, who were amazed by my ability to render accurate lines to represent the shooting of a tiger by His Majesty King Edward VII, or the arrival of Livingstone at Lake Victoria. 'Kenneth Brill,' I remember a little girl saying, 'you've done a painting and it looks exactly like the picture in the book.' No one ever said any such thing to Marcus Boone. Tallest, gingerest and cleverest in the class, he could no longer claim pre-eminence in the dominion of art.

It was the task of depicting a harlequin that proved his final artistic undoing. This was a little harder than usual because we were given only a short viewing of the image, then had to paint it from memory. The diamond pattern of the clown's apparel proved too much for most in the class, who let their colours bleed into each other. Mine was fast and accurate, edge-perfect, a cascade of watertight zigzags that curved and foreshortened to describe a human form, topped with a chevroned bicorne, as though Napoleon had been put through a kaleidoscope. I had discovered the subtle trick of allowing colours to dry before over-painting, and I had kept such profound and useful knowledge to myself. But Marcus Boone's painting was of a most melancholy jester who seemed to be drowning in his own muddy tears, his whole body a weeping mess of red and black. Even Mrs Higgins couldn't conceal her admiration for my effort, and held up my painting as an example to the rest of the class. 'Look at how little Kenneth Brill has done his harlequin. If he can manage it, why can't the rest of you?'

I found Marcus crying in a corner of the playground towards the end of lunchtime. But when he saw me he quickly put away his tears, unfolded himself and looked at me scornfully. He was holding his harlequin in one hand.

'Why are you crying, Marcus?' I said, with genuine bewilderment in my voice.

'Mrs Higgins threw my harlequin in the wastepaper basket,' said Marcus, realizing there was little point in trying to conceal the truth about his blubbing. 'When I went to collect it at the end of the last lesson it wasn't anywhere to be seen, and then I asked Mrs Higgins, and she just pointed to the wastepaper basket and said, "What do you want it for?" I said I didn't know.

So I said . . .' Here the emotions became too much for young Marcus: his lips trembled and amber tears sprang from his eyes, like little lenses that briefly magnified each freckle they traversed in their freckly journey down his face '. . . I said am I allowed to look in it for my painting, and she said she didn't see why not, though she couldn't see why I would want it. She said it was just a mess. But look.'

Marcus unfolded his painting to show me. A terrible swirl of colours that, in so thorough mixing, had lost their integrity and vibrancy and had become a dull, brownish aggregate. Not only had Marcus over-painted while the paint was wet, not only had he taken a wet colour right up to the edge of another wet colour so that the two had merged, but at the end of the lesson he had folded his wet painting. He had folded it in half twice. The procedure had, when unfolded, resulted in a far greater mess than had existed prior to folding, with the added complication of a muddy symmetry appearing, the clown having doubled itself around a horizontal axis, the messy clown's face appearing now down below, so that it was impossible to tell which way up the painting was meant to be. Furthermore, the paint having patchily dried after it had been folded, in unfolding it had produced great tears across the pigment, which stood out as shreds of brilliant white in all the chaos of colour, and arcs and ribbons of torn paper and paint were looped around the folds, rather like a Christmas decoration. Marcus's painting, appallingly bad to start with, had undergone a transformation into something of transcendent ineptitude. It not only signalled to the world that Marcus Boone could not paint, but that he was so bad he was a sort of anti-artist, who was only capable of producing things that were the opposite of artistic objects. And, like all clever boys who are bad artists, he was unable to comprehend his own badness. I truly believe that when Marcus Boone looked at that shredded mess of paint and paper, he saw a perfectly painted harlequin smiling back at him.

I didn't say anything, not straight away, but waited instead to see (in a spirit of scientific curiosity) what sort of effect my touch would have. And you, Marcus Boone, absorbed my touch instantly, there was no resistance to it whatsoever, but it was only a shoulder touch, not like I'd put my hand on your balls, as I suddenly have a retrospective urge to do now, from the almighty distance of my vantage point; nevertheless, you didn't flinch, not one bit, which meant you had accepted my consoling touch – must, in fact, have found comfort and security in it.

I can't think now how wavery and shimmery my feelings must have been, to have myself passing in and out of loathing for you and love, a chicane of emotions that I describe in order to excuse what I eventually did to you.

'Can't we just be friends again?' I blurted.

'Suppose so,' Marcus replied. Then his eyes flashed with excitement. 'Let's go in the toilets and do a strip, like we used to.'

I couldn't quite believe that the Marcus who had seemed suddenly so mature had reverted to this childish entertainment. 'What? Now?'

'Yes, come on . . .'

The idea of becoming nude for the sake of it seemed unbearably immature to me. It was as if in another life, idyllic and remote, we had indulged in such stupidity.

'I don't think . . .'

'You said you wanted to be my friend. Now you've got to do it if you want us to be friends.'

'I don't know, Marcus, it seems a bit of a silly thing to do now.' How wonderfully old I sounded to myself. Marcus eyed me with reptilian intensity. I was being put to the test. 'If you want to do it,' I said, 'I'll come in with you . . .'

I couldn't even finish the sentence before Marcus was pulling me by the elbow into the toilets.

This had never happened before, Marcus stripping while I remained clothed. But now I understand that this was the essential component of our nudity games: they had to be witnessed, even if only by each other. That was what gave them their thrill. Looking back I can see why Marcus was so keen to strip even if I remained clothed.

I stood there in the cubicle, my hands nonchalantly in my pockets, trying to appear relaxed and casual while Marcus busily went about disrobing. It was nearly the end of break. Marcus quickly lowered his shorts and pants, letting his long shirt-tails dangle. He then took hold of these and lifted them up to his chin in one brisk movement, revealing the length of his nakedness from his knees to his nipples. His torso was scant and mottled. His legs thin, kinked. For the first time I found my attention drawn to his genitals, still unflossed, still rudimentary. But I tried to resist the urge to look, and did my best to focus on his face, whose brown eyes looked back at me with a curious expression – how can I describe it? It was as though he couldn't see me, as though he couldn't see beyond the corona of his own excitement, blinded by bliss. And his mouth just visible, a little hamster tongue protruding sideways (he did this thing, when he laughed, of poking his tongue out sideways).

He still hadn't grasped that I had grown out of this childish delight in nudity, that I could see it now for what it was, an indulgence of the most puerile kind, belonging to the realm of potties and playhouses.

I felt like a bored father who's been asked to watch a son's performance of some trivial achievement (hopping, for instance) for the umpteenth time, the father who has become a little tired of expressing amazement and awe.

But this was only the first stage of Marcus's disrobing: the instant flash of fleshy revelation. He now intended to go on to full nakedness. He pulled frantically on the buttons of his shirt, and of his collar; he struggled to step out of his shorts and underpants, got them tangled up with his shoes and socks, had to hop about and bump against the walls of the stall. He was determined to strip down to nothing. But it was nearly the end of break, the bell would shortly be rung, and if we were to be late for our class we would both be in trouble.

Then, fully nude, he started doing a little jig, pirouetting, making the most of the fact that he was in the middle of school, without a stitch on, as nude as he could possibly be, and I was saying something like – all right, can I go now, please? And it was as Marcus was with his back to me, doing his silly nude dance, that I felt a need to pay him back for all those months of cruelty. He had cast me into the wilderness, and now I had an opportunity to thrust him into a similar hinterland. And so I did it straight away, a spontaneous act that involved hardly any conscious thought. While Marcus had his back to me, his little white buttocks protruding with blubbery impertinence, I snatched his clothes, which were in a little heap on the floor, and I left the cubicle and ran. Marcus didn't have a moment to think what was happening, and neither did I.

I ran without knowing where I was going, or thinking what I had done. The playground was emptying as children drifted back into the school building; we only had a few minutes before class started. Suddenly Marcus's clothes felt like a huge burden I was forced to haul around. Should I just throw them away? Should I take them with me into class, hide them in my desk? Should I backtrack and give the poor boy his clothes? The latter was impossible. I had embarked on a road with no turning. I had to follow it to its end. And it ended, somewhat to my surprise, at the coke heap by the boiler house, the chuckling, grimy mountain that had seen my most abject humiliation a few months before. It seemed most fitting, then, that I should bury Marcus's clothes on its lower slopes. I was taking a tremendous risk. Should Mr Egford suddenly appear from the boiler house, or round the corner from the playground, I would likely be taken to see the headmaster and suffer severe punishment. The coke was noisy as I pawed a hole, deposited the togs, then pawed the coke back over them. My hands were dirty, but not so bad that I couldn't wipe them nearly clean with some spit on the inside of my pullover.

I had to run quickly to be in class on time. I half expected to be pursued by a naked boy, but it seemed that Marcus had become trapped by his own nudity, as I had hoped he would, and was unable to leave the toilets.

And so I sat through an afternoon of lessons, imagining the turmoil that was happening at that moment in one cubicle of the lavatories – a little naked boy, imprisoned, unable to escape, confined by shame, the little boy who had, only a few seconds before, been revelling in the starkness of his social disobedience, doing that silly little jig. What must he have felt, turning round to see his companion and his clothes gone? I sweated at my desk with excitement at the thought of it. The world must have been utterly transformed for him, a place in which he dare not even set foot, as much as if it had suddenly been rendered in flame.

Mr Thomas was taking us through the intricacies of Euclid now, though his chalked trigonometry seemed meaningless to me, and as the minutes and hours passed I became increasingly anxious about the fate of Marcus Boone. From my desk, if I stretched myself vertically as far as was possible without snapping, I could get a view of the playground and the toilets at the far end. I monitored this view so frequently that it was eventually noted by Mr Thomas – 'Brill, if you want to live, you will look at the blackboard and not out of the window.' When this failed to check my window-gazing, he picked up the cane and rapped it on the desk. 'Brill, I will not tell you again.' By now my attentiveness to the view through the window had stirred others to crane their necks and peer into the empty playground. I realized this might cause me to be identified as the guilty party if anything did happen, so I resolved to fix my attention on the board and on my slate.

It seemed to me that many hours of baffling trigonometry passed before there was a noticeable commotion, and my heart emptied. People were standing up, deaf to Mr Thomas's prohibitions; there were cries of wonder, of horror. People were rushing over to the window to look out. I joined them.

I am haunted by what I then saw. Marcus Boone, who'd spent more than two hours naked in the toilets, finally emerging, his hands cupped over his genitals, staggering across the playground in a most melodramatic way, exaggerating the labour of movement so thoroughly he resembled Masaccio's depiction of the fall of man, moving with his eyes cast towards Heaven and a pleading look on his face. His body was filthy for he must have made all sorts of efforts to escape unseen from the toilet block by squeezing through narrow gaps – there were long scratches down his legs and across his chest. Everyone in the schoolroom was on their feet and at the window to see the great drama that was unfolding in the playground. Our teacher shouted at us to sit down, but when he saw what had drawn our attention, he was as dumbstruck as the rest of us. Who is that skinny little waif? Why, it's Marcus Boone. A thin strip of humanity crumpling up on the playground gravel, falling to his knees, a broken stick. It was Mr Thomas himself who was first to the rescue of the little boy. Ordering us to remain in the classroom, he charged full tilt into the playground unfurling his academic gown as he went. He then used this garment to clothe the naked boy. The sight of Mr Thomas without his robe was almost as startling as Marcus Boone without his clothes.

XII

'*Bastardo!*' I cried. 'You great fucking *bastardo*!'

They were the first words I'd managed to drag from my throat since our exit from the de Havilland where, I was later told by Somarco, I had sat huddled and rocking in the passenger seat like a thrashed child, refusing to speak or make eye contact. I have little memory of those moments; indeed, it seemed my mind and my memory had been left looping the loop in the troposphere while the empty vessel of my earthly body trembled on the ground, although I do remember, once the terrible mechanical whirr of the propeller had died down, the light pitter-patter of applause from the reception party that had gathered in the airfield, and I can remember a chorus of 'For they are a jolly good fellow', which sounded most awkward on the Arab tongue, and I can remember, when I was finally prised by Somarco from my cockpit, the shrieks of laughter and appreciative ululation that came when I tried climbing down the ladder that had been erected.

A beaming sub-sultan approached with a dish of dried dates, and burka-clad women continued their celebratory calling, but Somarco managed to excuse us by reference to some unspecified emergency and, apologizing for my behaviour, dragged me as speedily as he could to the truck. This was difficult because the experience up there had acted on me like alcohol: I was intoxicated from the pulling of my blood back and forth through my body, my heart felt like a paper balloon, my brain like burning wool, and I resisted Somarco's grip and tried to meet the respectable elders with their gifts, though could not keep on my feet for more than two seconds and, like a pitiable drunkard, staggered sideways and then over. Eventually I was dragged away. By now the welcoming party had fallen into a rather puzzled silence brought on, perhaps, by my repeated exclamations of *Bastardo!* At one point I managed to pull Somarco to the ground and grapple with him, which must have sent confusing signals to the locals, who perhaps thought one of us had turned enemy, and a sword was drawn by someone, though by then we were making our exit. By the time we reached the truck our only pursuers were a group of small children, who were filled with laughing as they launched little pebbles at us, some of which struck their targets and stung considerably.

'*Bastardo!* Filthy Italian *bastardo!*'

I was silenced by a smack in the face. Somarco had lost his temper. Pain always shuts me up, but I wept instead, cupping the blood as it came from my nose. The truck swung round so sharply I was almost thrown out of the open window.

'I'll run those little rats down!' said Somarco. The children were capering in front of us, still throwing their pebbles, and for a terrifying moment it seemed that he would carry out his threat. I had not realized he was so angry. Eventually we found our way back to the main road, and it was more than an hour before we spoke to each other again.

*

Our sulking might have continued for the rest of our time in North Africa had we not, very shortly after this, been brought up sharply against the reality of the war. The battle for Sidi Barrani had been won some weeks previously, but the devastation was still fresh. Many buildings were reduced to rubble, or were hollow shells. Oil drums were scattered across the roads and piled up in passageways. The town major lived in a dug-out in the centre of a heap of rubble, surrounded by ruins. Official buildings nearby bore inscriptions that even I, who knew no Italian but a schoolboy form of Latin, could translate – and Somarco could read with ease: 'Believe – Obey – Fight', 'Il Duce is always right.'

'So what do you think of that, you crazy, murderous Italian bastard?'

Somarco looked at me with scorn in his eyes. 'You should not talk to me.'

'You should not even look at me. After what you did I could report you for attempted murder of a superior. Is that it, Somarco? You're jealous of my rank?'

We were standing in the pitted and strewn town square. It was late evening now, the sun was beginning to set, and the shocking chilliness of the winter desert was starting to make itself known.

'I am not jealous of anything,' Somarco said, climbing back into the truck.

Our presence in the town was hardly noticed. Unlike the airfield, it was a place that had seen a regular stream of military vehicles in both directions and, after the recent battle, had become largely deserted of its civilian population. The town major was a weary-looking Australian, who advised us to press on as far as we could before nightfall, and to camp out. The town had no water supply, and few of the houses were suitable for occupation. He also advised us to head off the main road, the so-called 'Road to Victory', which the Italians had intended to use to convey their might into Egypt. The road was mostly unfinished, and would shake any vehicle to bits within a couple of miles. He said there was a parallel road that no one knew about, a little way to the south.

We couldn't find that road, but we were able to drive on the sand alongside the main road, raising our plume of dust to add to the many that were drifting across the blackening sky.

We erected our tent in the shelter of a small red outcrop. Before turning in, and after a meal of fried potato and onions with a mug of beef tea, Somarco made an attempt at reconciliation.

'Look here, Kenneth. We're out in the desert with no one to look after us but ourselves, a bloody battlefield up ahead, and all we have is a couple of guns. If someone comes out of the dunes tonight and tries to cut your throat, I will do my utmost to stop him. I hope you will do the same for me. Do you understand? We are each other's only protection.'

'All I'm asking for is an apology, Somarco.'

'For putting an aircraft through its paces? For not realizing you had unstrapped yourself?'

'There was no call for you to go through those aerobatics. We were on a reconnaissance mission, for Heaven's sake.'

'I thought you would think it fun, like being on a roller-coaster.'

I burst into tears. The terror of the flight had gained strength through memory. I tried to hide my sobbing. I didn't want Somarco's sympathy. He stretched out a hand to pat my shoulder, and I flinched away from him.

Somarco and I passed our first desert night together in the uneasy silence of a semi-truce. I slept only fitfully. The cold was numbing, and the silence was constantly interrupted by unexpected and inexplicable noises. I dreamt the tent was full of scorpions and woke in a state of panic, brushing them away. Later we heard heavy armour in the distance, and suddenly became aware of our vulnerability. The distant rumble, like an earthquake in another country, reaching us only as an aftershock, made us see how ignorant we were of the situation. They could have been enemy tanks heading east, or our own in retreat. We were lying swaddled like two babes in the shadow of vast armies that might trample us without even knowing it.

The next day we vowed we should not spend another night

like that, and that we should do our best to catch up with the forward positions, or at least attach ourselves to a convoy of our own people.

Early in our journey that day we found more evidence of recent battles. We passed through the area of Buq Buq where, we later learnt, the Italians had fought back but had been overwhelmed. The majority of ruined hardware was Italian, as were, we supposed, the charred remains of corpses that were scattered about the sand. I tried at first not to look too closely at them, but Somarco took an artist's interest in the scorched anatomy, and peered at any he came across. He even photographed some.

'There you are,' he said, indicating a curled, reptilian husk of a human, 'your first dead body. It has been a long time coming, eh?'

I had not told Somarco about the fallen aviator. Looking at these remains, I could not help but be reminded. When I had strength to look closely enough, I could see that nothing of the clothes remained, and what was left of the body tissue was carbonized as much as the spent logs of a fire. The clothes had vanished, or become one with the body.

'What use is it, photographing them?' I said, suddenly angry with Somarco. I'd raised my voice, and was alarmed by how far it seemed to carry across the silent battlefield. From the corner of my eye I saw movement, and turned to see a group of people, ghost-like in their white robes, standing and watching us, but in a second they were gone. I blinked, straining my eyes, already tired from squinting against the all-encompassing brightness, but there was no sign of them. From then on I could never feel certain that we were alone in the desert. Somarco said they were Bedouin, and that they were nothing to worry about, and moreover, that they were true masters of camouflage. From then on they became a familiar sight, at the most unexpected times, materializing out of nothing, seeming to step in at a moment of mental laxity to fill a gap in one's concentration. We could learn a lot, Somarco said, from their ability to blend into the landscape.

By now we had found the parallel road the Australian major had talked about, a wide, empty boulevard in the sand leading through a level landscape of caked mud and salt flats that eventually opened out onto the coast. We passed through the town of Sollum without stopping, then climbed the zigzagging road that ascended the Halfaya Pass to the plateau that overlooked Sollum Bay, the truck straining through its low gears all the way.

The view from the top was exquisite. At only a little stretch of the imagination we could have been looking down on a prosperous fishing village on the French or Italian riviera. We had an aerial view without the need for leaving the ground so I decided to do some studies of the terrain, with special attention to colour. The colours were particularly rich from this viewpoint – all the blues that had ever existed seemed gathered there, from the frailest forget-me-not to the most profound ultramarine. Against the beige edge of the monochrome land mass, it was all the more dazzling. I was rather surprised to find that Somarco was against the idea, and was anxious to press on westwards. He had had less training than I in the techniques of camouflage, but was suitably impressed by the work I had done in the de Havilland (I had hung on to the sketchbook with my teeth – there were bite-marks down one side). 'You see,' I said, leafing through the few pages I'd covered, 'the desert isn't a place of uniform colour and texture. From a few thousand feet it is a complicated arrangement of many different patterns. If we can devise a way of mimicking these patterns on our military vehicles or installations, they will vanish.'

In the end we both did some colour studies, seated on a rocky prominence with our backs to each other, surveying the opposite views.

Then we pressed on. The road was still mostly empty as we travelled across the plateau. We passed through the ruins of Fort Capuzzo, then crossed the barbed-wire boundary fence, patrolled by a single Australian sentry, and entered what only a few days ago had been Italian Libya.

This was when we met the first British trucks heading back east, packed with Italian prisoners of war. From some of the passing drivers we learnt that Tobruk had fallen and the army was surging on towards Tripoli. Truck after truck of Italian prisoners rolled by, all of whom seemed to have been officers of high rank, judging by the gaudy pieces of brocade and twinkling medals that flashed as they passed us. They hung on grimly in their lurching, swaying trucks, packed in so tightly they couldn't have fallen out if they'd wanted to. It was unnerving to see this human cargo being transported so roughly and carelessly across what would become hundreds of miles of desert roads. We had mixed feelings about the news – glad that Tobruk had been taken, but frustrated that we might be too late to catch up with the desert army. The war looked as though it would be over before we ever had a chance of doing anything useful.

As we approached Tobruk the desert lifted itself into the air, carried by a sudden powerful and persistent wind. A sandstorm, our first, had erupted, and we slowed to a crawl since our visibility at times didn't even reach the end of the truck's bonnet. Approaching vehicles appeared like phantoms, would swerve at the last moment and scrape our side. Debris of all kinds bounced out of the gloom and slammed against us and we feared something coming through the windscreen at any moment.

The storm didn't abate even as we arrived at the city, where the entrance was guarded by a group of Aussies who seemed nonplussed by our failure to produce passes, and shrugged us onward into the city. In the continuing yellow gloom of the storm we had an impression of ruined structures, of bomb craters into which we nearly drove several times. A sandstorm is a type of blindness by proxy – you imagine your eyes are failing you but it is the world that has become invisible, and in it you begin to see things that aren't there. When we first arrived and were steering slowly through the engulfed streets, I had the impression of crowds, of people pressing against the sides of the truck, of figures nearly falling under the wheels, and when only a little later the storm abated and the world emerged from behind its cloak, we saw that the city was entirely deserted. The army had moved on, the civilians had fled. From the town square we could see streets of shops, their walls pitted with bullet holes and their contents cruelly looted. Out in the harbour, the late sun had been given enough strength to bring out the rich azures, but this time darkly stained with oil. The listing hulks of sunken ships cluttered the water. There were ships aground, ships sunk by their bows, their sterns raised indecorously into the air, all their lower working – propellers and rudders – exposed. Others were leaning at drunken angles, their turrets knocked sideways and overhanging the decks. And among all this wreckage and confusion, our own little ships of war in their clean grey colours looked polite and a little embarrassed.

The city was patrolled by Australian sentries who this time took some convincing of who we were. Eventually we were shown to an abandoned Italian naval barracks where we were able to bed down. It was a grim habitation. The long, low-ceilinged rooms were, like the rest of the city, strewn and chaotic. Kitbags, white duck uniforms, suitcases, private letters and rations were scattered like confetti, ripped, trampled on and sticky with creosote that had leaked from some broken carboys. At the other end, sand had formed an indoor dune, having blown in through the broken windowpanes.

We backed our truck right up to the door so we could easily unload, then set the Primuses going and cooked potatoes, onions and bully beef. We made no comment on the paraphernalia of abandonment that surrounded us. I felt no urge to pick up any of the letters, the majority of which must surely have been love letters, and even with a translator at hand, felt no desire to pry into the private lives of lovers estranged and possibly dead. This was what the efforts to build a new Roman Empire had come to.

We ate in silence, then tried to sleep. But as the darkness came on so the wind, which had abated for some hours, returned. In its gusts we could hear doors slamming all over the city, near and far, loudly and quietly, all at different tempos. It was as though the houses themselves were protesting at their own emptiness, calling out for their owners. And then the dogs started up. Hundreds of abandoned dogs howling.

Nevertheless, we slept well, and in the morning the city and the harbour were revealed in searing clarity. In the small square near the sea we found some military police who told us where they thought the advanced headquarters might be, although they didn't seem very certain. All they could say for sure was that if we continued heading west we would eventually catch up with the army. No one seemed prepared for the speed with which the British were advancing, or for the lack of resistance from the Italians. So we travelled on towards the desert again, past rows of cuboid houses, some with their doors hanging open, others half reduced to rubble; shops, barbers, milliners, *ristoranti*, all with their sad contents scattered across the roads. On the walls, pictures of Il Duce, Victor Emmanuel and Balbo stared serenely down at us.

We climbed back up onto the plateau and forked right along the Derna road. There was little sign of any British losses, though we frequently came across ruined Italian armour. We tried to ascertain the whereabouts of the war by asking drivers heading in the opposite direction, but all gave conflicting information; even the sentry at an information post could do no more than show us a map of the desert, which seemed comically blank, and wave his hand vaguely over an area the size of Yorkshire. Around twenty miles west of Tobruk we found the command post of an Australian infantry brigade, who were bedded down in a wadi bridged by the road. They had gun positions a few miles further on. We made ourselves known to the brigadier when he arrived – a man full of furious energy and barely controlled rage, who conducted himself with the same disarming lack of cere-mony as his compatriots, smoking, chewing and swearing with an air of guarded insolence. To our amazement he seemed to know about us. Word had somehow travelled ahead of us, about a couple of artists travelling in an overladen charabanc and losing themselves in the desert. But he seemed to think we could be of use to him. He showed a place where we could camp, and told us to have a look at his gun positions the next morning.

We camped for the first time as part of a larger unit. It gave us an immense feeling of well-being, for until then we had felt alone in the vast desert. Maybe that was why, as the sun went down and the counter-landscape of stars opened up in the sky, Somarco was able to bring himself to offer something that sounded like an apology. 'For putting you through it, up there. I had forgotten that you are not used to flying.'

He had thought that was all he needed to say, but that little apology only chipped away at the mountain of grievances I held against the devious little half-Italian.

'So, now that I have got down on my bended knees before you, Kenneth, have you anything to say to me?'

'I think you'll have to stay on your knees much longer before I'm required to follow suit.'

I was expecting something more from Somarco that night, but I only heard him sigh as he swilled the last of his beef tea. I was too tired to push the matter further.

In the morning, for the first time, we heard the noise of battle

– shells exploding in the far distance, little bursts of machine-gun fire. At last we were nearing the war. We drove on and eventually found the two gun batteries mentioned by the brigadier. They were manned by six men each, in depressions by the side of the road just deep enough to conceal them. We now had our first opportunity to offer our services as camoufleurs. The gunners were surprisingly interested. We showed them our nets and garnish, like commercial travellers selling fashionable lingerie to lonely housewives. Somarco told them of how we could create false shadows with some canvas painted black and pegged down in the sand so that, from the air, it would look like one of the familiar cuboid buildings that marked the area, a ruin of which was nearby. A Reggiane was circling at about ten thousand feet and we thought it likely that the position of this particular battery was already well documented, although the fact that the Italian shells were falling well short of it and land-ing instead on an abandoned aerodrome in the valley below, which contained nothing but a few wrecks of Italian planes, sug-gested strongly that the Italian gunners were either hopeless at calibrating their guns or simply didn't know where we were. The gunners, interrupted every now and then by a command from the battery sergeant, were a little overwhelmed by our enthusi-asm. The sergeant was quick to point out a problem.

'Very clever idea, using painted shadows to suggest a building. But if their reconnaissance has already identified our position, might it not give the game away if you were to disguise us as a building? They'll then recognize any brightly shadowed building as a possible gun battery.' We debated for a while whether we could assume their position was already known, but eventually agreed with the sergeant that it would be better simply to conceal the batteries rather than disguise them as buildings. We should save that trick for a time when we knew we were working with an undiscovered position. We spent the rest of the morning blending the batteries into their surrounding terrain, using scrim, beige garnish and painted canvas.

It was then that it hit home to us the sheer quantities of materials we would need. Camouflaging those batteries had used perhaps twenty yards of netting, a litre of paint, several yards of canvas. All for just two placements. We would need to look seriously at procurement when we got back to Cairo.

There followed a day of confusion. We tried setting off once again in search of our armour, heading west and using borrowed maps, but we were quickly lost in a maze of tracks and became bogged down. We spent a good three or four hours trying to dig ourselves out of the sand, and then, when we were back on the main road, we saw armoured convoys heading west. No tanks, and not the advanced armour we were looking for, but Australian reinforcements heading for Derna. That city, we learnt, had already fallen, abandoned, like the others, with haste after what had promised to be a bitter battle. We followed, thick in the haze of the sandstorm kicked up by the three-tonners.

We passed a derelict aerodrome, the burnt-out shells of aircraft littering the cratered runways – the sight seemed to break Somarco's heart. Then, on the steep road that led down from the plateau and onto the narrow coastal plain, the Italians had blown several deep holes. The Australians we'd camped with were among the crews trying to clear the rubble and allowing one vehicle through at a time. We had to plunge through a switch-back of craters, carefully easing the gearbox through its full repertoire, while helpful squaddies pushed us forward.

Like Tobruk, the town had an air of panic-stricken abandonment, and the few Arabs who were left eyed us unemotionally from the pavements. The town had been ransacked, the shops were emptied down to their last packet of cigarettes, their last bottle of gasoline, and the houses had the now familiar door-banging emptiness of a forsaken settlement. We made our way to the pretty main square, where we found an Australian major acting as town commandant sitting in the shade of topiaried bay trees. This man told us we could pick any empty house we liked, and that there were some nice ones on the front towards the west end of the town where there might still be some water laid on. As we spoke, a group of soldiers passed by. Their arms were full of cauliflowers and aubergines while others were hauling a calf along by a rope round its neck, the creature setting its little hooves adamantly against the direction they were following. For a moment Somarco and I exchanged glances and wondered if we should be doing the same thing. We hadn't eaten fresh meat for some time.

*

It is an extraordinary feeling to be part of an invading army in a town from which nearly every last resident has fled. All notion of private property has disappeared: you can walk in and out of once-private houses with impunity, and if they are locked you can kick the doors in. Most of the doors had already been kicked in, it seemed to us, and the interiors casually ransacked. Linen, clothing, glass, cutlery, women's hats, children's toys, books, snapshots, saucepans, coat hangers were strewn across the gardens and pathways.

We eventually found a relatively intact white bungalow with running water and logs for the fire. It seemed to have belonged to a prominent Italian Fascist called Enrico Forino. There was a diploma on the wall that honoured the fact that he was a Cavalier of the Colonial Order of the Star of Italy. Photographs we picked up from the floor in shattered frames showed a wife a little past her years of beauty, and a trio of handsome children. Other photographs seemed to show that he was an engineer working on an irrigation project of some sort. In one of the bedrooms we found a military cap and uniform, lushly braided and decorated in the Italian manner, indicating that he was an important official. Perhaps we were staying in the mayor's house.

Without saying much to each other, perhaps without speaking at all, Somarco and I spent two or three hours tidying this house, restoring it, as far as we could, to something resembling its former domestic glory. We picked up everything that was strewn on the floor, brushed the dust off every item, and reset them on sideboards and shelves. We washed the trampled-on pieces of clothing and hung them out to dry in the small, pebbly garden. We washed the walls of their scuff-marks and smears. We did a good job, Somarco and I, two busy housemaids. We washed the sheets and hung them up to dry. Somarco found brooms, a besom for the garden paths, a soft one for indoors, and we swept like the good elves of a fairy tale until the dust was flying out of the windows. It was strange, the way we worked. Neither of us said anything, but we both knew what we had to do. Perhaps it was just a way of filling the time, or perhaps it was a response to the shock of seeing the aftermath of such recent fighting – although there was nothing as shocking as the charred corpses we'd seen on the other side of Tobruk. In Derna I felt the weight of civilian suffering. The petty differences between Somarco and me now seemed slight and insignificant, so we worked like a husband and wife to rebuild a domestic space, to resurrect a semblance of normal life from the confused threads of a war-damaged city. We hardly paused for breath, even though we were already exhausted from days of travelling in difficult terrain. We knew we wouldn't have been able to sleep in the villa of Enrico Forino without making it as respectable as we could.

When we had finished with the house we turned our attention to the garden. There was a vegetable patch among the rich blooms of bougainvillaea and azalea, and we found a whole row of purple-sprouting broccoli. Just as we were picking it a squaddie, who was staying in a nearby villa, came up and asked us if we'd like some fresh beef. The young chap looked as though he'd been in some pretty heavy fighting, until I realized the bloodstains on his face and shirt were animal, not human. He was one of the soldiers we'd seen earlier with the calf. We said we would very much like some beef and he handed us over the fence what appeared to be a whole calf's leg.

I had never thought I would respond so well to the smell of blood, but the freshly butchered meat aroused a yearning I had not recognized in myself before – a lust for animal flesh. It was all I could do to prevent myself sinking my teeth into the raw muscle there and then and tearing at it like a dog. Instead, Somarco was able to demonstrate his talents as a chef, and made a wonderful stew in a pot over an open fire. Perhaps a little spicy for my English tongue, but I was so hungry for good food that I would have eaten it no matter what it contained.

We spoke little during the evening. The only words Somarco said were, 'You're a difficult man to love, Brill.' I didn't bother replying.

The following day we were delayed because the Italians had blown up the road out to the west, and we had to wait while it was made negotiable. We spent the morning trying out our camouflage nets on the buildings, and holding more impromptu classes on camouflage for anyone who would listen. Eventually, when the road was cleared, we climbed the plateau and found ourselves in a very different landscape – green and grassy, with bushes, flowers and the elegant, slender spires of cypress trees. Somarco said it was very like southern Italy. We joined an Australian brigade and travelled along a decent road, making good time.

In this region there were some rather poignant reminders of

the Italian attempts to build a colonial empire. Mile upon mile of white bungalows labelled with the words '*Ente Colonizzazione Libya*', and a serial number. Each had a rain barrel, a wooden bench on the stoep and a green handcart. Rather heartbreakingly, perhaps more so for Somarco than for me, one could see the effort that had been put into creating precious spaces around the bungalows, little walled gardens and vegetable patches, where creeping plants were allowed to climb the sides of the bungalows, and the bright plants of the Mediterranean were flowering. And behind the bungalows, trim fields of crops and orchards. These were not the homes of conquering tyrants, but of mostly poor Italians who had been lured away from their Napoli slums with promises of a better life. The sight prompted Somarco to speak openly, for the first time, about Italian politics. There was no comparison, he said, between the Italians and the Nazis. The Nazis were on a mission of oppression and extermination based on racial hatred, whereas the Italians followed the British model of disguising their imperialist project as one of social improvement and aid.

I tried to imagine and continue to imagine, every night, Davies, those poor Italian families and what they must have gone through, how they must have packed everything they had into a cart and driven a sagging mule to haul their lives westwards, leaving behind the one thing they couldn't take with them, their land, for that to be picked over by looters, whom I saw with their sacks, casually but defiantly taking whatever they could.

They had been there for twenty years, at least. And that was bad enough for them. My family has been on the Heath for generations. Two hundred years, probably more. And you will brush us aside like a pile of human dust.

Davies was not a man to be easily persuaded. 'I think you are sentimentalizing the Italian colonists, Brill. They are parasites on the hide of a noble, sovereign state. They have tried to plant Roman Catholicism in the heart of a strong Muslim country. The British Empire never sought to impose Christianity on countries with well-established religions. The Hindu and the Sikh and the Muslim were free to worship in India. It was only to countries in the grip of heathen gods, in the heart of Africa, that missionaries went, but that was never a government policy, simply the strategy of individual Churches.'

'Well, I still say that these people were living in a mostly empty land. How long does one have to live on a patch of earth before one can claim rightfully to belong there, to call it one's home?'

Davies smiled but wouldn't answer.

One of the houses we stopped at, I couldn't resist taking a look around. They were such pretty, decorous dwellings, as you would expect from the Italian spirit of proportion and style, which was manifest even in the smallest, most trivial thing, a wheelbarrow, for instance. But I was particularly moved by writing we found on the side of a house, elegantly pencilled cursive against the white-wash. I had to get Somarco to translate – *melanzana*, *zucchini*, *lattuga* – they were plans, outlines, schemes of planting, showing the dates of sowing in the various fields, with proposed harvest times. 'They have linked it into the lunar cycles, it seems,' said Somarco. 'This here *novilunio*, they want to bring the artichokes in on the new moon. And, look, they have planted olives, with the date 1934. They planned to stay here for a long time. The olive is a very slow-growing tree. Even after twenty years there wouldn't be many olives from this little grove.' I looked at the brave little trees in their hopeful lines, and felt like weeping. Somarco did weep, as much for the infant olive grove as for the people who planted it.

I found all this far more upsetting than the children's toys, teddy bears and dolls, the little wooden cars, cradles and baby chairs we frequently came across in all the towns we passed through. It brought home to me my childhood on the Heath, with its hardy little fields and vegetable patches. Oh, I know it was riven with internecine rivalry, but there was a spirit of production, of earthy cycles and honest toil – yes, honest, Davies. They were doing what is most basic and elemental, growing food in a difficult land. And the same thing in the north Libyan desert – that was a pretty difficult land. And what do you think they were using to fertilize it? Manure. Where it came from I know not – camel, mule, donkey, chicken? But there were shit-heaps on that cultivated stretch, perhaps the most fertile stretch we had come across since leaving the flood plains of the Nile. They piled their manure and compost in the shade of vined canopies, essential in the piercing desert sun that would dry out the faeces in a matter of minutes – not a problem for the dung, so much as the rotting processes associated with any vegetable matter that was combined with it. Do you know what? I very nearly found myself wanting to settle myself in this Afro-Italian Garden of Eden, to take up residence in one of those Tuscan bungalows.

'We must talk some time about the Italians in Libya, Lieutenant Brill,' he said to me, 'I am not sure you would see the landscape through such sympathetic eyes if you were an Arab, especially not since Mussolini took over the running of things.'

'Somarco had a saying he liked to repeat. "We were all invaders once." Doesn't matter where you are, what part of the world or how long your ancestors have lived there, at some point in the past someone knocked someone else over the head for the right to be there.'

'Yes, for an Italian, he sounds as if he could express himself most inelegantly.'

'As I keep saying, he was born in Borehamwood.'

We were now part of a vast armoured convoy. For two more days we pressed westwards, the ways littered with abandoned Italian armour and technology, defensive positions abandoned, with heaps of munitions in ditches. Hand grenades, red as toffee apples, littered the fields. The villages had triumphal arches, as though Hadrian or Scipio Africanus had passed that way. We were held up occasionally by sabotaged roads but it was never more than a couple of hours before a diversion became operable. By now the convoy was straggling; our vehicles were disintegrating, bits were falling off. By the time we crossed the level plain into Barce, we were a ramshackle horde, comprising any vehicle that was capable of carrying a load, from little three-wheeled delivery vans, dainty little Fiats, to commandeered SPAs and Italian scout cars. We careered across the desert in the wake of the sunburnt Australians. It was as though a scrapyard had come to life in pursuit of some riotous carnival in the desert.

When the convoy came to a slow, creaking halt in the middle of a stretch of cultivated land, I went over to a group of Australian officers who'd just brewed up some coffee, which they drank from tin mugs, and asked a sand-blasted colonel if we might bivouac there.

'Probably best if you backed up about half a mile,' he said, having ascertained that we were camoufleurs.

I looked ahead towards some low hills in the distance, and asked him how far behind the armour we were.

The colonel looked bemused. 'There's nothing ahead of us,' he said. 'This is the front line.'

When I told Somarco he was thrilled. I had never seen anything quite like the look in his eyes.

'The front line, Brill. Who'd have thought we would ever get to the vanguard of the Army of the Nile? We must stay.'

'Don't be ridiculous, we're not in a tank. We should go back, like the colonel said.'

But I, too, was reluctant to turn back, even if only for half a mile. To drive in the opposite direction to that which we had pressed at so hard and for so long seemed an insult. Somarco pointed out we had two rifles, a tommy gun and a crate of ammunition. We were trained soldiers. If anything should kick off, we could do our bit.

I smacked him playfully in the face. 'Look at you, the eager little warrior. You can't wait to kill your first Fascist, can you?' I hesitated to say 'Italian'.

Somarco caught my hand and held it to his cheek. I withdrew it roughly. 'I might need it for fighting,' I said.

Somarco shocked me by producing a bottle of Chianti in a straw basket. He said he'd found it in the house of Enrico Forino and had kept it as a surprise. We drank it from tin mugs in big, clumsy mouthfuls. I had not had a drop of alcohol for many weeks, and with the exhaustion and dehydration, I became drunk very quickly. It was a form of drunkenness I had not experienced before – it made me aggressive and violently reckless. Somarco humoured me at first, but became anxious when I took up my gun.

'Why don't I just go over to that fine upstanding colonel and tell him you are a traitor?' I said.

'Kenneth, stop playing games.' Somarco took it all very calmly. He was lying propped up on one elbow like a good Roman, and had barely started on his share of the wine. He was smiling at me, and looked serenely beautiful. I noticed, for the first time, that he had a gold molar.

'I could go over to him now, and tell him the truth about you, and your life won't be worth a rat's breakfast.'

'It's more likely that you would be arrested for being drunk on duty. We are on the front line and could be facing an attack at any time, and you can hardly string two words together.'

'You can talk in that condescending tone as much as you like,

Arturo Fascisto. I would be doing a service to the British Empire if I blew your head off right now.'

'Well, then,' Somarco opened his arms wide, as if putting himself wholly at my disposal, 'why don't you just do it, Kenneth? Shoot your oldest friend's head right off, why don't you?'

By this time the aggression had been replaced by a wheedling sentimentality, and I burst into uncontrollable sobbing. Then I passed out. Thus was spent my first night on the front line.

*

It rained in the night, and the rain persisted all through the morning, opening up slicks of mud. The soil was red clay and the roads were bleeding a thick orange gore that sucked at our wheels. Vehicles were abandoned and their loads transferred to any other vehicle still moving. We slipped and slurped our way towards Benghazi, and soon heard that the city wished to surrender.

Although we had done our best to hang back from the front line, by chance we were among the first into the city. To avoid embarrassment we turned around and waited for the staff cars of the British and Australian colonels, so that they could take the applause that was being offered from the pavements and balconies, as the inhabitants greeted us with the kind of polite encomium they might offer a travelling circus troupe. Small guards of honour were assembled outside the town hall, guns and other heavy armour were paraded around the square in an impromptu victory parade, and then, almost immediately, we were pushing westwards again.

Beyond Benghazi the area of cultivation ends and the desert returns, but we were hardly out of the city before we met despatch riders coming back east, giving the thumbs-up signal as they passed. Then we saw ten-tonners and staff cars loaded with the glint and braided sparkle of Italian officers. The highest command had been captured; the Italian Army had capitulated. The war in the desert, in whose wake we'd travelled for nearly two weeks, was over, and apart from that little gun battery outside Tobruk, our camouflage skills had not been used once.

XIII

Marcus Boone had disappeared. Look for him though I might, search high and low among the fields and lanes of the Heath, the corridors, classrooms and playgrounds of St Saviour's, he was nowhere to be found. Some supposed, again, that he was dead, though this time the rumours were put forth with a little less conviction. Marcus Boone had already risen from the dead, and one couldn't help but expect a second miracle of that kind. The rumour-mongers were not deterred, and had in mind that he had caught a fatal chill in the unroofed toilets, exposed in all his flesh to the sky. He had caught pneumonia, they said. He had caught double pneumonia. He had caught triple pneumonia. (How many multiples of pneumonia were there?) I laughed off the rumours. Marcus Boone was clearly indestructible.

Then I was summoned to the headmaster's office and in there I found my mother and Marcus Boone's mother, sitting on stiff-backed chairs, wearing stiff-backed faces, and Mr Locke, as heavy and still as if he had been cast in bronze, sitting behind his desk.

'Kenneth, say you didn't do it,' my mother blurted instantly, then checked herself when the others gave her a warning look.

'Do what?'

'Kenneth Brill, a most serious accusation has been made against you,' said Mr Locke, his head a little offset. I was silent, unable to speak. The headmaster continued, 'It has been alleged that you executed a most perfidious crime in the school's toilets.'

'I know,' my father's music-hall voice pops into my head, 'we had to leave the windows open for three days.'

'It has been alleged that you stole the clothes of a fellow pupil while he was in the lavatory.'

'He hasn't said he did it,' said my mother.

'Let him answer himself,' said Mrs Boone, her mouth set firmly downwards. It was the first time I had seen Mrs Boone at close quarters. She had a gritty face on which there were the faded corpses of a hundred freckles.

'Well?' said the headmaster. 'Is this true?'

'No,' I said quietly. A look of disgust possessed Mrs Boone's face. 'I don't even know what you are talking about.'

'Oh, come, now,' said Mr Locke. 'There isn't a soul in the school who doesn't know what happened. The poor young man spent the whole afternoon trapped in the lavatory. With no clothes, he could do nothing but wait and hope to be discovered. He had tried worming his way across the back of the boiler house in a vain attempt to escape with his decency intact, but there was no way for him over the high wall, and as he knew, he would be in the full view of the high street if he made it to the other side. His only choice was to throw himself on the mercy of his fellow pupils and the staff, and so he staggered (for he was now quite exhausted with fear and humiliation) onto the main playground, where Mr Thomas was quickly on hand to provide the sartorial modesty of his academic gown. It is a token of how seriously this whole episode was viewed. I cannot think of any other circumstance under which Mr Thomas might allow a ten-year-old to wear the robes of a bachelor of science.'

Mrs Boone dabbed at a few imaginary tears as this vivid account was expounded. My mother was alert with anxiety. 'It's very serious, Kenny. You must tell the truth.'

'But how do you think I would have got the clothes off him?'

'The young man says you climbed in over the top while he was using the lavatory, and stripped everything from his body before he had a chance to react – the poor young chap being in the middle of his . . . you know.'

'A terrible thing to attack a child when he's most vulnerable, in the middle of his private functions . . .'

I cried.

'Don't think that act of irrigation will elicit sympathy, young man. I know all too well how little boys can turn on the tears and turn them off again, as if they had a stopcock behind their eyes. We have never had such a serious crime committed in this school, Mrs Brill, and this is not the first unsavoury incident involving your son. We are all too familiar now with this young man's fondness for knife-fights, and his recklessness with those weapons is a testament to his delinquency. A recklessness that landed the same poor boy in hospital not very long ago. And he himself has only just recovered from what I understand was a most serious injury resulting from another escapade with a bladed weapon. For this and the behaviour I have already mentioned concerning Marcus Boone, I have no choice but to expel your son from this school, with immediate effect.'

What? Mother – you've got nothing to say? You, you talkative woman, struck dumb by Mr Locke's decision? Why don't you cry out at the injustice? Even though I had done what I had done, it was not an evil thing. I was not dropping shells of poison gas on a pal's regiment. We thought we knew what evil was in those days, but we were wrong.

My mother, almost silent during the meeting, spoke incessantly on the way home. 'Do you know what, Kenny? I'm glad you've been expelled from that horrible little school. They have demonstrated that they are incapable of meeting your intellectual and creative demands. I have always been horrified by Mrs

Broad's piano playing, as if the quality of the piano wasn't poor enough in itself . . . As for their attitude to people who live on the Heath, I've long suspected they are prejudiced against people south of the Bath road. Well, if that's their opinion they don't deserve to have you at their school . . .'

The question that most preoccupied us, however, was how my father would take the news when he returned from his sales trip. In the end, my mother attempted to soften the impact of my expulsion by presenting it as an incidental pearl in the oyster of her dissatisfaction with life on the Heath. No sooner was he home than she lit the fuse on a blazing row.

'Glad to see you've been enjoying your gallivanting around the country while I've been stuck behind in this hellhole you call a home.'

My father's merry little comedian's moustache (which, like the bow-tie, he thought made him look like a medical man) drooped, as much as to say, 'Oh, no, not this old routine again.' And the routine was the familiar one of her bewailing the fact that she was trapped, stranded in a muddy demesne, cut off from the society of London, with mud-hoppers for neighbours and the constant stench of manure in the windows.

'And I'd like our children to go to a proper school, not to that converted barn where they still believe in witchcraft.'

'What? What's wrong with St Saviour's? It's a very good school.'

'And what evidence do you have to support that opinion?'

My father was momentarily flummoxed. 'Well, it's the only school for miles around.'

'Exactly.'

'Which means that they have all the children there, the cleverest as well as the stupidest.'

(Did my father glance in my direction when he said that last word?)

'Well, that stupidest of headmasters Mr Locke has seen fit to expel our little Kenny from his school.'

My father was holding in his right hand an artificial leg complete with sock and black boot and let this object drop from his grip. It clattered on the floor. He turned to look at me, his mouth open. 'Expelled? Little Kenny expelled?'

'Yes, expelled.'

'But Kenny's not a baddie boy. You've never been a baddie boy, have you, little Kenny?' He gave me the full brunt of his moustache before turning back to his wife. 'What do you mean, "expelled"?'

Now that the moment had come, my mother thought it best to tell the truth.

'Little Kenny stripped a boy of his clothes and hid them in a coke heap. The poor lad was trapped nude in the toilets for a whole afternoon.'

My father didn't seem to hear. 'He's always been a little Goody Two Shoes, haven't you, Kenny? You're a good little boy, always looking after your sisters, always helpful, a good little bugger.'

My mother had to repeat my crime, slowly and in more detail.

'Stripped a boy of his clothes? What had he done to you, Kenny, that you should take such retribution?'

'I didn't strip Marcus, he took his own clothes off,' I corrected my mother.

'Oh, this was when you were changing for games, or swimming, was it?'

'No, I just stole them when he undressed for me. In the toilets.'

Stole them when he undressed for you? In the toilets? My father didn't actually repeat my statements out loud, but they were written all over his face as questions. I could imagine him going into one of his music-hall routines: *What are you telling me, son, that your friend likes to parade about in his birthday suit just for you to take a peek at him? Who does he think he is – Lady Godiva? There's only one place for a nude boy, my son, and that's in oils on an art-gallery wall. Ooh, my word, I was in an art gallery the other day, ooh, my word, it was chilly in there, I'm saying it was chilly, yes, the Venus de Milo had a cardigan on, she did . . .*

'Well, you can kiss goodbye to any plans you had to be a brainbox, Kenny, because there aren't any other schools around here. You'll have to come out on the road with me, help me sell my wares . . .' he'd begun this speech as a diatribe but was beginning to warm to the idea '. . . might not be such a bad thing. Yes, little Kenny could be a model, a what-they-call, these days, a demonstrator. You don't mind if I cut one of your legs off, do you, Kenny, so that you can model a prosthetic? I'm only joking, Alicia, there's no need to give me that look. I'm the one who should be cross about all this.'

'No, Larry, Kenny is going to continue his schooling.'

'Where? You mean the Industrial School in Feltham? That's probably the only place round here that'll take a miscreant. I've heard they make a man out of you there – they've got their own gasworks and everything.'

My father would quite happily have seen my school education end at this point, but my mother was determined that it should continue. The only school of any quality she could find that was prepared to take me was Jacob College on the outskirts of Feltham.

Mother announced my new school career at the breakfast table one morning.

'I have heard from Dr Merryman, and he has agreed to take little Kenny.'

'Who the hell's Dr Merryman?' said my father.

'He's the headmaster of Jacob College – you know, the man

I went to speak to last week, the man you said you wouldn't touch with a barge pole. Well, he's written me a letter.' She waved a sheet of typed paper in front of my father's face.

'This is some kind of joke you are playing on us now, is it, Alicia?'

My mother gave one of her go-to-Hell smiles. 'You know I would not joke about our son's future.'

My father squared himself up at the table, laying both hands, palm down, on the cloth. 'Well, I never thought the following words would come out of my mouth at my own dinner table, sweetheart, but here they come. *I'm not having a Jew boy for a son.*'

'You're such a fool, Larry. Going to this school won't make him a Jew. I've told you before, there are hardly any Jews in the whole place. Does Wilberforce Merryman sound like a Jewish name to you?'

'No, it sounds like a bloody stupid name.' He turned to me. 'Kenny, forget any ideas about going to this daft school. You'll be coming on the road with me.'

I couldn't decide which was the bleaker prospect: years spent at this mysterious, alien school or years spent demonstrating peg-legs for my father, like the stooge of some snake-oil salesman on backwoods village greens. *Walk like a cripple, son, go on, hobble. Hobble!* My mother, however, clearly had the upper hand in this debate. Now she spoke to me.

'Kenny, you have nothing to worry about in going to Jacob College. The Jews have a lot more in common with your father than he realizes. Neither of them believes in Christ, after all.' My father made a half-hearted protest at this assessment of his religious sympathies, but my mother waved him quiet. 'Otherwise, Jews and Christians are more or less the same. The Jews' Bible is a little thinner, which can only be a good thing, and they have the richest cultural heritage, particularly in music.'

The argument went on for several days, my father's adamant opposition gradually losing ground to my mother's reasoned indifference to his objections. 'I never knew you felt so strongly, Larry . . .' He could see that she was simply not to be diverted from her plan. There was nothing he could do about it. My mother bolstered her argument by playing nothing but music by the great Jewish composers on the piano, and for weeks the house echoed to the sounds of Mahler, Mendelssohn, Offenbach and Gershwin.

One evening she came to my bedroom wearing one of the lacy embroidered gowns that had been bought for her when she was eighteen and which, she was always keen to point out, still fitted her. They were the gowns she would have worn for performances, if her career as a classical pianist had ever got under way.

'Kenny, you don't have to worry at all about Jacob College . . .'

'But what will they teach me?' I said, panicky.

She laughed. 'They will teach you what always gets taught in schools. Arithmetic, history, English, all the subjects you love so much. And a bit of Hebrew here and there, probably. Just a little. And who knows? It might come in useful one day. All knowledge is useful in one way or another.'

Over the weeks my mother made a great effort to introduce me to as much as she knew about the Jewish faith and culture, telling me the stories of Abraham and Isaac, of Joseph and his brothers, of the Exodus from Egypt and return to the Promised Land. These were all Bible stories I'd heard at St Saviour's. There were others I hadn't heard before – Jonah and the whale, Daniel in the lion's den and the story of David and Bathsheba, which my mother told with embarrassing relish. By the end of this induction I began to feel a certain amount of excitement at the prospect of becoming a Jew, but when I told Three Cylinders about it, his initial confusion turned into a peculiar hostility. I had run to him across the fields one day, barely able to contain my excitement – 'Three Cylinders, I have the most amazing good news for myself. I am going to become a Jew.' Unconsciously I had used exactly the same syntax and intonation Three Cylinders had used several years ago when he informed me he was joining the Boys' Brigade (a venture that lasted only briefly, for reasons that were never clear to me).

'Oh? How's that, then?'

'I'm going to Jacob College in September.'

'Jacob College? What's that, then?'

It was some time before Three Cylinders took in what I was saying, and he nodded with vague approval when I had explained fully what I meant, though he seemed more interested in keeping Lord Freddy, who eyed me darkly, well fed with monkey nuts. A few days later Three Cylinders came up to me in the fields and said, 'My dad says you got to keep off our land.'

'Why?'

'Don't know. He just said he don't want you near our crops. You might be bad for them, seeing as you're a Jew now.'

I had no idea what Three Cylinders or his father meant. I was used, now, to keeping out of his way, and thought little of it.

*

Though I was keen to embrace my new Jewish identity, the prospect of going to Jacob College terrified me, not least because it seemed so far from the Heath. It might as well have been in another country. Sipson was on the edge of the Heath, but Feltham was well beyond its boundaries, and Jacob College was even further, on the other side of the town. All that long, hot summer I felt as though I was in a constant state of mourning for my old life, for my childhood, and for the countryside in which I had spent that childhood. Even though I was to be a day-boy, I felt as though I was about to leave home. I spent the hot weeks cycling about the lanes bidding farewell to anyone and anything I came across. I said goodbye to the fields and I said goodbye to the crows (who seemed to reply in kind, I couldn't help feeling). I made many valedictory bicycle rides around the Heath. I even tried calling at Old Hall, but Marcus Boone's vanishing was complete when I discovered that his home was empty and that an estate agent's sign was up by the gate. So, I had rendered not only Marcus invisible but his whole family, their whole lives. They were gone, and Old Hall was slowly becoming dilapidated again.

I spent a lot of time with Marjorie Twelvetrees, although since my impaling our playing had become very restrained. I told her I was going away, and since she didn't know anything about Jacob College she believed me. But she insisted I take her with me. 'My destiny lies not here, Kenneth. It is most important that I escape the Heath as soon as possible. When you get to your new school, you must write to me and tell me where you are, give me directions, and I will come and join you. How far from London is your new school?'

'I don't know. I think it might actually be in London.'

Marjorie's eyes widened. 'You're going to live in London. It's not fair.' She nearly wept. Over that long summer we had many such conversations. She said we should both escape one night and go to London, hide in the back of one of the Joys' carts, beneath all the vegetables, but I told her not to be silly, that she should wait and that one day we would be together. This made Marjorie blush, and as a sort of reward for expressing such welcome sentiments, she unbuttoned her blouse and showed me her breasts. I was horrified, thinking that some terrible illness had swollen her chest, in the way that mumps will swell the face. She invited me to touch them, if I wanted to. I did so. How appallingly soft they were. How implodingly soft. But we both giggled away our uncertainties, and Marjorie rebuttoned her blouse.

VANISHING

I had a strong sense of passing out of other people's fields of memories, that I would be forgotten once I had left the Heath (even though, as I have said, I was not actually leaving), and I felt it necessary to do a constant round of the places and people I knew to remind them of who I was. So, almost daily I did a cycling circuit of Cain Lane, Heathrow Lane, High Tree Lane down to the ford, then back up to Perry Oaks, Tithe Barn Lane and Shepherd's Pool, along the Bath road through Sipson and past the Three Magpies, then the Old Magpie (or the Lord Freddy, as Three Cylinders called it), Palmer's Farm, Wild's Farm, Perrott's Farm, the Plough and Harrow, all the time making sure that people could see me, going right up to them as they sat on a bench outside their pub or rested their forearms on the handle of a spade, or brushed the dirt out of their horse's mane. To supplement the imprinting of my presence on people's memories, I began leaving as many physical traces of myself as I could. I carved my initials, or sometimes my full name, on trees and walls, or on the granite blocks of Mad Bridge. I wrote my name and dates on pieces of card and posted them in places where they were likely to remain undisturbed for many years – between the bricks of a house that was being built on Cain Lane, in the hollow nook of a tree, in the crevice of a bridgehead.

It was on one of these memorializing expeditions that I came across a figure I had not seen for a long time, and was nearly driven off my bike when, rounding a high-hedged corner, I almost ran into him. A solid figure planted on the tarmac in two hobnailed boots, the nails visible where the toes turned slightly up, scratched silver like horseshoes, the uppers chocolaty with mud. Then the leather gaiters strapped to each shin, tied with string around a worn leather knee pad, brown corduroy trousers, thick leather belt from the which a brace of rabbits hung, black pinstripe waistcoat, watch and chain, filthy white collarless shirt, sleeves torn and patched, and a medal on the waistcoat, the wrinkled neck, the thick grey moustache and the crumpled grey fedora – Tiberius Joy stood before me in the road, as solid an obstruction as if a tree had suddenly sprung, fully mature, from the tarmac. He was holding a shotgun in his hand, a single-barrelled Lee Enfield. I had seen him shoot a few rabbits in the days when I was his master of the shit-heaps, but I had never seen him hang them from his belt in this way. In their broken-necked, bloodstained misery, they seemed pathetic trophies to me. But looking up into Mr Joy's eyes I was struck by an expression I hadn't seen before, and I spent a long time trying to understand it. He seemed to have reverted to a primitive state. His face had the predatory stare of something pre-human, and for a moment he seemed to consider raising his gun and shooting me. I could see the thought pass behind his eyes. I could see myself as he saw me, reflected in those dark pupils, as a piece of quarry, or vermin. But then the human part of him reasserted itself, and I seemed to come into focus for him. He walked over to me, then looked at my bike. He pondered this machine for some moments, then stretched out his hand and touched the handlebars. I didn't like being so close to Mr Joy's gun, the barrel of which clicked against the front mudguard. Mr Joy touched other parts of the machine. He seemed fascinated by it, though regarded it with a certain detached seriousness, frowning.

'How long you had this?' he said, without looking at me.

I didn't really know how to answer, since I had no conception of how much time had passed since I had taken ownership of the bike, and for some reason I thought Mr Joy required a very precise answer. But then he seemed to have forgotten he had asked, and took a step back and to the side, as if to view the bike from a different angle. I felt like an exhibit in a museum, and held myself together, as though I shouldn't move. Then Mr Joy spoke very quietly.

'You want to make a few testies?' 'Testy' was a Heath word for sixpence.

I nodded. Mr Joy then walked off, indicating with a swing of the head that I should follow him. Unable to cycle at his slow pace, I got off and pushed the bike after him. It was only a little way up the lane before we were among what we called the back fields, which I didn't often visit. They were mainly given over to the growing of soft fruits and I presumed I was being conscripted into some picking of strawberries or raspberries. It seemed that he had forgotten about the prohibition he had issued through Three Cylinders only a few weeks before, or perhaps, when confronted with the reality of a soon-to-be Jew, he was too embarrassed to mention it.

In a corner of the field there was a large black carriage, a very old thing with big back wheels, some spokes missing, that had been there for years and was used as a storage shed. It was always full of punnets.

'I got to get this old cart going again,' said Mr Joy, reaching out his hand and brushing some of the dried mud from its side. 'Been out in the field since before my father's time . . .' In brushing the dirt off he had revealed ancient paintwork, and what appeared to be a coat of arms. 'This was a royal carriage many years ago. You see here? This coat of arms belongs to William the Fourth. He was king before Victoria.' I had heard this story before, and it was well known about the Heath that the old carriage in the back fields was a royal carriage of some sort, and we always thought it was funny that it was being used as a fruit store. No one knew how it came to be in the fields. 'You can begin by taking all the stuff out, and I'll go and get some other people to help.'

There were two doors at the back, which opened to reveal a complicated interior I had never seen before. A central corridor ran the length of the carriage, with small doors leading off on either side. I climbed in, and the rusted springs of the suspension creaked. A quail burst into terrified life from some hidden recess, banged itself against the dark walls before accidentally finding the exit. There was very little light, and when I opened the small side doors I had trouble seeing what was behind them, though the smell of sugar was overwhelming, the musty, golden scent of soft fruit. I opened one door and apples tumbled out, as though liberated, rumbling round my feet and down the corridor to the outside, a waterfall of russets. In another there were baskets of raspberries, mostly rotten, reminding me of my father's raspberry massacre, and making me feel uneasy to be inside such a private part of the Joys' empire. Nevertheless I took the bloodstained punnets, handling them as carefully as if they were sleeping babies, and carried them outside. Wasps and flies droned in and out of the cart as I continued this process. The vehicle must have fallen into disuse as a store because the produce in there had been left and forgotten. Most of it was rotten.

I was just stacking the last of the punnets in the open air, after an hour or more of backbreaking delving in the alcoves of the cart, when I noticed a team of women approaching from the lane. They were wearing the long dresses you didn't see women wearing so often in the fields now, with white aprons across them, and old-fashioned bonnets. They approached slowly but with a sense of purpose, carrying with them various items for the cleaning of the carriage, including several full buckets of water. Some of them I recognized as Three Cylinders's sisters – though they had been girls the last time I'd noticed them. There were cousins, who still bore the family resemblance, though in a diluted form. The Joys rarely flowered, and if they did it was in the male line (Three Cylinders excepted); the females of the dynasty were narrow-looking women, pinched and nipped, though strong and wiry at the same time. They seemed uniquely designed for work like this – the scrubbing-out of a dark and cramped interior. I could do little but stand back and watch as they took over the operation, giving no acknowledgement of the hard work I had already done, but setting to silently with their brushes and brooms and dusters. It was curious how little they spoke, those women. It was as though everything had been meticulously planned in advance, and each knew their role and purpose, and nothing had to be explained, or any commands given.

Then heavier, structural work was done on the carriage, and in this my help was needed, since it was considered men's work. Three Cylinders and other male members of the Joy clan arrived with carpenters' bags. The side panels were removed, with some levering and wrenching of nailed boards. Irregular pieces of the frame were sawn away, rough edges planed off.

These tasks carried over into the next day, when I returned, fascinated, to follow the progress of the restoration. I went to the field at noon, cautious in case I would not be welcome this time, since Mr Joy was not there, but only the women, who were working with long rolls of what looked like purple velvet and white lace, very luxurious materials to be out in the field. Some were seated on the ground with the velvet spread out before them, sewing the material industriously. This, clearly, was not considered work for a man, so I hung back a little. Still it was done in silence. Later some men arrived to work on the wheels and suspension. I helped with jacking the carriage so the wheels could be re-tyred, the axles oiled and reset. The coopers worked in the same solemn silence as everyone else.

By the third day the carriage was beginning to look resplendent. It had been repainted and revarnished, the royal coat of arms retouched so that it glowed gold against the black. The purple velvet had been used to cover the flat top beneath the roof, and the lace was arranged in draperies about the canopy.

The driver's seat had been reupholstered in wine-red velvet, and the hubs and spokes of the wheels glistened with the treacly blackness of fresh paint.

On the fourth day I went back again, and arrived just in time to see a most impressive sight: Mr Joy had arrived with two magnificent black horses. I had never seen them before and didn't know where he'd got them, and he harnessed them up to the carriage in line. Then, with some very gentle driving, the carriage moved for the first time in a hundred years. I wanted to raise a cheer, but everyone was still solemn, and it was only when the carriage was in motion that I could see what we had been working on all along. As it was steered around and rockingly pulled across the field towards the lane, followed by all the people who had been working on it, carrying their tools, their jackets and over-things draped on their arms – for it was a very hot day – it became very clear that we had been making a funeral hearse out of the old carriage, and I suddenly understood the sadness and desolation in some of the faces of the people I had been working with.

I ran home to tell my mother what had been happening in the field. And she seemed to know about it already.

'It's for Roddy,' she said, rather too matter-of-factly, without looking at me. 'I believe he went out into the fields and shot himself.'

*

We weren't invited to the funeral, even though my father was Roddy's step-uncle, and I was his step-cousin, and even though the funeral cortège passed right by the end of the drive at Swan's Rest. My father contrived to be away on business that day, but my mother couldn't help but take herself to the end of the drive, with myself and the two girls, to pay our respects, and I saw it trundle past, looking most elegant and lavish in its new purpose, so black and shiny it could have been made of liquorice, and that coat of arms brilliantly retouched, the whole thing lacquered, and short glass panels fitted round the open shelf where the coffin lay in its velvet and lace bower of flowers – there were many good flower-growers on the Heath so it certainly didn't want for a wealth of blooms, gladioli and irises and all sorts of petalled wonders. Tiberius Joy was wearing a black top hat, and the horses, black from head to foot and harnessed in black, were an impressive sight. And when Tiberius passed the end of our drive I'm sure he gave me a wink and a nod in some sort of acknowledgement of something – I'm not sure what.

No one seemed surprised by the death of Roddy Joy. And no one seemed particularly sad. Mr Joy had gone to great lengths with the funeral, but I never saw him or any of his family shed a tear when I was with them out in the fields. They had dealt with his death as a serious, practical matter. They had organized themselves and they had got on with it. It was like grief without sadness. And, furthermore, no one seemed to think that it was necessary to explain his death. If I asked why Roddy had done such a terrible thing, I was met with a shrug that seemed to say, 'Well, what do you expect?' But I was baffled.

I had spent some of my summer helping Roddy in his bi-cycle workshop, and I had even tried to make some money from him by taking him ruined and wrecked bicycles and bicycle parts, which had sometimes earned me a testy or two. Sometimes he would let me stay on and do some work, usually something simple like changing wheels, but he once showed me how to take a chain off and clean it in paraffin.

After his death I secretly went to his barn workshop just to contemplate the sacred space he had created – a sort of hospital for bicycles, like a place devoted to the worship of the machine.

I found a piece of chalk, the type that is used for dusting a puncture repair, to stop the glue adhering to the inside of the tyre. And I wrote on the tie beam of the roof, where the wheels used to hang, the words 'remember me'.

XIV

Jacob College was founded in 1870, after the discovery by archaeologists of what they believed to be a fourteenth-century synagogue near Feltham marketplace. At that time a small Jewish community lived in Staines and they founded the school with the aid of an endowment from the owners of Stein's shoe factory. What they built was designed to celebrate and revive an ancient Hebraic community, and the buildings possessed an appropriate pomp and venerability, tall, battlemented, ivy-strewn neo-Gothic, standing behind sweeping lawns a mile to the east of the town. Anyone visiting might suspect they had come upon one of the great English public schools on seeing boys on the playing fields in hooped shirts playing rugger, and mortar-boarded housemasters conducting choirs of angelic fourth-formers in the school chapel. Then one noticed the odd juxtapositions: the boys wearing skullcaps while singing Christian praises, or saying grace in the dining hall beneath an inscription, in Hebrew, from the Torah, which no one in the school, apart from the art master (a Jew) and the headmaster (a gentile, who'd studied ancient Semitic cultures at Oxford), could read. For the Jewish community that had once supplied the school with its intake had since moved on, with the closure of Stein's just after the Great War. Although the percentage of Jews in the school had never been much more than fifty, supplemented by the enrolment of many scholars from abroad when, in its heyday, the school was seen as one of the finest such institutions in Europe, the proportion had since declined almost to zero.

I was told all this in a private conference with the headmaster, who summoned me to his office a few weeks after commencement.

Dr Merryman did not quite suit his name. He was a tall, sucked-in sort of man, with a face that looked as though it could easily be taken apart and put back together. He was standing behind his broad oak desk in an impressively stately office, with a trinity of mullioned windows behind him. On the walls were maps of the world dominated by the pink spread of the British Empire, along with several others of Palestine and the Holy Land.

The main purpose of this meeting was for Dr Merryman to make plain that I was under strict surveillance.

'Kenneth Brill, it is with some misgivings that we have decided to allow you into this school. I have spoken to the headmaster of St Saviour's and he has told me the true nature of your misdemeanours there.'

A long silence during which it gradually occurred to me that I was expected to say something. When I didn't, Dr Merryman continued: 'One consolation is that the headmaster gave a rather impressive account of your academic achievements. Said he was rather sorry he had to lose you, as you were such a promising scholar.'

I had no idea the grim Mr Locke had thought this. Neither was I aware that my academic ability had been noted or measured in any way.

'Yes, sir.'

'Is that all you can say?' Silence. 'Well, I don't know what possessed you to perform the actions that led to your expulsion.

But I should like to impress upon you the three things that will not be tolerated at Jacob College, namely smoking, alcoholic consumption and acts of profanity. The last of those applies particularly to you, Master Brill. Is that clear?'

'Yes, sir.'

'Do you know what profanity means?'

Silence.

'Well, the act for which you were expelled certainly comes into that category. It should be interpreted as broadly as possible . . .' The faintest trace of self-consciousness had entered the headmaster's voice, as though he was onstage and in danger of forgetting his lines. He shuffled some papers on his desk.

'Now tell me, you are not of the Jewish faith, are you?'

I wasn't entirely sure if I was or not, but the doctor's tone of voice suggested the best answer was negative. I shook my head.

'Excellent. The classes that would normally be devoted to the Torah provide us with a number of opportunities for offering a wide range of alternative subjects. Master Brill, tell me, have you an interest in ballroom dancing?'

'I'm not sure, sir.'

'I see. Well, how about the game of bridge?'

'Umm . . .'

'How about the stars of the silver screen? Have you ever been to the cinema?'

'Rarely, sir.'

'Horse-racing? We have a class that runs during the flat season. No money is wagered, of course, that would be quite inappropriate, but the turf provides an excellent inroad into the study of mathematics. Not interested? Here. Let me see you turn.'

'Sir?'

'Turn around, boy.' He gestured in a circular motion with a knuckly right hand.

I turned around, and put my back to him.

'Keep turning, around and around. Rotate, boy, rotate!'

I did so, awkwardly.

'Yes, good poise, balance. Quite light on your feet, aren't you, for a Heath boy? No mud on your shoes, that's for sure. Well, do you know what? I think you will make a good little dancer. I'll put you down for Mr Starkey's class. Nothing too demanding, just a waltz to begin with, a two-step if you do well.'

I was dismissed.

'Can't I do the horse-racing class?' I asked a little audaciously, turning as I neared the door.

'Absolutely not. You have the perfect pivot for a master ballroom dancer. It would be a crime to waste you on turf accountancy. Away with you, boy— Oh, wait.'

He called me back.

'I almost forgot. The main reason for calling you here is so that I can provide you with— Now, let me look at your head.' He placed a hand on top of my head, just at the back, moved it around as if moulding it to the shape of my cranium, then removed it but held the shape in the cupped form, which he maintained as he walked across to a cabinet and opened a drawer. He tested several items in the cupped hand until he found the perfect fit. He came over and placed a soft velvet skullcap on my head.

'You should wear this at all times, especially if you see anyone in the school or in the street who looks like a rabbi. Now, away.'

The wearing of the yarmulke was just about the only observance of the Jewish faith in the school, that and the headmaster's insistence that we follow the Hebraic calendar, so it was then the month of Cheshvan in the year 5687. At morning assemblies we sang the Hatikvah, and there was other Jewish iconography pinned to the walls, lines of Hebrew none of us could read.

Who would have thought that a little circle of velvet could cause such consternation? Not only were my journeys to and from school impeded by those who thought it fun to mock and tease someone whose only difference from them was in this little piece of fabric. Sometimes my way was blocked so that I would be late for Mr Morris, whom my parents had enlisted to provide me with transport on market days. Then there was no alternative but to walk the lonely miles along the lanes. Then in Heathrow itself, men bending over would lift themselves from tending their kale and look upon me with eyes of wonder, or of fear, or horror. I could imagine the conversations that took place in the Plough and Harrow in the evenings – *What do you think I saw walking along the lanes this evening, coming up from the Feltham Road? A little Jew boy it was, a little Yid as I'm standing here, plain as daylight, with a skullcap on the back of his head like it was nothing unusual. Never been any Jews on the Heath, not for as long as anyone can remember or as long as history records. No, we've had everything here – Romans, Saxons, Vikings, Celts, but no Jews, not on the Heath, no.*

And it was a rather unexpected reaction I got from my father when I returned home wearing my new adornment. Afterwards I spent much time in thoughtful speculation on how I might depict his face in that extreme of emotion, how much white and red I would need, and how deeply to render the lines that appeared on his face, the way it folded itself diagonally – I hadn't seen his face, or anyone's face, do that before.

'You said they wouldn't make him Jewish,' he bawled at my mother.

'They haven't.'

'Well, what's that thing on his head?'

'It's just a hat. It doesn't mean he's Jewish. Anyway, I think it makes him look rather sweet.'

'Take it off, Kenny. If you wear that thing again I'll stop you going to that school for good and you'll have to come and work for me.'

I did as I was told. As an innately funny man, my father's anger was always hard to take seriously – even at the highest levels of his wrath one could sense a sliver of comedy behind the eyes, or expect that, at any moment, the rage would collapse into a shower of innuendo. But not this time. The rage was pure and burning, and self-consuming, as though, if I didn't comply, my father would simply burst into flames. On the other hand I was extremely fond of my kippah. I felt a perverse pride in the hostile attention it drew. My mother took me aside and explained how my father's feelings were probably the result of deep-seated anxieties about his land – with Tiberius Joy taking more than his share of their father's endowment, my father was naturally sensitive to what he thought might be other encroachments, in either the spatial or the social realms of his life. At least I think that's what she was saying. To lose a field to a stepbrother was a similar kind of deprivation to losing a son to a different religion, even if he had no strong religion in the first place. 'If Father has no strong religion, then perhaps he should become Jewish as well,' I said helpfully. 'Perhaps we all should.'

My mother said it would not be wise to put that idea to my father. 'That is such a sweet hat, Kenny,' she said, fingering the velvet. 'The embroidery is quite exquisite. I wish I could open your father's eyes to the beauty of things, but I think living on the Heath all this time has filled his eyes with mud.'

And so I removed my kippah whenever I was in the house, and on the journey home I would remove it as I entered the area of the Heath, and likewise I would only put it on to go in the other direction when I was clear of the last shit-heap.

I have Mr Morris to thank for the end to my bullying. One day he found me cornered just outside the marketplace by some thugs who were ready to go beyond the usual verbal taunts and were brandishing their bony fists close to my face. They were pulling at my lapel and trying to dislodge my kippah with bullets of spittle. Mr Morris was a big man with big carroty fists and they soon ran when he intervened.

'Jew boy or no Jew boy, you leave this one alone . . .' he bellowed at them as they scattered.

To my dismay, Three Cylinders and others of the Joy clan were among those who taunted me whenever I walked across the Heath in my kippah, and were another reason I removed that item of apparel whenever I was in their vicinity. I am ashamed now, as I look back on it, that I should so easily have capitulated to the bullies. Roddy, I am sure, would have come to my rescue if he had been alive, and I told Three Cylinders so when he gibed at me from a gateway as I walked past. It produced a look in his face; the yellow teeth and straw hair seemed to fade and wilt as I reminded him of his older brother, and he didn't mock me after that.

*

My studies at Jacob College consisted of a classical syllabus – Greek, Latin, history, art, English literature, mathematics, chemistry, biology and ballroom dancing. It was this last subject that I was looking forward to least, and when we assembled in the hall for our first lesson, I was filled with apprehension.

Mr Starkey was a dapper, delicately handsome man but for the strange twist his face took, as though he had been half turned during birth to come out with a slight corkscrew to his features. For our first class he assessed our bodily poise by making us walk in an endless circle around the hall, while he stood in the centre like a circus ringmaster, shouting all the while for us to use the whole of our feet, 'Heel to toe, heel to toe,' occasionally approaching a boy as he walked and roughly pushing him this way and that, as if manipulating a figure made of pipe cleaners, then pushing him away in disgust, the boy nearly falling over. After what felt like half an hour of such treadmilling, we were called to a halt and told to stand still in the centre of the hall. Mr Starkey then sorted us, starting from the front of the pack and working his way through, shoving each boy either to the left or to the right, until he had roughly divided the class into two groups, facing each other from opposite ends of the hall. None of us had any idea why this had happened, and assumed that some sort of teams had been formed.

Mr Starkey took his position in the middle, hot, dishevelled and ruddy-faced from his exertion. 'Now,' he said, in his booming stage voice (he had a very big voice for such a slight man), 'after carefully assessing the hideous and ungraceful gait and poise of you all, having located your centres of gravity and your lines of symmetry, I have divided you into two groups. Those to the west are the men. Those to the east, the women.'

We didn't immediately understand which of us was east and which west, but I had a sinking feeling that I belonged to the newly appointed females of the class, confirmed a moment later when a cheer went up from the far end of the hall. The men had realized their identity. From us, the women at the other end, there came a confused silence, followed by looks of disdain and haughtiness cast in the men's direction. In just a few seconds we had begun acting up to our roles, and were exerting our newly acquired sexual charm.

'Now, don't take it the wrong way, ladies,' Mr Starkey said to us, in a conciliatory tone, 'your role has been assigned purely on physical characteristics to do with your bodily frames. I am sure in spirit you will remain the full-blooded males that you are. However, for the purposes of understanding the art and craft of ballroom dancing, it is essential to grasp the different roles played by the male and the female in the partnership. Since there is not a single female person in this entire school, the onus has fallen on you boys to take up the challenge.'

We were then told that the 'men' would in turn pick a

dancing partner from the group of 'women'. We pseudo-females were expected to stand in a long line that nearly spanned the hall, while the boys, one by one, took their pick. Our female wiles became ever stronger, since none of us wanted to be among the last chosen. Unconsciously we began advertising our strengths as women, thrusting out our hips and chests.

How enviously we looked on Magnus Daley, the first to be chosen, for his lush golden curls no doubt, by Simon Clay, reputed by some to be the toughest boy in his year. What an excellent pairing they were – tall, elegant Magnus's wiry slimness the perfect counterpoint to Simon's burly, clumsy body.

I had resolved myself to the likelihood that I would be among the last to be chosen, but to my amazement I was among the first – perhaps the third or fourth out of more than twenty, but to my horror I was chosen by Eric Bennet. Bennet was a vile creature – a spotty, green-toothed, malodorous villain who had a reputation as a low-grade bully, meaning that he bullied only the smallest and weakest, his cowardice making the true toughs of the school, like Simon Clay, seem almost heroic by comparison. Though I was not in the least scared of Bennet, the thought of being within touching distance of him, let alone holding his hand or having his arm around me in a waltz, was almost impossible to bear. I could not help but recoil when he picked me, then shuddered visibly as he put his clammy hand into mine and pulled me out of the line. My feet turned to lead as he dragged me across the room to where the partnered dancers were gathering.

'Do we get to be the men next week?' I heard a pupil asking Mr Starkey.

'Certainly not,' he replied. 'These roles are assigned for the whole year. You cannot be a man one week and a lady the next. It would be too confusing.'

We could barely stifle our groans at this, a good proportion of us anyway, and I was resigning myself to the fate of clammy intimacy with Eric Bennet for a whole year, and beginning to devise plans to absent myself from the class, when a dispute erupted.

'Bennet,' someone called, 'I chose Brill.' It was a boy I didn't know very well, but one who had attracted a certain level of respect in the school, a boy of acknowledged academic and artistic abilities: Henry Manderley.

'What are you talking about, Manderley? I chose him.'

'No, you pushed in front of me. I had already made up my mind for Brill.'

'You're talking nonsense. I chose him fair and square.' There was a slight quaver in Bennet's voice. He, like the rest of us, was somewhat in awe of Henry Manderley.

'Give me Brill now. You pushed in front of me. Go and choose someone else.'

But Bennet wasn't going to be so easily beaten. He had found some inner strength and put on a show of defiance. 'You choose someone else – go on, before they're all gone.'

'I want Brill.'

'Why do you want him so much? What's so special about him?'

'I could ask the same of you, in the light of your refusal to give him up.'

This seemed to flummox Bennet, and after a few seconds of silence he suddenly pushed me towards Manderley, as though I were an old bicycle he no longer wanted. 'There's nothing special about him. Here, you can have him.'

So I was thrown into Henry Manderley's arms.

He gave me no indication as to why he wanted me so badly. He took me by the wrist and hauled me over to the dance floor, where by now the partners were getting ready for their first dance. He didn't say a word to me, and didn't even look at me, but treated me as some sort of inanimate prize he'd won. I had an inkling of what it feels like to be a silver chalice. Nevertheless, after some brief instruction from Mr Starkey, who prodded and pulled us again, making sure we were properly aligned and that our hands were in the right places (hand to hand, my other hand on Manderley's shoulder, his round my waist), and once Mr Jeremy had struck up on the piano, I felt myself carried across the dance floor on waves of gentle pressure, steered through the uncertain realms of a waltz by Henry Manderley's powerful, intelligent, delicious body.

*

Along with ballroom dancing I applied myself well to all classes, and even found myself enjoying some of the science subjects, but I was far more excited by the fact that we had double art once a week, which meant that we spent nearly two hours in the art room. I had by that time set my heart on becoming an artist, and planned to go to art school. Such an ambition was not looked upon favourably, even by the art master, who recommended I studied architecture. In fact this art teacher, and the department he ran, was the one disappointment of the school. Mr Kuratowski was a lean and acrobatic Pole, a man of fine, delicate features, who spoke English with the clenched grimace of someone struggling to contain his acid. As far as any of us could tell, he had no interest in art whatsoever, unless it illustrated the suffering and political struggles of his native country. His art lessons were history lessons. More specifically, they were lessons on the history of Poland. Occasionally Mr K (as we always referred to him) would remember his role, addressing himself to the task of our artistic education and mentioning the names of various Polish artists who'd endeavoured to depict the struggles of his country and its people in paint. So we became very familiar with the name Jan Matejko, whose *Constitution of 3 May 1791* was, according to Mr K, the greatest painting in the history of Western art, and one of the few paintings he mentioned that we could actually see, thanks to the large reproduction he had been able to procure and hang on the art-room wall.

'My father was great man,' would begin a typical lesson, Mr K standing at the head of the class, speaking through perfect teeth, 'killed by the Prussian devils in 1875. You not fit to spit on his boot. He was great man. Prussian Empire was evil empire, killed many of my people. Kingdom of Poland cleaned off the map for thirty years. New Constitution of May the third was first modern constitution, after American constitution. But America not proper country. Poland first proper country with constitution, to keep at bay Prussian devils. Now you continue painting Constitution of May the third, and remember my father. He was great man. You not fit to spit on his boot!'

Sometimes we could see a tear glistening in Mr K's eyes when he delivered these speeches – tears of anger or of sorrow, it was hard to tell. The only other feelings he gave evidence of were boredom, and a tetchy impatience. He showed no interest in our drawing and painting, and indeed rarely even looked at it. Once in a while he would stroll around the classroom and peer over our shoulders, but he offered no comments, though he would sometimes stand for many minutes behind someone, then do nothing but tut, or sigh to himself in a hopeless way. Sometimes he would chuckle quietly, but not in a manner that suggested he was at all amused. If I hoped for some helpful instruction, encouragement or approval, the best I got was some interested humming noises, little murmurs of surprise, as if to say, 'Good God, there is someone in the class who can actually draw.'

Mr K was fearsome in his discipline, and he struck us at every opportunity with a variety of artists' instruments – paintbrushes, rulers, T-squares. The bristle end of a hog-hair brush, with its metal shoe, could sting more than a cane. But I had some admiration for him. He was an extremely elegant man, with a handsome Slavic face; lean, though now creased with age. On the rare occasions that he smiled his face seemed to break open and sweetness pour out of it.

It might have been that the headmaster had had a word with Mr K about the nationalistic bias of his lessons because the following year our first term was dominated by a project to produce an advertising poster for a place he called the London Tower. None of us was sure what he meant – the Tower of London? Big Ben? The Monument? What about Nelson's Column? Or the Shot Tower? No one dared question Mr K, so the issue was never resolved. Some of us painted the Tower of London, some of us Big Ben, a few the Monument; Mr K approved them all. Whatever building he had in mind, he didn't know what it looked like.

Though he might have had as little regard for our artistic welfare as it is possible for an art teacher to have, he had no problem in regarding us as a possible source of supplementary income. To this end he operated a sideline as a pastel portraitist, offering his services to the boys (or their parents) at two guineas a shot. It was widely regarded among the more cruelly imaginative boys that this operation was a cover for a far less savoury activity. Mr K insisted that the portraits be done in his home studio and had a regular stream of boys visiting his house. Whenever a boy visited, he would be mercilessly taunted the next day.

For my part I couldn't be sure. Boys who'd sat for Mr K didn't seem to be in any distress afterwards – or did they? Perhaps there was a stunned deadness behind the eyes that had formerly been bright and cheeky. Perhaps they did bear a secret that couldn't be spoken.

Bennet was chiefly responsible for these rumours. He had,

since our falling out as dancing partners, decided to taunt me for my lack of masculine virtues, for the readiness with which I played the woman to Henry's man, quite forgetting that he had chosen me first and had been very reluctant to hand me over to Henry. He once passed a picture round the class, a hideous cartoon depicting me and Mr K (his Jewish features cruelly caricatured) naked, with our private parts corkscrewing round each other like intertwining serpents, and the legend beneath, *Together For Ever*.

This was because it had become known that I was to have my portrait done by Mr K, that I was to go to his house and suffer the terrible degradations Bennet liked to imagine took place there.

It was all my dear mother's fault. She understood how deeply interested I had become in art, so when parents' evening came around, she spent a long time talking to Mr K, who usually enjoyed a quiet time at parents' evenings and was rather unsettled by her enthusiasm for the subject. She recited long lists of artists' names, asking him what he thought of 'those Impressionists', telling him how she adored the work of Botticelli and Raphael. 'I have never really managed to get beyond the Italian Renaissance, you see, Mr Kuratowski, and I'm a little ashamed to say that even Turner seems a bit modern to me – but I'm sure you must know and understand so many of these modern painters. Tell me, what do you think of Mr Whistler?' Mr K had had enough and stood up, holding out his hand to be shaken, but my mother would not be put off. 'And what about your art, Mr Kuratowski? What sort of art is yours?'

Mr K seemed a little thrown by the question. It was almost certainly the first time it had ever been asked. 'I do the portrait,' he said, sitting down again.

'You are a portrait artist, are you?'

The familiar shiver of irritation passed over Mr K's face, as it did whenever he had to repeat or explain himself. 'I do the portrait. Your son. Two guineas. Frame extra.'

Mr K's poor English and his social awkwardness helped convince my mother that this wasn't an offer of a service but a compulsory part of the curriculum.

'Of course, Mr Kuratowski. That would be splendid . . .'

The usual procedure was for Mr K to take the subjects home with him immediately after school. He was one of the few people I knew to have a car, and I sat uncomfortably (he had the windows open, even though it was December) in his little black Ford, whose engine chugged along like a motorboat. Mr K turned to me and said, 'This will make a good little Christmas gift for someone, will it not? A beloved aunt, perhaps?'

When we arrived at Mr K's house I was astonished to find that it was a warm and welcoming family home, full of happy children. Twin girls of the most charming sweetness, two older boys, athletic and graceful, a kindly English wife who had taken Polish cuisine to her heart and served us smoked yellow fish in a cabbagy sauce, dumplings stuffed with strange cheese, then orange jelly with lumpy cream. I was guest of honour at the big dining table, but didn't feel under any guest-obligation to be sociable or on my best behaviour, other than during the brief blessings and silences that punctuated the meal, and during which the twins would giggle anyway. A friendly red setter wagged his tail at us.

The bleak, craggy gloom of the art room Mr K had vanished. The hollow, lean face now dedicated itself to the production of smiles and laughter. I had never seen any man so overjoyed to be with his family as Mr K. It was as though his tragic demeanour in the classroom was simply a result of his being forcibly separated from his wife and children. It made it all the more puzzling how he managed to generate such a pall of gloom from so warm and rich a home life.

I still felt an underlying nervousness. Bennet's warnings and stark visions of my imminent torture were too vivid to dismiss. When the time came for us to remove ourselves to Mr K's studio, I checked my pocket to make sure I had my jack-knife. But then it turned out Mr K's studio was the living room. Having seated me on a calfskin pouffe, he reclined in an armchair with a drawing board on his knee and began working from a box of pastels, while his twins performed a musical entertainment, on violin and cello, with their mother at the piano.

As if this wasn't enough amusement, halfway through his portrait Mr K, still with colour-stained fingertips, picked up a fiddle and launched into a folksy jig, which had everyone in the room dancing around me as I sat on my pouffe, until I was yanked up and made to join in the joyful capering, with mother, father, twin girls, athletic boys and red setter.

By the time I was driven home I felt the light-headed dizziness I would later feel after heavy drinking sessions at wedding receptions – my ears still full of music and my body tingling with dance. And yet this had just been an ordinary night for Mr K. Nothing in the art room could be the same again, I thought. How could Mr K manage to overlook my talent as an artist when I had trodden the carpets of his sacred home life, danced with his daughters and sons, eaten his smoked fish, been kissed by his beaming wife?

But I was to be disappointed. The next art lesson was as gloomy as all the others. There was to be no change. Mr K gave his lecture on the great Polish artists and the tragedy of Polish history, before setting us that lesson's exercise, which was to draw a cabbage, while he disappeared to the back of the art room. I have rarely been so disappointed in a man as I was in Mr K. The only time we spoke again was on two occasions, when he delivered the framed portrait for me to take home, and a few days later when he gave me a note to give to my mother, which turned out to be a receipt for her cheque.

Then something rather puzzling and shocking happened: Mr K died, along with his family, when his house burnt down. I only found out the details through my mother, when she read an account of the tragedy in the local paper.

'Oh, no, that charming man. This is too awful,' she said one evening. My mother only read the newspaper in the evening.

'What is it, Mother?'

Her face was grey. 'It is too dreadful. He was such a gentleman, Kenneth, and he cared so much about art, and he was so good to you . . .'

I had never spoken to my mother about Mr K's shortcomings as a teacher. His portrait of me, which gave me a glimpse of how I would look as an old man, now hung on the dining-room wall, an endless source of embarrassment for me.

'Wow!' I said, reading the article. 'They're all dead!'

My mother looked at me in horror for a few moments. 'Kenneth, human suffering should never be treated lightly. As an artist in the making, I would have hoped you would know that. It doesn't matter who is the subject of the suffering, whether they are our friends or our enemies, they deserve our compassion and our respect. And I will not have death acknowledged with the wide-eyed alacrity you displayed just now.'

'I'm sorry, Mother, it was just the shock, that's all.'

My mother's mood was tempered instantly by my contrition. 'Good little Kenny. I can see it must have been a shock for you to lose such a sweet art master.'

In truth I had been excited by the news, in my childish, boyish way. But later the poignancy of the event began to register itself in my mind. I thought of the tall, elegant pastel-portraitist weaving his acrobat's body through the flames to his dear little twins' bedroom to find them already ash in their beds, he and his wife roaring with despair as the flames closed around them. What a terrible thing for that pretty little family to be scorched so, for not just the individuals but the lore and rituals of family life – the prayers before meals, the merry little masques, the music-making, the joking and the dreams, all to be incinerated and silenced for ever.

But I continued to be bothered by what my mother had said about my apparent lack of artistic sensibilities and became anxious that I was missing some crucial component of the artist's mental make-up, an ability to sympathize, a sensitivity to suffering. I spent a long time encouraging myself to feel sad about Mr K and his family. I practised compassion in the bathroom mirror, looking into my eyes to see if any tears were forming as I replayed in my imagination the burning of that family. And, eventually, I did manage to squeeze out a few salty droplets, and was thrilled when they fell down my cheeks. Perhaps I was going to be an artist after all.

And that is all I know about the death of Mr K.

XV

Yes, Davies and his like will sneer at my practised compassion, my carefully trained sympathies. 'Those tears don't mean anything,' he will say. 'Without the emotion behind them they are just brine. You may as well prick your finger when you see a child die, if that's the only way to make the tears come.' But, then, how many emotions are truly felt? How many are not simply learnt responses? The watery etiquette with which we pay our dues to the world of feeling? Oh, I'm surprised at you, Kenneth Brill, painter of such tragic nudes, if you're saying there is nothing behind them but the levers and pulleys of a thinking machine.

Well, when it comes to the other end of the emotional range, I can admit to a singular lack of need for practice and rehearsal. I am someone who is innately gifted in the language of pleasure, and I learnt its vocabulary long before any of my fellow pupils.

Every Wednesday afternoon was, for me, a little spell spent in heavenly residence. A tenancy in the tenements of Elysium. In the grand hall of Jacob College, the third-year ballroom class tripped its way through a curriculum of waltzes, quick-steps, tangos, foxtrots, sambas, rumbas, *paso doble*s and cha-cha-chas, with Henry Manderley as the man, leading me on a journey through the most distant realms of physical delight. We had become the best dancers in our year, admired throughout the school. We would have won competitions, had there been anyone to compete against, but we were the only teenage ballroom dancers in England – there were no other schools that taught the subject. Oh, to feel the pull of Henry's tight, taut body as he led me through the sweet violence of a tango, to keep up with his gleaming spats as he trotted through a foxtrot. The exhilaration of being the woman to Henry Manderley's manly man, to be swathed in his sleeves, to feel his arm across my back, nestled in the small of it. Oh, God, the thought of it. I didn't under-stand what I was experiencing. I had never felt like that about Marcus Boone, even when he stripped for me in the toilets of St Saviour's and his little tapered thing had dingle-dangled before me. But to be led by Henry sent a tingle through me such as I had simply not experienced in my life before. Did it have a colour, this emotion? Yes, I think it had a resplendent redness, a searing, deep, blood redness, an overspilling tomato juice, a bloody-Mary-thrown-in-the-face type of redness.

VANISHING

I found myself now looking forward to the showers after games, those spluttering torrents that had so shocked me when I first encountered them, to see Marcus Boone's downfall duplicated a dozen times and made compulsory. So shocked that at first I sought any excuse to avoid joining the crowds beneath the boiling rain, until I caught a glimpse of Henry's tessellated solar plexus and the big serrifed *o* of his navel, wide and deep enough to take an exploratory tongue. He was downy with the first crop of adult hair, the tangle given a scrolled symmetry by the water. It was a great effort not to fall to my knees in adoration before Henry's body. He would saunter past me in the shower throng, unaware of my ardour in that stinging water, when we were all soap-blind, our ears looped with echoes, and I would position myself so that his prick would brush against my thigh, an action that registered nothing in his face, the same if I managed to brush my own against his.

I can't remember how it came about, probably as a joke in the first instance, but after dancing an elegant and deft waltz, he would kiss the back of my hand in conclusion, an action that drew appreciative laughter from everyone who saw it. And no one teased us for it, no one even seemed to think it odd when we kissed each other on the lips after a dance. Though it shocked and delighted me. I had kissed no one on the lips before, not even Marjorie, and I was astounded by the softness of that part of the face – lips look such raw, hard, tough things. But being kissed by Henry was like being kissed by a little cloud. Again the laughter. We were just taking our roles to their outer limits, except that no one else did it, and even in the world of adults, kissing in such a manner between dancing partners would have been thought forward, or even downright insulting. And even Bennet, who was a dreadfully gauche waltzer, a quite insultingly bad performer of the two-step, had nothing to say about our kissing, but laughed along with the others.

Henry came to my house only once, and it wasn't a successful visit, though it had begun exquisitely with a cycle ride together across the Heath from Feltham, Henry stopping every now and then to read aloud from the large library of poetry books he had packed into his saddlebag.

'Did you really need to bring all that poetry? It looks very heavy.'

'Yes, but it lightens the soul, by way of compensation.'

We had a picnic en route during which Henry was keen to make a display of his cultivated personality, reading from Palgrave in a declamatory tone, and smoking a cherrywood pipe. He dared me to take a puff and, thinking back to Roddy Joy's cigarette, I thought myself up to the challenge. I took a deep draw. This time I felt as though a demon had entered my throat and was somehow strangling me from within. Henry chuckled at my tribulations and gently picked the pipe out of my weak hands.

To my delight, he seemed enraptured by the landscape of the Heath, his reaction so strongly in contrast to the disparaging remarks usually made by non-Heath people that I had endured all my life from St Saviour's onwards.

'I should have brought my selected Wordsworth with me, Kenneth, to help me celebrate the gloriousness of Nature's work here.'

Reading aloud the words of Keats or Coleridge seemed to have a visible effect on our surroundings. The countryside, my rotten, muddy, putrefying countryside, praised so, hailed and addressed as though it were a creature sensitive to affection, glowed in response. The leaves filled with deeper greenness, the sky acquired new layers of light. It seemed to me that the attention of a beautiful man triggers beauty in the thing observed. The love I have for the landscape of the Heath dates mostly from that day we spent bicycling around the lanes. I realized I lived in a beautiful place from that moment.

When we got home I was embarrassed to find that my sisters were very eager to meet Henry, and he was rather pleased with their attention. They had dressed themselves up in their finest clothes and had clearly spent hours on their hair, curling and backcombing it; the oldest, Angelica, had even applied some make-up. Of course, it was a rare thing for me to have a friend round for tea. Since the days of Marcus Boone I had had no friends to visit, and Marcus now had become a distant memory.

The girls were clever enough to know that it was a dangerous strategy to make obvious your attraction to a fellow so, as was so common with their annoying sex, they overcompensated and went to the other extreme, hurling sarcastic comments and downright insults at Henry whenever they had the opportunity. And Henry, I was even more displeased to learn, was well acquainted with this topsy-turvy world of male-female flirtation, and responded to the girls with equal sarcasm, just as they would have expected, as was evidenced by their tedious tittering and blushing.

They thought his habit of reading poetry to himself at the dinner table quite hilarious.

'In our house we don't allow reading at the table,' said Prudence.

Henry affected not to hear this.

'In fact we consider it the height of rudeness.'

Henry said, without looking up, 'To prohibit the reading of poetry, at the dinner table or anywhere else, is an act of extreme barbarism, wouldn't you agree, Mrs Brill?'

My mother, who had not been taking notice of the conversation, being deeply engrossed in some food-related domestic matter, and having just returned from a consultation with Mrs Rossiter, stared blankly at her young guest before saying, 'I have always promoted good reading tastes in my children.'

The girls tittered.

'Why don't you go and titter elsewhere?' I suddenly snapped, while Henry turned a page of his Shelley, the food turning cold on his plate. 'Mother, can you send them to their playroom? I don't think guests should be subject to such tedious whinnying.'

But to my dismay the flirting continued all afternoon, much as I would have liked to take Henry to my room and persuade him to pose for me in the get-up of Lawrence of Arabia (our shared hero at the time). Instead I had to join all three of them for a walk around the orchard and an inspection of a little fairy bower they had made. And when I did finally separate Henry from my sisters, I could do so only by challenging him to a cycling race, which liberated Henry's boyishly silly side: he began cycling far too fast for his own good, and indeed came to an ignominious end, head down in Mr Morris's shit-heap, having swerved to avoid his plodding dray, Daphne.

Then, washed and in a set of borrowed clothes (but still faintly reeking, for ever from then on), Henry Manderley was driven back to his home in Mr Morris's truck, with his bicycle (front wheel buckled) in the back.

A terrible thing happened shortly after what was to be Henry's one and only visit to the Heath. We were separated as dancers. There seemed to be no rhyme or reason to Mr Starkey's decision, except that he liked to mix the partners up now and then, especially if they had been together for a long time. I would have thought that Henry and I, being such successful dancers, would be spared that arbitrary rearrangement.

I now found myself partnered to an awful clodhopper, a barely bipedal oaf called Mick Barking, who not only trampled my toes to splinters but his horrendous clumsiness actually had us falling over and landing in an ungainly heap on the parquet floor of the gymnasium. Henry, meanwhile, had been partnered with a slender, golden-haired, blue-eyed thing (the least Jewish-looking member of the whole school, probably) and continued to swan around the gym with all the grace and flow of a pair of swallows.

But they didn't kiss. No, at the end of a class no kisses passed between Henry and the blond boy, not even demure chivalrous ones on the back of the hand. Kissing, it seemed, was something uniquely our own, and I was gladdened by that. I remained, as far as I knew, the only boy to have kissed Henry. But I was never to kiss those lips again.

*

The death of Mr K meant that we found ourselves (after a spell of stand-ins from the other departments, all of whom, despite their lack of training or expertise in the subject, proved far more competent and enthusiastic teachers of art than Mr K) with a new art teacher. He was called Mr Toynbee and he was Mr K's opposite in every way – young, enthusiastic, dynamic. I later learnt he had only just graduated from the Slade, a place I had never heard of but with which I was soon to become familiar.

No more projects on irrelevant advertising campaigns, or depictions of nineteenth-century Polish history, no more lectures on the cruelty of the Prussian Empire or the injustices of the Russian tsar, art lessons now became adventurous experimentations with varieties of media. I made an owl out of bits of an old clock. I made a jack-in-the-box, puppets, collages from newspapers. We painted from our imagination and from life in equal measure. Mr Toynbee brought into the classroom a life-size human skeleton, which we drew. In fact, I became quite obsessed with this skeleton, and over my remaining years at Jacob College I drew and painted it as many times as I could.

Mr Toynbee even looked like an artist – he wore trilby hats and dandyish suits, would smoke in class using a cigarette holder, and occasionally liked to affect a consumptive air, when he would lounge across his desk with his shirt unbuttoned, and cough into a frilled handkerchief. To my delight I was recognized at last as having a serious artistic talent. Frequently my work was held up to the others in the class as an example, and this had the unexpected effect of making me popular. By now the art class was made of pupils who had chosen art over other options. The bullies and no-hopers, like Eric Bennet, were off doing metal-work and learning to be ironmongers, and we were left to form the artistic elite of the school.

*

I had mentioned my ambition to go to art school to my parents. They reacted, as I knew they would, very differently.

'Art school! What a wonderful idea, I'm so proud of you, Kenneth.'

'Art school? Why do such places even exist? What purpose do they serve?'

My father wasn't wholeheartedly opposed. If I wanted to go to art school, fine, but he wasn't going to pay the fees. I felt it unlikely that he would pay the fees whatever subject I was study-ing.

I applied anyway and, to my amazement, I was invited to London for an interview and was able to present my parents with a *fait accompli*. I had secured a place at the most prestigious art school in the country.

'But where will you live, or do you intend to commute from Heathrow? You know there is no public transport and you'd have to walk up to the Bath road and catch an omnibus, then a train. And how will you pay for your accommodation? And have you thought about the fees?'

'No. But I'm going to go, whatever it costs. I'll steal the money if I have to.'

'No, Kenneth. Listen to me carefully. I can pay for you, if you're sure it is what you want to do. I have money.'

'What?' my father burst out.

And she had, the wonderful woman. All those years of piano lessons, and she had been squirrelling the money away, just for me. All those sour little pusses and their clumsy Moonlight Sonatas, little had they known they were paying for my future education.

'Why do you want to leave home so much,' said the former scholar gypsy, changing tack and introducing a note of hurt, 'just when things are beginning to go our way, Kenneth?'

My father was, at this time, building his sludgecake empire and putting enormous pressure on Tiberius Joy to concede some of the land that he believed was his. Productivity on my father's own land had increased as much as the price of sludgecake, and he was beginning to exert his influence about the fields of the Heath. I suppose he imagined he was founding a new, powerful dynasty on the back of his stacks of sludgecake, and that I was to play a key role in its development.

'Hah, first you try to turn him into a Jew and now you're trying to turn him into a nancy-boy artist. Kenneth, what's wrong with you? All those years you loved to go and work with Three Cylinders, against all our wishes, doing Tiberius's donkey work for him, but when your own father starts to make good with his own land, you want to leave the Heath altogether.'

The arguments went on like this for several days; my father could not be persuaded that my future lay in training to be an artist, but neither could he influence my mother against her conviction that it did. And since she had, to my father's shock, sufficient means to help me in that direction, there was little he could do in the end but sulk, which he did for several years.

Financial matters were assisted greatly by my mother's negotiations with her sister Mary, who lived in Holloway. I was never fully to understand the nature of this arrangement, but it seemed that she was deeply indebted to my mother for some past favours so she agreed to provide me with free lodging in London. There was talk that I should supplement my income by working in the market at Covent Garden (my father's idea), but my mother would not hear of it. 'Kenneth could not possibly be expected to work with all the other mudlarks on the stalls while his fellow students are taking tea at the Café Royal. He would be an utter laughing stock.'

XVI

Have you ever had the experience of meeting someone who is wearing exactly the same clothes as you, right down to the last button and trouser crease? No? Well, try joining the army. Ha ha.

Davies came to my cell carrying something on a large hanger. 'There you are. Don't say I never bring you anything.'

It was a rather smart suit, in pinstripes, along with a shirt and tie.

'Hard to get it just right – we don't want you to look like a car dealer, but then we don't want you looking like a tinker either. Smart civilian, that's how we want you to come across.'

I took the hanger of clothes and inspected the jacket. 'These lapels – they look a bit Jimmy Cagney. But wait a minute – shouldn't I be wearing my uniform?'

'We have been unable to obtain one – and, besides, we will be arguing that this hearing should be taking place in a civilian court. You were on extended leave at the time of your arrest and your activity was not connected with your role in the army – this should really be a standard case of criminal law. I think we will stand a much better chance of success, a lower sentence if the jury decide to convict and a fairer appeals process, of course. By appearing in civilian clothes you will strengthen my case in this respect.'

'Have I been charged with anything yet?'

'Brill, please don't be vague. You know exactly what you've been charged with – breaking defence regulations and assisting the enemy by attempting to pass information to them. This is easily refuted, but we have yet to see what evidence the prosecution will provide.'

After he left me I contemplated the clothes for some time. I arranged them on the bed so that they looked like a poor soul lying there, his body evaporated. Little fellow. Thin little fellow. When I summoned up the resolve to dress, it was an agonizing process. Never before had the act of putting on a set of clothes felt so akin to stepping into someone else's body. Not even when I put on an army uniform for the first time had I felt such a strong sense of my bodily self being consumed by a sartorial self. The very act of getting dressed, it seemed to me, was becoming a task of towering difficulty: more and more I felt the naked self was the true self, and that clothes were a kind of parasite that clung desperately and pathetically to the body, sucking the life out of it.

An hour later, my body firmly in the grip of that dark suit, the knotted tie like a fist at my throat, a group of armed guards came to my cell and I was escorted to the main hall, which, to my astonishment, was crowded with people and had been transformed into something resembling a court of law. Long tables had been put out, arranged carefully and draped with red cloth. A Union Flag and an army banner were hanging at the back of the room, behind what I took to be the main bench. Down either side, officers in service dress sat behind desks, while others stood at doorways in sentry mode. I was the only person in the entire room not in uniform.

I was told to sit in a chair that stood exposed in the middle of the room, facing the main bench, as yet unoccupied. I sat as I had been told, and noticed how no one in the room seemed to be taking any notice of me whatsoever but was deeply engrossed in various documents and legal tomes. I could see Davies, smarter than I had ever seen him, sitting in close consultation with his companions. On the other side of the room, and facing them, the prosecutors, Cunningham and his sour-faced colleagues.

There was a brief bit of ceremony when an usher called for the court to stand, and we stood as four men in uniform walked in and took their places at the main bench. The judge advocate seemed to be an amenable fellow, a civilized look about him, and an air of gentleness on his face. After sitting down I was immediately told to stand, confirm my name, rank and number, then made to swear an oath on the Holy Bible. I was told to sit down. An officer read out the charge.

'The accused was arrested in fields to the west of Cain Lane, in the district of Harmondsworth, Middlesex. It is alleged that the accused was engaged in covert surveillance activity, gathering information on the proposed military airfield at the said location, including information regarding its fortifications and defence structures, with the intention of passing this information to the enemy.'

The judge advocate then turned to Captain Cunningham and asked him for a brief statement regarding the prosecution.

Cunningham stood and allowed a moment's silence. He was a lean, coppery man, with yellow eyes. I was surprised to find that he spoke with a strong Yorkshire accent.

'The defendant was arrested as described in the charge. He was seen, over a period of several days, making drawings, diagrams and more detailed plans of the fields surrounding the Great West Aerodrome. This aerodrome, and the land around it, has been requisitioned by the Air Ministry under the Military

Land Purchase Act 1892, for the construction of a new military air base, which will play a vital role in the future prosecution of the war. Prior to his arrest, the accused was seen to be in conversation with a number of individuals. Several of those individuals have been traced and will be called as witnesses. The accused was seen at several locations in the fields surrounding the proposed air base over a number of days. On the occasion of his arrest the accused was observed to be making drawings and diagrams of an area of particular strategic sensitivity, namely an anti-tank fortification off the Bath road to the south of the village of Sipson. A squad of sappers were working on this fortification at the time, and the sergeant went over to the accused and asked him his business. It was at this point that the accused was brought into custody.'

The judge advocate thanked Captain Cunningham, then turned to Davies and asked him for a brief statement for the defence. Davies stood up and began to speak.

'Your Honour, the accused does not deny that he was making the drawings, paintings and sketches, though he would dispute that any of these could be called diagrams, at the times and in the places described by Captain Cunningham. However, the purposes for which these images were made are quite different from those proposed by the prosecution. Your Honour, Lieutenant Brill is a distinguished artist. He was trained at one of our most prestigious schools of art and has exhibited his work in well-known London galleries. We will later be calling witnesses who can testify to his importance and standing as an artist. Since the outbreak of the war he has served with distinction in the Royal Engineers and has risen to the rank of lieutenant in the Camouflage Corps. Not only has Lieutenant Brill planned and directed some extremely important camouflage operations, he has played a leading role in developing new camouflage techniques for use in desert environments. He played a vital role in giving the Allied

Forces a decisive advantage in the battle of El Alamein, and was subsequently injured in the course of his duties and invalided home. Here, after convalescence in various hospitals, he spent some time at his family home, which, you may be surprised to learn, is very close to the locations mentioned by Captain Cunningham. In fact, the land surrounding that home has been requisitioned for the purpose of building the new air base, and his family has been ordered to leave the house and the land that surrounds it. The whole area will shortly be redeveloped. Neither Lieutenant Brill nor his family has raised any objection to this, understanding that the necessity for sustaining air power will be crucial as we move towards victory in the war. He did, however, feel it would be important that he recorded the landscape as it exists now before it is destroyed by the new development. This is the reason why Lieutenant Brill was out in the fields painting the landscapes he has known since early childhood. He was merely trying to make a personal record of a cherished landscape that will soon be lost for ever.'

Davies sat down. I couldn't have felt more affection for him, in those moments immediately after his speech, if he had been my own brother. I felt that he not only understood the facts of my situation but that he understood their emotional substructure. It was almost as though he'd written a poem about me, in which all my anxieties and doubts had been detected and given expression. And the rush of gratitude and affection I felt was all the stronger when I considered how Davies had produced this eloquence out of those long hours of gruff, tedious interrogation, when I had thought, in my muddled way, that he was out to prove some sort of case against me, rather than conduct my defence.

Captain Cunningham now opened the case for the prosecution. 'This case revolves around a set of paintings and drawings that the accused made at the places and times earlier described.

I would therefore like to present these items to the court, so that the jury can make an assessment of whether they contain sufficient detail to be of any use to an enemy, or conversely whether they appear to be a personal record of a landscape soon to be lost, as Captain Davies has put it.'

Then, to my astonishment, the courtroom became something like an art gallery. Ushers brought in various easels, lecterns and other supporting apparatus and arranged them in a line at the far end of the room, behind the row of judges. Then my paintings, those that I had done on canvas, were brought in and placed on the easels. There were twelve in all, and some works on paper, which were laid out on tables, along with two spiral-bound sketchbooks. The judge and his acolytes on the main bench spent some time in close inspection of the work, muttering and murmuring and pointing out details to each other. I couldn't quite believe it – perhaps it was my insurmountable ego – but they seemed to be making appreciative noises to each other: they actually enjoyed looking at my paintings. After they returned to their bench, the officers on another bench, whom I presumed were the court-martial equivalent of a jury, went over to have a look as well. More appreciative murmurings. I wondered if I might even make a sale.

After everyone in the courtroom had had a good look at my work, Captain Cunningham began to make his case that my paintings could be useful to an enemy. He talked the court through several of the images in detail, pointing out specific features and how they related to the geography of the future air base.

'There is an existing civil aerodrome at the location of the future air base, which you can see in some of the paintings. This, in relation to the other features, makes it quite easy to orient these paintings with regard to a map. But the really important fact is that they contain disguised information. For instance, if you look at this painting here, you will see a most odd structure that clearly has no place in the painting.'

The court looked closely. It was a view across Butler's Field with the aerodrome in the distance. I was rather pleased with how I'd captured the play of light on the cabbage leaves.

'Please note the small grey cuboid structure in the far corner – you see? A building of some sort? Well, the maps of that area show there is no building at that location. There are very few buildings anywhere on that section of the fields.' Here he produced a large map he had had made of the area depicted in my painting, and placed it on a display stand. He then produced a plan of the proposed new aerodrome, which he displayed alongside it. 'The hangar of the existing aerodrome is to be retained as part of the new air base. We can therefore use the hangar as a convenient way-finder on the new plans. As you can see, the location of the grey cuboid structure in the painting can be plotted on the corresponding map, here.' He pointed with a stick. 'Then, if we look at the plan of the proposed air base, we can see that there is a building marked in exactly the same spot.' Again he pointed with his stick. By showing the position of the old hangar in both maps he did indeed seem to identify a correspondence between my painting and the plan. 'What we have here, in Lieutenant Brill's painting, is a depiction of a building that does not yet exist. This grey cuboid structure so carefully painted is, I propose, a depiction of a building that exists, so far, only in the plans for the new base. Moreover, this is an extremely important building – it is the main fuel depot.'

To my horror, this revelation produced some gasps of amazement around the courtroom.

The judge advocate then spoke up. 'Do we know how the accused managed to acquire such detailed information regarding the new air base?'

'Well, we have no evidence that he has procured any plans or blueprints to that effect, but we can surmise that a certain amount of information has been made known to the residents of the Heath in the process of land acquisition. The layouts of the runways and holding areas can be easily ascertained from comparing land-purchase orders, and it may be the case that more information has been given to the land owners than would be appropriate. It is also the case that the accused has managed to glean a great deal of information from casual conversation with the surveyors and engineers he has encountered while out in the field doing his "landscape painting". Again, there is evidence that some members of the engineering project had been rather careless regarding the imparting of information to members of the public, but it has become apparent that the accused has used his obvious talents as an artist to beguile those members, and has used his charm and eloquence to glean information from them. I understand those members are facing appropriate disciplinary measures. And to further our case, Your Honour, I would like to call the prosecution's first witness.'

After due court process, the first witness was called, and there entered into the room a man I vaguely recognized, a man in all respects a person you would have guessed was some sort of public-service lackey. He came in with his mackintosh over one arm, his yellow, balding head re-covered with combed-over hair, a fussy, unnecessary little moustache and round horn-rimmed spectacles. After stating his name and profession he then went into description of our supposed encounter.

'I was with two colleagues, surveying an area to the north of the A30, when I came across a person I took to be an artist. He was standing at the edge of a field and had an easel, and a small trestle table on which were arranged his paints and other artist's materials. He looked very professional, very genuine. After we had been surveying the area for about half an hour he came over to me and began talking. He introduced himself as Kenneth

Brill, and said that he was a local artist, and that he was painting the area to provide a visual record before the land was destroyed for the new air base.'

'And did he ask you for any information regarding the layout of that air base?'

'Yes, he asked me where, precisely, the perimeter of the airfield would be. So I'm afraid I said to him something like, "Well, if you were standing here when the new airfield is built, you'd be about two hundred yards inside the boundary fence, on the main runway." I understand it was very foolish of me to divulge such information.'

'It certainly was,' the judge interrupted. 'However, I am sure you now understand the import of your lapse, and you can go some way to atoning for it by being as clear and as detailed as you can in your recollections of your conversation with the accused.'

The man looked extremely uncomfortable, fiddling with the collar of the mackintosh he was holding, looking down at his feet like a scolded schoolboy. 'Yes, well, we spoke a great deal, and I'm afraid I divulged further details of the new layout of the aerodrome, such as where the observation tower would be, in relation to the existing buildings, and the location of the fuel depot, and the munitions dump. He wanted this information so that he would know what in the landscape would change, and what would stay the same, so that he wouldn't waste time on painting views that wouldn't be changed. It seemed reasonable to me. I did have some sympathy with the local residents. The land was very rich in produce, and the artist told me that his family had worked on the land for at least two hundred years. Lieutenant Brill told me they were getting very little or no compensation for the loss of their land.'

Two other witnesses were called, a policeman and a sapper, who barked his answers as though on the parade ground. Both confessed to having had long conversations with me in which they divulged just about everything they knew of the future air base. All three were invited to examine the paintings and comment on their topographical accuracy.

'I did wonder,' said the sapper, in the puzzled tones of someone unused to thinking, 'why on earth anyone would want to paint those fields. It's not a pretty place, and it stinks to high Heaven.'

A whole day was given to this sort of evidence. At the end of it Captain Cunningham spoke to the jury: 'You will have seen from the testimony given here today that the defendant had an exceptionally keen interest in the layout of the future air base. This interest goes far beyond what would be reasonable to expect from someone who was merely recording a landscape for sentimental reasons. It is extremely regrettable that such information was so easily and thoughtlessly given, but that is a separate matter. What remains is the fact that Lieutenant Brill had acquired an extensive knowledge of the plans, and was incorporating these into the apparently innocent landscape paintings he was producing.'

But Cunningham had so far only been able to point out one feature in my paintings that could be seen as providing information about the new air base – the grey cuboid structure that supposedly depicted a future fuel depot. So great was my frustration at being unable to speak that I could do nothing but look helplessly at Davies. I was the only person in the entire courtroom who knew what that structure was but I had to remain silent until it was my turn to take the stand. I would savour that moment greatly, when I would be able to say that that grey structure was not a future fuel depot: it was a stack of sludgecake.

PART TWO

I

I am thinking of the myth of Orpheus, with Norman Learmouth in the leading role. I can see him strolling through the under-world in his stylish flannels and loose tweeds, and I can hear the evil gravels crunching under his Oxford brogues. He has the look he carries so well, as though a Surrey stockbroker had washed up on the Left Bank. At a glance you think he has long hair that drapes over his shoulders, but look again and he has a respectable cut. He is ironed and polished, but at the same time sewn and patched up. He carries a palette of paints instead of a lyre, and soothes the advancing demons by means of deft portraiture. A few strokes and dabs, and a stoical reality has appeared on his canvas. The demons can do nothing but scratch their glinting horns and wonder at how the fire has gone from their breath.

I first met him in a very unlikely Hades, the tiny basement store of Rowan and Black's, suppliers of artists' materials, off Long Acre, where it was recommended that students of the Slade equip themselves with the tools of their calling. I had brought with me the list that had arrived at Swan's Rest earlier in the summer and which had caused my parents such consternation when they read it over my shoulder (a shoulder each), marvel-ling at the long inventory of arcania – 'What do they want you to buy all that rubbish for?' my father said. 'I don't even know what half these things are – titanium dioxide? Cochi– whatsit? What do you think you're doing, a science course or something?'

Cochineal. Chrome powder. Ultramarine. They were as much a mystery to me as to my father. *One jar of linseed oil. Retouching varnish. A length of leadstick. One bottle of turps. One box of charcoal, pencils of every grade from 6H to 6B, a square of pure latex, a spirit lamp, a wrap of horsehair, rabbit skin glue, cow glue.* I had to work hard at persuading my father to give me some money for these, but he agreed, in the end.

The basement of Rowan and Black's was dimly lit and consisted of narrow passageways between shelves filled with boards and rolls of canvas. The proprietor kept most of his smaller stock in a back room, the entrance to which formed a serving hatch where he stood, guardian-like, staring with angry, forget-me-not eyes. This man was a well-known figure of hate among the students, someone with whom one had to negotiate and strike bargains, a simmering gatekeeper who seemed constantly about to spill out of his barely controlled civility. He had arranged a discount with the school, and this seemed to be the principal among the many resentments he nurtured. He would demand to see proof of our student identity, interrupting our polite conversational parries with an order that we should produce our 'chit', then tossing the piece of paper back at us, saying that it needed to be stamped by the school bursar. It was a horrid experience. Everyone came to dread visiting the dreary basement of Rowan and Black's.

Only Norman Learmouth could charm this bristling Cerberus. As I stood there nervously in a queue, watching the brutal treatment of those who went before me, listening to Mr Wheel's barking, counter-slamming fury as each customer was dealt with, then to scurry away with the little parcel of artistic provisions, he sailed into the basement and strolled straight up to the counter, nodding and smiling at the rest of us with such charm that we didn't mind his butting in with a jovial request for some sable brushes and, sorry, he was in a bit of a rush. Mr Wheel turned into someone else entirely: his creased face was pressed into smiling, his eyes widened and softened. 'Certainly, Mr Learmouth. How nice to see you again.' I assumed Learmouth was a regular customer, a senior lecturer at the university, or perhaps a fellow, who knew? If not, then some club-dwelling member of London's artistic elite, if it were not for the absence of pomposity. In fact, I was baffled eventually to discover he was one of us, a freshman, a first-year undergraduate in the fine-art department. While Mr Wheel went busily about his business of fetching paintbrushes, Learmouth smiled again at me, whose place he had so adroitly taken. 'Saddens me to think of all the Russian polecats who gave their lives for the good of the English watercolour. Still, better that than lining the gowns of the tsars. Damned hard to get real sable now, though – they won't let them out of the country. Although someone told me the other day that Lenin used to wear a sable hat.' He took a moment to pause and examine who he was talking to, and noticed the piece of paper I was holding. 'Oh – I see you've got the dreaded list. You know you don't need half the things on it, don't you? Let me give you a hand.' He took it from me and started crossing things off and scribbling new things down. 'All these raw pigments – you'll never use them. They used to have a paint-making course. This list hasn't been updated since the days of Professor Alphonse Legros. A secretary sends it out every year, and has done for the last three decades, without anyone bothering to change it.'

Being a friend of Learmouth's was an advantage in life, I was quickly realizing.

We walked together down Long Acre, Learmouth taking big, confident strides, easily sidestepping the many obstacles – horses, people, street vendors, coalmen emptying their black sacks, delivery men, postmen, people spilling out of pubs – how I loved the crowded streets of London. He was talking to me all the while – where are you from, how are you finding the Big Smoke?

I hadn't grown used to explaining my origins. Heathrow, Sipson, Feltham – I was surprised, at first, to discover these names meant nothing to anyone much beyond the Heath. Now I was beginning to use the broken little county in which those villages resided as my *fons et origo*, even though I had never really thought of myself as being from Middlesex.

Learmouth told me how his family were from the Welsh marches, how his father was a county-court judge, and how he'd already spent a year as a law student in Oxford but had dropped out, having realized, so he said, his true vocation as a painter.

'The law was my father's idea, so I thought I should at least give it a try, just to please him. Oh, but it's the dryness of the law that so depresses me. All human life is there, but crushed and desiccated down into dry, crisp pages of parchment. I pleaded with my father to allow me to change my course, and after much discussion we came to a sort of arrangement. He said if I could make fifty pounds in my first year as an art student, he would allow me to continue. If not, then I have to go back to Brasenose, if they'll take me. In fact, I've made six pounds already, by selling a painting to my landlady. Where are you living?'

I went through the sad story of my lodgings in Holloway, and the misery of living with a woman who was technically my aunt but who showed no kindredness to myself in body or spirit in any way, and was as different from my mother as it was possible to imagine. Along with her husband (the pair of them had had no involvement in my life up until then), she reluctantly provided me with board and lodging in return for that ancient favour of my mother's. I had no idea what my uncle did for a living, except that it was something that caused the hands that had been scrubbed pink in the morning to be a soft black by evening. I was under a strict regime of early nights, evenings out only on Fridays and Saturdays, and then to be home by ten o'clock at the latest, and to take my meals with the family, the meals being greasy, lukewarm fare that was rarely edible – pork chops and potatoes fried in dark brown lard on a stove encrusted with a black hoar frost of carbon. The children, two sons and a daughter of teenage years, barely looked at me, let alone spoke to me.

'Do you have a good view from your bedroom window?'

'Just rooftops, chimneys and a gasometer.'

'Perfect. Why don't you do a painting of it, realistic? You know, the sort of realism that is attractive to people who don't like art. And give it to them as a gift, framed – we can frame it at college – and they'll love you for the rest of their lives. That's the joy of art. It can instil goodness and warmth into even the coldest heart. I'm a bit of a believer in the Orpheus myth, aren't you?'

*

So, I stuck close to Learmouth in my first weeks in London, which was sometimes a difficult task because of his energy and his gregariousness. He could talk to anyone, chatting as happily with shopkeepers and porters as with senior academics and distinguished visiting artists. A real man of the people. That was certainly how he liked to think of himself, and his beliefs about art were eventually to follow the same line – art for the people, art that people can understand and relate to. But in the early days of our friendship he flirted with the Continental influences as much as any of us, away from the inhibiting studios of the Slade.

Through Learmouth I became established in a small circle of friends who met regularly after classes in various Fitzrovian drinking holes – the Newman Arms, the Adam and Eve or, most usually, the Flag on Tottenham Street, with its sumptuous Byzantine interior. There was David Natland – another refugee from Oxford, where he'd read divinity and had been expected to enter the priesthood. He painted religious subjects as a way of appeasing his father, who was sub-primate of all Ireland and

Bishop of Iraq, though we doubted he would have looked kindly on the tortured, Expressionist scenes his son painted. There was Barbara Owen-Jones, founder of the University of London Ladies' Fencing Club, and one of the few females to associate with us. She always had her sports bag with her, and would sometimes arrive in class in full fencing costume, minus the face shield.

Of the many original minds among us perhaps the most original was that of Alfred Knell – broken front tooth, a dark, assertive beard that was iridescent, like cat fur, in certain lights. He wore grey flannels and a cricket pullover, and was an avid disciple of D. H. Lawrence, and claimed he was in correspondence with the great man – 'I'm in a sublime mood today, my fellow artists, for I have had another missive – Herbert has written to me . . .' He scribbled poetry in his hours alone, but he would show it to no one. He claimed to be working on translations of the Chinese masters, even though he knew no Chinese – 'I base it on the feel and appearance of Chinese script.'

We first met in the Flag, sitting round a table of dimpled copper with some others, each with halves of watery bitter, though Alfred had a pint of stout with a head as white and fluffy as Garbo's cheek. Alfred always managed to find the money for pints: he claimed to have an account behind the bar, though it was more likely he could simply charm beer out of certain barmaids, especially the motherly ones. Feeling sorry for his less endearing colleagues, he offered his pint around the table, and I was the only one to accept as it passed from hand to hand, though it was the first time I had tasted stout and nearly spat my mouthful across the room. The others laughed at my reaction, and at the frothy white moustache I had grown, when I handed the glass back, shivering with pain. I had quickly developed a reputation as an innocent among my friends, all of whom seemed familiar with the brown, malty interiors of pubs or, when they had the money, with navigating the protocols of the classier restaurants, snapping their fingers at waiters (Learmouth, that man of the people, was a very adept finger-snapper), whereas I always felt ill at ease with the very idea of being waited upon since to me it seemed a relic of the days of serfdom and slavery.

Knell seemed charmed by my rejection of his stout, and came to sit next to me. He asked me if I thought animals had any religion. 'Because the other week I went to the zoo, and was looking at a baboon in its cage, when suddenly it made the sign of the Cross. Now, if that is not an indication that animals believe in a God, then I don't know what is.'

'And is it the same God we, or some of us, believe in?'

'Well, my theory is that God manifests himself to the animals according to their species. So, the baboons have a baboon-like God, the mice have a mouse-like God, and so on down to the worms and the ants.'

'And did the God of the worms send his only son, et cetera?'

'Yes – the baboon's sign of the Cross indicates that the baboon-Jesus was crucified just like the human Jesus. I have written to Herbert about it. He says I should become a close observer of nature, and see if I can identify anything among the ants and the worms that looks like a church.'

I noticed Learmouth, a little distanced from the rest of us, leaning with his back against a lady of gilt wood with golden nipples, sketchbook on his knee, vigorously rendering locals at the bar. I loved the way he drew, with a little chip of black chalk pinched between finger and thumb, making bold, vertical strokes to catch the hanging folds of an overcoat and scarf on a drinker, turning his hand to vary the thickness of the line. He drew so quickly. In the time we were in the pub he must have filled half his sketchbook.

'And what will you do if you find one?'

Knell thought for a moment. 'I would probably worship at it.

Mind you, a week later I went back to the zoo and looked at the very same baboon, and this time he was vigorously playing with his genitals. And I wrote to Herbert, and do you know what he said? He said it meant that religion and sex were the same thing.'

Knell said his ambition in painting was to capture the essence of pure energy. He dreamt of artistic materials that would transcend their materiality. He hoped one day to be able to paint without paint, and instead mould forms from pure light. His paintings became madder and madder. He painted mythological scenes, sometimes in the style of Blake, sometimes in the style of Samuel Palmer, sometimes Richard Dadd. When he told us that he had started mixing semen and blood into his paint we were expecting things of transcendent madness, but curiously his pictures that incorporated these substances looked the least passionate, the most static and entropic of any of his work.

The Slade's curriculum was not quite what I was expecting. A great deal of our education consisted of lectures delivered in an academic manner, in a traditional lecture theatre and without illustrations. There were lectures on the evolution of the pencil, the colour wheel, optics, the psychology of perception, the behaviour of light, a history of solids. One grey-bearded, wing-collared elder delivered a talk called 'In Pursuit of Active Seeing', which at least included a demonstration, with the elder drawing a fully clothed student on the platform. Then we would spend long afternoons in the studio investigating the architecture of a bowl of pears or, on one occasion, a batch of live lobsters. We had a term on landscape painting, when we would freeze and tremble in the nearby squares of Bloomsbury before an icy canvas. And all this time the second-year students sat in the cosy, sweaty, paraffin warmth of the life room drawing some ageing Venus or other. I had still not seen a nude figure, but I had seen the regular life model, Naomi, walking around in her Oriental silk dressing gown. She was a middle-aged woman with blonde hair and vulgar make-up and a seedily bohemian demeanour. She would sometimes sit in the refectory, still in her dressing gown, eating a pomegranate and reading a book of French poetry. Sometimes she would be chatting to a louche character with long, floppy hair and a pince-nez.

*

Halfway through our first year we became concerned about our lack of access to the life room. Learmouth, in particular, was keen to express his frustration.

'I came to the Slade because it's the only art school in England that teaches drawing from life. If I wanted to paint statues I could have gone to the Royal Academy or the Royal College.' He had made this point to Schwabe himself, on one of the professor's rare trips around the studios, which he liked to do as head of a little team of tutors, rather like a chief surgeon making the rounds of a medical ward, offering a withering analysis of a student's work as though the student wasn't there.

'Professor Schwabe, I wish to make a formal complaint,' said Learmouth, making the professor and his entourage take a step backwards. 'We have been students of this institution for a term and a half and have still not been given access to the life room. I chose to attend this school because of its emphasis on drawing from life, and its kinship with the principles of art education as practised in Europe. Can you reassure us that we will be given a chance to draw the human figure from life before the end of the Lent term?'

'And you are?' said the professor, after a lengthy pause and inaudible conference with his colleagues.

'I am Norman Learmouth, sir.'

A hush seemed to have descended on all the studios. One could sense many ears turned in our direction. As Learmouth's studio neighbour, I had a close view of the exchange, and could hear one of the tutors murmuring into the professor's ear, words to the effect that this was the outstanding prizewinning student they had all been so excited about.

'Well, Mr Learmouth, I am glad to see you are so keen to pursue the study of the human form, and I am sure that you are aware that such study is not to be undertaken lightly. There is a great deal of preparatory training necessary before a student can cope with such a complex subject as the nude.'

'I think you underestimate us, sir, if you don't believe we are ready by now.'

At this point the professor turned his attention to Learmouth's work. The prolific student had crammed his modest studio space with an array of paintings and drawings in the style of the post-Impressionists – landscapes in Fauvist colours, a Chagallesque mythological scene, weightless characters floating in the air, tentative Cubist still-lifes.

'So I see, from your work, that you are trying to run before you can walk. And that you are at risk of encouraging an undisciplined imagination. We are not in the business of allowing imagination to contaminate empirical observation – and I can see that the contagion is spreading . . .' At this point the professor's attention was turned towards my own work, which was executed in similar styles.

'All the more reason, then, that we should be subject to the rigours of life drawing . . .'

The session concluded, after some heated discussion, with an assurance that our group would be allowed into the life room within the next couple of weeks.

*

We laughed, Learmouth and I, about the boldness of his complaint – 'I think you underestimate us, sir!' – and we doubted that it had had much effect; we had probably been scheduled to go into the life room soon anyway. It didn't prevent the enormous feeling of anticipation when the day finally came, and we were quietly ushered through the grand mahogany and brass doors to meet our first nude model. The event seemed to cause us physically to shrink back to childhood (a sensation perhaps enhanced by the large proportions of the room and its doors), and we fell into the collective hush one usually associates with sacred spaces like chapels of rest or the saloon bars of country hotels.

All the more startling, then, was the brilliance that lay beyond the heavy doors. Out of the shadowy, gas-lit corridors we found ourselves in a large room that was windows on two sides, flooding the space with grey light and giving onto a view across the chimney pots of Bloomsbury to the pretty white steeples of the City beyond. Within, Corinthian pilasters punctuated the high walls, and fruit-laden plasterwork adorned the ceiling, all heavily and carelessly whitewashed, which gave it the same clumsy and numb quality you get in an orchard after heavy snow.

The room was part hothouse, part fabric emporium, part museum. There were plaster casts of classical statuary dotted about the space (someone had placed a Yorkshireman's flat cap on the head of a small Hercules), there were draperies of every pattern and colour hanging from the walls, and there was vegetable matter – pot plants of extravagant foliage, a cactus in a corner that nearly reached the ceiling. The focal point of the room was the set-up for the model – a dais, a chaise-longue, a chair and, in a corner, a Japanese screen for the model to disrobe behind.

Two paraffin heaters did their best to supplement the warmth provided by the radiators, which was very little. Two of the windows had been opened, and I could watch the crimped heat rise from one of the stoves and flow directly out of the open sash.

The first thing I learnt about a life room is how conscious it makes one of one's own body. I felt this even before the model had appeared. Simply being in a room whose function was to provide study of human topography made one aware of the weightiness of one's physical existence. My mind dwelt on the matter that my body had processed over the years of its existence, all those vegetables, all that soil. And what was my mind apart from the intelligence of that soil? I looked down on myself and wondered if there wasn't still some brick earth in my clothes, some clay clinging to my shoe soles, a trench of loam in my turn-ups. Though I doubt the others in the class had such earthbound thoughts, though they were all, in their way, as apprehensive, as body-trapped as I.

Almost directly opposite me was Learmouth. He was well prepared for this moment, having campaigned for it for so long. In fact, he was already working. He had set up all his materials and was mixing colours, putting some of the background in. I had thought this to be a drawing lesson, but Learmouth had his paints out, not even watercolours but oil paints. And that thing on the easel in front of him was not a drawing board with a sheet of paper pinned to it, but a canvas, on a stretcher. We had barely been taught the art of canvas stretching, let alone used one.

To my left was Knell. He was nervous, though tried to hide this fact by giving all his attention to the single fly that was blundering quietly through the air, occasionally crackling against the glass of the windows. David Natland was seated further to my left and was reading a book.

Then our lecturer arrived. This was a man I had not met before, but whom I had heard a great deal about. Arturo Somarco, born of an Italian father and a Spanish mother but raised in Borehamwood. An extraordinary figure in the Slade at that time, proponent and promoter of all the strange -isms that had swept the Continent in the last few decades, but which had yet to receive much acknowledgement in Britain. It was rather apt that we were standing in a pre-concert hush because he had the appearance and demeanour of a musical virtuoso – a wing collar and narrow black tie, arranged in a foppish, Yeatsian bow, and an Edwardian tailcoat worn dandyishly tight. Thick dark hair, daringly long. Big, soft, lazy eyes. He was smoking a cigarette, which itself seemed to be drawing seductive grey shapes in the air.

A porter, the large fellow who, we presumed, had set up all the equipment in the room and had since been sitting on the chaise-longue reading a newspaper in expectation of further instructions, removed himself when Mr Somarco arrived. With a considerable sense of effort he lifted himself up and, with a gardener's bent-kneed roll, ambled slowly towards the screen. We looked at each other. Some of my fellow students couldn't suppress a smile, others a look of alarm. Learmouth was perfectly calm, as though he'd known all along the porter was in fact our model. The enormous man, his head and shoulders towering above the screen, was beginning, in a tired and methodical way, to get himself undressed. I was feeling great discomfort. I was shocked that such a large man could so willingly make himself vulnerable. It was like watching the Black Prince unscrew his magnificent armour and step out a pallid, hairless waif. I felt the room had been filled with a spirit of wrongness and I looked to Mr Somarco for some sort of reassurance that everything would be all right. He was deeply engaged in a technical conversation with another student. I looked back at the screen to see our large man remove his tie and collar (some difficulty with the stud), and now his naked shoulders were visible.

I looked at my fellow students. One or two had red faces, but for the most part they seemed nonplussed. Knell was still watching his bluebottle. Natland continued to read his book.

The enormous man emerged. The blaring shock of nakedness

was not dimmed by the slow preparation we'd had. Perhaps in my heart I had been expecting him to have protected his modesty somehow, with a loincloth perhaps, but no, he was as naked as a pin. He had an excellent physique, his musculature perfectly defined, not a scrap of fat on him; he was solid and compact and as white as marble, but for his hands and his face, which were a rusty colour, and his genitals which, compared to any that I had seen before, were a giant's apparatus, the scrotum tucked underneath like a little woven basket, then draped over it, the shaft in its veined sleeve. I looked across at Learmouth. He was already making preparatory marks on his canvas, even before a pose had been established, drinking in the whole spectacle with untroubled ease, holding out his arm with thumb flexed, getting the proportions sorted out.

'Now, Hector, how shall we have you today, hmm?' said Mr Somarco, once the model had stepped onto the dais. Hector stood there, inert and compliant as Somarco began to position him, using his hands to turn him, pull him, push him. Hector seemed to have lost all will, to have become something like a human puppet. I found the spectacle of the man being manipulated quite horrifying. Eventually a pose was assumed, a pseudo-military, heroic pose, the man standing, one hand on his hip, the other holding onto a pole; he could have been a gladiator or some such.

With the man settled in position, I found I was confronted with his nudity head-on. I hardly dared look into his face, and when I did, was horrified to find that he was staring directly at me. Oh, such a handsome face, but handsome in an unexpected way, not like Michelangelo's David, not at all, or like Donatello's; here was something more brutish, probably the sort of face that had confronted the Romans at Richborough, and sent Caesar back across the Channel; the low, dense brow, the fixed, deeply recessed eyes, the square gills, the pouting mouth. But he was looking at me with contempt. Holding his spear, he seemed ready to pin me to the ground.

Looking from the spectacle of this nude man to the bareness of my paper was a type of void-shock, a glimpse of a stark abyss. All around me came the sound of graphic creativity, the slashing sound of bold pencil or charcoal strokes, the knock-knock of chalk vigorously applied, the busy back-and-forth gnash of hatching. Learmouth was already deeply engrossed, taking in the spectacle with long eye-gulps, then working in short bursts at his easel, then another long eye-gulp, closing one eye, measuring proportions. He was in a sort of observational trance. Others were working with similar deep concentration, a dozen different Hectors slowly forming on easels all around the room. But it was all right for them: the object of their observation wasn't staring back at them, like Hector was at me. I was sweltering under the fixed gaze of the nude man, so how was I to look at that giant's apparatus? How could I look down there while his eyes were drilling into me? Pale blue eyes, sharp and slightly resentful.

I tried everything I could think of not to look at the fellow's privates, and I knew I was being insufferably foolish in getting so fixated by them, and I knew all I had to do was concentrate on other parts of the body and gradually work my way down to that problematic area, and I knew I was wasting the opportunity that I had come to the Slade for, but I had not prepared myself for the reality of a confrontation with the flesh of an ordinary man. I simply didn't know where to look. Whatever I looked at seemed to stare back at me, even those parts of the body that didn't have eyes. And, what was more, the last time I looked at his face he gave me a wink, I was sure of it, and a wink from an unsmiling face is a most disconcerting thing.

The only safe place to look was at the blank paper on my drawing board, but this possessed a whiteness that seemed to engulf me. I held a chalk in one hand, and gripped the side of my easel with the other. Heat was travelling up my legs slowly from my feet. The room was becoming dim. I was short of breath and my mouth felt sticky. What damned fool, I remember thinking, what damned fool thinks it's a good idea to turn the lights out, in a life room of all places, to turn the lights out in a life room? What a damn-fool idea . . .

*

When I came round I found myself lying on some cushions and blankets on the floor of a store-room. There were large canvases arranged on wooden frames, like toast in a toast rack; some ponderous items of student sculpture; on the wall in front of me a rather naive portrait of women harvesting apples in an orchard. My face felt sore.

'Do you wish to be sick?'

I suddenly realized I was not alone. Sitting beside me was the tutor from the life room, Mr Somarco.

'Do you wish to be sick?'

'No, I don't think so.'

'Because I have procured a bucket for that purpose, if you need to.'

I tried sitting up.

'You should remain lying down. You have a cut on your chin. I have applied a bandage.'

Mr Somarco, it seemed, had had some training in first aid. The pain in my chin suddenly registered. I must have winced quite badly.

'It'll heal. We thought you might have to go to the doctor for stitches, but it'll be OK. You'll have quite a scar, though, I should think. You collided with the corner of your easel on the way down.'

It was a while before I could gather enough mental strength to speak in sentences.

'You must understand I've never done anything like this before,' I said.

'I wouldn't really regard fainting as "doing" something. It's not as though you had any choice.'

'But everyone must have taken me for a proper fool.'

'I don't see why. I suppose you're thinking that fainting is something only women do. But I have seen soldiers faint.'

'But I feel such a fool. Did anyone else faint?'

'No, why should they have?'

'I don't know. I thought perhaps it was the lack of air, and the paraffin fumes.'

'Oh, I thought you fainted because you were embarrassed at having to look at a chap with no clothes on.'

I tried to affect a surprised, disdainful laugh. Me? Faint through embarrassment? At a male nude? What did he think I was? Some silly virginal schoolboy?

'The life room can be quite a shock the first time,' Somarco went on, 'especially if you've never encountered such open nudity before. It is only recently that life models were permitted to remove the *cache sexe*, though the males still wear them in the female class. Extraordinary, really, that a female student can graduate from one of the world's finest art schools without ever having drawn a penis.'

'I wasn't shocked,' I said abruptly, though feeling myself redden at Somarco's frankness. I coughed to provide an alibi for my blush. 'It was the lack of air.' Then, after a pause, with affected nonchalance, 'Shouldn't you go back to the class? How long have I been in here?'

'Just a matter of five minutes or so. I will let the class carry along on their own for a while, then go and put them right.'

'I expect they're all laughing about it at this very moment.'

'You are rather self-centred if you think you are such an object of fascination to your fellow students.' He said this with the sweetest, most affectionate smile. 'I am sure they are more interested, at this moment, in the surface anatomy of Hector. Hector is a very fine life model: because he eats so little, his skeleton is clearly visible. I often think we should starve our life models so that we can see clearly beneath their skin. Sorry, am I making you feel unwell again?'

'No, I just need some water.' I reached for the jug.

I was thinking back to my few experiences of male nudity. The showers at Jacob College had poured their scalding rain on youthful torsos, and since I had given up sports at the age of fifteen, when the male body is, for the most part, only just beginning to define its adult proportions and detail, I had to concede that perhaps I hadn't ever viewed a fully mature male body before. My stomach turned, I lurched, and heaved a mouthful of nothing. I was almost sick.

'No,' I said, after Somarco had brought the tin bucket a few inches nearer. 'I've never seen anything quite like it.'

I hated saying it, because it seemed to confirm something for Somarco, about my innocence and naivety.

'While I have never seen someone react as strongly as you, I am surprised it doesn't happen more often. But you will get used to it, over the weeks.'

'I will get used to the paraffin fumes,' I said. 'That is what made me ill.'

Somarco smiled, patronizingly. 'Would you like a cigarette? It might make you feel better.'

'I don't smoke.'

Again the smile. 'Perhaps you weren't expecting a man.'

'What?'

'In the life room. You were surprised to be presented with a naked man, rather than a female.'

'I don't know.'

'You were hoping for your first sight of a naked adult woman.'

'Well, I suppose I was a little surprised.'

I felt ready to return to the life room, but Somarco advised against it. He said he thought I should go home and have some rest. I was glad not to have to face my fellow students so soon after such a moment of humiliation and thought, after all, that perhaps it would be better if I didn't return immediately.

I went home to the cold little house in Holloway, and stayed in my room for the rest of the day. I declined the repeated calls for dinner, unable to face the warm, dark grease that awaited me in the parlour. When the smell of frying onions came up the stairs I heaved emptily again. My aunt, unable to bear the thought of me not eating anything, and hearing of my ailment, came to my room with a bowl of junket and left it on my side table.

The next day we were scheduled for another session in the life room, but I still felt queasy. My aunt expressed surprise at my green complexion. I decided to take the rest of the week off, and instead of going to college went for slow walks around the streets of my neighbourhood and up as far as Hampstead Heath with a sketchbook under my arm. What a relief it was to draw landscapes again, to have human presence reduced to a pinpoint. A relief, but a frustration. All my artistic life I had wanted nothing more than to tackle the human form, but hitherto I had had to make do with simulacra, Mr Toynbee's faithful old skeleton. Now, when the moment arrived, I had failed myself miserably.

And I was dismayed also to find that absence was taken rather seriously at the Slade. The lack of my presence had been noted and I was required by the secretary to provide an explanation. Had they not heard about my fainting in the life room? Luckily Mr Somarco came into the office just as I was, in rather blushing tones, trying to explain myself to the secretary, and was able to vouch for my ill-health.

'Well, you are looking much better, Mr Brill,' he said to me, once we were in the corridor. 'I trust you are ready to take your place in the life room again?'

I nodded. He placed a reassuring hand on my shoulder. 'And we'll have no more feminine swooning, will we?'

I shook my head.

No one among the students was surprised that I had taken the rest of the week off, though I was disappointed that I had missed my chance of drawing Hector. My fellow students' renderings of the enormous chap were on display all around the studios. Hector's form, in graphite and charcoal, could not be avoided, and seemed to mock me from its drawing-pinned perches in every direction. How could I have been so childish as to find fright in something so still and dignified? Knell had produced a Hector bubbling with muscle, a torso that was like ribbed sand, pectorals like cliffs of flesh. Learmouth's Hector was rather more restrained and delicate, but all the more impressive for suggesting the musculature through a sensitive outline. How I would have loved to have my own effort on display, when I had talked and bragged for so long about how I had drawn skeletons. Now I hardly dared mention the fact.

It was an agonizing wait for my second attempt at the nude. Groups were given life classes on a rota basis, and our next turn in the life room wasn't for several days. At least that meant whatever illness had affected me the first day would have gone, but on the next occasion I was dismayed to see that it was another male we had to draw, although not the giant of our first class. This man was skinny, somewhat older, with a severe short-back-and-sides and bushy moustache, and a general air of defeat and servility. He might have been the owner of a down-at-heel tobacconist, or a clerk in a railway office. It certainly seemed odd that he should have fallen into such abject employment as that of an art students' model. He was sitting fully clothed in wait for us, reading a newspaper. He was wearing an over-starched wing collar in an unconvincing attempt to signal his respectability. I took my place at my easel, feeling quite calm and settled. No one, I observed, was paying any attention to me. I was half expecting concerned looks in my direction – is he going to do that every time he sees a nude man? But no one, apart from myself and Somarco, who was in charge of the proceedings again, had linked my fainting to the presence of male nudity.

I took deep but silent breaths as our little tobacconist went behind the screen, and averted my eyes as the naked version of that person pitter-pattered where he had previously clip-clopped. I was conscious only of a white shape passing across the room and mounting the dais. I concentrated instead, as others seemed to be doing, on lining up my materials, straightening my paper, adjusting my easel. When the time came to look at the model, I at first tried to convince myself that I was looking at nothing to cause any sort of disturbance to my well-being. But immediately I felt that lack of air again, as much as if someone had punched me in the chest and pushed the gases out of my lungs. My eyes lost their power to focus, or to work in unison, and I began to have bouts of double vision. Christ, surely it wasn't going to happen again. I had to steady myself at the easel, pretending to adjust its height, in reality hanging on to it for dear life. My head began to hurt: a most awful headache had brewed in my brain. I took one last look at the little tobacconist. Through a mini-flood of tears he was a blurred image, splitting and doubling, forming and re-forming in my weakened eyes.

I was going to be sick. I became instantly certain of that fact, and knew as well that I had but a matter of seconds to get out of the room before it happened.

I was too late. I managed to get past Learmouth, but it seemed that a forest of easels separated me from the door to the corridor, and then these easels began swaying like the masts of a drunken flotilla. I fell to my knees and began heaving. I gushed with vomit: it streamed from my mouth and from my nostrils in a triple fountain of vitriol, and when empty my stomach pumped its own emptiness, making me moan rhythmically like a sea lion, to bring forth tiny spurts, then nothing. It was like a lesson in vomiting for the uninitiated, a demonstration of its most extreme expression. In fact, I am told that at least three students took the opportunity to do a quick sketch of me while I was down on the floor. I had become the model in the life room, a depiction of a soul in torment in the basements of hell, a subject for a pastiche of Bosch or Goya.

I didn't pass out but couldn't help thinking that this was worse.

I was summoned to see the professor the next day.

II

Every human activity leaves its trace. Every journey has its footprint, every sojourn its flattened grass. Life naturally goes against the grain of its surroundings. A man walking across a clover field will leave a mark that lasts for days, and can be photographed from thousands of feet. But there is a peculiar character to the marks made by an army, there is something about the very way they move, that distinguishes them from the movement of civilians and peaceable men. The army generates a great terrestrial mess, but in the mess there is a pattern. A gun battery or a fuel dump will leave its own kind of texture on the ground, dictated by its strategic purpose. From ten thousand feet a gun battery and a fuel dump present two strikingly differ-ent patterns. You could call them signatures. There are people in both armies whose job is to interpret aerial photographs. They can spot these signatures with great ease.

The desert offers almost no natural cover, as we had learnt on our journey to and from Benghazi. But there are patterns ranging from gentle italics to rigid striations that can be used by anyone who is aware of them. And there are also the scars of previous battles, which can be used as hiding places. But, even so, they are few and far between.

What seemed to be the most useful role for camouflage in the desert was not so much the concealment of what existed, but the display of that which didn't exist.

*

I had taken rooms in Gresham House, having grown tired of Garden City with its art-deco villas and walled gardens, and I was so seduced by my new-found privacy that at first I didn't tell anyone where I was living. We were able to avoid each other now. I kept out of Somarco's way as much as I could, and in the uneasy lull that had fallen on the war in the desert since the arrival of Rommel, we didn't always have much to do. Although our army had destroyed nine Italian divisions, captured countless numbers of men, guns and munitions, the western regions of Libya had been left poorly defended. A token force had remained in Tripoli while the main fighting forces were drawn back eastwards along the coast roads they had, only a few weeks before, ridden victoriously in the opposite direction. The attention of the Allied Forces was now turning towards the threat to the Balkans and Greece, and a new fighting force was slowly being assembled for their defence. But things were happening too quickly. Rommel had landed in Tripoli and within weeks he had assembled a colossal invasion force, the embryo of the Afrika Korps. At the same time, German tanks swept through Yugoslavia and Greece, driving the British regiments back through Thermopylae to the beaches of

Kalamata. In North Africa the five hundred miles we had gained from the Italians was wiped out within weeks by Rommel's lightning advances, only a pocket of resistance holding out at Tobruk, which came under prolonged siege. The two prongs of a vast Axis invasion, north and south of the Mediterranean, seemed focused on the Middle East and Egypt as the kernel of the nut it was trying, without much trouble, to crack.

My veranda looked over the courtyard of a Jewish orphanage. I would spend hours leaning on my railing gazing down, like someone sitting in the gods of an enormous theatre, on whose stage little children performed. At first the children were nothing more to me than little points of energy, like ball bearings rolling around in a box. But gradually, even from that distance, I could begin to resolve the points into individual people, and slowly, over the days and weeks, a narrative began to emerge. I would spot groups forming, teams and cohorts who played exclusively among themselves. I could spot the child who'd been ejected from one group and I could watch them tentatively try for admission to another. I followed the tiny dramas of rejection and triumphant inclusivity. If the wind was in the right direction I could hear their voices above the traffic noise. I fancied I could hear their names being called. From the distance of an unknown language I Anglicized the noises I heard, or invented others – Lizzy, Dick, Johanne, Rameses. One afternoon I found that I had been sobbing while watching a little girl being teased by her former friends. She probably longed for the adult world where she thought such petty rivalries are put aside and everyone gets along together. Then I looked up at the pinnacled cityscape beyond the orphanage walls, the minarets, domes and cuboids of a clamouring population, and wondered how the little girl could ever hope to find her way among it all.

A letter from April had, after many redirections, arrived. It was brief and had been written to inform me of a single fact.

That April had given birth to a son. My son. And that she had called him Sebastian.

Above and beyond the orphanage, the rooftops of the city. Aerials had formed a thin, attenuated upper level, among which birds of prey moved and roosted. They fed mainly on trash from the city streets, which they would carry up to a high ledge as though it was the most coveted treasure. Sometimes, if I was in bed, they would perch on the railing of my veranda, and do their butchery there. At such times I couldn't bring myself to go anywhere near them. I couldn't even watch them. But I could hear the soft ripping and tearing of a body being consumed. The hawk was not to be disturbed at such times. To do so would have been like interrupting my father while he was doing his accounts. Then later I would see the blood and feathers on the balcony.

I would try writing a letter in reply to April, but every time I sat down to write, it seemed the children of the orphanage raised their voices to call me back to the balcony, and I would go out and observe them, anxious to know how little Lizzy's plight was developing – had she been taken back by her old friends, or had she found some new ones?

'Dearest April, I can't tell you how delighted I am to hear your news. Your letter has taken some time to reach me, so I estimate that our son is now nearly four months old . . .'

I went for walks, utterly seduced by the city and its anonymity. To be away from Grey Pillars, to be able to walk freely along the grand boulevards and around the parks, or by the great river, was an intense luxury for me. I found the loneliness invigorating, refreshing. The Egyptians were extraordinarily friendly and hospitable. The young men had such a grace and delicacy about them; they were slender, smooth, finely carved, a quality that endured all their lives, as even the elders retained it. I might find myself drinking tea and smoking a hookah with strangers, who welcomed me into their intimate-seeming cafes – or were they living rooms? It was hard to tell. In the parks I would often fall into conversation with friendly locals. They would tell me how much they hated the British, but seemed remarkably skilled at separating the political and the individual notions of British-ness. In the Fish Gardens, whose wonderfully crude landscaping I had come to adore – it was like walking in the type of papier-mâché landscape a child might make for his toy trains – I met a chap who that very afternoon took me out to the river marshes north of the city, where we spent a few hours hunting for quail. I enjoyed the chance of some target practice, though I deliberately aimed away from the birds, and we didn't kill anything.

I came to love the carved and decorated city; its pierced panels of intricate repetition, behind which female eyes watched as you walked down the street, seemed to speak of a great respect for the private life.

'Dearest April. I miss you very badly. I loathe this city and its inhabitants. They are beasts . . .'

I had taken to drinking in certain bars in the areas around my new quarters, which were more European than I had ever thought likely – at first taking the odd dry sherry or a shot of brandy in establishments that seemed respectable enough, then later in the shadier dives favoured by Australian servicemen, who plied me with thin but powerful wheat beers, and gibed and teased me in a good-natured way that I found rather charming. Through these fellows I was able to discover that there were such places as nightclubs in Cairo, large ballrooms in which drinking and dancing went on into the small hours. The men vastly out-numbered the women in these places, and getting a dance with a girl meant competing with a posse of lustful Aussies. I longed to dance, but instead would spend the hours drinking carafes of wretched Nile wines that tasted painfully sweet and destroyed my senses for a day and a half. I began to find myself waking up in such odd places as beneath the towering palms of the Ezbekiah Gardens, and would have to stagger home in the freezing dawn, imbibing as much iced water from the street vendors on the way as I could.

I was able to spend so much time away from Grey Pillars because I had been assigned the task of producing a general-purpose booklet on camouflage, to be distributed to all troops in the desert. I found that after a few meetings with the others, I had all the material I needed and could best work on it from home. I was delighted that our brigadier had approved funding for it, and he even liked my title, *On the Art of Invisibility, a field guide to camouflage techniques*, by Lieutenant Kenneth Brill. That book was to be the first guide to camouflage published since the Great War.

'Dearest April, how I long to be with you, to meet little Sebastian. You must tell me more about him – what sort of baby is he – how big – what colour eyes, hair? Has he any teeth yet? I am going mad here in this city. There has been no action for many weeks now. The armies of both sides are regrouping. Why have you not written to me? You should have written again by now. Why the silence?'

I had begun dozens of letters to April; I had posted none of them. Nothing I wrote seemed adequate, up to the mark, appropriate. How does one write to one's wife when one doesn't even know if she can truly be described as such, or if she is the mother of your child? I drank.

Dearest April,

There is a chap out here, Arturo Somarco, I may have mentioned him before. He has threatened me that he will write to you, and I can imagine that his letter will be full of great lies about me. He will say that our marriage is an impossibility, that it is a sham. He has told me many times

how he will begin a letter to 'Dear Mrs Brill' (you would
have to hear how he says those three little words to understand
his loathing of the idea of our marriage), and you must not
believe anything he might say in such a letter, in fact I would
advise destroying it before you even read it, for it will contain
such powerful poison even you, the most rational, intelligent
person I know, might be contaminated . . .

Dearest April,
            Forgive me. We cannot be married. I cannot be a
father to our child. I am a disgrace. You will not see me again.

'Do you realize your actions could be interpreted as desertion?'

Learmouth was crouching over me, holding an empty glass whose icy contents he'd just thrown in my face. I thought at first that I was outside, but slowly realized I was lying on the floor of my living room. I didn't know how long I'd been there. Learmouth lifted me up by the shoulders and shook me. He had been transformed by his years in the army, far more than any of the rest of us. He slapped me lightly about the face with warm hands.

'Desertion?' I said. 'What are you talking about?'

'To disappear like that. To move out and not leave any forwarding address . . .' By now he was lifting me onto a chair. 'How long have you been living here? When did you last report to the office?'

'I was there a few days ago, I assure you. Do you think you could get me some more water, and let me apply it internally this time?'

Learmouth went to the kitchen and returned with another glass. I drank deeply. The pain in my head eased a little.

'And I had to act the detective to find you, walk halfway across town. And now I find you blacked out? This could be a court-martialling issue.'

I had never seen Learmouth so angry before. Like everything else, he did anger very well. Just the right amount of control, just the right volume.

'Don't be a fool, Learmouth. I've been working from home. *The Art of Invisibility*. It's nearly finished. I think it'll be a best-seller.' I pointed to the stack of paper on the table. 'I was going to show you – it's the final draft. I need to get your comments.'

Learmouth looked at me doubtfully before going over to the table and perusing the manuscript. He was very quickly absorbed in the detail, reading quickly through the introduction and chapter headings. While he was reading I went to the bathroom and splashed water over my face. Then I went to the kitchen and started making some coffee.

'I just needed some time away,' I said, finding Learmouth still engrossed in my book, 'get things in perspective, you know . . .'

Learmouth looked up for the first time. 'You've put quite a lot of work into this little book, haven't you? In fact you've done too much. This is far too big to be practical for wide distribution. You were supposed to produce a pamphlet, not *War and Peace*.'

It is a simple thing to create, on the ground, a pattern in black paint that, when viewed from high altitude, will resemble the shadows cast by a house or other building, and so will suggest the presence of those structures. By this means the true nature of the terrain can be disguised. This method is particularly useful for disguising airstrips. A simple template can be fabricated from board, or even cardboard, and the paint applied with brooms. (see diagram XX)

'Well, that section can come out for a start.'

'Your wonderful shadow-houses, Learmouth? Why?'

'For one simple reason. They do a very good job of concealing an airstrip, to such an extent that our own pilots can't locate them to land. We're working on a new idea anyway. Trying to devise a way of giving the effect of bomb craters, so that the airstrip will appear to have been destroyed. At least then our pilots will be able to see them.'

We sat discussing the book for a while, before Learmouth came to his main point for visiting.

'Things have been changing very fast at Grey Pillars. We're expected to be making a move against Rommel in the next few weeks, and I've managed to persuade the authorities that camouflage could be of some use. So they've allowed me to recruit as many people as I like, and to procure as much in the way of materials as I need. They've given us a small compound over the road, which we can use as a sort of workshop and laboratory. All this,' he pointed to the manuscript, 'is just theory. Very soon we'll be given the chance to put it into practice.'

*

Learmouth's intervention brought me back to reality. I returned to Grey Pillars sober and with some energy. Camouflage had been given new offices on the first floor, occupying twice as much space as before, and the workshop over the road was buzzing with new personnel. Newly trained officers had arrived from the centre in Wiltshire and were keen to get to work. There were filmmakers, set designers, potters, signwriters, carpenters, stained-glass artists, furniture-makers. A panoply of artisans, Learmouth called it. He remained in overall charge, and was granted the title of director of camouflage under the control of the director of military operations. Myself and Somarco were his deputies. I was in charge of large-scale strategic planning, Somarco and Knell in charge of research and development.

All about the place there was an extraordinary sense of anticipation, though no one knew quite of what. Rommel had been held back from making further advances eastward through

Cyrenaica, and Tobruk was holding out effectively. Apart from a back and forth pushing at the front line, there had been no progress on either side. Rumour and counter-rumour were rife. We heard stories that Rommel was building up to a new major attack, and counterwise we heard the opposite, that his supplies into Tripoli had been heavily bombed, and that it was the Eighth Army who were preparing to mount an offensive. The arrival of General Auchinleck, replacing General Wavell, seemed to signal a new impetus in the long stalemate that was unfolding throughout 1941. We witnessed the slow build-up of supplies, the slow growth of food, ammunition and petrol dumps, and how they were moving, inch by inch, further west, closer to the front.

Eventually Learmouth called me to a meeting upstairs at Grey Pillars, and I was surprised to find myself reunited with Somarco, whom I hadn't seen for several weeks, and hardly at all since our return from Benghazi. He had been out to Palestine and the Holy Land with Knell, on an extended reconnaissance mission. There were many faces in the briefing room I didn't recognize, newly recruited officers, eager and full of energy, their faces still bearing only the first wave of sunburn, lacking the deep, penetrating tans of those who had been in the desert for many months.

The purpose of the meeting was to outline the forthcoming offensive, and to discuss the roles for camouflage. A massive operation was planned, one that would push the Germans back as far as Benghazi and relieve Tobruk. For that purpose a new railway was being constructed in the desert, with a railhead at Fort Capuzzo. With a casual swing of the arm, Learmouth assigned Somarco and me the task of camouflaging the railhead.

We thought at first that he was joking. When we were shown aerial photographs of the railhead under construction, we realized immediately that concealment was not an option. A great loop of track in the smooth, unwrinkled desert, with roads and lines radiating from it, like spines on a sea urchin, the whole complex covering dozens of empty acres of sand, was far too prominent to be hidden.

It was Somarco who came up with the solution. If we couldn't conceal the railhead, then we should construct a dummy railhead, closer to the front line, and even bigger than the real one. If we could construct something that could fool a pilot a few thousand feet up in the air, then it could lure the bombers away to let their bombs blush unseen on the desert air.

His idea was met with laughter at first. The scale of what he was proposing seemed to exist in the realms of fantasy. But if the army could build a real railhead in a week or so, surely a dummy railhead would be a simple task, by comparison, and given that our resources were now almost without limit, perhaps it could be done.

So sweet was Somarco's idea that in the darkness of a tamarind grove, later that evening, I let him kiss me.

III

'Mr Brill, I have called you in here because I am rather concerned about what has been happening in the life room recently. Can you offer an explanation?'

There were more books in the professor's study than I had been expecting. One entire wall was given over to shelving, and the mostly small, fussy-looking leather-bound volumes gave the room a sterile atmosphere, in a way that I have never observed books to do in any other room.

'How do you mean, sir?'

Professor Schwabe did not seem comfortable with enforcing disciplinary matters. His notorious stammer was aggravated by the tension of the situation. When this became obstructive, he would take up his pencil and scribble something on a sketchpad on his desk, a quick rendering of himself issuing the desired word in a speech bubble.

'Well, I've been told that on two separate occasions you have been taken seriously ill, that on one occasion you f-fainted, and in so doing sustained for yourself a nasty gash on the chin, whose scar is still quite distinct, I can now see,' the professor peered at me, 'and that on the second, you were overcome with nausea to the extent that a major clean-up operation had to be carried out and the life class postponed for the afternoon. Now, are you telling me that those incidents did not occur?'

'No, sir.'

'So – an explanation?'

'I can only say that, by pure chance, I have felt a bit queasy on both my sessions in the life room so far. I would suggest it is something to do with the ventilation, and those paraffin stoves . . .'

'That would only satisfy me as an explanation if other students had been similarly afflicted. Yet they haven't, neither now nor in the past. In fact I cannot recall a single incident, in all the years that I have been here, when a student has been taken ill, in the way that you have, quite so suddenly and violently.'

We were silent for a few moments while I tried to think of something to say, but could do nothing except shrug and smile in an apologetic way.

'I've been looking at your record,' he said, lifting a buff cardboard folder. 'There is no mention of any medical predispositions. I think it is very unlikely that your adverse reactions are anything to do with the air supply in that room. I am more concerned that you have some sort of moral queasiness about the arrangements there.'

'I don't follow.'

'Well, let me put it this way. We are not living in Caravaggio's Italy or Homer's Athens. For the last hundred years the sight of a naked body has been rarer than at almost any other period in human history. You are more likely to see a ghost or a visitor from another world than you are to see a naked human being, outside the confines of a marriage – and even then the spectacle is not necessarily c-commonplace. As such it can be a shock to the system when one is confronted by such a sight. Artists, doctors and undertakers are perhaps the only people in the whole of society whose profession entails the frequent viewing of the naked body.'

'I'm not at all embarrassed by the naked body, sir,' I said, feeling slightly bolder than I had realized.

'Then why can't you control yourself, man?' The professor, standing up from his desk, wincing briefly with the pain in his joints, fumbled at the loose, floppy bow-tie that hung at his neck, and half-heartedly thumped the desk with his fist as he made this point.

'I don't think it's anything to do with the presence of nudity, sir.'

'Well, that's not how it appears from my vantage point, and indeed from the point of view of anyone else. Look here, I know what a shock it can be to see a man in full-length nudity, with not a stitch on – but there is nothing to be embarrassed about what-soever. The human body is the greatest achievement of all God's creation. We do it a great disservice, I would even say insult, to conceal it in clothing at all times. Male or female.'

'I suppose I agree.'

'You may agree intellectually, but physically it seems you do not agree. Your body reacts most strongly to the presence of nudity. I cannot allow a recurrence of the events of the last few days. Yesterday's display caused some of your fellow students enormous distress. And the earlier incident not only caused distress all round but injury to yourself.'

'You can't—'

'I am going to withdraw you from the life classes, and restrict your life-drawing instruction to the depiction of the clothed human form.'

*

It was rather like being sent down a year. While others continued their studies of the nude, I would sketch alone in the plaster-casts room. My isolation was such that at times I felt on closer terms with Hercules and John the Baptist than I did my fellow students. I joined them only if the model was clothed. There was a regular session that used clothed models; mostly they were people of the lower orders, recently sacked footmen and chambermaids, out-of-work navvies and dockers, match-sellers looking for some extra cash. They shambled in in their scruffy clothes, and they were usually very poor models, rarely able to keep still for long. I remember one old chap, ten minutes into a session, took out his pipe and went through the lengthy process of filling and lighting it, oblivious to our tutting and sighing.

Somarco tried to persuade me of the value of the clothed subject, and would insist that depicting clothing was a far greater challenge – the skin, he said, clings to the body in a most uninteresting way whereas clothes possess a life of their own: they form folds and creases that have nothing to do with the musculo-skeletal system. He would point out how a detail of the figure I was drawing was wrong because I had not thought deeply enough about the structure of the folds in a trouser leg or skirt, that my drawing displayed a lack of understanding of corduroy or crêpe de Chine. Clothing generally has a much coarser, more open texture than the skin. The knit or weave of a garment is like a ploughed field compared to the skin's tightly clipped lawns.

'There is a grain to people,' Somarco said, 'just as there is a grain to fine cloth or seasoned wood. And the skill in drawing a person is in identifying their grain. Do you understand?'

'No. Say it again.' It wasn't so much that I didn't understand but that I liked hearing Somarco explaining these odd theories of his.

'There is a fine, hardly visible texture to a person, composed of a minute repeated pattern. This pattern runs in a certain direction, like the grain of a piece of wood. Once you detect this direction, you have captured the person.'

'But isn't the grain the same for all people? Surely we all have basically the same skin.'

'Oh, how little you understand, poor boy,' he said, laughing. 'No wonder your drawings are as dead as doornails. You think people are all the same, when in fact in some people the grain flows from top to bottom, or from south to north, or diagonally, or in a spiral. Oh,' he sighed, 'you have so much to learn about people.'

Well, I am not sure I ever understood the grain of Mr Arturo Somarco.

My frustrations mounted. I was desperate to draw the male nude body, but the life room had become an exclusive club. I was not even allowed to peep inside its doors. Instead, the only thing I saw was the drawings and paintings that the students had done when they brought them out to display in their studio spaces. I was fiercely jealous. To see Hector's granite anatomy beautifully rendered by Learmouth, Knell and others, while I was prohibited from viewing him myself.

I was the subject of light mockery by my colleagues. 'Eva, that neckline of yours is a bit low. We don't want young Kenneth fainting/throwing up again – you should cover yourself. Roll your sleeves down, Angela, Kenneth is going green in the face again.'

In the Flag, over meagre half-pints of stout, I would bemoan my exile and its unfairness.

'How odd, young Kenneth, that you should have this strange sickness,' said Natland, 'I should think it is the worst sort of illness that could afflict an artist, apart from blindness.'

'But, then, I suppose you could say it is a form of blindness,' said Learmouth. 'Kenneth here is unable to see the naked human form without convulsing or falling unconscious. He refuses to see. His eyes cannot behold what the artist must behold.'

'As for myself,' said Knell, 'I have the opposite affliction in that I cannot look at a clothed human being without their vestments dissolving before my eyes, and I behold them in all their nakedness. And it doesn't matter who – male, female, young or old. I have become abnormally conscious of the naked body we all carry beneath our clothes.'

'And without which those clothes would be pancake-flat, crumpled, wrinkled puddles of fabric adhering to the floor like scabs.'

'How long is it now, Brill, that you have been banned from the life room?'

'It's nearly a month. I can't tell you how much this upsets me. You may think it's all a great joke but like you, Learmouth, I came to the Slade because it was the only school to place such emphasis on drawing from life. My most burning ambition is to master the depiction of the human form. This situation is intolerable to me.'

'Why don't you speak to the professor? This ban can't go on indefinitely.'

'I can never find him. He never makes time to speak to me.'

'But surely, I mean, Mr Somarco wouldn't object if you were to come in with us. Who would know?'

'I spoke to Somarco. He said if he let me in, he could lose his job and I could lose my place at the school.'

Just at that point Mr Somarco entered the saloon bar of the Flag. It was an extraordinary moment, to see our lecturer there, as none of the academic staff had ever been seen in a public house before. It was also odd to see him alone. Somarco was such a gregarious man that one usually saw him as part of a group. Heads turned as he shimmied between the dusty-coated regulars, his face suddenly refracted through the barroom mirrors, then split a dozen ways, before he happened upon us.

None of us was quite sure if he had come into the pub in search of us or whether it was by chance that he was there. He showed no surprise when he saw us. In fact, he looked as though he had found what he was looking for.

'Mr Somarco,' said Learmouth, 'we were just talking about our friend here's plight, and his ongoing ban from the life room.'

Somarco shrugged, as if to say that there was nothing to worry about, everything would sort itself out in the end. 'I am here because I am told this is the only pub in London that sells good manzanilla.'

We looked at him blankly.

'Manzanilla is an Andalucían sherry. If you will allow me, I will buy you some.'

He went to the bar and ordered glasses of the desired drink, and returned with them on a tray. This action attracted comment from the customers, who had never seen such petite drinks in such quantities before. Some whistled, as if at an attractive young lady. He was like a waiter from Fairyland, delivering pixie-sized beverages.

We had all changed since we had been at the Slade. Even Learmouth, that charmer and man of the people, that forthright and stolid inheritor of the mantel of Augustus John and others, had been affected, and affected is the right word, for some of us at least. We had begun to think of ourselves as artists, and to adopt what we believed to be the artistic protocols of the time, which was to drink large quantities of alcohol, inhale large volumes of tobacco smoke, and to ravish as many females as we could land our paint-splattered paws on. We were doing well at the first two, not very well at the last one.

'Mr Somarco, we need help with young Brill's predicament.'

'And what is his predicament?'

'Before we say, can we drink to your good Hispanic health, sir, for providing us with these delightful beverages?'

'Hard to imagine old Schwabe doing the same thing, isn't it?' said Natland.

'Very.'

'Well, to your health.'

Somarco sipped from the tulip-shaped glass. I sipped. It was the flavour of stale honey.

'His predicament, like we said, is that he has no access to the nude ladies of the life room.'

'Ladies?' I said. 'You've moved on to ladies?'

'We have been painting ladies for some time.'

Somarco laughed at me. 'Bless the young fellow, the way he tries to assert his interest in the female form.'

'Carmichael gave us a demonstration last week,' said Knell, 'a brilliantly stupid class, in which we had to sit back and watch the man draw a Bermondsey Venus with breasts like two sleeping dolphins.'

'He did a decent job, though.'

By this time Learmouth had wandered off. He was always doing that in pubs, drifting about, sketching, chatting.

'I think it's doing my artistic education serious harm,' I said, now that I had more of Somarco's attention. 'I'm falling behind in my training.'

'Well, there is a solution, if you're serious about it.'

'And what is that?' Knell and Natland were listening as attentively.

'You want to pay women to take their clothes off for you? There are two places you can go. One is a school of art. The other is . . . ?'

We looked at each other and sniggered.

'A nunnery?'

'No, you fools. A whorehouse.'

It was as though Somarco had exposed our innocence in one swift drawing back of a stained sheet. We were so shocked by the single word that we fell into a laughterless silence, glancing at each other from downturned faces.

'I know those places,' said Knell, with sudden resolution.

'I doubt that you do.'

'I can't quite believe my ears,' I said. 'A distinguished artist and lecturer at the University of London is advising us that we should avail ourselves of the services of common prostitutes?'

Somarco gave me one of his lyrical smiles, his lazily beautiful sneers. 'Have I shocked you, young Brill, have you really lived ere long without overstepping the traces? This is a great city, full of great things . . .'

'If my mother—' I began, but was immediately cut down by roaring laughter.

'Oh, his mother,' said Somarco. 'Should his mother find out, we will all be for the high jump, no doubt. Is she as formidable as she must seem to you, you poor sweet boy?' The laughter continued as Somarco patted my head and tousled my hair. I shook off his hand and drank my stout, frowning with hurt.

'How about we look at it this way?' Somarco said. 'That we would be doing something noble. That we'll be saving a woman from a night of prowling the streets, that for one night, at least, she'll earn her pay in an honest manner. That she will, while she poses for us, be safe from the dangers of the capital's ravenous bank clerks and tobacconists, or whoever it is who uses her services – and I doubt that it is artists. I will bet you whatever woman we might find will have never posed for an artist in her life.'

'Somarco, you are clearly devoted to the cause of female emancipation,' said Learmouth, who had just returned from a distant corner of the pub. 'I salute you.'

'As Nietzsche said, what if the truth was a woman – what then?'

'Well,' said Learmouth, 'I have a different and much more wholesome proposition. If you look over there, in the far corner – don't all look at once . . .' we took turns to glance casually in that direction '. . . you will see a man with a grey beard and a Homburg on his knee, sitting alongside a young woman with thick-rimmed spectacles and a glass of brandy . . .'

'I can see the man but I can't see the young woman. All I can see is an old lady with grey hair.'

'Well, from a distance she might look somewhat older than her years. She is twenty-one. Anyway, the poor creature is a German half-Jew. She has been living in London for some time, but her passport expires in a month. She risks being deported. Sent back to Germany.'

'Nasty,' said Knell. 'She'll be maltreated. Slave labour. A concentration camp.'

'What – even for half-Jews?'

'Quarter-Jews get maltreated. If there's any trace, basically. So I've heard.'

'Learmouth,' said Somarco, 'are you proposing that this unfortunate young woman pose for us?'

'No, I'm proposing – appropriate word – that one of us marries her.'

'Marries her? Are you insane?'

'Not at all. She needs to claim British citizenship. She'll pay any future husband fifty pounds for their trouble, and she'll pay for a divorce as soon as you want.'

'I'll do it,' said Knell, putting down his drink and straightening his tie. 'Take me over, introduce us . . .'

'Wait a minute,' said Learmouth, placing a firm hand on Knell's shoulder, 'let's not be too hasty. This is marriage we're talking about. There are lots of angles to consider.'

From my position I had a good view of the couple. They were occupying a crowded corner of the pub, and seemed awkward amid the noise and jostling. Although pushed close together by the other customers, they seemed unaware of each other's existence. They looked like a father and daughter who'd been forced to socialize. The man, I presumed, was some sort of Jewish authority figure, if not actually a rabbi. They had come to the pub, it seemed, for the sole purpose of making contact with a possible suitor. The woman did look much older than twenty-one, with her prematurely grey hair. She glanced about herself continually, as if afraid to let her gaze settle on any one thing for too long.

'The ideal candidate has been described to me. He would be – one – unmarried . . .'

'Obviously.'

'Two – in need of some quick and easy money . . .'

'That covers just about all of us . . .'

'And three – he should be a committed homosexual.'

'I say, that's not fair,' said Knell.

'Well, it counts us all out.'

'Oh, really? I thought there were at least two homosexuals among us.'

'Are there? Good Lord.'

'Are you counting yourself, Learmouth?' said Somarco.

'Me? Heavens, no. I would certainly marry the poor woman, but I think my fiancée would have something to say about it.'

'Oh, you and your fiancée, you're far too unusual to have a fiancée.'

I tried to speak up but the words shrivelled in my throat. I wanted to say what Knell had just said – to take me over and present me as a candidate for a marriage of convenience. But Learmouth's third proviso silenced me. I could not believe that anyone imagined I was a homosexual – and whom had he meant when he said he thought there were two among us? Knell? Somarco? Natland?

I looked again at the couple. We all did. I was too afraid by now to ask anything about her, though Learmouth went on to explain.

'She is a writer. Rather well known, apparently. But, like I said, marriage is rather a big step to take.'

'I don't see why,' said Knell. 'I would happily marry her.'

'But you would also fall in love with her. And she's a lesbian.'

'Christ, Learmouth,' I suddenly blurted, 'keep your voice down, would you?'

'Keep his voice down?' Somarco was smiling.

'We don't want to get thrown out.'

This produced more laughter from my colleagues. I felt stupid again.

'I don't think that young woman has anything to worry about,' said Somarco. 'For one thing, she probably won't be repatriated. And if she is, well, I'm sure she'll find a friend of her own kind who can swing things in her favour.'

'Of her own kind?' queried Learmouth, as a little hush fell on us.

'Yes,' said Somarco. 'Her own kind. I mean other writers. Why are you looking at me like that?'

*

It might have been the following night that we embarked on our mission to engage the artistic services of a prostitute. There were four of us – Somarco, Learmouth (looking far more nervous than I had ever seen him before), Alfred Knell and myself. We met up at the Salisbury, St Martin's Lane, with our sketchbooks and drawing materials in satchels, like the innocent personnel of any undergraduate sketching club. After a quick, nervous drink, we set out, led by Somarco. Learmouth had pulled his hat down so far he could hardly see where he was going. I felt a curious thrill in my stomach, a nervous jumpiness. Only Somarco looked calm, strolling casually along Charing Cross Road as if he hadn't a care in the world.

He gave no indication of where he was taking us, and we imagined that we were headed for some sort of singing and dancing club, behind which the prostitutes might ply their trade, but he took us to an amusement arcade near Cambridge Circus, a gaudy little place full of pinball machines and one-armed bandits.

'What the hell have you brought us here for?'

'Just start playing the machines, Norman. You've got some coppers, haven't you? Start playing, enjoy yourself, go on.'

Learmouth and I hesitated, but Alfred sauntered quite happily into the neon grotto and started playing, looking awkwardly proportioned and postured.

'I don't like this,' said Learmouth. 'We're on view to the whole street, lit up like dummies in a tailor's window. Anyone could walk past and see us.'

'Go to the back,' said Somarco. 'This place extends for miles. No one ever sees anything that goes on at the far end . . .'

And he was right. The arcade unfolded in pace with our exploration – the further we ventured in, the bigger it seemed to become.

'And what happens now, when we start playing the machines?'

'Someone will come and talk to you.'

'What do you mean, "someone"?'

'A lady of the night – a whore, a tart, whatever you like.'

'And then? What do I say?'

'Whatever you like. You know what to ask for. Anyway, she might not come up to you first . . .'

We played the pinball machines. Learmouth didn't even know how to operate them, fumbling for the slot and the lever. He looked painfully uncomfortable, with his satchel awkwardly held beneath his arm and his collar up. It was rather heartening to know there were things even the great Learmouth couldn't do, to see him so far out of his depth. I almost felt sorry for him.

We played the machines for an hour, until we had run out of coins, and no woman of the night had come to visit us. On the other hand, we had to agree that we had thoroughly enjoyed ourselves. Learmouth and I had accumulated impressive scores on adjacent tables, and Knell, it appeared, had become addicted to gambling. We therefore agreed to try again the following day.

Somarco suggested we try earlier in the evening. Prostitutes, he said, were often at their most active in the late afternoon. So we returned to the same amusement arcade, this time with extra pocketfuls of copper coins, and were so absorbed in our machines that we didn't notice when a prostitute came in. I was only alerted to her presence by a sharp elbow nudged into my ribs. Knell was breathless with excitement at having spotted a real live tart. She looked terrifying, a concoction of cheap furs and glaring lipstick, a ridiculous pillbox hat and veil perched crookedly on her stiff black hair. But she was already talking to another man, a chap almost invisible behind his high collar and wide-brimmed hat. Very quickly they walked away together.

'We must play the tables nearer the entrance,' said Somarco, 'to make sure we are the first to be approached.'

Eventually we had luck. A woman in a blue leather coat and a straw hat marched in and went straight up to Somarco, who was at a one-armed bandit, and began talking to him. They had a long conversation, during which the woman frequently threw back her head and laughed. Then she looked around at us, while Somarco whispered smilingly into her ear, and laughed again.

Somarco and the woman linked arms and began to leave the arcade, Somarco gesturing for us to follow them. We formed an odd procession as we left, the three of us following about ten yards behind the happy couple. We turned off the main road and were shortly in Old Compton Street, a part of the West End I hadn't visited before. It had a shabby, run-down, seedy feel, though at the near end there were some rather intriguing food shops. Somarco, we observed from afar, was fascinated by them, and couldn't help going into one, an Italian delicatessen with peculiar-looking sausages in the window. Learmouth, Knell and I waited on the corner with nervous impatience, while Somarco and his vulgar consort perused the delicacies on offer. He then emerged with brown-paper bags under his arms, a bottle of wine in a wicker sleeve, wedges of cheese and a string of dried sausages around his neck. A little further down the street the woman disappeared into a doorway, and Somarco came back to talk to us.

'Take a smell of that, my friend,' he said, offering one of the paper bags to our faces. We recoiled and were too nervous to sniff, suspecting strong unsavoury odours. 'Go on, put your nose in. The finest Parmesan I've ever seen outside Italy.' I did sniff; the vitriolic tang nearly made me retch.

'Oh, you silly little Englishman. Never mind now. That sweet woman I was talking to is called Mags, and she has agreed to do our bidding, and is indeed rather intrigued by the prospect of being immortalized by a group of soon-to-be-world-famous artists – she has an abode here, above a Continental coffee house, which she shares with two fellow workers in her trade, and believes they might be amenable to the type of work we envisage.

I think it would be an excellent evening – the question of payment is negotiable, but she is expecting about five shillings from each of us, to compensate for the amount of valuable time we might be using. That will buy us about an hour, I believe. But these comestibles are on me – my, I never even knew this place existed, and there are other shops, Parmigiano, whole rounds of it, and mortadella, Puttana truffles. It is Paradise, gentlemen.'

We were advised not to enter the building in a group, but to go in singly at three-minute intervals. After Somarco, Learmouth was the first, and I was the last. When through the street door, I found myself in a dimly lit place that went immediately up a flight of uncarpeted wooden steps. On the landing I turned down a passageway, recognizing the tart's laughter in the distance and following it. On the way I passed an open door through which I could see a plump blonde woman of about forty, and a man wearing nothing but a vest down to his knees. He was sitting on the bed, and she was standing in front of him, and seemed about to unfurl the shiny dressing gown that clung to her tightly. I walked quickly on, trembling at the sight of such intimacy, so casually exposed.

I followed the laughter of our tart to another room, the door half open, beyond which I could glimpse the people I knew. Entering, it was as though a party was in full swing: Somarco had opened the wine and was sharing it out in an assortment of drinking vessels – tin mugs, china teacups, a pint jar presumably stolen from a pub. The room was full of smoke from freshly lit cigarettes, the tang of match sulphur, and the stench of Parmesan cheese.

'And now young Brill makes our party complete. Beware, my good woman, Brill is the reason we are all here, for he has twice disgraced himself . . .'

'Leave it,' I snapped. 'Let's just do it, shall we?' I threw my five shillings on the stained carpet.

'Oo-er – listen to him. Someone must have pissed in his milk,' said the tart.

'Well, my dear, perhaps we should make a start. Time is money, after all.'

'So what do you want me to do? Just take me clobber off?'

'If you would be so good.'

She had already removed the blue coat. The rest of her was contained in a low-cut red dress that thrust a quivering cleavage upwards.

'Well, I'm not what you think and I don't care to undress before a lot of prying eyes, so if you don't mind I'll disrobe in the bathroom and see you all anon.'

With that, she disappeared through a peeling yellow door.

This left us in a curious state of silent contemplation. Learmouth took the opportunity to whisper loudly, 'If a word of this gets out to anyone, we're all finished, do you hear?'

'I don't see why,' said Knell. 'This is surely just extra-curricular, extramural study.'

'He means if a word gets out to his precious fiancée,' I said.

We looked about the room. There was a plate on the floor, on which was the chewed perimeter of a bacon sandwich, and some Petit Beurres. Our whore emerged shortly wearing a silk dressing gown. She stood in the centre of the room and lit a cigarette. 'So what shall I do? Just plonk meself down in the chair – or shall I lie down?'

'Perhaps you could do a standing pose?' Learmouth tentatively suggested.

'What? Stand on me plates for an hour? After all that walking around? No, darling, I'm used to working lying down, so if you want me to stand, you'll have to pay double.'

She took some cushions from the settee by the window and made a little bed on the floor. Then she removed the dressing gown and threw it onto a chair. This movement was so sudden and unforewarned it was as though night had turned to day in an instant. Her nakedness had erupted in the centre of the room like a fountain of milk. Her whiteness was dazzling – it was like staring into a blinding light, only to find that your eyes can cope with it, after all. And then, in the after-image of her glow, you could see the imperfections and the stains. The moving, hinged parts of her – knees, ankles, neck – had the same wear and tear of any well-used mechanism. A hard little scab, no bigger than a currant, on each elbow. Plum-coloured bruises on her belly, fat as thumb prints, like the purple ink-stamps on bacon. There was a tide-mark of dirt halfway down her thighs. She had soaped her loins but had got no further. Her pubic hair was light and healthy-looking, though slightly grey with talcum.

Then, as if this wasn't enough to take in, there was movement. To one used to painting mannequins and statues, this was more of a shock than the flesh itself – the swaying of her dirigible breasts, the waves of her abdominal flesh, the ground-shocks rippling up her thighs with each step. The mere act of walking seemed a miraculous accomplishment, an act of bodily orchestration. She then dropped herself onto the cushions and turned on her side, rested her cheek on the back of her left hand, draped her other arm over the plateau of her hips, and lay there, twiddling her toes in boredom.

I felt a great sense of triumph in the fact that I had retained my consciousness. More than that, I had retained my calmness of composure. Perhaps it was the suddenness of Mags's disrobing, perhaps it was the nerve-soothing effect of Italian wine, or perhaps it was the calmness of Mags herself, who had that special quality I saw common to all the prostitutes we were to meet – an ability to allay fears, to soothe, calm and quieten the nervous hearts of men.

One thing that Mags lacked, however, was an ability to remain still. After only ten minutes the arm was lifted from its position on the hip and flopped out across the floor. We looked at each other, wondering who was going to tell her. In the end Somarco went over to her and gently moved the arm back into position.

And so we embarked on our journey into the mysteries of female topography. We came away from that first one-hour session elated and bubbly with the experience. We were fervent and effervescent as we walked back up Old Compton Street, practically skipping along – almost as though we'd had the benefit of a sexual marathon with the tart, though nothing of a sexual nature had happened, or even seemed likely to happen. When the session was over, Mags lifted herself as abruptly from the floor as she had earlier dropped to it, gowned herself and said, 'Here you go, time's up,' and reached out to smack the head of the little pink alarm clock she had set to go off. She had, by that time, obliged us with several interesting poses that in total gave us a circumnavigation of her anatomy, both horizontally and vertically, and had taught us valuable lessons on foreshortening and perspective generally. Somarco had assisted us on some of the finer points of representation, and had helped me with my grasp of proportion.

But at the end of the session we were quickly ushered out to make room for new clients, who were hanging around on the landings and the stairs, and all turned away from us as we trooped out, hiding themselves behind their hats. Mags showed no interest whatsoever in the artwork we had done, did not even ask to see anyone's rendering of her.

Out in the street we couldn't stop proclaiming to each other how beneficial the exercise had been, our sketchbooks were noticeably heavier with applied graphite and pigment, and we all agreed that we should return for another session.

We spent the rest of the evening in a Soho pub and that night was the first time I'd been late back to my aunt Mary's. I had no key but the problem of gaining entry didn't occur to me until I was at the front door, and noticed how all the lights were off. An unusual, forbidding darkness seemed to fill the house behind its lacy windows, and my tentative knock on the little Greek-urn-shaped brass knocker was sent like a bolt of lightning into that darkness, which instantly swallowed it. In my innocence I thought my aunt and uncle and their three sour children must have been exceptionally deep sleepers, and only much later realized they had not been asleep, but had allowed me to stand on the pavement knocking hopefully, with gradually strengthening resolve, for nearly half an hour, just to make their point. By that time I was working the knocker like a blacksmith at his forge, and banging on the windows, shouting through the letterbox, rousing the neighbours all down the street, though my aunt's house remained stoically dark.

When my uncle finally appeared, pulling the door open to reveal himself in all his wiry, flannel-pyjamaed glory, I was given a good talking-to in the hallway about the scarcely believable level of selfishness I had attained in my living habits, that didn't I know he had to be up at the crack of dawn for work the next day, while it's OK for the likes of you, swanning off to your fancy art school at any time you like – what time do you say classes start, ten o'clock? By that time I'll be having my first tea break, if I'm lucky enough not to have to work through it. I don't know what they do on the Heath, but in this house we keep respectable hours.

'What is that terrible smell?' my aunt said, as she came downstairs in a cross-stitched dressing gown, her hair up in curlers and her face pale and creamy. 'Has he been drinking?'

The aroma of Italian wines and cheeses filled the hallway.

'What do you think your mother and father would say if we told them their boy came home near midnight reeking of alcohol? Look at me, boy.' My uncle took me by the shoulders, gave me a light slap on the cheek and stared into my eyes. 'I thought so. This boy is far gone, Mary. Far gone.'

I had not known I was so intoxicated.

'Let me paint you a picture,' I slurred, trying to unbutton my coat. 'I'll paint you anything you like, free of charge.'

*

On only our third visit to Old Compton Street we were some way into the execution of our drawings when there was the sound of a commotion from a nearby room. The noise of laughter and the chortling of a male and female together was quickly replaced by angrier exchanges, until at last there came some veritable screams, at which point our model suddenly stood up, regirdled herself and went out into the passageway. More shrieking. Some angry retorts from a disgruntled male, some invective of a colourful nature against the male race, before she returned, dropped her gown and resumed a pose entirely unrelated to the one she had adopted before the interruption. We made do as best we could, or started afresh.

Another prostitute put her head round the door shortly after, to see what we were doing. She smiled, or leered, with her painted mouth. This was the same woman I'd seen earlier, with the vested gent. That time she had seemed as lifeless as a mannequin. Now, animated, she was truly terrifying, full of aggression and violence and indifference, all of it, at that moment, channelled, thankfully, into humour. She laughed at our set-up. Claimed that she would insist on us 'doing' her next time. 'I can hold a pose with the best of them. Here, why don't you do me as Britannia with me bosoms out? That would be a good one, eh?'

Soon Viv and Mags were doing poses together, though they rarely stayed still but partook of the food (Somarco always stopped at the delicatessen on the way), treating our room as a cafe, a sort of retreat they could use if they weren't otherwise occupied. Others joined us. Lucy was a younger and prettier prostitute, a slim, semi-transparent blonde who tried to conceal an educated accent when she spoke.

One afternoon we got very drunk and Viv brought along a catapult, which she used to fire olive stones at us. We retaliated (all but Learmouth who tried to capture the scene in charcoal) by pinging rings of salami skin across the room. Try to picture us, the stern, studious art students in food battle with a trio of naked whores, half drunk on Chianti – I felt that at last I had discovered the true Bohemian life of London.

*

We visited the tarts as often as we could, and much earlier in the day. Always we were guided and corralled by Somarco. It seemed vital that he was there because his presence as a lecturer made our visits legitimately educational, in our eyes at least. Somarco was Italian-smooth, controlled and calm in the presence of lucid female skin, of hard-nubbed nipples, of thickly thatched pudenda. When the girls all but gave up the project of stillness, he seemed to relish the chance to draw them in continual motion, but I found it very difficult to cope with – I would look into the horizontal tessellation of a smile, then be puzzled by the braced-brackets curve of a pair of vaginal labia, and marvel at how one whore had lipsticked a red heart onto her flesh at the fringe of her floss, and another had plaited her pubes and done them with a delightful butterfly of bowed silk. On my own pages a kind of *Demoiselles d'Avignon* emerged: the forms began to split and reassemble according to the movement of their bodies through time. I had long discussions with Learmouth about the direction our painting should head, that our experiments with capturing movement and energy in painting should ultimately find their fulfilment in a mode of expression that transcended form altogether, and consist of nothing but energy – as Knell had once envisaged. But Learmouth was troubled by the prospect, and didn't think it would help our careers at the Slade at all.

Without the presence of Learmouth and Somarco, who knew where our sessions would have ended? It was clear that Knell, for one, was keen that we should conclude our classes with private 'consultations', for which we could pay extra. 'Consultations' was Mags's term. She would often say to us, 'Here, if you feel like anything extra, I can offer you a private consultation in my room. A lot less boring than sitting here doing nothing.'

'My dear girl,' Learmouth had grown in confidence during the visits, and would happily lord it over the tarts, 'if you think we are doing nothing, you are quite mistaken.'

'No, I meant me. It would be a lot less boring for me.'

Sometimes Learmouth would talk aesthetics while we drew, and analyse the tart as we drew her, as though she were an uncomprehending creature. He was adamant that it was a much harder task to draw the female body than the male because it had no angles. A woman is just planes and volumes, whereas a man has structure: he has ridges and lines and corners. In that sense he is much easier to draw because he has something to be measured; a woman's body is mysterious and elusive – there is no underlying musculature to give it structure; its only lines are at its extremities; the interior planes are that much harder to depict.

'Well, I don't see it myself. You might suppose the male and female body are very different things, but you're thinking of their classical, idealized forms. In reality, most men lack the Herculean muscular substructure, and most women lack the mysterious curves and planes you talk about. In reality men's bodies are flabby and full-breasted, while women's may be emaciated and angular, with hard ribcages and collar bones from which hang tiny little titties as negligible as a couple of prunes. The differences are much less obvious than you suppose, if you were to actually look at the reality.'

'That's quite a shocking thing to say, Brill, if you think there is no difference between men and women's bodies. It shows an utter failure of discernment and susceptibility. I worry that you be given access to artistic materials at all . . .'

Knell was the most deeply affected by our experiences with the Old Compton Street Tarts, as we came to know them collectively. He fell in love with them, both individually and as a whole. Learmouth and I tried to talk him out of his infatuations, but his attraction to them was both primal and spiritually complicated. When we tried to point out to him that he was risking a great deal in even considering directing his affections so inappropriately, he was affronted.

'You mean you think it is bad of me to feel anything because she is a common whore? But that is what makes her so attractive. She devotes her life to sex. No form of love is wrong, as long as it's love.'

'But it's sex without passion. I thought passion was everything to you.'

'True sex is impossible without passion – that is the glory of their calling.'

'Look here, Knell,' said Learmouth, using his retired-solicitor voice, 'it won't do any good if you pay one of these girls for a night of passion. It will only disappoint . . .'

'And what do you know about passion, Mr Learmouth? Just because you're engaged to the daughter of a friend of the director of the National Gallery, or whatever the blasted relationship is . . .'

Later, he asked us our advice on whether he should propose to one of them. He had Lucy in mind, the least ferocious of the three. The others, Mags and Viv, seemed wild and dangerous, their make-up extra thick to hide the bruises and scratches that always marked them. Viv was the oldest, and her age became shockingly apparent when she was naked, the paint on her face making it contrast with the untinted flesh below the neck, as though a marble statue had been given a bronze head. Her stomach was lax with childbearing and scored with birth scars. The buoyancy of her breasts had long since been replaced by a sort of clinging emptiness.

'If sex was a religion, she would be its goddess.'

'Well, sex is god, god is sex. That is the lesson I learnt from the baboons. You know I went to the zoo again? I saw a gorilla praying . . .'

IV

'What are you so worried about, Kenneth? You had a train set when you were little, didn't you? Well, it's just the same thing, on a bigger scale.'

In fact I never had a train set. Toy planes were my thing. I didn't tell Somarco this. He was so enthusiastic about the idea of the dummy railhead it was hard not to be drawn along by him. I had to concede, in diagrammatic form, the operation looked achievable. Railway tracks were surely an easy thing to fake – wooden poles laid end to end would be enough, we thought. Or rope. Then the station buildings, the sidings and loading bays could all be manufactured using our well-established methods of painted cloth pinned to wooden frames. We worked on plans for three days, did some calculations of materials required, then asked Learmouth for sufficient quantities of wood and canvas, and for extra men to help us. We were assigned a working party of around thirty people, consisting of anyone with the slightest experience of working with their hands.

We left Cairo by the usual route, but in a convoy this time – seven three-ton lorries, carrying all our people and equipment. It felt good to be out of the city again, to be among the lone and level sands, though Somarco was growing tired of the barrenness of it all. 'How do you think it feels for a man like me, who has devoted so much of his time to the raising of plants, to their depiction in paint, to have to live in a world where all plant life has been banished? I would give a thousand pounds to see a deciduous tree out here.'

As we neared Fort Capuzzo we saw the real railway under construction, teams of men, including large numbers of Italian PoWs, working flat out to construct the new track and loading ramps. They made me think of the men who had built the Pyramids, toiling in great teams under a relentless sun to raise an impossible structure out of the empty desert. At that moment, the terminal of the railway seemed as ambitious a project for these men. All the more so for us, who had to create something on the ground that would exceed all we saw before us in scale.

Somarco proved himself to be a very good gaffer, overseeing little teams of men and managing the workforce in such a way that they respected and feared him in roughly equal amounts. We'd plotted a route from the real railhead towards the enemy lines along a flat stretch of desert, and so avoided the need for cuttings or bridges. In half a day we built a mile of track, using up nearly all the wood we had brought with us, but the first aerial survey showed that these tracks were not at all convincing from above – they were too thin, could not be kept straight, and they didn't have a metallic shine. A test track of rope was even worse. There was no real track to spare and, besides, we didn't have the manpower or equipment to handle the weight of real rails. And as someone explained, there was no point in building a dummy that was in fact real.

In the end Somarco had the idea of using jerry cans and oil drums. They could be quite easily cut up, opened out and hammered into shape. Their inside surfaces were unpainted and shone like fresh steel. There were vast quantities of these items scattered all over the desert. We sent parties out in lorries to form a continual supply chain, collecting cans and drums from every base in the area. It was slow, painstaking work, but the resulting rails were indistinguishable from real ones, when seen from on high. We were given more men, siphoning off some of the workers on the real railway, including a large contingent of Italians. A genuine rail gang seemed to emerge, with men squatting in the sand, hammering their metal into shape as the sun beat down on them, and slowly, mile by mile, the rails took shape, along with points, sidings, junctions, signalling.

The lines of Ozymandias kept coming back to me, in the most annoying way. So many times I was struck by the way our fragile constructions resembled relics of a lost civilization, rather than the ingenious products of an advanced society. We made things that looked, up close, as though they could be blown away on the wind. We were working in the loneliest and flattest parts of the world, far from any settlements or roads, just Somarco and I and our work parties, over two hundred men at times. We were building not just the railway lines but everything that went with them – cookhouses, depots, shelter trenches, supply points. It was as though we were the few people charged with building an entire civilization out there in the sandy nothingness. Oh, I had these horrible dreams as well, that I was in a photography plane in flight over the Heath and looking down on the patterns of habitation, the quadrilaterals, the twisting rivers, the cuboid cottages, the lumpen shit-heaps, and wondering, are they real, or are they merely canvas and wood? Is that whole land nothing but a sham? Ha! In my dream I had the blinding thought that it was – and that those farmers down there, those toiling gardeners, those shit-heap tenders, they were men of straw, rigged up and left out there to fool whoever might look down on them.

I didn't tell Somarco any of this: he was too busy building a train. A whole train, with dummy locomotive and thirty-three freight cars, eighteen flat cars, a brake van. And not just one train, but another on a siding. He had made a busy train terminal. And lorries as well. Lorries and trucks and tanks and DMVs.

I became proud of Somarco – the sheer energy he was putting into the whole project. He was a benevolent slave driver, pushing people to their limit. But somehow he got every last drop out of them. They loved him. And I had become nothing more than his assistant. He had taken command of the whole operation. The frustrations were huge – sandstorms would blow away our flimsy dummy installations, or bury them. I remember seeing a whole locomotive complete with tender, truck and brake van floating through the air like a barrage balloon, to land half a mile away, crushed to matchwood. Moustachioed brigadiers would drive across our tracks and ruin them. At the railhead, Somarco was using every scrap of palm frond and timber, hessian and canvas to create more buildings and vehicles, as many as he could muster. 'We have to build something huge, colossal,' he said. 'At least twice the size of the real railhead. It has to dwarf it.'

After many days of toil – everything had to be carefully orchestrated with realistic slowness; to have constructed everything too quickly would have given the game away – we had managed to create what we felt was a perfect simulation of a large railhead. There were the phantom trains and the phantom carriages, the phantom fuel depots and the phantom cookhouses.

We had built a city with our bare hands, and now we could only wait to see if it attracted enemy bombs. We were in the unusual position of willing the German bombs to rain down upon us. We had rigged the whole place with explosives. We had constructed pools of engine oil to ignite during a raid and give off the black smoke of burning vehicles.

By this time there were only a few men left to maintain the dummy. It was almost as though we were alone – sole inhabitants of the city we had built. I told Somarco how proud of him I was, and he seemed not to hear me. His work was not finished, he said. He insisted that the dummy vehicles be continually moved and their positions changed. If the enemy took two photographs, even a few minutes apart, and noted everything was in an identical position in both, then the sham would be exposed. So we were continually occupied by the task of moving our enormous but lightweight fleet of dummy vehicles into new configurations.

In the desert, bombing raids could be carried out only in daylight. The first two days passed without incident. The skies remained disappointingly empty of enemy planes. But on the third day the bombs fell. We had some real anti-aircraft placements to add realism, and suddenly the world was alive with the most apocalyptic colour and noise. We ran out into the open and rejoiced at the devastation, as though we were merely the participants in some carnival of flame, and gave no thought to our own safety. We danced amid the fire, our own explosions complementing the useless bombs of the Germans perfectly in a choreography of destruction.

Over two weeks there were regular raids on the Capuzzo Dummy, while the real railhead, six miles away, was left virtually untouched.

V

Do you think God wears any clothes? The idea is nonsense.

God is nakedness.

I have not had this dream, but wish that I had, that a woman gives birth to a fully clothed child, that he slips from the womb wearing a little person's Sunday-best suit of clothes – tweed shorts, blue woollen socks, brown polished sandals, a shirt with a red bow-tie, and a little baby-sized tweed sports jacket, all miraculously clean.

*

We were spending nearly every penny we had on our prostitutes. The afternoons and evenings at Old Compton Street had become a social occasion, as much as an educational one. The girls took us out of our swaddled and complacent selves and presented us with new selves – ones that seemed five years older, and an inch or two taller. The regular companionship of harlots burnished our confidence, emboldened us, galvanized our self-esteem. We strode around London with the swagger of giants; we strutted the corridors of the Slade like visiting nobs of the art world; we became bossy and demanding.

London nights held no anxieties for us. Sometimes our sessions with the girls carried on into the late evening. If they were so disposed they allowed us an extra half-hour at no extra charge, or even an hour. Those half-hours would be spent in nothing but drinking and laughter, for we would have given up trying to draw the bodies that themselves had given up any attempt at remaining still, and afterwards, we would sometimes accompany the girls off the premises as we made our way home and they made their way to work, quite drunk, our guts swilling with Chianti and salami and Parmigiano. I would be too drunk to care that I would be late again for Aunt Mary and that I would have to hammer on the front door for half an hour before being let in, if they let me in at all. I recall one night, walking the girls back to the Charing Cross Road (as they said, they didn't care to walk the streets alone like a pair of common whores), Viv became utterly and hilariously foul-mouthed. We passed an elderly gentleman in the street, and she yelled at him, ''Ere, Grandad, cheer up, what's the matter? Someone put vinegar in yer spunk?' Then she clung to me and brought her glazed red mouth right up to my ear (I'm sure the amount of lipstick on her labia muffled her voice slightly).

''Ere, Claude,' to protect our identities we had all assumed false names, borrowing from the artistic pantheon of modern masters, 'you want to know a secret?'

'Not really.'

'No, go on. You want to know a secret?'

My companions, Paul, Vincent and Pablo, had walked on ahead. I could hardly see them.

'Yes, then. I would dearly love to know a secret.'

'Well, I'll tell you.' The coated lips were brought up to my ear again, but there was no whisper, rather a shrill cry that hurt not just my eardrum, but my cochlea, and those three little bones. 'I ain't got no knickers on!'

'Fascinating.'

'No, it's true. Look . . .'

And she ran a few steps ahead of me, lifted her long skirt and bent over, flinging the skirt up over her back and down over her head, so that her upper upside-down body was concealed beneath her inverted skirts and petticoats, and her legs (clad in hooped knee stockings) and her bare arse were visible. Mags reeled with laughter, ran over and gave Viv's left buttock a slap.

'Madam, really,' I said. I was by now very much acclimatized to the naked female form, Viv and her friends having proved singularly uninhibited in their modelling, to such a degree that we doubted certain of our drawings could ever be shown in a respectable gallery. Even so I could not take my eyes off the cleft vision before me, exposed as it was to the whole street, which was still busy and bustling, and I wondered, drunk even as I was, how I would appear to others in the company of such a woman, as Viv reached behind herself to pull the two halves of her arse apart and reveal the richer, darker depths, then self-slapped her buttocks and beckoned to me with a finger poking out beneath the buttock archway (a rather clever feat given her orientation). It allowed me the freedom to swagger, to feel that I was one able to master a shrieking, clawed woman of Viv's sort, from whom most men would cower. And these feelings might last for a week, until we were back in the upstairs room with the girls again, when we would withdraw into our former muted selves, at the mercy of these women, able to be terrified of them once more.

Our situation changed one day when our drawing class was intruded upon by someone we came to know as Mr Lacey. It was during one of our sessions with Viv and Lucy together, Viv sitting on a chair while Lucy stood beside her, head declined as though she was looking for her reflection in the carpet, when Mr Lacey entered the room. He was, by all appearances, a very respectable gentleman, wearing a heavy brown overcoat and a grey bowler hat with a golden band. He had a round, dish-like face and full lips.

He was someone we were later told not to 'worry about', by Mags and others, someone whom we were assured was not a 'violent man', and who was, indeed, as gentle and as nervous as a kitten 'on the inside'. We might have believed in the veracity of such statements more had not the girls themselves so visibly shrunk in his presence: the assertiveness of their flesh became weak and vulnerable when he entered, as if all their nerves had come on display. They trembled like unfledged birds fallen from their nest.

Of course, these remarks were made only because they had to be made, because we needed that reassurance, because he seemed to us at first to be a very difficult and potentially dangerous man. He seemed very unhappy with the set-up in Viv's room, and in my innocence I thought this was simply because he was the landlord of the premises and didn't take kindly to it being used for something as Bohemian as an artist's studio. He asked us all how much we were paying to do our 'scribbling'. Learmouth was at first affronted, saying our business arrangements were none of his affair, to which Mr Lacey didn't take too kindly. 'If you're drawing one of my girls, she's got to get a price appropriate to her situation and standing,' he said. I was still naive enough to think that by 'girls' he meant his daughters, and this man was the women's father. We looked to Somarco for guidance, but he had suddenly become rather quiet. Though now he piped up, offering Mr Lacey a glass of good *vino*, suspecting, I think, that the gentleman bore some Italian blood.

'You think this lot are no better than the Hyde Park girls? This Lucy here, she was untouched when she came to me – worth her weight in cold roast pork she was, though filthy from sleeping in the park. Had to hose her down like a motor-car.' He gave a gargling laugh and pinched Lucy's chin, so that her bottom lip was dragged down, displaying the filled and drilled lower front teeth. 'I'm not happy about it, four young men doing their sketching – what are you? Think you're all Leonardo da bloody Vinci, do you? You think you can chip in and pay for two of my girls – how much you paying? If she was on the street you wouldn't get a look-in, you lot. You think she can't earn more than the hourly rate with a single gentleman? Let me tell you, Viv here has had three on the go at once, all paying the full rate. Haven't you, my darling? Regular little acrobat you were, weren't you?'

'What do you take me for? I'm a fully trained tailoress, I am. That's my true profesh.'

'I can assure you they wouldn't earn any more if they were on—'

'You think how many clients Dusty Kate can get through in an hour – why, she once had fifteen, if you include the three-somes, each at ten shillings a go. What's that add up to? More than seven quid for an hour's work. As for Viv, she's a lazy little tyke, aren't you, my darling? Sitting on your backside like a statue for an hour. Anyway, what do you lot call this? My little cousin could do better, and he's only seven years old.' He was looking at Somarco's Cubist interpretation of Viv's reclining figure. 'Looks like a lot of smashed crockery. And what's this? All this smudging and rubbing out, and you haven't even done her hands.' He was offering these comments to Learmouth. 'Suppose you got the proportions right. Yeah, not bad. But do the face, and the hands, and get rid of all these lines all over the place . . .'

Later, Learmouth was to remark that he had never before had art tuition from 'a small-time ponce' – that was Viv's term for him. 'You don't want to worry about Mr Lacey – he's just a small-time ponce. Thinks he owns us, but we're the ones with the money, we can give him what we like.' Indeed, Mr Lacey was very concerned about money, and tried to get more out of us, convinced, because of our accents, that we must be gentlemen with cash to spare, no matter how much we protested that we were but penniless art students. 'I been keeping an eye on you lot, and I don't like what I'm seeing. You book out three of my girls at a time, sometimes for two hours. Three hours. And all you're doing is laughing and eating the cheese. And they don't charge you no extra. What you don't understand, my little Rembrandtinos, is a girl like Lucy gets gold sovereigns stuffed up her slit on a good night, and I come round to collect, just like on the one-armed bandit, hold my hat out, the coins come tumbling out of her fanny like a jackpot. But when she's sitting here, that quim's as empty as Fingal's Cave, echoing like the catacombs of St Peter's in Rome.' He threatened to throw us out and ban us from coming back, and I was greatly heartened by the fact that Mags, Lucy and some of the other girls rallied to our support and stood up to the bowler-hatted man, and a sort of uneasy truce was formed between us.

He professed to be a religious man, a devout Catholic, and he brought in with him once some paintings that he'd done in his youth and which he had carried about with him, images of the Crucifixion of childlike naivety, one of Jesus holding a large rose, another of the Virgin Mary and a bowl of bananas. To our dismay he had not brought in these paintings so that we could give him some advice and painting tips, but rather as examples to us of how to paint properly. His more important objective, we believed, was to make sure we stayed only one hour, and didn't try to extend our time period, seeing as how lazy he thought his girls were.

Despite his meanness of spirit and his flat face, we soon realized we had little to fear from Mr Lacey – in fact, we found him amusing company, entertaining in the most unintentional way, so it didn't seem out of character for me to feel that I could afford him a favour, if it so happened that he needed any help, which was how it came about that I claimed his name for myself when I was questioned by a police officer.

The world had changed during a visit to the lavatory, in a way that I have found worlds often do after visits to that place. The lavatory in Old Compton Street was a narrow cell of yellow paint lit by a bare gas jet, and one evening, after rather a lot of Italian wine, I dallied in there rather longer than normal, feeling a swimmingness in my head and only half aware of what seemed to be a thundering beyond the door, a stampede of feet going back and forth down the passage, up the stairs. Through the small window that gave onto the back alleyway, the sound of breaking glass and a police whistle. Still I did not connect those sounds and commotions with any predicament for myself, so I was alarmed when I opened the door to find a police constable standing in the hallway, as if waiting (as indeed I assumed) to use the facility I had just vacated. But, no, he was waiting for me. 'Good evening, sir,' he said, touching the peak of his helmet, and in the light from the lavatory I noticed an odd thing – a red lipstick imprint on his right cheek.

As if from the other end of a tunnel, a voice called to us from the far reaches of the landing, 'Mr Lacey! Anton! Darling!'

Mags, I realized, was offering me the chance to disguise my identity, and as she approached us was putting on a drunk act. I then noticed that other members of the constabulary were moving around the property – in and out of doorways, up and down the stairs. Suddenly from a room there burst forth a little balding man wearing a French maid's outfit and a sulky expression. 'Leave little Mary alone,' a female voice was calling from the room he'd just left. 'He's only come to dust me boudoir,' followed by a hail of cackles.

The original policeman ignored the commotion and called to a fellow officer, 'Sidney, we got the Johnson here.'

'Lacey,' I said, in what I thought was a very polite and measured voice, 'the name's Lacey.'

'Mr Lacey,' said the second police officer, 'such a pleasure to meet you.' He was holding out his hand to shake. I took it, and in a moment was spun round on my heels and pressed face first into the damp wallpaper, my arms painfully yanked backwards. Mags paraded up and down the passage and up and down the stairs with a furry stole and a cocktail glass in her hand, as if directing the guests around a society party. She showed no concern at all for what was happening to me. There was no sign of any of my colleagues. When I was taken to the living room, where some plainclothes men were picking through the contents, it was evident that they had been afforded an escape route through the back way. They had taken all their belongings with them. Only my sketchbook was left, on which a half-finished drawing of Lucy, in a rather provocative legs-open pose, was folded back for display.

*

It took me some hours to establish my true identity to the police, and then for the innocence of my relationship with the prostitutes to be established. The police seemed deeply baffled by my story. When I tried explaining that I was employing the prostitutes as models, they wondered why I didn't pay professionals for the purpose, a question I couldn't satisfactorily answer. They wondered why I wanted to protect Mr Lacey by assuming his identity, when he was a very nasty criminal with a history of violence towards young women. I was told he had once thrown a small phial of acid into the face of a young girl who'd strayed onto his patch. 'She wasn't even on the game, poor thing, just a runaway from a remand home who'd taken a wrong turning off the Charing Cross Road. Now we go round to Lacey's girls every now and then, just to sprinkle some of the frightening powder, but we never expect to find him there. And you do look similar.'

Another detective pitched in: 'What do you want to get yourself mixed up with women like that for? You're talking about them as though they were friends. Let me tell you, every mug thinks they're the whore's special one, the one who's not like all the rest, but you're not, you're just the same. All right, you didn't pay them for sex, but in their terms that just makes you easy money, an hour off the streets. They have no feelings for you whatsoever. You're just another steamer to them. Women like that don't have any feelings. They're as cold as statues, and would see your face razor-slashed without an ounce of pity.'

It was established that I hadn't done anything wrong at Old Compton Street, apart from giving the police a false name, which they thought worth prosecuting me for. I appeared at Bow Street Magistrates' during which the circumstances of my arrest were given in detail, and I was fined two pounds.

*

For some reason, during the events at Old Compton Street, I had lost my shoes. For my appearance at court the police could only provide me with a pair of ancient wellingtons with cobwebs inside them. It was these wellingtons that helped distract Aunt Mary from the question of my overnight absence when I returned to my lodgings later that day, near to tears with the stress of the whole thing.

'Listen, I'm sorry, you were probably wondering what happened last night . . .'

'I'm more puzzled by your wellingtons . . .'

The pair of shoes I had lost was my only one.

'Yes, you see I went to stay with a friend who lives in the country . . .'

Aunt Mary showed her disapproval by turning her back on me and going into the kitchen. I followed meekly.

'Listen, could I borrow . . . How can I put this – do you have any spare shoes?'

Aunt Mary looked me up and down again, without speaking. The thought that I might be asking to borrow her husband's shoes was too embarrassing for her to give reply to or even contemplate. He had several pairs, neatly lined up in the cupboard under the stairs. Their vigorous and meticulous polishing was a Sunday-night ritual, when they would be spread out on sheets of newspaper and Mr Brown would be seated on a low stool with his handyman's apron spread over his knees, tins of polish open and reeking all around him, and thick black brushes in his hands. But he was a small-footed man. His feet were mere hoofs compared to mine.

Aunt Mary was kind enough to ask no further questions, and to provide me with something in the way of tea – a boiled egg and a dish of pilchards. I prodded with my fork at the cooked vertebrae and shredded silver of the headless fishes, and decided that my only option was to go back to Old Compton Street and confront the tarts. Mags and Viv had to be responsible for my plight, and they might even have kept my shoes. They were probably waiting for me to collect them.

'And where are you off to now? You've only been here five minutes and, look, you haven't even eaten your pilchards.'

'I had the egg, thank you.'

'You make sure you're back in time, or my husband will be very cross with you. And get some proper shoes.'

It was a long walk from Holloway to Soho in heavy wellingtons. I got some funny looks. Someone asked me where I'd parked my tractor.

I wasn't looking forward to the prospect of a confrontation with Viv and Mags: they could be sullen she-devils when they wanted to be, spitting and clawing at the least provocation. I had seen the way they treated difficult clients – talons flexed, jaws jutting, and words of such profanity flowing forth. Mags was rumoured to have blinded a customer in one eye with her sharp nails. Even the police were nervous of her.

Lucy was walking the streets near Soho Square when I found her. She showed no interest or surprise when I approached, and seemed utterly unconcerned at how I'd been dealt with by the police. Like Aunt Mary, her only interest was in my footwear. 'Why, Claude, you look like you've been gardening.'

I tried to show anger, explaining that I believed she and her friends were responsible for my predicament – why had they pretended I was Lacey and got me to join in the pretence?

'Why? For your own protection, of course. They wouldn't want to touch Lacey, not with a barge pole. They were looking for the proper steamers, like you. It's what they do now and then. How were we to know they'd changed their mind and were wanting to put old Lacey away?'

She was so convincingly innocent that I didn't even question her about my shoes. Her lack of interest was simply a factor of her familiarity with the police. Raids on their lumber were, as she'd said, a regular event in their lives. So were occasional nights in the cells. All part of their overheads. 'It's best you finish with this art-model game. It was fun for a while, but Lacey was right. It was bad for business. And if you get caught again you'll be in trouble with your people, won't you, up at that college?'

I'd hardly given any thought to what would happen if the news got through to the Slade – but, then, why should it have? Lucy was having a slow afternoon so she took some time out to help me get some shoes, as she knew a good little second-hand shop in the East End, whose owner owed her a favour. I was given a free pair of very good Irish brogues.

When I got home later that afternoon, the worst had happened: the news of my arrest had made the evening editions, and my uncle was full of silent fury. He would not even speak to me. The paper had put a particularly salacious slant on the story. In court I had pleaded that I had been taking extramural study, at my own expense, to supplement my university work, naively thinking that would show me in a good light, as a hard-working, industrious student. The papers preferred to say that I was running a brothel for students in a notorious Soho bordello. Just one look from my uncle's grimy eyes told me I should go to my room and remain there. A little later Aunt Mary came up and told me they could no longer accommodate me. I could have a week's notice but I had to be gone on the seventh day. 'Believe me,' she said, in an anxious whisper, 'I had to work very hard to persuade my husband to allow you that grace. He was all for throwing you out of the house tonight. I do suggest you avoid using any of the downstairs rooms while he is at home. I will bring you your meals. He is particularly concerned that you do not have any communication with the children.'

I thought this was funny, since they had taken no notice of me at all in my tediously long months of residence.

My life, it seemed, was collapsing about my ears. I took some time away from college, unable to face my fellow students, unsure if I would be subject to mockery or disdain. But shortly I was compelled to go because a letter came from the principal demanding my presence.

Professor Schwabe had never looked so thin and brittle. He wasn't alone this time. Two others flanked him, men of a similar age and hoariness. Governors, I supposed. Their presence boded ill, though I was slow to recognize this. I had thought I was merely in for a telling-off.

'You have put me in a most difficult position,' said the professor, using the well-worn catchphrase of the artists' model. 'Art schools generally have a certain rather unfortunate reputation, Mr Brill, and it is not one that we want to encourage. The board of governors, in particular, is keen to avoid the reputation of the Slade being brought into disrepute. To be brief, they have asked that you be expelled from the school. I don't take this decision lightly.'

For a few seconds I could barely breathe. I shook my head. 'But it was all a terrible misunderstanding, sir.'

'Mr Brill,' said one of the other people, 'we might have been willing to overlook what might seem to be a misunderstanding, as you call it, but the news that has been reported, that a group of our students and one of their tutors has been regularly visiting what the papers call a bordello for the purpose of extra-curricular study . . . Well, need we say any more? We are already a laughing stock. Soon the laughter will die away and a more serious form of censure take its place.'

There had been further reports in morning editions. The story wouldn't stop running. Journalists had been poking around the studios of the Slade itself, knocking on the professor's door. The presence of a tutor at these classes seemed to give the newspaper licence to assume the visits were approved of and indeed organized by the Slade itself. I was quite horrified at how my remarks had been so misinterpreted, and saw instantly that my position was hopeless. In fact, I was rather surprised that the professor and his colleagues were not all the more angry.

The man sitting to the right of Schwabe spoke from behind a white beard. 'Can you tell us, Mr Brill, which tutor it was who organized these visits to Old Compton Street? And which other students were involved?'

I opened and closed my mouth, fish-like, as I thought about how to reply.

'I can understand your unwillingness to provide us with that information,' said the professor, 'but I can promise you, Mr Brill, that you will be finding life difficult from now on. With your reputation and record you will find many doors closed in your face. However, we can do something to make those doors less firmly closed than would otherwise be the case. Perhaps we could provide you with references that make no mention of your misdemeanours. In return, that is, for information regarding your colleagues on these sordid expeditions.'

A bargain was being sought. A deal. I was shocked. My inno-cent endeavours to improve my drawing skills and understanding of the human form seemed shiningly noble in comparison to this grubby attempt at blackmail.

'We didn't go to the bordello for sex,' I exclaimed, my temper aroused. I noticed six pairs of eyes close in a suffering way at the mention of the word. 'We went there to improve our drawing skills. Because you had denied me access to the life rooms I had no alternative. Well, I suppose I could have employed a life model – but where would I have painted her? Brought her back to my aunt's house in Holloway? You haven't met my aunt but I can assure you it would have been quite impossible. Well, then, employing prostitutes for this platonic exercise meant not only that I had a model but a studio as well, and shared between four of us the cost was negligible – although their ponce did try to make us pay extra, claiming they could get through three or four clients in an hour on a good night, but that was simply untrue. In fact, they were making more than they would normally for an hour of doing nothing.'

'That's quite enough, Mr Brill,' the professor burst out. 'I don't give a damn what you went there for, and I certainly don't want to hear about the pecuniary arrangements. You've just made our task a little easier, in that I can now expel you from this school fully confident that I am acting fairly. I will have no further discussion on this subject and I expect you to leave immediately. If you are found on these premises again I will have you removed, by force, if necessary. Good day to you.'

*

After two or three days (which I spent in solitary contemplation of the galleries of London, weeping tearlessly before the Dutch masters and their scruffy landscapes) I went to Learmouth's. He opened the door to me wearing an expression of crushed euphoria. He hesitated when he saw me, then, rather begrudgingly, invited me in.

'We're having a little do,' he said, as he led me up the stairs, 'to celebrate the marriage of true minds.'

I could hear polite laughter coming from behind the closed dining-room door. We paused in the privacy of the passageway.

'I heard about what happened,' he said.

'Which bit?'

'All of it – your arrest, the fine . . .'

'Did you know I've been thrown out of the Slade?'

Learmouth looked genuinely surprised. 'Is that why you've been crying, Kenneth?'

I had not realized but my face must have been streaked with tears.

'Partly. My life has ended, Learmouth. The Slade has thrown me out. My aunt has given me a week's notice. I've got no-where to go but back to the mud of Heathrow, dragging my palette behind me. I'll have to give up on the whole idea of being an artist.'

'Why should such a thing prevent you being an artist? All it means is that you'll lack a piece of paper . . .'

'I just want to know what the hell happened that night.'

'You must believe me, Kenneth – it's a complete mystery. All we heard was a banging on the doors downstairs, and suddenly Viv was up off the floor and ushering us out through a window at the back of the kitchen. Knell, Somarco and I were scrabbling down a fire escape, knocking dustbins over, with policemen jumping out at us from every corner. I don't know how we got away, but we did, still with our sketchbooks under our arms.' He couldn't suppress a little laugh. 'It was all really quite thrilling.'

'Thrilling for you. But you didn't have to spend a night in the cells, or be brought up before the beak.'

'Oh, Brill, you're talking like one of them, like an underworld character. How wonderful. Think what it'll do for your artistic development. I almost envy you, Kenneth.'

'Well, if that's how you feel I'll pass your name on to the police, if you like, and you can have the same experience.'

Learmouth suddenly became serious, lowered his voice even more and removed us a little further down the passage, away from the dining room, from which the sound of polite laughter continued to trickle. 'Kenneth, did the professor say anything about – you know – who else was involved?'

'Yes, he certainly did. And he wanted names. Tried bargaining with me, said he'd give me good references if I told them who else was at the bordello.'

'And did you – did you tell him?'

I could see that Learmouth was absolutely petrified. He was blushing so much I thought he would begin sweating blood. I understood that I had a kind of power now. Disgrace for Learmouth was unthinkable – not only because of his stern, overpowering father, but because of his own ambitions within the art establishment. Learmouth saw a brilliant future for himself – perhaps as a Slade professor or something like that. He couldn't countenance the thought of falling out of favour with the authorities.

'No. Don't think of me as a saint, but his bargaining price was set too low. There would have been little advantage to me in revealing your name. Of course he was especially interested to know who the tutor was.'

Learmouth was humbled. He wanted to hug me with gratitude but could see that to express too much relief would only deepen the acknowledgement of his moral wrongness. Instead he ushered me into the dining room where I was confronted with a scene of post-nuptial celebration.

I had thought Learmouth was joking when he mentioned a marriage, but in fact he was being literal. A wedding tea had been laid out on the extending table that filled half of his dining room; an empty bottle of champagne chilled in a bucket of ice. This was the only item of extravagance in the whole spread, the rest of which consisted of scantily filled sandwiches. At first there was no indication that anyone had been married, apart from a single posy of pink roses that sagged in a pot of water by the kettle. And there seemed to be no females in the room, until one particularly severe-looking figure stirred, and coughed, revealing a feminine vocal structure in the sound. I was taken aback. This female, attired as a man, had had her greying hair cut short and sharp. She wore a black silk jacket, a man's shirt without a collar, black trousers and solid-looking shoes. She was smoking a French cigarette and eyed me indifferently through her steel-framed spectacles.

The little white dot of confetti that clung to her hair just above her left ear was almost comically inappropriate, like a July hailstone. The groom, a scholarly man in a crumpled dark suit, was lounging on the floor, his head propped against his wife's armchair, his knees raised and legs crossed extravagantly in front of him. He seemed intent on occupying as much space as possible.

For a newly married couple they seemed somewhat less than romantically preoccupied. I had interrupted a discussion on pacifism that resumed once they had acknowledged my arrival.

'The problem with pacifism, of course, is that it would entail a complete overhaul of the economic system. If a state were to adopt a pacifist stance it would also have to take over the distribution of capital and abolish private property. I don't mean there has to be a Communist revolution, but something like it, where the relationship between government, industry, religion, education and the philosophies of life are realigned.'

'It is not the destruction of material things that matters,' said another of the small number of guests in the room. 'The Germans could destroy every building in the country, but if the population remained intact, then they would have destroyed nothing. Our culture and our ideas would have survived, so long as there were minds to think them, remember them. And why should they destroy a population that offers no resistance?'

'Oh, you are a funny fellow, Bryce. Do you think your philosophes of life can exist without buildings? Do you think a population without shelter or food will have any thoughts beyond those of mere survival? A pacifist state can only work if there is nothing worth defending.'

'You have a very poor regard for the human imagination if you think it is so dependent on material comforts. I'm surprised at you, a poet. What about the ascetics? There are holy men in India who live on nothing but ashes and have higher thoughts than you or I are capable of.'

'Well, in that case I don't understand why you don't go home and set fire to your little library this minute. In the whole of the last war, around fifty tons of bombs were dropped on London. I read that the Luftwaffe is now capable of dropping that amount in a single night. Technology has now advanced so far as to make warfare incapable of anything but annihilation. There is no longer such a thing as a defensive war.'

'There you are, Brill,' said Learmouth. 'You don't have to worry about being thrown out of the Slade. In three years' time this city will be nothing but ashes, and our culture will have vanished.'

'You haven't introduced us properly to your friend,' said the lounging one, regarding me directly for the first time. 'Has he really been thrown out of the Slade? What for?'

'I'd rather not go into it at the moment, if you don't mind,' I said, sitting uncomfortably on one of the dining chairs.

'Well, I do hope it was for something outrageous. So tell us instead where you stand on this matter of pacifism. Do you subscribe to the pacifist league, like Mr Bryce here? Progress for Peace and all that?'

'I haven't really thought about it. I always hoped that people would just see sense before it got to the point of starting a war.'

This remark seemed to deaden the room for a few moments. I felt instantly ashamed of it, wishing I could somehow suck it back into my mouth.

'That is what is so lovely about artists. They are so ineffectual. I myself am in favour of the strategies adopted by the Tudors – marry your enemies. Form international alliances through marriage. It should be the duty of every Englishman now to go to Germany, woo the nearest Rhine maiden he can find, and marry her. Do you think the Luftwaffe would drop those fifty tons of bombs on London if they realized they were dropping them on their own daughters and grandchildren?'

'Good strategy. How many marriages do you think there would have to be before the Germans began to think of us as significantly part of their own families?'

'I love champagne but it makes my piss smell of rotten apples,' said the man called Bryce, who had just returned from the lavatory.

'Probably about twenty-five per cent of marriages should be Anglo-German . . .'

'I say, are you serious? You've actually thought out the per-centage?'

'Well, as a sort of thought experiment. I know it's never going to happen. But we should encourage it. That is why our marriage is so important and should be celebrated.'

'My race unfortunately means I don't count in your master-plan. I am only an incentive for Germany to drop more bombs on London, as long as I am here.'

This was the first time the bride had spoken, and by so doing revealed her strong German accent. It was only then that I realized this was the woman Learmouth had petitioned some of us to marry, to save her from repatriation, though she looked rather different now. Affronted and shocked as I then had been by Learmouth's assumptions about my sexual preferences, I suddenly felt all sorts of odd pangs of jealousy, regarding the lounging one as an arrogant usurper. Though I supposed he fitted all the criteria, including that he be a committed homosexual.

'This twenty-five-per-cent idea is nonsense. We should follow the medieval example more literally, and find an English maiden to woo and marry Hitler himself. Preferably a Jewish maiden.'

'Yes,' the German woman said. 'If such a thing were possible it would be the most ample testimony to the redemptive power of love. Imagine it, Hitler in love with a Jewess. The world would stop, and run backwards.'

I couldn't understand why I found this woman so attractive. The straight edge of her nose, the way it made me want to get out a pair of drumsticks and rap out a little tattoo on it, the pleasant curl of her sideburns; though they were no such thing, I couldn't help but see them as such. And I wondered about her body for which her masculine clothes gave no evidence. She was, it seemed, made perfectly for me.

'Well,' said the lounging one, lifting himself up, 'in the light of the approaching thermite and vesicants, we should make the most of our married life and go our separate ways.' The woman smiled sadly at this little joke.

'No honeymoon?' said Learmouth.

'Maybe we'll go on separate honeymoons. Goodbye, Mr Brill, so pleased to have met you. I expect Norman will tell me exactly what kind of immoral conduct you have been engaged in. I'm sure I would approve . . .'

When they were gone I turned to Learmouth. 'Why didn't you let me marry that woman?'

'I asked you, you declined.'

'But you didn't even introduce us. Now she's married to that awful man who has no intention of acting as husband . . .'

'Which is exactly how they both want it. I doubt they will even see each other again, unless it is to arrange a divorce. And, by the way, that awful man is one of our country's finest poets.'

'Well, pardon me for scorning a versifier. Besides, I could have done with the money now that I'm getting thrown out of my digs. I've got nowhere to go, Norman. Nowhere.'

Learmouth told me to sit down and stop pacing about the place because I was making him giddy. He made a fresh pot of tea and lit a curious scented stick, which filled the room with Catholic-smelling smoke. All this gave him time to think up some sort of solution, a plan that would avoid the necessity of my moving in with him.

'How soon do you have to leave your aunt's place?'

'End of the week. I have just a few days. I've got to find somewhere else to live. I've got to get my paintings out of the Slade. Dear old Bo's looking after them at the moment but sooner or later they'll be dumped. I don't know what I'm going to do.'

Learmouth was such a fixer, such a setter-up of things. I still felt my life was governed by him, for no other reason than that we had happened to bump into each other in Rowan and Black's that day.

He suggested I call on Somarco who, he happened to know, was soon going abroad for several weeks. He had a nice place in Chelsea with lots of space. Seeing as he was the responsible member of the group, and that he would be in deep trouble if it ever got out that he had been involved, Learmouth seemed to think he would have no choice but to agree to put me up. And if he was going abroad, he might even be glad of someone to stay at his place as a caretaker.

'But I can't just turn up on his doorstep, demand that he allows me the use of his home.'

'Well, why not? I'd let you stay here but I have my sister coming to stay with me tomorrow. And, besides, you said your-self how Schwabe was very keen to know which tutor it was who led you and me astray. If you let Somarco know how interested Schwabe would be in this information . . .'

'I see. You mean I should blackmail him.'

'No, I mean let it be known that he owes you a favour, after what has happened.'

VI

It is a curious thing to discover that someone has taken your paintings and made a map of them. It is almost as though a hand has reached down from the sky and plucked you from your foot-ing on the ground, hauled you up into the air before you've had a moment to think what is happening, then to look down and see the world you had previously viewed from eye-level stripped of its third dimension to become as flat as – a drawing. As I looked at those little maps, admiring their lines – a draughtsman had taken great care to get every detail of the land right – I was back in the de Havilland with Somarco, in free-fall with a ghost of vitriol suspended beside me. I was almost sick, looking at those maps.

But there were to be more exhibitions of my work. When I next entered the courtroom I was stunned to see that a verit-able retrospective of my paintings had been carefully mounted. Landscapes, male running nudes, still-lifes, allegorical scenes.

Mostly they were exhibited on chairs, which gave me the sense that my life's work was seated politely as an audience of itself. Up and down the rows of paintings the military men perambled stiffly, hands behind their backs or canes beneath their arms. If I half closed my eyes I could make the insignia and braidery of their uniforms disappear and imagine that these were ordinary men, civilians in civilian clothes, taking in the details of my works, discussing them in muttered and murmuring undertones, and I could imagine – entertain the fantasy – that I was a successful artist enjoying my first one-man show in a well-known and respected gallery. In all, I felt pleased. My art, for whatever reason, was being taken seriously, perhaps more seriously than art was taken for any other artist. My art was evidence.

After the paintings had been thoroughly and closely inspected, and everyone had returned to their seats, Cunningham held forth again.

'We are none of us, I believe, experts in the field of art appreciation, which is why I would like to call my next witness.'

A rather stormy little man was brought into the courtroom, a brow ploughed with parallel wrinkles, wispy black hair half covering his pale scalp; he wore a bright yellow bow-tie, a most incongruous item of apparel. He stated his name and profession.

'My name is Albert Wyre. I am professor of painting at the Royal Academy.'

'And you have been given time to examine the paintings that are on display in this courtroom?'

'I have.'

'And could you share with the court your assessment of the work?'

The professor gave an almost embarrassed chuckle, which led directly into speech. 'I would say they are the work of an accomplished amateur. I would say they are the work of an unformed artistic sensibility, someone who is either too young or too inexperienced as an artist to have found a viewpoint and vision with which to view the world. Some of the work is of a technically very high standard, some of it of a woefully dismal standard. There is an uncertainty about subject matter. The artist clearly cannot decide whether he is a landscape artist or a portraitist, whether he is a painter of still-lifes or of allegorical scenes. Likewise the styles are many and compete with each other. You can see a sort of old-fashioned, traditional realism that we might associate with the Victorian painters, alongside what I can only describe as modern art. In these he seems to have submitted himself to the foreign influences of the latest generation of men who call themselves artists, and who exert considerable influence on the Continent, less so here, and none at all at the Royal Academy, I can assure you.'

There was polite laughter around the courtroom.

Cunningham then pressed the professor to say a little more about the Continental influences.

'Well, I don't propose to be an expert in what goes on in the salons of Paris or Rome, but I believe that some of the works that you can observe to the left of that line over there are painted in the style of a movement I believe is called Futurism, which celebrates the energy and momentum of the modern age of machinery and automation. It also celebrates war and violence.'

The judge turned to the professor with renewed interest.

Davies stood up to raise an objection. 'Your Honour, the counsel for the defence fails to see the relevance of the accused's past artistic output.'

'We are simply trying to establish the accused's artistic credentials, Your Honour. This may help the jury form a judgement about the accused's motivations in painting the scenes for which he was arrested.'

'Continue,' said the judge. Cunningham then asked the professor if he could elaborate on the school of Futurism, since he was quite sure that there were few people in the courtroom who would have heard of it.

'Well, I can tell you what little I know. I don't much care for these so-called schools of modern art, as you might have gathered. Futurism, I believe, was a movement that was founded by a group of Italian artists before the Great War. After the war it became closely associated with Italian nationalism, and was naturally drawn towards Benito Mussolini's Fascist Party. The leader of Futurism, a fellow called Marinetti, is, I believe, a prominent member of the Italian Fascist Party.'

'Thank you, Professor Wyre.' There was a pause in proceedings while the professor left the witness stand. 'If Your Honour will allow me, I can expand a little on what our witness has said. I have undertaken a certain amount of research in this area, and there are some striking aspects of the accused's work that link him to the Futurist movement – most notably his interest in aircraft. As you know, the accused was arrested while painting an airfield. As a camouflage officer he has undertaken many flights in order to survey the land from an elevated perspective. The Futurist movement has placed great emphasis on the importance of the aeroplane in offering humanity a new viewpoint upon the world. If I can quote from what rather grandly titles itself as a manifesto for aeropainting . . .' Cunningham here produced a pamphlet and began reading aloud, ' "The changing perspectives of flight constitute an absolutely new reality that has nothing in common with the reality traditionally constituted by a terrestrial perspective—" '

Davies interrupted, 'Your Honour, the defence cannot accept that an interest in aeroplanes is proof of Fascist sympathies. My client grew up near an airfield. He has been interested in planes since he was a little boy.'

'Let the prosecution make its point. Continue.'

Cunningham smiled rather endearingly in my direction. 'I

have no doubt that Lieutenant Brill had an interest in planes as a child. He could hardly be called a normal little boy if he hadn't. However, he also has an interest in that new viewpoint upon the world, as described in the document I just quoted. In 1938 he took part in an exhibition called New Beginnings, which was a Futurist exhibition in all but name, curated by a man who was later trained as a pilot by the RAF. That man's name was and is Arturo Somarco, the accused's colleague in the Camouflage Corps, and prominent member of the Futurist movement. Indeed, he was a signed member of Marinetti's Fascist Futurist council as late as 1939, which he seems to have kept secret from all his friends and colleagues in this country. We will be glad to hear the accused's views on his close friend's involvement with this movement, when he is later cross-examined.'

*

Several other 'experts' were brought in to offer bleak appraisals of my work, all agreeing on its poor quality and on its suspiciously Continental influences. When it came to the defence's turn to call witnesses, only a single person could be found to offer a contrary view, and I was shocked, a little breathtaken, to see Captain Norman Learmouth enter the courtroom. He, too, had lost his desert complexion, far more so than when I had seen him in Oxfordshire. The English climate was far more suitable for his skin, which glowed white above the green serge of his uniform. I felt myself melting before this vision, though I had never before felt any physical attraction towards Learmouth. It was the presence of an ally that moved me so unexpectedly, after all the weeks and months of nothing but criticism and hostility. Learmouth arrived like an emissary from the lost continent of friendship.

He remained adamantly professional throughout the proceedings, barely glancing in my direction, let alone offering any sort of gesture of greeting or recognition. He was asked to give an account of his service thus far, and he gave a detailed summary of his work in camouflage, and more recently how he had been working in camouflage alongside a branch of military intelligence, but that he could, for security reasons, elaborate no further.

Once his credentials as an exemplary officer in the war had been established, he was asked the usual question about my artistic oeuvre.

'My opinion is that Kenneth Brill is one of the foremost painters of his generation. His career has been hindered by some personal difficulties, but he is still a young man, and I am sure, once this war is over, his name will become a prominent one among contemporary artists.'

When Cunningham had his turn he was scathing: 'Well, Heaven forfend that the war should interrupt the career of a young artist. In the meantime perhaps you could offer us an opinion on these particular works, the ones here. Would you call them more – what is the word that is used these days? – abstract?'

'No, I would not say they were abstract at all. They are figurative. It is just that the subject matter has been interpreted according to a certain way of seeing.'

'And could that "way of seeing" be described as Futurist?'

'No, I don't think so. Futurism tends to be more hard-edged – the shapes sharper, more clearly defined. If anything, I would call these works expressionist.'

Cunningham seemed to audibly groan. 'Another foreign movement. Would you care to tell us where the expressionist style of painting originated?'

Learmouth opened his mouth ready with the answer, but left it hanging open for a few seconds before saying, quietly, 'Well, Germany . . .' A ripple of disquiet passed around the courtroom before he continued, 'but the Germany of Hindenburg and Weimar. The Nazis were highly disapproving of this kind of art. They called it degenerate . . .'

'That is all very interesting, Captain Learmouth, but I think the jury should take note that the two principal schools of art identified as important influences on the accused happen to originate from within enemy territories of the Axis Alliance.'

Learmouth tried his best to give context to what he'd said, but the court had heard enough and he was asked to leave the witness stand. He gave me an apologetic glance as he left the courtroom, while I tried to let him see that he had done nothing wrong, that he couldn't be blamed for the blind stupidity of his interrogator.

VII

Arturo Somarco resided in long-haired Chelsea, a part of the capital I had not yet explored and which, when I arrived on top of a number 17 bus, cold and shivering like a refugee from some other city, seemed ominously different from the crowded parades and chophouses of my aunt Mary's Holloway backwater. It even seemed at a remove from the high-treed squares of Bloomsbury. It was both more moneyed and more bohemian. Down Cheyne Walk lords in top hats and tails emerged from limousines just as tattered composers strolled back from their smoking salons, sheaves of unfinished string quartets under their arms.

I walked the streets of the district with a feeling that at last I had discovered where everyone had been hiding, for it seemed that everyone of any importance in the arts, finance, politics lived down here. Everyone I saw, whether they were in brushed velvet or corduroy rags, seemed possessed of a supreme confidence and swagger. How appropriate that Somarco, who possessed those qualities in abundance, should live here. He had a wonderful pad on the banks of the Thames, down a backstreet from the King's Reach, with the newly built Battersea Power Station fresh and majestic in the distance across the river. One reached Somarco's place through a cobbled mews, then a flagstoned alleyway and several flights of steps, in and through other buildings until one came to a sort of rooftop garden, behind which a red front door marked the entrance to what Somarco called his *grande maisonette*. He greeted me with a singular lack of surprise, almost as though he'd been expecting me. When I saw a telephone in the hallway I imagined awkward, forewarning calls from Learmouth, and again I fell into a stew of resentful feelings, imagining myself pushed and pulled by powers more shrewd and expedient than I.

But my impulse to let fly upon Somarco a tirade of accusations and charges was dampened by the fact that he seemed to have emerged from what I could only think of at first as an indoor forest. The house seemed to contain trees fully foliate, palms and ferns, the sort that graced Kew. Somarco at that moment was holding a ceramic pot from which grew some sort of many-flowered shrub, the petals a shade of deep purply red, which made me think (I couldn't help it) of bullet wounds.

'Kenneth, what a pleasant surprise.'

He was wearing a loose silk dressing gown with a red paisley motif, and sandals that could barely contain his long, over-spilling feet.

'I hope you're happy now,' I said. It was a feeble parley. But it amused Somarco.

'Happy? Why, yes, I think I can say that is exactly what I am.

Whenever I'm allowed to spend time with my plants. It's the oxygen, you know.'

'What is?'

'The reason plants make you happy. They fill your house with oxygen. Do you have many plants in your house, Kenneth?'

'My aunt has an aspidistra,' I said sullenly. Then, as if waking myself out of a vegetative state, 'I don't understand you, Somarco.'

Somarco looked about himself, as if trying to see what was puzzling me. 'Oh – are you disconcerted by my foliage? Has no one ever mentioned to you that I am somewhat interested in the lives of plants? Come on, follow me round, I will give you a tour of my arboretum,' and I followed Somarco as he moved through his maisonette. The large, high, glass-ceilinged hallway gave on to a living room with a mezzanine reached by a spiral staircase. Plants of all sorts filled this space, which was lit by an array of skylights. Creeping plants climbed the pillars that supported the mezzanine, and entwined the banisters of the staircase, or trailed in viridian cascades from the balcony. Spiked things – cacti, succulents, agaves. The room was filled with an intense warmth that came from under-floor vents. 'I spent three years reading botany, Kenneth, following in my father's footsteps. He was a great Italian botanist, classified many of the plant forms in the Dolomites. My interest in art grew out of a desire to be a botanical illustrator.'

I found the interior gardens of Somarco's maisonette profoundly soothing. I was so charmed by the exotic greenery everywhere that I forgot my anger, and when I told Somarco about my double expulsion, from college and home, it was more as a lament than the fulmination I'd been planning. And I didn't need the leverage of threats to persuade Somarco to allow me the use of his flat. I didn't even mention the fact that the higher authorities at the Slade were demanding the names of those culpable in the Old Compton Street meetings before he offered me the accommodation. 'I am going away for three months, from next week, and I need someone to look after all this. I have already made arrangements for someone to care for my plants, but they can easily be changed. The person who stays here must be good with plants. Are you good with plants, Kenneth?'

'I think so. I grew up surrounded by gardens.'

'On which you grew things?'

'Sometimes. I've got manure in my veins, you might say.'

'Well – there are many different types of plant here, some tropical, some alpine, many with very strict requirements. You will need to use my special liquid fertilizer – I will show you. And I will have to draw up a timetable. Some plants need to be fed twice a week, others once a fortnight. Get them the wrong way round and they will both perish. This plant needs its leaves moistened once a day. It lives normally in the rainforest, which is why the paraffin heaters have to be on all the time. They get through a gallon of fuel in a week so you have to replenish regularly. That means carrying a can to the garage on the King's Road. This one must not be watered from above – you need to sit it in a saucer of warm water once a week. This one must not be watered. I water it only once a year. This one is due to flower in a couple of weeks. As soon as the flowers are finished you must pick them off. I would like you to take a photograph when it blooms. I will write it all down for you.'

*

When I got back to Aunt Mary's later that day I slunk into the house as quietly and guiltily as their fat ginger tom, and huddled myself in my room, only to discover that there was a letter from my mother on the bed. Struck cold with dread at the thought of having to tell her about my expulsion, I couldn't bring myself to open it, not till the following day. This was unfortunate because it contained the news that she would be visiting London tomorrow and would 'call in on me' at my college.

> *You will think I am barmy but I so much want to see you and to see the wonderful paintings you have been telling me about, and I miss London so much that I can wait no longer. Mr Morris has offered to drive me to Feltham and I will take a train from there. I trust you will be at the college? I would rather meet you there; I don't want to come out to Holloway Road, and I doubt if my sister will be keen to have me at her house.*

She then went on to mention the train she was intending to catch. She said she would get a taxi from Paddington. What was she thinking? That she could just swan into a school of the University of London to take tea with her son and the professor without making an appointment? I now recalled the letters that had preceded this one, and the long-term intention she'd had of visiting me when the time was right. I had assumed I would have many weeks in which to think how best to frame the news of my expulsion to my parents. Now I was faced with the need for instant confession and explanation. But more horrible was the thought that my mother would hear the news first from the school itself, and that she would receive the full, unedited version of my crisis, including my court appearance, news of which I didn't believe had so far spread beyond the London newspapers.

I therefore saw my first duty as the interception of my mother before she reached the Slade, and on my way think how to explain my crisis.

*

It all went rather horribly wrong. My bus was delayed by heavy traffic on Oxford Street. I tried the tube at Oxford Circus, but there were delays there as well. I stumbled into Paddington a full ten minutes after my mother's train had arrived with infuriating punctuality. I quickly searched the bookstalls and coffee shops but, no, it appeared she had hopped straight into a taxi and was probably already halfway across the West End. My last hope was that a return journey on the tube would overtake any traffic-bound hackney carriage, but there were more delays on the eastbound line. From Euston Square I sprinted down Gower Street and was just in time to meet my mother at the entrance to the Slade courtyard.

'Kenneth, you look as if you've been running.'

'I tried to meet you at the station but I was held up. I didn't get your letter until this morning. I didn't think you'd find your way here so quickly.'

She kissed me on both cheeks, something she hadn't done since I was a little child. 'It wasn't difficult. I simply asked the taxi driver to take me to the most famous art school in the world. Unfortunately he dropped me at the Royal Academy, but from there it was just a short hop in another taxi. Kenneth – you're such a horrible colour . . .'

I could have said the same for her. Oh, the poor thing, she was wearing the most ghastly parodies of up-to-the-minute fashion, purchased, no doubt, during one of her manic shopping expeditions to Hounslow or Slough. She had on a sort of bonnet that wouldn't have looked out of place on Little Bo Peep, and a long dress with puffed shoulders, a little tweed roué jacket, spiked heels and a parasol. When I had been in the company of women who wore such daringly modern clothes, my mother was nothing short of an embarrassment.

'As I said, I've been running.'

'You've run all the way from Paddington?'

'Mother, you haven't been in there yet, have you?'

'To your school? No. It does look impressive. Can you show me your paintings?'

I began steering my mother gently away from the school entrance and towards the Euston Road. 'It wouldn't really be convenient at the moment – perhaps later. Why don't we go somewhere and talk?'

'Well, as long as we'll have time. I have to catch a train at six o'clock. And I want to see some of the sights. Where are we going?'

I didn't know. 'How about a tea room somewhere? Or there is quite a nice coffee shop not far from here.'

My mother turned to me, her face bright and silly as she held both my hands, as if we were about to sing 'Ring a Ring o' Roses', and burst out, 'I would love to go to a pub.'

'A pub?' I was shocked. As far as I knew my mother had never visited a pub in her life.

'Well, why not? I believe there are some that allow women. And from what I've heard, you must be quite an expert on them.'

What had she heard? She couldn't have heard anything – or had she read the newspaper reports, and was withholding the fact, teasing me for my ignorance? When I looked at her quizzically she gave me the girlish face again, eyes twinkling, as she skipped along in a manner I thought a little too frisky.

We went to the Grapes, one of the more congenial establishments on the Euston Road. Bravely as she tried to seem at ease, I could see she was uncomfortable. She looked furtively around, her gaze settling on a languorous copper nude entwined around a lampstand at the far end of the bar. The chaste nymph was something I had always regarded as a paragon of ugliness, with her cupreous callipygian rump, so regularly caressed by the drunkards of eleven o'clock that her buttocks were noticeably brighter than the rest of her body.

I tried distracting my mother by asking about home and the Heath. She obliged by telling me how well my father was doing with his new sludgecake business, how things had been smoothed out between our family and the Joys. 'Do you know, as soon as I got off the train at Paddington I could smell your father's cabbages, even from there? It's even stronger now, with Covent Garden so nearby – it is nearby, isn't it? Do you ever go there?'

I had to confess I had not once been to the market since moving to London.

'Oh, Kenneth, I'm a little bit disappointed. Have you shunned your past so thoroughly?'

'No, not at all, Mother, but do you think a young art student has time to go shopping for cabbages? Even if they are his father's.'

'Well, I didn't think art students were such busy people.' My mother took a long draught of her dry sherry, nearly finishing it in one go. I looked on in mild shock, waiting for the shuddering response of someone not used to alcohol, but it never came. 'And I'd have thought you'd like to keep in touch with the people there. You are such a poor letter-writer, Kenneth. You've been quite neglectful of your family.'

It was during this visit that my mother expanded on my father's past as a music-hall entertainer, and on the tragedy of little Miller. The stories took up so much time that we had each had several drinks by then, and the atmosphere had lightened between us in such a way that I was beginning to feel I had no real worries: if I could get my mother drunk enough on sherry I could send her home on the train from Paddington and she would have forgotten all about her intentions of visiting my college. However, things changed again when she took a letter out of her handbag.

'Do you know, Kenneth? I'd almost forgotten why I came to London in the first place. Now what is all this about you and a house full of prostitutes?'

'Mother!'

'But is it true, Kenneth? Can it really be true?'

317

'I don't know what you mean, Mother.'

'Oh, well, it's all in this letter. I was rather surprised to get a letter from Mary. Naturally when I saw the handwriting on the envelope and the postmark I thought she was writing to tell me some awful news about you. And she was – but not quite what I was expecting. She said her husband could not stand to have you about the house any more, and then she said that it was because you had been arrested by the police and that you'd been running a sort of artists' brothel in Soho . . .'

She had the letter out of its envelope and was referring to it and quoting from it as she spoke. I tried to read it as well, craning my neck to get a look, but my mother held it apart.

'That's just a lot of gossip, Mother, a big misunderstanding. Nothing of the sort happened in Soho. Just a lot of rumour and innuendo.'

'That's what I was hoping, but unfortunately she enclosed a cutting from the *Illustrated London News* – look – quite a long article, mentions your full name several times. I must say I was a little bit thrilled to find that my son had made his name in the national press, but of course I would have liked it to be for more savoury reasons. And your uncle is not the sort of man who would take kindly to someone conducting himself as you have done. He's an odd fellow, they both are. But I'm not surprised that they decided to evict you.'

'She's told you that? Of course I was going to tell you my-self . . .'

'Were you, Kenneth? And would you have told me that you had been thrown out of the Slade too? Yes, no need to look so shocked. I had a letter from them as well. It only arrived this morning.'

I was suddenly indignant. 'Look here, you've known this all along and you didn't say anything?

My mother, as if not hearing me, suddenly stood up and,

rather swayingly, walked over to the upright piano that stood in a corner of the bar, a dusty, beer-stained instrument with a snapped music rest. 'Mother!' I hissed, but she had already settled herself there and had run through a speculative series of chords, ending with a trill at the very top of the keyboard. She then played a languorous waltz, leaning back as she played so that she was almost facing the ceiling. Old men with oily moustaches looked up from their tankards with a sort of grudging approval, and a bickering argument that had been smouldering in some far corner of the pub for most of the time we'd been in there seemed to melt away. She called me over to the piano, but only to ask me to get another round of drinks. When I asked her if she really believed that was a good idea, she said I'd been living with my aunt Mary for too long.

So we drank until closing time, and a little bit after, thanks to the generosity of the landlord, who insisted, by then, that my mother return at half-past five to continue her musical extemporizing, for she had begun taking requests and had, in a short time, attracted a considerable crowd into the bar, tripling the pub's usual takings for the afternoon.

By now my mother was a woman I had not met before. She had long since removed her bonnet and one half of her hair had collapsed, but in a rather charming way. She walked with the over-confidence of the inebriated, refusing my guidance and veering dangerously.

'Your father wants you to come back to the Heath. He made it my mission that I should bring you home. Ridiculous man. He still thinks you would want to dig furrows for him. And I was afraid you would think you had no choice, but I am sure, Kenneth, that if we went in there and reasoned with them . . .'

'What?' I said, gripping my mother's soft elbow. 'You mean go back to the Slade?'

'Yes. I'm sure they can be made to see reason.'

'No, Mother, we can't go back there. It won't work.'

'You see, they can hardly hold themselves up as paragons of morality if one of their tutors is organizing trips to a local brothel, like the paper said. It should be the tutor who is thrown out, not the student. It stands to reason.'

'Mother, it's not as simple as that. You see . . .'

But she could not be held back, and threatened to scream at the top of her voice if I stood in her way. Since I was sure she would do this, and since the last thing I wanted was more involvement with the police, I allowed her passage down Gower Street.

'My blood is boiling, Kenneth. When I think how long it took me to save the money to put you through a good education . . . Oh, I'm so angry. You must give me the name of this tutor.'

'Listen, Mother. You can't go in there and start accusing people.'

'Oh, why am I wasting my time talking to you? I should go straight to the office of the headmaster, or whatever he's called.'

I made further attempts to divert her from her course of action, but she had a drunkard's determination to see a thing through. I spent most of our journey down Gower Street walking backwards in front of my mother, pleading with her not to make a fool of herself, but it was useless. By the time we reached the gates, she brushed past me, and I left her to it.

I heard later from Learmouth and Somarco what had happened. They were in the life room, quietly engrossed in rendering the reclining nudity of Hector, the model I had first seen and whose powerful physique had had such an unfortunate effect on my metabolism. Propped up on an elbow, his other arm resting on the apex of his raised knee, he looked like a very noble Roman, Learmouth said. 'And then in walked this extraordinary vision, a picture of indignation and contempt, all wrapped up in the figure of a woman in her most bizarre heels and jacket, a parasol most incongruously on her elbow. The amusing thing is that she seemed to have entered the type of room in which one does not expect to see a naked man sitting. She came in with the stomping determination of someone who intends to make a complaint in a department store. She looked at us all, the students arranged in their circle, trying, one supposes, to pick out the tutor, when her eyes fell on the naked repose of Hector. I would not have previously believed that a woman's eyes could pop out of her head, but they very nearly did. There was utter silence for a full ten seconds, before she picked up a piece of drapery that was bunched on the dais, and threw it over poor Hector, covering him completely, like a parrot that has been put to bed for the night. And the funniest thing was, you know, Hector was so deep into the meditative state he achieves when he is posing for us that he did nothing in reaction, but just continued holding the pose, even though he was completely invisible, except as a vague, lumpy outline beneath the brown hessian. Well, this delightful woman didn't know what to do after that, and instead just bellowed at the room in general – "You'll be better off, all of you, if you follow my son's footsteps and quit this place for good." And then she clumped out with the same shop-complainer's bluster as she'd entered.'

VIII

Lucy, the sweet little thing, offered to put me up in Old Compton Street – 'Just till you get yourself sorted out, like.' And I would have agreed, had it not been for certain forebodings concerning my mother and the reputation I now had to work so hard to restore. If she was to learn that I had become a tenant in a house of sin, co-habitant of common London prostitutes, well, I could hardly imagine how it might have affected her. Learmouth, too, was very concerned about my continuing friendship with Lucy.

'We should cut off all contact with those women, Kenneth. None of us should be seen within a mile of Old Compton Street.'

'Speak for yourself, Norman. I no longer have a reputation that can be damaged.'

I was half minded to move in with Lucy just to put the wind into Learmouth's flannel turn-ups. Instead Somarco came good on his promise to let me stay in his maisonette while he was abroad. So, after some days spent sleeping as a rather unwelcome guest on various couches and floors around London, I returned to Chelsea, this time with two suitcases in my hands.

'Learmouth will bring my paintings over in a few days' time – he knows a chap with a car,' I said, putting down my suitcases in the tropical hall of Somarco's luscious quarters.

'I hope you will do many more while you are here, my little expelled friend,' said Somarco, who showed me, for the first time, his studio, which was at the top of the house behind the room with the mezzanine. It was a glass-roofed terrace that actually jutted out over the river, and had the most glorious views across the Thames to the trees of Battersea.

Somarco's work was, of course, evident everywhere. I had seen very little of it until now. It was like a survey of modernist schools – there was cubism and Fauvism, Futurism and abstraction, and then the succulent Georgia O'Keeffe realism of his botanical paintings. When questioned about this range of styles, Somarco said they represented different stages of his career, though he wouldn't say much about the present stage.

*

Somarco left London the next day, with very little by way of farewell. He provided me with a breakfast of toast and a boiled egg, and by the time I had emerged in my dressing gown to eat it, he was fully dressed and packed and waiting for a taxi to take him to Victoria.

'Are you going to tell me where you are going?' I said.

'Why should I? Are you my mother?'

I was too tired to muster a reply.

'There. I have written a list of instructions regarding the plants. Please don't forget my African snails. They need wiping with a damp cloth three times a day. Do not feed any cheese to the cheese plant. The acanthus will need some ash mixed into its soil in about three weeks.'

'You went through all this the other night, Somarco.'

'Yes, well, there's the taxi.'

Before he left, he kissed me on the cheek.

*

I felt like an artist who had eaten his own still-life, though without the benefit of satiety. I had eaten the still-life, but there was nothing to compensate for it. Instead there was an empty table, a fruit bowl full of apple cores and orange peel, an empty wine bottle, an empty wine glass. I had a sense of hunger that seemed fugitive and unfixed – sometimes it was in my guts, and sometimes my heart. Sometimes the hunger travelled up into my head, and I felt nothing but hollowness there, a cradled blackness that grew bigger the more it was fed.

I intended to use my time in Somarco's flat productively. Still stinging from my expulsion, I wanted to demonstrate that I didn't need the Slade. In fact, I liked to think that I had simply graduated ahead of time. I was now an artist, while my former colleagues were merely students of the subject. I sensed my friends felt the same way. I had moved into the real world and I was determined to show that I could earn my living as a painter.

But I had eaten my still-life. I had no subject. Nothing I could paint about. The world I had entered was too huge and varied for me to understand, and I longed for the guidance of a curriculum, for the directing hand of a tutor, for a life room.

I made visits to galleries to get an idea of the kind of work that was selling. A dreary realism seemed to prevail. There were pictures of shabby London streets, dowdy music halls, gloomy, gas-lit living rooms. I decided I could specialize in such subject matter without too much trouble, and in a fortnight had amassed some suitably murky watercolours, which I eagerly presented to a gallery near Bond Street. The woman in there peered at them coldly through chained spectacles.

'Why would anyone think the back end of a bus a worthy subject for painting?'

'It's rather sad what young people today consider picturesque,' said her colleague.

'Absolutely astonishing. Look at this. Rooftops, chimney pots. All we need is a washing line and we can start singing "Knees Up, Mother Brown" . . .'

They were so pleased with themselves after making these comments that they were still chuckling quietly as I left the gallery.

I tried other galleries, and met with similar responses. Hawking my portfolio around, I began to feel closer to my father's profession than the artist's, and wished I had his talent for salesmanship, that I had inherited the quick wit and the playful, friendly patter. I began to wonder if good salesmanship is founded on a profound love of humanity.

I soon gave up the idea of trying to paint what I thought the galleries wanted. Instead I began working on a series of studies for what I envisaged would be a very large work. I wanted to paint a running male nude.

My first problem was lack of an available model, but I soon realized there was quite a simple solution to that problem: I could be my own model. The thought thrilled me. There was a good mirror in Somarco's flat – a cheval glass, about three feet long, and hinged in the middle to a frame so that it could swivel back and forth. I arranged things carefully, chose the best spot for the light, then regarded myself, fully clothed at first. It was as though I had suddenly magicked a stranger into the room. I had never seen myself so clearly and squarely before. I must have spent half an hour just staring at my clothed form, thinking that I was not such a bad-looking fellow, still very much a young man then with a young man's emptiness of physical form, yet to fill out. The clothes hung loose on me, any looser and they would be of a scarecrow looseness, and I was pleased that I seemed to choose clothes with plain, simple lines; everything seemed to hang and crease at just the right point.

So, the moment came when I bared myself to myself. Untying my tie, unbuttoning my shirt – gosh, I was so thin: I was ninety per cent air, it seemed. Then, off with the vest and, yes, myself naked as a chess piece, and as still. I did some drawings, marvelling at the dismal, pinhead smallness of my nipples, though I could trace a pleasingly cruciform shape in my anatomy, the vertical line that follows from the Adam's apple down to the navel, and even lower to the two-for-one symmetry of the genitalia.

I did many drawings, experimenting with different poses. Sometimes I would achieve an aphoristic mood and blurt out little chunks of meaning that I would write in the corner of my sketchbook so that their wisdom would be preserved – some examples:

Man is an emperor in a palace of meat.
Behold, above the equator, it all comes together.
No two faces are the same, yet a thousand bodies
may be identical.

I considered myself in relation to all the nudes I had seen in my life, and it was a peculiar thought but until that moment I hadn't been aware of the common property we share: the body. We all have one, and unless there are mutations, then they are closely enough identical in everything but the face. The anatomists must be in a constant state of amazement to find, for instance, in the complex river network of the lymphatic system, every little curl of a capillary has its twin in every other body, every vein is repeated a billion times throughout the human species. I became, if you like, species conscious. I possessed the equipage that identified me as a human. A feeling that both excited and dismayed me. Dismayed because it made me think, where is the individuality if we are replicated down to so many details? Anatomical awareness puts you in mind of a production line: the mould is turning out the same bodies again and again and again . . .

And what did I learn about Somarco in my time as a resident of his wonderful, frond-rich and leaf-dappled flat? That he might have been born to live in a jungle, perhaps, and that he was a great admirer of the British royal family. In one glass cabinet I found an Edward VII dessert service, nine pieces in Paragon china, which I occasionally used for the drinking of his Spanish liqueurs. That he had an exceptionally sweet tooth – in his larder I found several tins of molasses whose lids bore my friend's fingerprints: he was evidently in the habit of finger-dipping the succulent treacles and was clumsy with excitement when he did so. That he was a voracious reader of current affairs: his book-shelves contained more on this subject than they did on both art and botany, though I enjoyed lingering over his volumes on Brueghel, Leonardo, Uccello, with their large monochrome plates. I was less interested in articles such as 'What we can learn about colonial administration from Italian East Africa'. Or 'The crisis in the German Church. Now that blood is replacing religion as the driving and binding force in modern Germany, what is the role of the clergy?' What an intriguing question, and one about which, at the time, I couldn't have cared less. But I learnt more, in reading Somarco's library, about the international situation than I had ever learnt anywhere else. One article in the *National Review*, which someone had starred with a red pencil, proposed a triple alliance between Germany, Britain and the United States. Many articles I read dwelt on the importance of building up good food reserves, and feared that Britain would starve in a future war with Germany. Well, one could hardly move without hearing such sentiments echoed. I persisted with my Orpheus school of thinking, that the artists could best prevent war by ensuring that human beings could see each other clearly and steadily (yes, I hear my future self reply, 'See them clearly and steadily, so they can get a good shot at them!'), see them whole and complete, see them as people with hearts and minds and feelings and emotions. I wonder, then, what I was doing with my self-portraits, because the more I drew myself naked, the less personal I became. I might as well have been drawing a landscape, for all I was seeing in my nude body was a vista of shapes, and forms. Nevertheless, by the time Somarco returned, I had filled his studio with drawings of myself in the nude, in many different poses, some of them approximating a run.

Somarco sent me postcards now and then, mostly reminding me to care for his trailing fuchsias and to feed them with bone meal and phosphorus. The postmarks were of various European locales, from his Piedmontese homeland, reminding me how proud his people were to have driven Napoleon out of their lands, to Austria and Germany. He sent a card informing me he was on a shooting trip in the Bavarian Alps, and that he had come across several rare species of orchid.

Even though he was absent by many hundreds of miles, I was finding Somarco's presence a little hard to live with. I felt as though I was trapped in his life. His influence entwined me as much as the convoluted necks and stalks of his plants. And in the studio there was, of course, his work to contend with – the blurred Futurist concatenations, the constructivist squares and rectangles, the cubist still-lifes, Fauvist animals, the rigid social realism. During my sojourn in his maisonette I was particularly drawn to his paintings of botanical subjects – romantic, sumptuous flowerscapes, where the petals grew into gigantic structures, the stamens and pistils became rampant throat-dwellers, seed-bearing pods that had the hand-grenade look of barely contained potential energy.

In the end I had no alternative but to hide Somarco's work. I took down any of his paintings that were on the walls. Those that were propped against the sides of the studio I turned round. Only then was I able to get into a truly free rhythm of creative activity, and I began to replace the work of my absent friend with my own. My nude self-portraits, mostly done on paper, in charcoal, chalk, gouache and watercolour, now hung from the walls. I drew myself from every angle, sometimes peering intently over my shoulder to draw my own spine, my buttocks, the pallid backs of my legs. Or I would strike a complicated pose with legs and arms thrust out, torso twisted, which I would have to redo every time I stepped back from my drawing board and returned to the mirror. The mirror-self became almost like a companion, lit in odd ways from the skylights, bestowing peculiar colours that were the double reflections from the river off low-cast clouds – sometimes my skin would be a sickly yellow, at others a radiant gold. Blues and purples would sometimes drop down from above and adorn my paps, or my skin would be sewn all over with green sequins.

I realized the only way to capture my body in motion was to sprint across the studio and take in as much as I could of my naked image as it dashed past the mirror. It was little more than a flash of flesh in the cheval glass, a blur of pale yellow and white, but it was enough to give me a sense of angle and momentum, and to try to capture these on paper. I had a sense of the movement of limbs, of the movement of genitals, the back and forth and up and down trajectory of my cock, the brief flight at the moment when both feet were off the floor. I became very interested in the movements my body was capable of, and I recalled my dancing days with Henry, and attempted to capture that movement as well. I had a rather extraordinary time, drawing myself while dancing. I could do that quite easily, executing a little solo tango before the mirror and drawing it as I did so. Sometimes with a bottle of sherry I could pass a very pleasant session with my paints in this way.

It was characteristic of Somarco that he should enter the room quietly, making as if to surprise me. When he returned he did just this, walking with a cat-light tread up the stairs, placing his suitcase with silent delicacy upon the floor, then coming right up to me and placing his freezing hands on my buttocks. I cried out, nearly fell over in shock and, hardly looking at Somarco, ran to the bedroom and closed the door behind me.

'What's the matter, little Kenneth?' he called, through the door. 'Don't hide yourself away. You can't think what a pleasant homecoming gift it is to have a naked man in my *grande maisonette*.'

I opened the door, once I had covered myself with a sheet. Somarco's face fell a little as he saw how I had concealed myself.

'I left my clothes in the studio,' I said, hurrying over to them.

I took them back to the bedroom to get properly dressed. Somarco followed me closely all the way.

'And these drawings, Kenneth. They have such vigour and *joie de vivre* I could eat them.'

'They're just attempts at doing something . . .'

'And they do it so well.'

I was dressed now, and emerged from the bedroom, red-faced and wild-haired, as I could tell from the mirror. I realized I had not spoken a single word in over a week, apart from the briefest of exchanges with shopkeepers. I wondered if, in that time, my voice would actually die, and was rather surprised when, at the lightest request, it sprang into life again. 'Thank you, Somarco.'

'You must keep doing these, Kenneth. As your former tutor and current mentor, I command you to do so. Now, in absence of rent, I expect you to be my slave. Will you make me some of this German coffee?'

He pulled a tin from his bag and shook it. The soft sift of ground coffee gave a little samba. I took the tin. I didn't understand coffee, I had never made any, and treated it like tea, putting some in a pot and then covering it with boiling water. The room smelt of warm gas.

'Did you have a good . . .' what was it? '. . . holiday? Tour? Journey? Voyage? Mission?'

'I had a most wonderful journey. Ah, you got my cards.' He saw the little row of sepia prints with their dainty cursive labels in white ink (which I loved) that charted his progress north from Italy.

'My main purpose was in collecting seeds. It is not a good time of year, of course, though some plants are producing seeds in early summer, and there are others that still bear seed pods from last season. I have enough specimens to keep me occupied.' He delved into a knapsack and extracted a stack of German tobacco tins, including one called Constantin Kaiserpreis, the lid showing a German officer languidly smoking in front of a fleet of battleships, though mostly they were rather peaceable-looking containers. Not like the tobacco of a nation hell bent on conquering Europe, I remarked to Somarco, who only smiled lazily in reply, as he began opening his carefully labelled tins to display their contents. They were filled with kernels, nuts and pips of all sizes and colours, from dust particles to conker-sized things. (In fact they were conkers, German conkers.)

'The nations of Europe may be in crisis over their borders, but the plant kingdom has never known such restraints – trees and flowers march without hindrance from country to country, and no one proposes pacts or treaties, or declares war on the forests of oak and ash.'

'Wasn't it a rather strange thing to go to Germany? We may be at war with her before long. What do the Germans think of us? Did they say?'

'Everyone was very friendly. It was a most enlightening trip. I see it as my role to encourage as much interchange as possible between our two nations, so that it will be that much harder to go to war, if ever that situation seems likely. There should be whole missions going from our schools and universities. There should be exchanges between factory workers.'

'Yes. I suppose the trouble with that is, if any of the workers were Jews, they wouldn't be allowed in.'

'No, and of course the ideology falls down at that point. The problem with racial purity is that there is no such thing, only national purity.'

I looked at Somarco with alarm, as if several disparate elements had fallen into place to create an image of sudden unsavouriness.

'Somarco,' I said, 'you're not some sort of – you know. I mean, you're not actually in favour of the Nazis, are you?'

Somarco laughed so sweetly it was almost an answer in itself, but he backed it up. 'Dear little Kenny, just because I have brought some German chestnuts home with me? No, I am not a believer in Nazism. I am a believer in a natural order. Our politics should come from the natural world. The Nazis believe this too, at root, but they are going about the realization of this new order in the wrong way. They are trying to engineer a natural order, when in reality they should let it simply emerge. By engineering it, you create suffering. You cause conflict and war. If, for instance, they want to get rid of the Jews, they should simply introduce a procreation law, forbidding Jews to mate with each other. Such a law would extinguish the Jewish race within a few generations. And no one would have suffered. The Jewish identity would simply have been swallowed and subsumed by the stronger race.'

'That sounds like engineering, just as much as what the Nazis are doing now by expelling everyone or putting them in camps.'

'But the Jews could go on living with all their freedoms and rights, as long as they marry out of their own kind. There will be some heartbreak, of course, but there will be as much unexpected love. Do you think that when you graft a red rose onto a white bush it cries for the loss of its red companions?'

'Plants don't have feelings, Somarco. They can't cry about anything.'

'Oh, Kenny, how can you say that when you have been living in my *grande maisonette* for so long? Have you not heard the voice of the agave?'

'It's cruelty, Somarco. Your scheme would be cruel, inhuman.'

'What? Compared to the alternative? You would rather bombs and bullets and gas? I am talking about love as an instrument of politics. Marriage as the vehicle for invasion. There would be nothing inhuman about an invasion that consisted of the relentless courting and seduction of a population's women-folk over the generations. That is the difference, Kenny. Time. If we see the world from plant time, where hours last for weeks and weeks for years, then a battle should take centuries, an invasion millennia, and consist of nothing but seduction, lovemaking, childbirth and child-rearing in a loving family, until one popula-tion has replaced another. The end result is the same, the means of getting there very different.'

*

I felt distinctly awkward after Somarco's return. Knowing that I had nowhere else to go he insisted I stayed on – 'We can't have you sleeping in the streets now, can we, Kenneth?' But I felt out of place. He wanted me to share his narrow bed, but I insisted on sleeping on the couch. 'How very English of you,' he would say, kissing me on the cheek, which I thought excusable given his Latin provenance, but the awkwardness persisted. He began lav-ishing gifts upon me, mostly of a comestible variety – silly little chocolates and daintily wrapped packets of sweets from Fortnum & Mason. He was treating me like a concubine or catamite, I now see, though at that time I was far too innocent to suspect any-thing. We would spend evenings drinking very splendid red wines and nibbling chocolates so dark they were almost black. He spoke of how he would help me forward in my career, that he felt a sense of obligation after what had happened at the Slade. He said he would take me to a lunch of lobster thermidor with the director of his gallery, that he would get me into his Pall Mall club and give me afternoon tea with his dealer.

I was thrilled at the same time as feeling rather cautious about Somarco's schemes. He was clearly trying to impress me and going far beyond the call of duty in making reparations for the damage that had been done to my career, but I failed to see the true ambition of his scheming. I failed to see it right up to, and a little after, the moment I woke up in the small hours of the night to find the half-Italian kneeling naked beside my makeshift bed, bent down at the task of swallowing my prick.

Climbing ladders of wakefulness I was suddenly perilous on the vertiginous tip. I exclaimed, 'Jesus,' or some such profanity, and felt my cock withdraw from his lips with an audible *schlepp*, and a gagging response from Somarco's throat that sent him into a fit of coughing. My cock felt as damp and cold as a pulled whelk. I clutched the blanket to my body, like Diana at her bath, and nursed my sucked member.

In my naivety I had no idea that I had just taken part (though not consciously) in a sexual act. I could only understand Somarco's behaviour in terms of madness, and even then I was left with questions. Perhaps he had been sleepwalking and had imagined that I was some sort of food, or perhaps I had suffered a terrible medical collapse and he was performing a little-known first-aid procedure, restoring life to my body by blowing down the urethretic passages. You can think me ridiculous if you like, but there were other obstacles, internal walls, of which I still have only a vague understanding, that prevented me from achieving a clear perception of my situation. The trouble was, I had an awareness that at some level, far below the conscious one, my mind had responded favourably to the act.

For a moment I was speechless, as if Somarco had sucked all the language out of me. There was a full moon and the light on the landing was on. I could see Somarco, his face loose with passion, his lips wet, a long string hanging from his chin, sitting on his haunches.

'Kenneth,' he said, 'don't be stupid.'

'What are you doing? What's wrong with you?'

'Nothing's wrong with me. You were crying out in your sleep. Moaning. It was hurting you. Why are you getting so upset?'

In a moment he had asserted his presence and was on to my body again. He found a patch of my midriff and kissed it. The kiss interpreted the earlier act for me. Now I knew what was happening, that I was being made love to. He kissed again, short sharp ones, like a pecking finch. He located a nipple, licked it. I was aroused a little but pushed the feelings away, refusing to accept I had any interest in this kind of love. I tried telling Somarco, as his face reached mine, but he swallowed my words and filled my mouth with his. 'Don't try and pretend you like women . . .' I let Somarco kiss me as punctuation, licking me in commas and colons '. . . your drawings of the brothel displayed no passionate interest in the female form, yet you fainted twice at the sight of a naked man. Why did you faint? Because the blood was rushing to your groin to swell it, but you diverted it through your inner repressiveness, thus flooding your heart and depriving your brain.' I was not revolted by the half-Italian's kisses, his spittle was sweetness in my mouth, but still the urge to resist what I felt to be a profound wrongness was too strong and I pushed him back.

'No, Somarco, stop it,' I said, in the voice I used to talk to dogs. Somarco laughed. I stood up from the couch. Somarco stood up as well, his nudity unfolded itself before my eyes. 'Here – have a look. A naked man. You feel faint? You feel your head swimming?'

I tried not to look at his body because I was afraid that I would indeed find it irresistibly beautiful.

'I am glad that you are still conscious. Are you feeling nauseous at all? Look at me, Kenneth. Look at me.'

I had my back to him and was struggling to button the fly of the trousers I had just pulled on. I turned to look. Somarco was gorgeous. He was standing in the middle of the moonlit room with his arms behind his head, dainty little elbows tight and bloodless bracketing his face. His physique was distinctly Italian in a way I hadn't realized a physique could be, but I saw a figure I had seen before in a hundred paintings of the Renaissance, the delicacy of line, the lightness of stance. How easy it was to think of a man defying gravity when he looked like this, to be borne aloft on dirigible clouds – cherubim could bear his weight on their podgy backs, an arrow could pass through that coffee flesh and leave no trace. And then the soft geometry became apparent, as though Nature's working drawing was made visible beneath the finished work – a series of triangles, the two nipples and the navel formed one. The tufts of underarm blackness and the matching floss of his pubis formed another. On his chest there was a little embroidered isosceles. And the pattern was repeated beneath the skin, the bas-relief of his pelvic bone like a Corinthian capital – I could almost count the acanthus leaves that curled by his hip – then the inversion of the same at the apex of the breastbone. For a moment I understood how all art aspires to the condition of sex, even architecture. Oh, my mouth watered, even more so as Somarco lowered his hands and started moving them across his body, smiling directly at me as he did so. I had to turn away sharply as he began touching his lower half. I ran into the bedroom and shut the door behind me.

'Silly, silly boy,' Somarco said, through the door, taking a different tone, framing me as the foolish one, as the one who'd done something outrageous. 'Why are you being so foolish and ignorant, Kenneth?'

'Somarco, I've got nothing to say to you. You are the one who's doing stupid things. I'm not opening this door until you put some clothes on.'

I heard Somarco's dismissive laugh. But he didn't know what to say for a while. I tried again: 'Do you always take advantage of people when they're asleep? What's the matter? Is it too difficult to seduce a conscious person?'

'Oh, Kenny, Kenny, Kenny,' came the voice, again the sense of weary disbelief, 'how can you be so foolish? Listen to me. How can I put any clothes on when all my clothes are in the bedroom?'

'Get a towel or something. Put an overcoat on.'

'But this is absurd. You think I am going to attack you?'

'No . . .'

'Well, what is it, then?'

'It's just not right for you to be parading around in the nude . . .'

Eventually Somarco put on his overcoat, but said he had only done so because he was starting to 'feel a bit chilly'.

I realized that it had become impossible to continue living with Somarco so I cleared my things out of his flat and left the next day.

IX

After the success of our little masquerade with the dummy railhead at Fort Capuzzo, camouflage operations were taken with increasing seriousness by the higher echelons of command.

After many months of having to plead for materials and manpower, suddenly we were given whatever we asked for. The supply routes were still a problem, the ships coming from England still went the long way round, so competition for space on those vessels was fierce; every gallon of paint had to earn its place against shells and mortars, food, medical supplies and engine parts.

But Learmouth was mysteriously brilliant in the arts of procurement, and was able to charm as much as could be taken from local traders and suppliers at knock-down prices. We veritably stripped the markets of unbleached calico, which meant a chronic shortage of clothing for the fellahin. It was remarked in the local press that the British Army was stripping the nation bare, that soon there would be no materials left for clothes and that the population would be confined to their homes for lack of covering.

More promisingly, Learmouth's charm had penetrated the heavy doors of the War Establishments Committee, and he had been granted permission to recruit sergeants and privates from as many different areas of operation as he could, and had been given funds that enabled us to acquire excellent materials.

With these we began buying and importing wire, fabrics, nets, mild steel, rush matting, hurdles of split cane or palm frond, special substitute paints and distempers made from local materials, pickets and poles, wire gauze, gelatine wafers, brushes, tallow, fire-proofing materials, balloon fabric, spun yarn, shellac . . .

If we were to form an effective operation, the quantities of material we required were quite staggering. Learmouth produced what he estimated we would need for a year's worth of operations.

8,000 tons of paint

250,000 fathoms of cordage

120,000 nets of cotton string

2,500,000 square yards of rabbit fence with steel wool woven into the mesh

5,000,000 square yards of white cotton fabric

120,000,000 square yards of coloured hessian cloth for garnish

We were granted a dedicated training and development centre and were given a camp within the boundaries of the

Union Defence Force, a complex of sixty huts, some of which had been refurbished to act as lecture halls, workshops, stores, offices, cookhouses and mess huts for officers and NCOs, and living accommodation for a hundred and fifty students at a time. A university of deception, a college of camouflage out in the desert at Helwan, south of the city. Learmouth was in overall command, but now a range of other experts was brought in, the camp given a commandant from the centre in Wiltshire, and a number of other staff from that section (which had itself grown considerably) came over to provide training in the desert.

What had begun as a four-man operation now involved hundreds, with all the attendant paperwork and administrative chores. Our offices in Grey Pillars grew proportionately. Learmouth was now on several important strategic committees and had regular meetings with the highest in command. Somarco and I divided our time between Grey Pillars and Helwan, developing ideas for camouflage, which were put to the test in the camp. A visit to Helwan was now like visiting the site of some great primitive enterprise: everywhere one was met with the spectacle of men carrying long planks of wood, sawing things on carpenters' tables, hammering and planing and pinning, painting and staining and sewing, and all on such a colossal scale that it was as though a city had been dedicated to the arts and crafts of the ancients. There was an emphasis on manual work, an absence of machinery that strongly suggested the age of medieval craftsmanship. These men could have been making the scaffolding and cranes for one of the great cathedrals. The camp itself was carefully camouflaged with nets and other fabrics covering the workshops, so that from above it looked no more than temporary.

I found myself increasingly bogged down in the paperwork that was being generated by the new scale of operations. We had no secretary of our own, and every new recruit had to have his transfer papers signed and the duplicate filed, every tin of paint to be accounted for and entered into the accounts book. We were now dealing with a budget of thousands. Learmouth kept promising to recruit administrative staff to take care of it, but in the meantime I spent a lot of time in the office trying to keep track of everything.

It was during one of these filing sessions that I came across a piece of paper, a transfer form for a young private who was working as a mechanic in one of the tank regiments, that gave me a moment's pause. Evidently the fellow's skills as a mechanic were rather wanting for he had been transferred to camouflage, where his abilities as a carpenter (his occupation before the war) could be put to better use. There was nothing remarkable about the form – I had countersigned hundreds of them over the preceding weeks, sometimes pausing to note a suggestion of the person behind the form: the 'any other comments' section might contain a hurriedly written snippet of relevant biographical material, such as 'Was a scenery painter at Sadlers Wells' or, once, 'Too bloody slow'. The form that caused me to pause was not one that had any interesting comments, but I was caught by the name of the commanding officer, whose signature had been dashed across the bottom of the form: *Major M. J. Boone*.

I might easily have missed it, for the name that had once passed my lips more frequently than my own, that had danced on my tongue like a jewel of spittle, the very utterance a kind of conjugation, had been dead there a long time. I had not spoken it in all the years that had passed since that curious day at St Saviour's, and when I said it aloud now, alone in the office at Grey Pillars, I felt a revival of the old thrill for the name I had loved.

I held the form in my hand for a long time, looking for any clue in the way the name was written that this might be the very same Boone I had known. The signature was bold, bursting out of itself, the two *o*s like a pair of balloons in the centre of the name, the jagged and emphatically vertical initials shoring up the entire structure, a flourish underlining the whole. It was the signature of someone who valued his name above all else, who gave it only grudgingly on forms like these, and then did so with a mark of authority that insisted you remember that fact.

It was not a difficult thing to track down the owner of the name. I had his regiment and knew where he was stationed. I began to frequent the areas close to his staff headquarters. In this spell between campaigns, while the armies of both sides regrouped and waited to see who would make the next move, men would return to Cairo from the front line for respite. There were now hundreds of thousands of Allied troops in Egypt. At times it felt as though they outweighed the native population.

And then I saw him. He emerged from his headquarters in Garden City, not far from the embassy, and walked along one of the leafy boulevards as part of a group of three officers. Even though in my memory he existed as a child, the adult form was unmistakable. The walk, the hair, the voice. I followed at a distance. They were heading north towards the European district, as unhurriedly and casually as if there was no war on and they had all the time in the world for taking in the pleasant evening aromas of the city. They passed my block, and paused outside its door. I noticed they were talking to an Arab child. I hung back and slunk into a doorway, like some cheap gumshoe. The officers were bantering cheerfully with the boy and tousled his hair before moving on.

Eventually they turned east onto a street full of clubs and once-grand hotels, and finally turned into the Windsor, the most imposing of these, one of the favourite haunts of off-duty British officers. I had been there myself several times, and loved the old colonial style of the place, which still maintained a dignified air of deferential grandeur, with its befezzed waiters and bellboys.

Now that it contained Marcus Boone, however, it seemed to acquire a new layer of exclusivity. The beaming doorman in his embroidered kaftan seemed a gatekeeper of towering authority. Nevertheless, he let me pass, and I entered the ceramic beauty of the Windsor's lobby.

PART THREE

I

Berryman's, six miles north of Taunton, Somerset, was an impressive-looking school. Built in the Palladian style, an imposing series of limestone cliffs, hewn into symmetrical arcades and porticos, rose above an infinity of lawns and playing fields. Above the sculpture-filled pediments an enormous copper-green dome seemed to hover, lending the place an air of divine authority to such an extent that you could not believe it had been built solely to educate children but that it must do something else as well – house bishops or store great works of art. But no, it simply housed the children of the rich and landed, labouring over their equations and Latin compositions.

As I stepped out of the motor-bus that deposited me discreetly at the end of the drive I was immediately aware of a change of scale. The playing fields opened out before me; the towering facade of the school rose behind them as fresh and clean and proud as if it had just that moment risen out of the ground. It took one's mind a moment to adapt to the new proportions of this world. I felt like a fly crawling on the face of a great statue.

The spaces were filled with people at ease with the broad dimensions – the troupes of boys in hooped rugby kits jogging in formation across the driveway (several, even through their fatigue, offering me polite smiles as they clumped past); the team of young men hauling a vast iron roller across the grass, like termites carrying a cocoon to the nest; the gowned masters billowing on pedestals as they directed some operation or other.

They all conveyed a sense of being at ease in a place where the true business of the world was being sorted out (Berryman's had produced two unmemorable prime ministers).

'I'm so sorry, there should have been someone to meet you at the end of the drive. Though you don't look as though you've expended any energy at all.'

Anthony Cossins was, like most of the staff, vastly over-qualified for teaching young boys, whose efforts were never likely to amount to much. He had seen me from an upstairs window walking up the drive 'looking like some rake who's just been sent down from Oxford', he later told me, meaning that I was walking with the nonchalance of someone who doesn't really care about anything, my cardboard case in one hand, my other casually tucked into my pocket, my college scarf wrapped loosely around my neck.

'Let me take your case. Norman was so effusive in his letter, we're really pleased to have you here. He said you had to leave the Slade because of ill health?'

'That's right,' I said, after a pause. Learmouth had not told me about that.

'But not something that will affect you here?'

'No,' I said, thinking quickly. 'It was a bad chest brought on by the London smoke, I think. That's why I'm keen to work away from the city.'

'Oh, the air here is very good. And the light, of course. I try to teach the boys about the light. We get the most extraordinary shadows here – you've probably noticed already.' I nodded vaguely. He went on, 'Norman was very keen for us to take you. I'm a great admirer of his – both as an artist and as an individual. I don't think I've ever met someone whose judgement in all things I've so wholeheartedly respected . . .'

I thought back to the panicky conversations I'd had with Learmouth after leaving Somarco's flat. I'd told him I was desperate for somewhere to live, for a job, for anything, and to my surprise he'd already been working on my behalf to make arrangements for me to leave London altogether. I had been about to tell him that that was my strongest desire, and that if he didn't help me I might have to tell Professor Schwabe who else had been a regular at the bordello. But in the end I hadn't needed to use blackmail at all.

'Brill, I was just about to write to you. I have some wonderful news. I have managed to find a position for you.'

'Oh?'

'Yes, as a teacher of art at a school down in the West Country.'

'Really?' I was taken aback. I knew Learmouth was a man with good connections, but I hadn't thought he could pull off something like this. 'I have no experience or qualifications . . .'

'No matter. The fellow there is a good friend of mine and an excellent artist, and he has almost complete power over what happens in the art department. He would be delighted to have a Slade graduate. I wouldn't mention the fact of your expulsion – but even if it did become known I don't think it would matter. The reputation of the college is enough credential, at least in the eyes of a school like Berryman's. It's rather a nice place, I hear. They'll even provide accommodation.'

I was still worried about never having taught children before. Learmouth was reassuring. 'You have a gift for seeing goodness in things, Kenneth. You will see the good things in the ghastly daubings of young artists, and they will love you for it.'

'How many people in the art department?' I asked Cossins.

'Oh, just you and me, now. We have a very selective and small group of students. Unfortunately art isn't a popular option for boys who have set their sights on a career in the City or the law. They say it won't be any use to them.'

'And what do you say to that?'

'I mostly agree. The majority shouldn't be allowed anywhere

near a set of paintbrushes. I've hand-picked the few talented boys in the whole school.'

Cossins was a very handsome man a few years older than me. His thick dark hair was swept straight back, though stray locks kept springing forward and hanging lusciously over his forehead. On the way to my rooms he gave me a brief tour of the school. We passed through the vaulted entrance hall, with its soaring oak panels on which there were many lists in gilt lettering – of prizewinning scholars, the captains of rugby and cricket teams, champion sprinters and rowers – dating back a hundred years. Then there were the heroes of the Great War and their regiments, several with post-nominal honours for bravery and valour. Portraits of past headmasters stared coldly down from the great staircase. Two had had their likenesses done in marble; one was bare-shouldered and crowned with laurels.

We passed through the empty dining room over which the interior of the copper dome hung. Gazing upwards was like looking into a coffered and gold-trimmed view of Heaven. Then out onto the quadrangle, the biggest in the world, so Cossins said.

He waved his arm casually in various directions as he described the buildings. 'Boys' dorms down that side and that side, chapel and classrooms over that side. Masters' accommodation on the top floor of that wing. If you look up you'll see your windows – those three at the end there.'

We went through an archway, then up several flights of creaking wooden stairs to a corridor high in the wing, and I was presented with my rooms.

'Here you are. Lived here myself when I first arrived. Loved it, but it gets on top of you in the end – doesn't give you any space to breathe. Especially once you get married. Once I'd done the deed we had to find a place. We've got a lovely little cottage in Grantley now, thatch, the lot. So what about you? Have you got a sweetheart, a special girl in your life?'

'Me? No.'

'Oh.' Cossins looked perplexed. 'Well, I mean there aren't many around here to choose from. There's Miss Card, but she's a bit . . . you know . . . like her name.'

'You mean she's a bit of a joker?'

'No – I mean she's flat-chested.'

I was taken aback by Cossins's assumption that finding a wife was at the top of my list of priorities, or that the chests of females was the key criterion for selecting one.

'Don't look embarrassed. I'm a bit of a Rubens man myself. I like them full and a little bit flabby. Don't tell my wife I said that. I take it you're more of a Botticelli man. Well, Miss Card's probably got something of the *Primavera* about her.'

I was beginning to take a mild dislike to Cossins, which deepened when we talked about art and I saw some of his paintings. Despite his married status he had too much of the sixth-form common room about him, concerned with petty trivialities and stupid rivalries, and a poorly developed sense of humour. He had a lack of wisdom that only comes with a long career in education.

He was a brilliant draughtsman and technical painter, but had no imagination. I could see why he was friendly with Learmouth. Cossins's paintings, some of which hung on the walls of the art department and adjoining corridors, seemed to lack any discernible brush strokes. They had no texture, other than a sort of enamelled flatness.

*

My first few weeks at the school were bewilderingly delightful. I was lost in a confusing welter of classes and meetings, lunches and dinners at high table where I was introduced to scores of fascinating people. Many of the staff were leading experts in their field, people who more properly belonged in a university department. The music master, Mr Coke, was one of the finest organists in the land, had studied at Leipzig and was a friend of Elgar, whom he'd once managed to persuade to conduct the school orchestra in a performance of *The Dream of Gerontius*. The English master was William Hoppen, who had studied at Oxford under Quiller-Couch, and was engaged in an interminable project to catalogue the works of various eighteenth-century playwrights. He put a great deal of effort into staging school plays, and had a fondness for revivals of commercially successful pieces that had fallen out of fashion. The latest of these was *The Scarlet Pimpernel*, which he planned to stage later that year. It was traditional, so he told me, for members of staff to take some of the roles, new staff, in particular. I made it as plain to him as I possibly could that I had no interest or skill in acting.

Lessons were a delight. It was clear, from my very first class, that the boys regarded the art class as a social club where they could chat and gossip as much as they liked, and that the production of art played only an incidental role. They would gather round me and ask me questions about myself, and in the first instance I answered far too candidly, particularly when it came to questions about my love life.

'Is Sir married?'

'No.'

'Does Sir have a sweetheart?'

Why the obsession with matrimonial matters? I was bewildered.

'No, Sir does not.'

'Has Sir ever had a sweetheart?'

'Well, I suppose not, not really. I was very friendly with a little girl once, but you could hardly call her my sweetheart.'

'Does Sir think true love is possible without the suppression of the ego?'

Most of these questions were put by one particularly beautiful and precocious young man called Mountfoot, who, it was asserted by everyone but himself, was entitled to be addressed as the Honourable Julius Mountfoot, on account of him being the son of a baron. He was a very poor artist. His riposte, when this was pointed out to him, was that art was of no use to one whose destiny lay in the upper strata of political service, Home Office, Foreign Office, prime minister. 'Does Sir really think an ability to draw apples will be of use to someone who signs treaties with foreign powers?'

I could only smile at Mountfoot's teasing. He was one of a group of boys who regularly invited themselves to tea in my rooms. I was only a few years their senior, and they possessed the confidence of someone much older, which made them seem roughly my coevals. The relaxed approach of the school to the teaching of art, my elegant rooms with their splendid views across the quad, my decent salary and my little coterie of charming and beautiful boys made me feel as if I had landed rather firmly on my feet. I wasn't sure that I had ever been so happy.

*

It was several weeks before I came to the attention of the headmaster. Even though Dr J. F. Pontefract and I had attended the same meetings, though I had sat three seats away from him on the school stage for assembly and speech day, though his billowing gown had several times caught me full in the face, my existence had passed him by until, for some undisclosed reason, he sent for me, using a prefect as a messenger. To be called out of class presaged something urgent, I supposed, so I was expecting Pontefract to have finally read some sort of report on me, that he had perhaps found out about the circumstances of my exit from the Slade, or had seen my police record.

'Just thought I'd bring you in for a little chat,' the great man said, standing up from behind his desk and holding out a hand to be shaken. The office was everything I would have expected –

book-lined walls, a view across the playing fields, a reproduction of Gainsborough's *The Blue Boy* behind the desk. 'Rather ashamed not to have said hello before. I like to meet all the new members of staff, but it's damned hard trying to find the time these days. Running a school like this is becoming more and more like running a big company. So, you're the new art teacher, are you?'

'Yes.'

'And how are you finding things?'

'Very good. Everything's excellent.'

'Ever taught in a school before?'

'No.'

'How's behaviour been?'

'Not too bad.'

'Good. You've probably been told this, but we don't practise any form of corporal punishment here. We believe that a boy can be trusted to behave, if put on his honour to do so. We try to instil a sense of moral duty and responsibility instead.'

'I see.'

'And no doubt you're wondering how we go about doing that.'

'Well . . . yes.'

Pontefract seemed to swell slightly when given the opportunity to expound his educational philosophy. His moustache thickened, his shoulders broadened.

'In my experience, the best way is to begin as close to home as possible, rather like St Paul in his letter to the Thessalonians – won't you sit down? – when he entreats that we control our bodies in holiness and honour. I'm sure you know the chapters I'm referring to. We strongly discourage indulgence of any kind. We don't have a tuck shop here, you will have noticed. I know, the Bible has little to say on the subject of tuck shops. We are not complete Stoics, of course. We believe in allowing a certain amount of fun. Now, I know this might sound rather draconian to a gentleman of an artistic persuasion, like yourself, but it is really quite simple. Our boys need rigid discipline – they need rules, rotas and regulations. You may be rather surprised by this, but many of our boys – the vast majority – come to us without any idea of how to wash themselves.'

'Really?'

'Yes. Often they are really quite smelly, even the ones from good homes, though nearly all of them are, and the titled ones are often the smelliest – you might have noticed if you have come across any first-formers. Do you smoke? No? Finest Havanas. The trouble is they have always had someone to wash them, if not their mothers, then nurses and nannies. They are expected to pick up the technique simply from memory and observation, but of course they aren't up to it.'

For one horrid moment, as Pontefract momentarily vanished behind blue cigar smoke, I thought he was going to tell me that I would have to wash them myself, but no.

'My plan is that we should teach our boys the art of washing. Masters can prepare lessons to be given in times of private study.'

It was assumed that all the masters were themselves experts in the ablutive arts, but I doubted it. I had seen some extremely dowdy, crusty-looking masters, reeking of pipe smoke and liquorice. The idea of such people giving lessons in hygiene was hideous.

'You don't have to look so worried. I am not asking that you give a practical demonstration . . .' He paused, as if he hadn't previously given that thought any consideration until now. 'No – well. You know, in the army, we learnt that an efficient fighting force begins with the war against dirt. Now, where I think you could provide me with great assistance is in the provision of visual illustration. I have in mind some large drawings, perhaps pen-and-ink on white board – don't really know how you fellows work but a large, poster-sized illustration of the various stages of washing, each one illustrating a particular technique.'

'I see,' I said thoughtfully.

'Do you think you could manage that? Or should I ask Mr Cossins? I would have, but I thought this would be a good opportunity for us to get to know each other a little. Have you ever been in the army?'

'No.'

'No, of course not, not really sure why I said that. No, what I have in mind is, say, five illustration boards. Number one shows a boy sitting upright in a bath. Number two, a boy in a bath in reclining position, with only head and kneecaps above waterline. Number three, perhaps a sponge applied to an armpit. Number four, a boy standing up in a bath, perhaps a sponge covering the private parts. Number five, a boy drying himself, viewed from back, towel covering seat.'

I agreed to undertake the commission. But I was not completely sure I was up to the task. In effect, I was being asked to produce five nudes, when painting or drawing the male nude was the one aspect of my artistic training that was significantly lacking. Other than the self-portraits done in Somarco's flat, I had no experience, and using myself as a model would not have been practical. I could attempt the project using only my imagination, but feared that the resulting works would look amateurish, and expose me as an ill-trained artist. Would Pontefract notice? The alternative was to get some boys to sit for me.

When I suggested the idea to Mountfoot, he seemed quite keen.

'So Sir would like me to pose naked for him. Is Sir quite sure he is ready for this? We haven't even kissed yet.'

I smacked the boy playfully on the crown of his head. 'Sir will put you in a half-nelson if you say such a thing again.' I had never before indulged in such outrageous boy-flirtation, and found it quite hilarious. Mountfoot was very skilled at it, and I presumed he used it, as I did, as a rehearsal for the real flirtations of the future.

'I have no objection at all if Sir wants to see my naked flesh.'

'Well, as a matter of fact, I'd rather you wore something, perhaps a pair of bathing trunks, to save us all any unnecessary embarrassment.'

When, a few days later, Mountfoot arrived for his first session as my model, the playfulness had gone, to be replaced by a brittle anxiety. The mood was partly fostered by my own apprehension, recalling those awful episodes in the life room, then the business with Somarco, which was still strong in my mind. I was keen to undertake the task of depicting the nude Mountfoot for the opportunity it offered of helping me understand my relationship with the male nude. I filled the bath, and was glad to find that Mountfoot had followed my suggestion, and was wearing bathing trunks. His exquisiteness was edited a little by this piece of fabric, though he did give me a questioning look as he was about to step into the bath – as if to say, *Are you sure you don't want me to take these off as well?* He seemed to understand my little shake of the head.

As he sat in my bath and displayed a sumptuous armpit, I managed to view Mountfoot dispassionately. He was infuriatingly handsome, displaying all the perfections of a recently acquired adult form – equine, athletic, perfectly groomed. Yet I was able to look on my subject as a specimen of anatomical perfection, with the same awe I might regard a newly opened orchid. As he held the required poses (sponge to armpit, towel to seat, etc.) I was greatly relieved to find that I was no more aroused than if I had been looking at a sculpture by Michelangelo. In fact, it was this artist who came to mind most frequently as I worked on the drawings, bringing to them, I believed, a level of attention to sinew and muscle worthy of that old master. I used cross-hatched shading of such density that my sketches had real depth and solidity.

I took the drawings to Pontefract when I had finished the last.

'Oh, most excellent work, Mr Brill. Yes, indeed, these will be a most excellent illustration for our lectures on the art of washing. There will be a meeting shortly to discuss this matter. In the meantime, I will look after them.' He perused the drawings, then placed them under his desk. He said he would take care of them, and whenever a form master was to deliver his lecture on the art of washing, he could come and collect them from him.

II

It was well into the Michaelmas term before I saw a woman. In Berryman's, it seemed, such creatures simply didn't exist. Even in the dining hall our meals were served up by a bulging, bearded Scottish chef and his team of weasely, unshaven undercooks. Cleaning and carrying was done by porters, who were mostly ex-military men, some with medals chinking on their chests. It was said that there was a woman somewhere in the administrative building, and occasionally I received official letters from a 'Miss Staples', imagining something prim and spectacled behind the accurate typing. And there was a school nurse, who occupied a room whose door was always closed, a sign hanging on the handle saying 'Back in ten minutes'. These women kept their presence so discrete they had little more impact on the life of the school than fairies. So when I came across the sight of a real, living woman after all that time, the thought crossed my mind that it was someone playing a joke, that one of the masters had donned a skirt and was wearing a wig. April Card didn't have the most elegant walk; in fact, she strode down corridors with the heavy footfall of a policeman on the beat. She also had a squareness of face and prominence of jaw that could make her seem quite masculine, but when seen head on, her visage had a very pleasing symmetry, the high cheekbones balancing the low, wide mandibles, a bone structure that seemed to reach the very boundaries of beauty. A fraction of an inch further in either direction, and April Card would have been a horse or a frog.

We first met by chance when we were waiting outside Mr Pontefract's office. I couldn't help looking at her, and she eyed me with a curiously assertive stare. I found this quite thrilling. Then she spoke. 'My mother would say something like, "Have you had an eyeful?"'

'I'm sorry. Am I staring?'

The coldness went from her eyes and she smiled sweetly. 'Rather a lot, actually.'

'It's been a long time since I've seen a woman.'

April sprayed a laugh of incredulity through near-closed lips. 'That sounds perilously close to a cry of despair.'

I could feel myself reddening. 'No – I mean, it's just odd, you know. In a place like this it suddenly strikes you, after a while, that one half of the human species is absent.'

April changed the subject. 'You're the new art teacher, are you?'

'Yes. What do you teach?'

'Mathematics. Don't look so horrified.'

'I just feel it's a shame we don't have more in common.'

'Oh. Have you not pondered on the relationship between mathematics and art?'

'I didn't think there was one.' I said, half laughing, thinking it might be a joke.

She turned away, half in order to hide, I later thought, the look of disappointment that must have been forming on her face. I came to realize that April found most people disappointing. She said it was because so few of them seemed to share her view of the world. When asked to say precisely what that view was, she gave a sigh and said it didn't matter. She was quiet and didn't participate much in conversations in the staff room. Most of the men thought this was because she was slow and couldn't keep up with the fast-paced talk. I came to see that it was quite the opposite. She was usually a few steps ahead in the dialogue and was simply waiting for people to catch up, by which time she had moved on again and probably seen the conversation through to its inevitable and disappointing conclusion.

'So what is the relationship between mathematics and art?' I asked her.

'Well, for instance, I've always thought the theorem of Pythagoras would make rather nice wallpaper. It was said he formulated his theory after looking at the patterns in the tiles of the bathhouse floor. The relationships between numbers express themselves as patterns. I'm quite convinced that the beauty of a flower can be expressed as a simple mathematical equation.'

'Are you?'

'Yes.'

'What about a colour? Is there a number that corresponds?'

'I'm sure colour could be expressed as a number. All colours are defined by a wavelength of light, and that wavelength can be expressed as a number. It's quite simple. You artists always underestimate sciences, don't you, yet we're trying to do the same thing, examine and describe the world.'

April and I quickly became friends. The curriculum at Berryman's meant that our paths rarely crossed, and even on the occasions when we were brought together in the same room or hall, we would be widely separated at opposite ends, or would have too many others intervening to be able to talk. Our departments used different staff rooms, and even lunchtime was difficult because April brought her own sandwiches and ate them alone in her classroom. I began to engineer opportunities to socialize with her, happening to be in the quad at the precise time she left the science block to make her way to the bike rack. This gave us ten minutes of friendly chatting every day, and before long she accepted an invitation to my rooms for tea.

She was a little reluctant at first, fearing that 'people might talk'. But the comings and goings of visitors from the staff residences was little remarked upon. Most staff had a frequent traffic of friends, staff and boys from their rooms, some holding regular soirées on Friday evenings.

I felt tremendously privileged when I first managed to get April to my rooms. She exclaimed with delight at the few paintings of mine I had managed to get framed and hung on my walls, one of which was of Lucy, my Old Compton Street model, a back view with a frilly camisole round her waist.

'That's not one of yours, is it? That's a famous one surely. I've seen that somewhere before.'

'Well, I take that as a great compliment, April. It is one of mine, but I have to confess I was rather heavily influenced at the time by Toulouse-Lautrec.'

'I think I've heard that name. It is rather shockingly good. Not at all what I was expecting.'

'What were you expecting?'

'Oh, something befitting Berryman's philistine ethos – landscapes in the style of Claude Lorraine, or portraits in the style of Gainsborough.'

I laughed. 'I must have made a pretty poor impression on you if that's all you thought me capable of.'

'Well, I haven't paid much attention to you so far, it's true. So who was the model for this painting?' She still couldn't take her eyes off Lucy.

'Just a model at the art school,' I replied hesitantly.

'I didn't think they allowed such risqué poses at art schools. She looks like a tart.'

'I expect many of them were. Some of our models were very hard up for money.'

'Poor things.' April said this with a certain amount of genuine feeling in her voice.

I was enchanted by April, and enchanted by the idea that I was on the verge of forming what might be my first proper relationship with a woman. I looked hard into her face whenever I could, trying to decide what I felt about it, whether I enjoyed what I was seeing. I noticed how large and dark her eyes were – but was that a good thing? Was it beautiful? The lashes on those eyes, were they sufficiently thick? There were few, in fact. She had very sparse eyelashes, reminding me of a stretch of raspberry canes in winter. At other times I would concentrate on the mouth. Again the problem was deciding what those lips meant. When at rest they formed a heart shape, the lower being plumper and rounder than most. When she drank tea she left big lipstick imprints on my cups.

She came from the Derbyshire Peaks, where her father owned a cement factory. What would your expectations be of a *sui generis* Derbyshire cement magnate? A solid, towering, dusty figure spouting wise saws and homespun philosophies of self-control and common sense? When I finally met him I was surprised, not to say flabbergasted, to encounter a slim little northern aesthete, delicately featured, a man who could easily have passed for a frightened little schoolmistress if so attired, who wore a smoking jacket in a smoking room lined with leather-bound books of poetry and philosophy. April's physical solidity and squareness came from her mother, who had Italian blood. The binding together of two such disparate elements as her parents was responsible for her singular appearance, as it was for her personality, where reason and imagination seemed to lie together so comfortably. April said that her father's only resemblance to cement was in the way he seemed to set if he stayed in one place too long.

I spent a pleasant few days there one half-term, and was invited to immortalize the family home in a series of watercolours. But I was more interested in the cement works, with its peculiar clusters of windowless buildings, its cones of brilliant white spoil, its conveyor-belts, cylindrical ovens and mysterious chugging machinery. I was able to secure a day of sketching in the works. April's father was quite understanding of the artistic sensibility and how I was in thrall to the arts of observation. I managed a little watercolour of the house as well.

April and I had become close friends, but we were not lovers, not yet. Back at Berryman's we spent the evenings in a kind of innocent flirtation, discussing everything from Kierkegaard to Franklin D. Roosevelt. And then I began sketching her. While we talked I would take out a small sketchpad and a Black Prince pencil. It would have been very unlike April to raise any objection to my drawing her: to do so would have been to confess to a strain of vanity, and she was quite strongly against any form of it. She was quite cynical at first that I would be able to render a convincing likeness.

'I'm not going to stay still for you, you know. If you expect me to stop talking just because you've got a pencil in your hand, then you can think again.'

I told her I didn't need her to stay still: I was quite capable of drawing her from my observations while she moved normally. When I had finished I was expecting her to be greatly impressed by my ability to capture the still essence of her face and head amid all the movement and agitation. In fact, she was disappointed.

'I can see this is a very well-made thing,' she said, 'but what you have drawn surely bears no resemblance whatsoever to the experience you've had of me.'

'Do you not think so?'

'Well, how could it? There is nothing in this drawing that registers the fact that I have been opening and closing my mouth non-stop for the last twenty minutes, or that I've been drinking this very fine claret, or that I've been turning my head this way and that. What you have drawn is a statue who happens to look like me. You have killed me in order to render me.'

At the time I laughed off her criticisms, saying I was not really interested in capturing the movements of our mundane conversation: I was more interested in the essence, the platonic thinginess of April.

'Why must it be still? Why must the essence of anything be motionless? Surely it is the other way round. Life is motion. Only in death do we become truly still.'

Soon April began to be a little more enthusiastic about my drawings of her. She began to pose properly, keeping herself still for twenty minutes at a time. She began to wear the sort of clothes she thought might be of interest to an artist – lighter, flimsier materials that were able to display the form of the body beneath. Then, by degrees, she began wearing fewer and fewer clothes. She posed in a low-necked dress, then a shoulderless dress, then a camisole and knickerbockers, like someone from a Toulouse-Lautrec portrait. Finally, she allowed me to draw her with one breast exposed. I didn't encourage her. It seemed inevitable. At some point, she would have to expose one of her breasts. She was wearing a low-cut dress with a rather gaudy lacework rose at the centre of the bosom, and nothing underneath. As she sat on the bed, her legs folded beneath her, she glanced down at herself and, after a moment's shrugging thought (left, or right?), she drew down the shoulder of her dress to expose her left breast. It glowed and quivered, and took some time to settle. The nipple was large and dark, reminding me of those bicycle-repair patches. Of course I knew a great deal about the alleged attractiveness of the female breast to the male eye, and I could see that April's was an excellent specimen: in size and shape it had a fullness that was most impressive, making nonsense of Cossins's joke that she was flat-chested. I suppose I thought of it in the same way that women might think of a well-developed bicep, not sexually attractive so much as an impressive display.

Halfway through my drawing I put down my pad and moved over to join April on the bed. She covered herself quickly as I did so, but allowed me to place my hand on what had so recently been on display. I was intrigued by the softness, the sheer collapsibility of it. It seemed to draw the hand into an endless progression of softness, and no matter how deeply you probed, there seemed to be no core to the thing. We kissed. April smelt strongly of burnt toast and metal. It wasn't a displeasing smell, but it didn't seem human. To my surprise, when I drew back I saw that she was flushed and breathless, her face shiny with sweat, her eyes unfocused. We kissed again. I could only think of it as an exploratory thing, an act of curiosity, but April was clearly taking it differently. It shocked me to see that rational, intelligent woman suddenly seem so blurred and helpless. It made me aware of how dispassionately I had just acted. Realizing I should somehow contrive to appear the same, I put on a convincing display of being in the throes of physical ecstasy, knowing full well that there would be no opportunity for going any further. We were taking a rather bold risk as it was: to have gone so far as making love on school property would have been too dangerous for either of us to contemplate.

April said to me in horror, one day, 'Ponty wants me to give a lecture to my boys on the art of washing. He has given me a set of illustrations to use. I told him I cannot possibly do it.'

'And what did he say?'

'He said I was talking nonsense. I said, didn't he think it rather awkward for a female to be asked to do such a thing? He said it could be just as embarrassing for a chap. "We all have to do it. I'm all for equality, you know." '

'He's got a point.'

'And have you seen those pictures? They're absolutely appalling. They're nothing more than homosexual pornography, and he keeps them in his office. Salacious, sentimental, they look like little coy nymphs rising from fairy pools. It's quite shocking. I don't think young boys should be exposed to such images.'

'Surely they're harmless.'

I was taken aback by April's reaction. It had not been my intention to produce anything that could be thought titillating, and her apparent repulsion at the very concept of homosexual attraction put me on my guard.

*

To my alarm, the whole school soon appeared to know about our friendship. I learnt this from Mountfoot, who, with an amused and perfect smile on his face, mentioned the fact one day when he came on one of his uninvited visits to my room.

'So, how are you getting along with Miss Card?'

'What do you mean?'

'Have you been, as they say, intimate with her yet?'

'Will you wash your mouth out, Honourable or not? What sort of a question is that to ask a man, let alone a schoolboy his teacher, or any gentleman?'

'That's a very roundabout way of avoiding the question. It is of interest to us because no one in the school believes that Miss Card is human.'

'Enough of that. Show me what you've brought with you.'

Mountfoot undid the laces of his small portfolio, still eyeing me with a knowing expression. Poor Mountfoot – he couldn't draw for toffee. He'd been copying reproductions of a Titian he'd found in the school library, a matchstick-man version of *Bacchus and Ariadne*, and of course he thought his efforts were indistinguishable from the old master's.

'Mountfoot, I suggest you give up any hope of an artistic career.'

'Oh, you're just jealous, and how can you think of banishing me from the art department? I know how much you enjoy my company.'

'You are a very presumptuous boy. And what do you mean by that thing you said about Miss Card?'

'Well, either that she is some sort of miraculous mannequin, designed to work to maximum efficiency at the expense of any such distraction as humour or emotional warmth, or that she is of some other species disguised as a human, I suppose.'

'I think that is grossly unfair. April – Miss Card has a very good sense of humour.'

'So there is something afoot between you two . . .'

'A very good sense of humour, and have you ever thought what it must be like to be the only female in a place like this?'

'Yes. She didn't use to be the only female, you know.'

'No?'

'No, there was another teacher. The wonderful Miss Bowness, with the accent on the second syllable. Oh, she was adorable, if a little too Aryan. One always expected her to bring a cow into the school and start milking it in the quad.'

'What did she teach?'

'English. But she wasn't very good at it.'

'Why not?'

'Because no one in the class could take her seriously. She was too beautiful. And, apart from that, she didn't know her subject. She thought Ophelia was Hamlet's sister, for Heaven's sake. She thought Dr Johnson was the brand of cold remedy. Take Dr Johnson for night-time relief, that sort of thing. It was quite embarrassing.'

'I'm surprised my hip hasn't become dislocated, the number of times you've pulled my leg.'

'Oh, but she was such a sweet and pretty fool. You'd have liked her. Quite masculine.'

'Why did she leave?'

'Well, that's the thing. No one knew. She left halfway through term with no warning and no explanation. Our lazy and ill-informed but endlessly enjoyable English classes were suddenly presided over by Dr Lewes and his revolting dog. Lewes, as I'm sure you know, is ill-informed on all literature apart from that produced in the classical era. Every lesson was devoted to translating *The Aeneid*. "I sing of arms and of the old man". He thought he was terribly funny. His dog did too . . .'

'Any theories as to why the Aryan milkmaid left?'

'Well, I was coming to that, you see. As soon as she left, Miss Card went into a decline. For maths lessons she would set us an impossible problem in algebra, then retreat into the stock cupboard, sobbing, while we tried to work it out.'

'That doesn't sound like the Miss Card I know.'

'No, it wasn't the Miss Card anyone knew. And this went on for weeks. We could only come to one conclusion, that she was lovesick for the milkmaid. And I mean lovesick in every sense.'

'How many senses are there?'

'As many as you want.'

'Are you saying that they were . . . you know?' I'm damned that, even at that mature age, I wasn't sure of the word for it.

And Mountfoot was so frighteningly precocious, so knowing. I assumed he had knowledge of these things.

'Your busy Lizzies are coming along well, aren't they?' he said, teasingly changing the subject and sauntering over to my windowsill. '*Impatiens*. You don't really do still-lifes, do you? Why don't you like painting plants?'

'Tell me more about Miss Card and the milkmaid. Are you suggesting they were lovers?'

'Surely you can see she's a bit of a Tom.'

'I don't know what you mean.'

'Just look at her square jaw. Her cheekbones. Her shoulders. She has the physique of a good prop forward. Think about it – would you like to tackle her on the rugby field?' He came at me with a playful parry and knocked me onto my chaise.

'I find that description very insulting, and get off me, you insolent boy.'

'And that's why it's quite interesting to see that she's falling in love with you now. She can't quite be the Tom we all thought she was.'

'Falling in love with me? Are you mad?'

'Don't deny it. She's been seen leaving your rooms at all hours. You can't do anything here in secret, you know. I expect Pontefract will have a word with you about it soon. He doesn't like staff fornicating on the premises.'

'We've never fornicated, and wash your mouth out, you sleazy little boy.'

I had become somewhat exasperated by Mountfoot's endless sexual teasing. I was quite horrified that this elegant and refined young man, from one of England's noble families, should have such a lavishly delinquent imagination. It is very disconcerting to be with someone one's junior who seems more sexually experienced than oneself. I resisted the temptation to talk further about the stories he frequently spun, each one calculated to test me on some point of sexual morals or other. I took with a liberal pinch of salt his stories of Pontefract's sexual incursions into the boys' dorms, though I couldn't help being amused by his tale of the dummy schoolboy. It was said that one pupil became so averse to the nightly episodes that he constructed a dummy of himself, using, among other things, a football bladder, and when Pontefract went up to the usual bed he performed his deed without noticing any difference. Mountfoot claimed furthermore that Pontefract practised shunamitism and that the poor young boy involved had actually been prescribed by the school doctor.

Much as I had come to distrust young Mountfoot, I did concede that the friendship between myself and April should be conducted more discreetly. April didn't have a room in the college. She lodged at Mistress Appleby's, an antiques shop in Cysterow Fitzherbert, and came in every morning by bicycle. Unfortunately Mistress Appleby, a hefty woman with an unexpectedly pretty face, lived downstairs and kept vigilant guard over the comings and goings of her tenant, and was as strict as Pontefract about overnight visitors, or male guests at any time of day.

'Couldn't you say I was your brother? How would she know?'

We did try this, and it worked a few times. Mistress Appleby gave us cold, suspicious glances over her glass cabinets of cameos and leather bottles, as we shuffled in and out of the shop, and reluctantly allowed me permission to go upstairs. Then she took to making unannounced visits to April's rooms, entering without a knock, always in the hope of finding us *in flagrante delicto*, and showing deep disappointment when she found we were not. The threat of such surveillance, however, made it impossible for us even so much as to kiss while on the premises so we had to find alternative arrangements.

We were by now so hungry for intimacy that we resorted to the natural cover of the surrounding countryside. There was a little wood about half a mile's walk from the school, along an overgrown hedge-lined path that took many twists and turns. The wood was dense and tangled and the domain mainly of partridges and pheasants, who would burst screeching from their cover when you were almost on top of them. In order to justify my excursions in the unlucky event of meeting anyone on my travels, I assumed the habits and appearance of an ornithologist. I would set off with a pair of binoculars dangling from my neck and a field guide to British birds under my arm.

April adopted no such disguise. For our first liaison in the appointed hazel grove – a wood within a wood – she arrived wearing a silk dress beneath a heavy trench coat. But she had made up her face to such a degree it took me a moment to recognize her as the same woman: her rouge had brought out the already prominent cheekbones; the heavy mascara had thickened the lashes so they seemed to beat like wings when she blinked. I thought the effect rather brilliant, and was jolted by her film-star glamour. No one seeing her could have thought she was entering the countryside for rural pursuits. When she saw my binoculars she stumbled with laughter.

'Well, I never thought I'd make love with a bird-watcher. What are you going to do, note me down as a rare species?'

'Well, funny you should say that. I've noted several rare species while I've been waiting for you. My father once tried to interest me in bird-watching, but I've always preferred aeroplanes. It's a very frustrating hobby.'

It was true that my disguise had unearthed some awkward and uncomfortable memories of the Heath, and of trying to build enthusiasm for a new hobby. Birds are such shy, secretive creatures, always appearing with the sun behind them, hiding furtively in leaves or behind a tree trunk. Then, when they were actually observable, how to tell the difference between a reed bunting and a brambling, or a tree pipit and a meadow pipit? I was happy with the strikingly individual birds, like the wood-peckers and the nuthatches, but all those brownish, sparrow-like birds in between – I couldn't be bothered with them.

Our relationship entered what Knell would have called its Lawrentian phase, by which I presume he meant D. H. rather than T. E. The bearded one would have been quite proud of us, the way we went about our lovemaking, bedding down in a grove of saplings, stretching out in dappled sunlight, opening our rough clothes and revealing our soft skins to each other. It was the first time I had lain with a woman, and I was immensely relieved to have done so.

April was nearly ten years older than me, but it transpired that she had not before had a relationship, a physical relation-ship, that is, with a man, at least not one that went as far as ours was to go. We were both virgins, and neither of us knew what to do with the other, quite. I must admit I couldn't help being somewhat shocked by the absence of anything down there when, after our third or fourth visit, she allowed my hand to rove south of her navel, through the weak elastic of her undergarments. (I had my eyes closed and my hand's progress was blocked from view so I did not quite understand the geography of her cloth-ing. It seemed there were several hemmed and frilled things that had to be negotiated before the forest of thick, springy hair was reached. This I was prepared for, thanks to the generosity of the various prostitutes who'd posed for me back in Old Compton Street, but as my hand reached ever further, it was still a surprise for it to be confronted with an anatomical absence, a lack of apparatus. There was nothing down there but a soft looseness, a tangled sort of dampness.)

April was returning the exploratory gesture, her hand having weaved itself through the layers of my trousers and underwear, and had, with a gasp, struck her fingertips against my stiffening member. Once she had grasped it, she did not seem to know what to do with it, but held on to it, as though it was the lever of some vehicle that would halt if she let go. A dead man's handle.

On the first occasion of our lovemaking I could not help but allow the surprise of sudden bird-proximity to distract me: a trembling presence had alighted on a nearby bough, which I glimpsed with one eye (the other being closed and touching lid-to-lid with one of April's), and I felt a rush of passionate curiosity. It was as though the blood that had gone to work building up my manhood had now urgently regrouped itself in my bird-watching brain, and my penis dwindled rapidly in April's light grip. It had turned to ashes in her hands, but I didn't think she would notice or care that much. But she did seem to care when I retrieved my left hand from the vicinities they had begun so tentatively to explore and to reach with those same shining fingers for the binoculars that were by my side and train them upon the little bird, which seemed, to me, to be wearing a moustache.

My action had a decisive effect on April: she withdrew herself completely, looking at me in horror as she adjusted her clothing.

'What on earth are you doing?'

'Sorry, but this little bird just flew into view . . .'

'But you just said you had no interest in bird-watching. You hate it.'

'I do – well, I did. Having to keep up this pretence, and reading these bird books and trying to identify the little blighters, now I'm getting a bit obsessed with them.'

By now the bird in question had flown away, and with it, our sexual desire.

This happened on several other occasions. At some crucial point in our lovemaking a bird would interrupt us, and I would get my binoculars out or, more worryingly for April, I would be unable to draw myself away from bird-contemplation to begin lovemaking at all.

'There's a tree pipit. I must just watch it while it's there – they're quite rare, you know.'

'I'm beginning to think you have no desire for me. It's quite insulting, you know, to be passed over in favour of a scrawny little bird. Do you actually find birds' bodies more attractive than my own?'

'Of course not, but you are not likely to fly away, are you?'

'I wouldn't bank on it, dearie,' she said, in a sudden horrible parody of streetwalker's talk and, indeed as swiftly as a little dove, upped and left.

I suppose the psychologists would call it a displacement activity. I was transferring my sexual energy into the observance of birds, which allowed me to avoid confrontation with the fact that I felt no sexual desire for April. More than that, it helped me avoid the precipitous moment of full sexual intercourse, which otherwise seemed an inevitable outcome of our serial liaisons. I could look upon that prospect as nothing other than a trial and ordeal. I could discern a type of beauty in April's bodily presence, but only in the same way that a work of art is beautiful. I could no more make love to April than I could to a painting by Constable or Turner. I did not, at that time, make any connection between my lack of desire for April and an aversion to the female body in general. I still thought it was simply a matter of April's individual body type. Perhaps a different type of female body would work its spell on me. As Cossins might have put it, perhaps I was a Rubens man, or a Michelangelo man, or a Velázquez man. In truth I had no idea in which school of painting April belonged. There was something of the northern Renaissance about her, with her hemispherical bosoms and her bicycle-patch nipples. But, whatever it was, I felt I had to employ every strategy I could think of to avoid the moment when I would have to conjoin with it fully.

Otherwise I had a sense that I was entering into some sort of contract, the small print (or even the large print) of which I hadn't been allowed to examine. It seemed there were countless rules waiting to be broken, indiscretions, points of order, sub-clauses, articles of which I was presumed to have knowledge. I had not been aware of any such protocols in my friendships with men, and I began to long for the easily understood, uncomplicated world of male friendship. Perhaps I should not have allowed things to develop with April as they had done, but I did seem uncannily drawn to her for her intellectual companionship, her wonderful insolence and disregard for authority, her mimicry, her wit. Her boldness and bolshiness.

And so I persevered with my attempt to kindle something between us. Our woodland assignations continued, but we wondered for how much longer this particular routine could be maintained. Our worst moment was one Saturday afternoon when we found ourselves, by chance, lovemaking within ten yards of the path that was being used for the school cross-country run. Straggled out, the procession of exhausted boys in their white gym kits took nearly half an hour to pass, and all the while we had to lie as flat and as still as stones in the undergrowth, hardly daring to breathe.

It became my duty to see April home every evening. I walked with her up to the end of the drive and round the corner, she wheeling her bicycle like a darling little metal pony. We would kiss lingeringly in the twilight, April always the first to open her mouth and send her wriggly little tongue against mine (there was no chemistry in that spittle, it was just that, a chemical), before she would kick herself away on the bike, and I would watch her flickering red lamp shrink into the gloom of the lane. Could it really have been so soon in our knowing of each other that we first discussed the possibility of marriage?

Yes – what madness when two youngish people are thrown together as the only two kindred spirits in a vast community of others. No, I hadn't actually proposed marriage, and she hadn't accepted, but a sort of conversation had begun in which it seemed an assumed future event. We would talk about a life of shared dwellings, of shared beds, of twinned pursuits of art and mathematics. We would show the world that the two halves of the human spirit can live together, work together, love each other. The marriage would be a marriage of intellectual polarities: she would teach me the higher reaches of her subject, would fill my ignorant recesses with whispered quadrilaterals and pouted algebras; I would likewise teach her the art of seeing, of shapes and patterns and of translating these into the form of marks on a surface.

My friendship with Mountfoot acted as a sort of counterweight to my romance with April. In an odd way, it was all the more charged with flirtatious energy since the boy insisted on testing my loyalty to the heterosexual realm by teasing me mercilessly with his horseplay. In inadvertent furtherance of this, Pontefract had had me into his office again to discuss my hygiene illustrations and to say how useful they had proved to be. 'I can sense the school has become a cleaner, more wholesome place since we began using these drawings in our instruction, Mr Brill. The corridors are now filled with the perfumes of coal-tar soap and brightly scrubbed skin, and I can sometimes pass a whole day without seeing a single dirty fingernail.' He had in mind for me to execute another set of drawings – along similar lines but covering certain aspects of washing so far left out. 'We need a diagram to illustrate the washing of hair in a shower,' he said. 'Perhaps a diagram showing how one boy can assist another in the process. We also need a diagram showing how boys can assist each other with drying.'

I recruited Mountfoot again as the model for these drawings.

'You do realize, don't you, that you are simply supplying Pontefract with his own custom-made pornography?'

'That is an outrageous thing to say about your headmaster. And I fear for someone with an imagination as corrupt as yours to be able to think such a thing.'

Mountfoot was standing before me, naked but for a loincloth, on the middle of my living-room carpet, while I sat on my couch, rendering him with pen-and-ink. I had asked him to hold his hands to his head, as if soaping his hair, and was trying to get the detail of his two luscious armpits.

'You know what the next stage will be, don't you?' he said to me.

'No, I don't.'

'He'll be asking you for drawings of our lower parts in all their detail, for the sake of our sexual education.'

'I think that is unlikely. And I would refuse to cooperate anyway.'

'Would you? I should be most offended. Why would you refuse?'

'Because there are certain boundaries that must be maintained between master and pupil.'

'Oh, really? I've always thought of the relationship as being rather similar to that of husband and wife.'

'In which case I have great pity for your mother.'

Mountfoot laughed. 'I wonder what she would say if she were to step into this room now, and see me here like this.' He thought for a moment, then spoke in a high-pitched parody of her voice: 'Julius, girdle yourself this instant! We don't want Mr Brill falling down in a faint.'

I had been foolish enough to tell Mountfoot about my

experiences in the life room, and he had teased me about them ever since.

'The sight of your puny little self will have no effect on me whatsoever, I can assure you, and anyway, it was the paraffin fumes.'

'Shall we put your constitution to the test, sir?' Mountfoot was teasingly pulling at the knot of his loincloth. I ignored him, and thankfully he stopped. I was perfectly able to resist Mountfoot's charms, and often felt like rising to his playful seductions, just to see his terrified reaction. But I did enjoy his attention. We played at being lovers, and he seemed to realize that, though his master, I was only his senior by a few years and had very little advantage on him. As I have said, I always took our flirtations as a rehearsal for the real thing when it came along, and felt nothing of the shock and danger I had experienced at Somarco's maisonette. Here things were innocent and, it seemed to me, honourable. The foolish thing was to put our playacting down in written form. We had taken to writing each other parodic love letters. I would sometimes mark his art-history essays with a kiss and 'Good work, darling'. Mountfoot's mother might have seen the innocence of such missives, but not his father.

III

In the Lent term April and I were so well established as a courting couple that the English master thought it would be an awfully good idea to cast us together in the school's end-of-year production – *The Scarlet Pimpernel*. Oh, how I came to loathe that play, with its undisguised contempt for the common people, and its unashamed championing of wealth and privilege. I was made to take the part of Citizen Chauvelin, the envoy in search of the Pimpernel. April was given the part of Marguerite, wife of Sir Percy Blakeney, the Pimpernel himself. We protested at length but no one would hear a word said against the idea, and Pontefract seemed positively in favour. The tradition that staff should have roles alongside the boys in the school play and that new staff should take part as a sort of initiation was to be strictly observed.

The school possessed an impressive theatre, a proscenium stage with tiered seating and some baroque ornamentation on the various balconies, balustrades, pilasters and columns, where naked cherubim and bare-breasted Britannias cleaved the wind with their nipples. The curtains were thick velvet with luxurious fringes and tassels, the whole place in sumptuous contrast to the bleaker austerity of the Palladian exterior, with its rigid verticality. Backstage there was all the equipment you would expect to find in a Theatre Royal: gantries of catenaries, pulleys and weights, and rigs of lighting, trapdoors and dressing rooms. As we went through the rehearsals and got to know our parts, I began to warm to the project a little. I found that I could do a cod-French accent that would have the audience in titters. And the particular adaptation had been so crafted to allow for some romantic entanglements between Chauvelin and Marguerite at the beginning of the play, and we had some fun with those scenes. April was a natural actress – somewhat to her own surprise – and seemed quite at home on the stage, while I was shrinkingly nervous, and suffered terrible bouts of stage fright as we entered full dress rehearsals.

Our first performance was a tremendous success. My French accent had the audience in tears of laughter and I somewhat upstaged the poor boy who was playing the Pimpernel. The applause at the end took me wholly by surprise. For some reason

I had not expected any, but it seemed to pour over me in waves, and when I took my individual call, to have all that noisy praise heaped upon me, with whistles and cries of 'Bravo!' I lamented the fact that the visual artist never experiences such appreciation, though they may be more famous and celebrated than any actor. It didn't seem entirely fair.

I was swept up in the whole mood of the thing. There was a week of performances. People came from all over the country to see us. My acting grew in confidence as I began to learn exactly how to draw the right response from a crowd. I began to be critical of some of the boys in the cast, and would point out when they were placing the emphasis on the wrong words.

'Kenneth, try not to get carried away. I think you rather upset Sir Percy just then, with your scolding.'

'I wasn't scolding him, just giving him some helpful advice.'

'From the great, famous actor Kenneth Brill.'

It was rather nice to be forced to spend the evenings with April. After our performances I would walk her to the end of the drive. One night she even dared to sneak back to my rooms, and we spent the night together for the first time, though April insisted on sleeping on the floor.

One evening she remarked to me how conscious she had become of ageing since she had been a teacher. 'It gets to you, in the end. You become aware, as the cycles of the academic years pass, that you get older with each turn of the wheel, but the boys – because some are replaced each year – stay the same age. It is quite terrifying.'

I was on the verge of proposing to her when she said this, but something made me hold back, and I delayed asking the question.

So, no firm arrangement had been made, no ring offered, no knee bent, but a shared future had been tentatively mapped out and I was too full of the life of the schoolteacher in love to think about anything.

There was a special audience for the last night, which included many invited dignitaries. Members of the board of governors, pillars of the local community, a bishop. Everything went as before, but in Act Two, when I had a short moment alone on stage to give a brief soliloquy before Marguerite entered, things went catastrophically wrong.

Marguerite didn't enter. Instead, a man from the audience climbed the steps onto the stage, and marched towards me with big, purposeful strides. A man who was dressed for the occasion, in wing collar and frock coat. I was thrown by the intrusion. I could see April offstage, hesitating in the wings. Before I could think what to do the man had arrived at a spot directly in front of me, so close I could see the precise point where the whiskers of his handlebar moustache disappeared into his skin. He did nothing for a few seconds, but stare at me with the fixity of a statue. The audience, knowing no better, assumed him to be a part of the play, and were keen to hear the next line. Fearing things would never move on, I improvised a line, in *sotto voce*, 'Monsieur, *voulez vous* return to your seat, *s'il vous plaît*.' The man gave no response, but turned to face the audience.

'Ladies and gentlemen,' he said, in a voice strong with actorial projection, which made my own acting voice seem frail in comparison, 'be not deceived. Evil communications corrupt good manners. This man you see before you, this "inspector" so-called, is nothing less than the devil in disguise, a corruptor of innocent flesh, a devourer of innocent souls.'

I looked about me. Puzzled faces were watching from the wings, but no one seemed to think of dealing with the intrusion. As for the audience, they seemed to be enjoying this moment of direct address. The man continued, 'He has infected the sanctity of this school for young gentlemen with a brand of filth beyond the comprehension of decent people. My own son has suffered unspeakable torture at the hands of this man, and indeed may be permanently scarred by exposure to his depravities. I will now perform a rather violent but necessary act of purgation. Please avert your eyes if you are sensitive to acts of violent punishment.'

Before I had had a chance to comprehend the man's speech, or recognize that Mountfoot's illustrious father was standing before me, he had swung round and delivered to my solar plexus a blow of sickening force that had me doubled up in a second for my face to meet with the man's knee – a classic rabbit punch, the dirty trick of the street-corner fighter. I have only confused memories of events from thereon – I remember falling to the floor and blows raining down upon me: Mountfoot seemed to have produced a cane and was beating me thoroughly. I sensed an audience commotion before Mountfoot and I were carried offstage in opposite directions.

*

Beyond some bruising, I was not seriously injured, though the pain of my beating was severe enough for me to pass out of consciousness, and the savagery of the attack had been enough, so I heard, to make some in the audience rise up and come to my aid, realizing by then that they were not seeing a part of the play but witnessing some extraneous act of vengeance. By the time I had gathered myself enough to take in my surroundings, I had been returned to my room having been treated for my cuts and bruises by the school nurse, who administered her first aid with the same brusque bossiness she dished out to the boys. Lightly bandaged, I lay on my bed, alone, for what seemed hours, only vaguely aware of a general hubbub happening somewhere in other parts of the school, an uncharacteristic sense of disturbance and disorder in the quad.

Finally, Pontefract called on me. He had never been to my room before. He was not angry, or outraged – just panicky and a little puzzled.

'Look here, Brill, you cannot stay here a minute longer. I want you gone first thing tomorrow morning.'

I propped myself painfully on an elbow. 'I'm thirsty,' I said. This seemed to cause Pontefract more consternation, and he looked impatiently about the room for a water source, finally offering me a glass he'd clumsily poured from a jug on the sideboard.

'I've had to do everything in my power of persuasion to avoid having the police called here tonight. The reputation of the school might never recover. For Heaven's sake, the Bishop of Bath and Wells was in the audience, with his wife!'

'I swear to you, sir, this has all been a terrible misunderstanding.'

'So you may say. Lord Mountfoot is taking his son out of our school, and others are likely to follow. Oh, this is a catastrophe.' Pontefract was pacing up and down the room, his gown swishing and twisting. 'Apparently His Lordship came across some amatory letters between you and the boy . . .'

'That was just fooling around – playacting.'

'And some drawings – what you might call erotic drawings of the young man . . .'

'Those were the drawings you had asked me to do,' I winced, as a spasm of pain passed through my neck, 'preparatory sketches, for your hygiene talks.'

Pontefract lost all colour in his face. 'Good God, man, you mean you've been drawing boys in the altogether for that purpose? Oh, God. He was in my office for an hour – the drawings not three feet away from him. This could have been the end.' He suddenly stood still, as though everything had become clear. 'All the more reason for you to be gone tomorrow morning. I will call you a taxi myself. If you are on the premises after eight o'clock I will have the police come and arrest you.'

'I see. I suppose it would be too bold of me to suggest that it is Lord Mountfoot who should be facing arrest.'

Pontefract cast a look of genuine pity upon me.

'Would you at least allow me to see Miss Card? I need to talk to her.'

'Certainly not. Miss Card is a respectable teacher and has been grossly insulted. I can tell you that she has no desire to see you.'

*

I didn't believe Mr Pontefract, but there was nothing I could do to see April. A taxi was booked for seven thirty that morning to take me and my suitcases to Taunton, and the headmaster personally and wordlessly supervised my departure. Once I was in the cab, he slammed the door emphatically behind me, having mockingly acted the role of an overzealous porter and footman throughout my departure, eager to remove me personally from the school. I thought about reasoning with the driver, asking if he could take me to the village so that I could call on April, but I thought better of it. It would be too soon. My plan then was to stay in Taunton a few days, perhaps send her a letter, then go back and try to see her.

I stayed at the King's Head, a rather shabby establishment near one of the fine church towers. I drafted a letter.

Dearest April,

I have not had a chance to speak to you since yesterday's unfortunate incident, and as you will know by now, Ponty has dismissed me from the school with immediate effect. I am writing this on Saturday morning in a hotel in Taunton; my room reeks of dead fish and pipe tobacco. In the high street it is all very Victorian, with horses clattering on cobbles all day long.

April – I must see you.

I cannot explain in a letter what happened yesterday evening but, fearful of the prospect of having no alternative, I will make an attempt. Will you believe me if I say that what happened was all the result of a serious misunderstanding on the part of the boy's father? He came across some letters between us, and misinterpreted them. It is really as simple as that. That he should have reacted as he did can only point to a rather poisonous imagination and a violent lack of self-control. April – I am fearful of what you might be hearing from others about young Mountfoot and myself. I know only too well how rumours spread – in fact Mountfoot was one of the most despicable gossip-mongers and slanderers in the whole place. It wouldn't surprise me if he had fabricated the whole thing as a way of getting himself taken out of the school. As for his father, it astounds me how he can think public displays of violence are morally superior to the private displays of affection he believed were taking place between his son and myself – which they were not, at least not in the way he believed. I can still hear the screams of children in my ears! What a dreadful thing to have ruined the innocence of so many in a single swoop. But I say again, it was not of my doing.

This is such a tangled web now that I become confused myself. Perhaps you, with your wonderful mathematical brain, can find a solution to this puzzle. Ponty, of course, will not listen to any such apologies or explanations, and is as disbelieving as any rational man might be. You are supremely rational as well, but as we have always said, the world of the imagination is of as profound importance in science as it is in art. It will take a great imaginative leap on both our parts, April, to explain what happened last night, and I don't propose to be able to do that in a single letter. Would you allow me a visit to talk this through with you? I believed we had a

wonderful future ahead of us and now everything seems in
doubt because of what happened. I will try and call to see you
in the next few days.

Yours ever lovingly

        Kenneth

This letter took me several drafts, and most of the day to complete. By then it was too late for the post, and the following day was a Sunday. I decided to do nothing until Monday, when I would go to the village and deliver the letter in person.

After a desolate and bleak Sunday, and a Monday spent awkwardly in Taunton, drinking rough local cider in a pub and perusing the lace and china in the market square, I took the evening motor-bus to Cysterow Fitzherbert.

Mistress Appleby of Appleby Antiques was the biggest gossip in the village and would almost certainly have heard about my disgrace – she might even have been in the audience. Nevertheless, I went there directly, wishing the coiled bell that hung over the entrance wouldn't ring so loudly. Among the leather bottles, Oriental vases and little naked figurines carved in black gneiss, Mistress Appleby stood in all her chinny glory, twinkling with adamantine necklaces and cameo brooches. She might as well have used a broom to sweep me off her premises.

'Is Miss Card at home?'

'Out. Get out of my shop.'

'But I need to see Miss Card.'

'Would you like me to call the police?'

I removed myself from the shop, but lingered outside for a while, wondering if there was any way I could make contact with April, if she was in her rooms. Her window faced the back, over-looking a walled garden. I dared not trespass there.

Walking around the village green I could feel eyes trained upon me from beneath every thatched roof. I had missed the last motor-bus back to Taunton so had to take a room at the Shepherd's Arms. I was conscious of a mixture of sniggers and outrage as I made my way through the crowded saloon. 'Bloody disgrace,' I heard someone mutter.

'The nerve,' said another.

Were they talking about me, or were they discussing Chamberlain's latest budget? I could do nothing but shut myself away in my room, not even daring to venture out to find something to eat, in case I should meet some offended, wrathful farmer.

I devised a plan, while in my room, of setting up a sort of ambush. After a rather scanty breakfast at the inn (porridge and burnt bacon), I set off down the lane, the only route between the village and the school, found a spot where it passed through a wood and hid myself in a little gateway.

The problem was how to apprehend her while not at the same time scaring the life out of her or, worse, causing an accident. It was a difficult manoeuvre. At the first sight of me she wobbled. I moved across the lane to block her path, holding out my arms. She tried to steer past, a look of horror on her face. I forced her gently off the road and luckily she applied the brakes in time to avoid plunging into a blackthorn bush.

'I've got to talk to you, April.'

'Well, I don't want to talk to you.'

'But you must let me try to explain.'

'I don't think any explanation would be sufficient.'

'It's all been a terrible misunderstanding.'

'No, I think everything is perfectly understood.'

'Look, I've got a letter for you. It explains everything. The boy and I – we were just playing at being lovers . . .'

'Oh, really? Well, what about you and me? Were we just playing at being lovers?'

'No, of course not – how can you think that?'

'Very easily, Kenneth. From my perspective it's impossible to tell the difference. And besides, regarding that boy, I think you have behaved outrageously. I think Pontefract was quite wrong not to call the police – but, then, I think he's got enough to hide himself. The two of you disgust me. Let go of my handlebars!'

She wrenched them with such vigour I lost my grip. I felt weak and stupid, wobbling on the edge of a bramble-filled ditch, while April remounted her bike. I still had the letter in my hand, and was waving it desperately.

'April, you must give me a chance to explain properly.'

'I've had all the explanation I need, Kenneth. If you do this again, or persist in hounding me, I will call the police.'

'I'll see a doctor!' I called to her departing figure, as it slowly regained speed. I had no idea why I'd blurted that statement – it seemed the only thing left to me, to appeal once more to science and the rational.

'Perhaps you should.' She was well away from me by now, and although I had trotted along a little way behind her, I realized there was no point in trying to keep up. Before long she rounded a bend and was out of sight. I was left alone in the lane, the letter still in my hand, and nothing but a sense of emptiness within me, which caused me to double up again, as though I had been punched in the midriff.

IV

After several days of drab and dreary testimony, of having my work appraised and analysed by people without the necessary critical skills to appreciate it, and after hearing so many distortions and falsifications and outright lies told about me in court, I was only too willing to take the stand and face cross-examination. This was something of a turnaround for me, because all along I had dreaded the prospect of cross-examination and pleaded with Davies in our private conferences to engineer things in such a way that I wouldn't have to submit to the procedure.

'Lieutenant Brill, your defence has gone to great lengths to convince the court that you are a celebrated artist. We leave it to the jury to decide whether the evidence that has been provided to support this fact is sufficiently strong. I myself do not claim to be an expert on aesthetics, and I have no doubt that there are some people in the jury who share my lack of expertise. And so we have had several witnesses brought into the court who do possess expertise in this field. Again, it is up to the jury to decide on the strength of this testimony, but I can't help being reminded of Professor Wyre's assessment of your paintings as being the work of "an accomplished amateur". "An unformed artistic sensibility", I think, was another phrase he used. Correct me if I'm wrong.'

'That was just one opinion. You heard others who spoke highly of my work.'

'Captain Norman Learmouth. Yes, he did give some very high praise for you, didn't he? But then, as you say, that is just someone's opinion, and in this case the opinion of a very old friend of yours. How long have you known Captain Learmouth?'

'A few years. Perhaps five years.'

'And where did you meet?'

'We were fellow students at art school.'

'Yes, the Slade School of Art. That is another name that has recurred constantly throughout this hearing as further evidence of your standing as an artist. Because the Slade School of Art has a very high reputation, hasn't it?'

'Yes, it has.'

'Yet you didn't finish your studies there, did you?'

'No, I didn't.'

'You left two-thirds of the way through your first year. Why was that?'

'I was asked to leave.'

'Why?'

'I'm sure you know why.'

'I am giving you the chance to explain to the court in your own words.'

'I was expelled for bringing the university into disrepute. I had been taking part in life-drawing classes which a group of us ran, using prostitutes as models. It has never been suggested that anything untoward took place during those classes, and although I was arrested during a police raid on the premises, it was decided I had not broken any laws, other than giving the police a false name, which I did in the rather futile hope of avoiding any bad publicity for myself or the university.'

'Thank you, Lieutenant Brill. What you have said fully corroborates our own investigations. May I ask if you ever had any doubts or misgivings about using the services of prostitutes in this way?'

'Not at all. Drawing the human form is a vital skill for the artist, and the Slade was providing me with insufficient tuition in this area. I was taking it upon myself to rectify the matter.'

'It didn't occur to you that spending large amounts of your time in a brothel in a run-down and insalubrious part of London might not be the best way to spend your time as a student?'

'No.'

'Again I will leave it to the jury to decide on what it says about the moral integrity of an individual who can avail himself of the services of prostitutes with no apparent compunction, no moral doubts, no practical doubts.' He cleared his throat. 'How many students were in this group that visited the brothel?'

'Not many. Three or four.'

'Would you care to name them?'

'No, I would rather not.'

'Was Captain Learmouth among them?'

'I would rather not answer that question.'

'You have sworn to give a truthful answer to all questions put to you.'

'Yes, he was.'

'Thank you. Again I leave it to the jury to decide on the reliability of a witness who evidently has such a casual attitude to matters of morality. Now, Lieutenant Brill, let us move on to other matters. Can you tell the court why you decided not to wear your officer's uniform?'

'I was advised that as I had been arrested as a civilian I should be tried as a civilian. In fact, I do not recognize the authority of this court to try me in this case. I should be tried in a civilian court.'

The judge spoke out in a tone of incredulity: 'Did the accused just say he did not recognize the authority of this court?'

'He did, Your Honour. Perhaps your preference for trial in a civilian court is related to the fact that you are already rather familiar with those places, aren't you, Lieutenant Brill?'

I had already been told by Davies that these issues would come up. In a court-martial court, antecedents could be made known to the jury at any time. I made no verbal answer, just shrugged.

'Speak up!' said the judge.

'Yes,' I said.

I couldn't help but notice that one of the jurors was doing the *Telegraph* crossword.

'We have already heard about the case concerning the Soho brothel, which shows us that not only are you a person with a questionable attitude to sexual morality but that you are some-one who can easily lie to a police officer. Is that not so?'

'I didn't find it easy to lie to a police officer, no.'

'And since then you have appeared before magistrates on a charge of criminal trespass, in a notorious case that earned you a custodial sentence. You are, in fact, a somewhat seasoned criminal, are you not?'

'I would hardly say that.'

'Then how do you explain your string of offences?'

'I have on a number of occasions found myself in situations that have been misconstrued as . . .' I struggled to find the right words '. . . at odds with the law.'

Mr Cunningham paused for a moment and smiled to himself, as if savouring the phrase I had just used, then repeated it with a slow, lingering emphasis, turning to the bench, who smiled in a knowing way. 'At – odds – with – the law. A phrase that I'm sure will become a useful part of legal discourses in courtrooms of the future. One might find oneself "at odds with the law" in many situations not of one's making – but to be three times at odds with the law, including this latest circumstance, in the space of just a few years speaks less of ill-fortune and more of habitual criminality, wouldn't you say?'

'I can see that it might look like that to the outside world, yes. But that doesn't mean it's true.'

'So you attribute your law-breaking to bad luck and unfortunate circumstances?'

'Yes.'

'Would you say there is any common theme or recurring motif to these circumstances?'

'Yes. I would say they can all be attributed to my life as an artist.'

'In what way?'

'Well, I should say that this latest case is a good example. In pursuit of an artistic cause I have strayed into forbidden territory. Unwittingly I have painted scenes that should not be open to the public gaze. I fully understand now how that act could have been misconstrued. I think the same thing applies to the earlier case concerning the Soho brothel. In pursuit of an artistic goal I had strayed into forbidden territory. And on that occasion, as with this, my purpose, my intent, has been misunderstood. I think it is a condition of being an artist that one walks across boundaries, sometimes not even knowing they are there. For us the visual world contains no boundaries – to us a fence is not an obstruction, it is an illustration of perspective, giving depth to the landscape. A trench is not a tank trap, but a right-angled quadrilateral that accentuates the curvature of the land into which it is cut.'

The court fell into silence for a few moments. This was mainly so that the stenographer could catch up, as I had spoken rather quickly. Then Cunningham said, 'I invite the jury to consider the accused's remark about boundaries. Wars are fought over boundaries – men and women die. Might not such disregard for borders and boundaries be evidence of an indifference to political and ideological boundaries as well?'

'I have a great respect for ideological boundaries.'

'And moral ones?'

'Of course.'

'When you were called up, you put your occupation down as "failed artist". Can you explain?'

'I had meant it as a sort of joke. I wasn't feeling very good about my success as an artist at that time.'

'Oh, really? Yet your defence has gone to great lengths to establish your success as an artist. What was it the morally stout Mr Learmouth said – but for the war, terrible inconvenience. You remember his remarks?'

'I was not referring to my success commercially.'

'I see. So what sort of success were you referring to?'

'Aesthetic. Intellectual. I had begun to question my ability to see things clearly. I could no longer decide what was beautiful.'

'And what brought about these doubts, these uncertainties?'

I paused. 'I don't know.'

'Surely you must have some thoughts.'

'Perhaps the war. In a time of war the artist must consider what use they are, or their art.'

'You felt, in other words, that art is useless.'

'In a time of war, yes. That is, until I became involved in camouflage. Then I found that all my skills and training could be put to good use, that they could save lives, help win battles.'

'It must have been a great relief to you to find that your art has a use after all.'

'Yes, it was. I found that art could do more than just make moral or political statements. It could have a strategic purpose. I had never thought about art like that before.'

Cunningham paused. 'Perhaps what you mean is that you were made fully aware, for the first time, of art's power to deceive.'

V

I began drinking heavily for the first time in my life, far more heavily than I had ever drunk as a student. I would go into a pub and drink a gallon of beer in half an hour, a procedure that led almost directly to unconsciousness, and would wake hours later in some damp, ratty place to which I had been dragged. I was back in London but too ashamed to make contact with any of my old associates. I felt naked and exposed, and had constant visions that I was literally so. I would imagine that I was walking down a street and that my clothes had melted away, and I would run for cover, seeking shelter from the affronted gaze of passers-by, before realizing with intense relief that I was dressed as normal.

I once woke in a hostel among the dreary and unwashed, the men of meths, the Tolstoy-bearded down-and-outs, and from above the rough fabric of my covering, I thought I was being assailed by a figure who straddled me, like a child on a rocking horse, but with empty cuffs at my throat instead of hands, and it was nothing but clothes, my clothes, wrestling me, trying to kill me. Another dream, of course.

My life had entered its most turbulent phase. I had decided to leave Somerset straight away, but there seemed nowhere for me to go other than to the capital. I couldn't bring myself to beg help again from Learmouth or any of my former friends who still, presumably, were deep in their student lives. For more than a year I had lived outside their circle, and had felt myself to be far ahead on the road to artistic fulfilment. It was partly a reluctance to fall back to their level, to be among the amateurs and the apprentices, to be among those who previously had looked up to me (so I thought) as a person living in a reality beyond their comprehension, that kept me apart from them, and instead I drifted among the homeless of the capital, from the Salvation Army hostel in Spitalfields to the railway bridges of the Embankment or the benches in Trafalgar Square. I spent odd nights in the outbuildings of abandoned factories, or on half-sunk barges on the lower reaches of the Thames. I remember picking rashers of cold cooked bacon out of solid blocks of grease at the back of Claridge's, going through discarded monkey-nut shells outside a cinema. I stole milk from doorsteps. I begged.

In part I was conducting a conscious exercise in purgation, believing that in putting my body through such trials and punishments my soul might be cleansed of the idiotic tendencies that had seen me fall from grace with April and Berryman's. I wandered eastwards, or south of the river, places where none of my old friends ever set foot, and found a strange comfort and solace among the rough types who dwelt in those regions. In fact it was they who managed to shake some sense into me when, after months of a vagrant lifestyle, I was taken in hand by a kindly old mother who could see I was out of my depth. She was someone who made it her business to keep an eye on the destitute, and was used to seeing disgraced clergymen or fallen businessmen sleeping among the usual tramps but was surprised to find an educated young man like myself, someone who had not lived long enough to fall so far, as she put it. I don't even remember her name. She took me in to live, for a short while, with her own family, a noisy but happy mob crammed into a tiny house near Surrey Docks, and for a while I took my place, shoulder to shoulder with her other chicks. After some stern dressings-down and a severe curtailment of my drinking, I sobered up and began to remember who I was.

I recollected that I should have a decent amount of money put by in my bank account from nearly a year's employment at Berryman's. With few living costs, nearly all of my salary was saved. With this I was able to find a room, and leave my saviour a parting gift. Knowing she wouldn't accept money, I bought her a Chinese tea service, at the time a popular domestic novelty, which puzzled her so much she was unable to refuse it.

I rented a spacious attic in Southwark behind some wharves. A very desolate and eerie spot, that I couldn't help thinking of as a little corner of Hell. The pubs were full of boatmen and river-side workers. I liked it. And I had plenty of light and space. If I stood on a chair I could see St Paul's Cathedral and Tower Bridge. I wasted little time in converting it into a workable studio, pushing all the furniture to one end and opening up the space by the tall windows. I bought a good easel and the best-quality paints and brushes. I bought wood, canvas, carpentry tools and began making my own stretchers. I spent a small fortune on properly equipping myself, but for most of the time in the studio, I sat and brooded. I tried some half-hearted sketches of the view from the window, I charcoaled a St Paul's, I did a translucent watercolour of Southwark Cathedral, but they were nervous, timid little renderings – my buildings looked as though they would topple over with fright. So I sat and brooded some more. All of this material at my fingertips, and I couldn't touch it.

Dearest April,

This is the eleventh letter I have written to you, and I hope it is also the first one I will actually post. I am trying to be brave. I am trying to see things clearly. Sometimes I think I am a hollow shell, that the body that inhabits these clothes is made of nothing, and that I am just a set of garments walking around. Like one of those suits of armour you come across in old country houses. I have just read that back to myself, and it sounds mad. I am not mad, but I think I have lost a part of me since circumstances separated us. I will not go over again how wrong everyone has been about the relationship between myself and that young man whose name I cannot bear to put down on paper. The world has mistaken natural horseplay for something more sinister. But I will not go over it. What must you be thinking? I really must send this letter to you if only so that you have an address to reply to – if you want to reply. I hope that you do. Well, now that I am settled, I can write properly. For a good few weeks I have had no fixed address. In fact I returned to London entirely destitute and lived among the down-and-outs for a while. I think I had what they call a breakdown. I think I went through it all to help me forget you. But I can't forget you, April. You keep coming back into my thoughts. In fact you hardly ever leave them. You are the only ~~girl~~ woman I have ever had any feelings for, and who I have ever felt understands me.

*I have found permanent lodgings near Southwark
Cathedral, a part of London unknown to me before now – the
address is at the top of the letter – a rather rough place full
of navy types, but I like it. I have converted my room into a
studio – it is an attic with wonderful views and I have become a
proper garret-dwelling artist, except that I find I cannot paint.
I can put paint on my brush, but the moment the brush touches
canvas, the colour seems to drain out of it – sometimes I think
my artistic talent is draining out of my body through the soles
of my feet. Art was once the thing that filled me. Now it seems
to be draining me. Oh, April, how I miss talking with you,
especially about painting – you brought such freshness to the
subject. I have never heard anyone say the things you say
about art. What can I do to convince you that I have done
no deliberate wrong? Well, please write to me.*

Kenneth

*

When my savings ran low I started looking for work, and had
some unhappy, enervating experiences in factories and shops.
I spent an intolerable spell as a door-to-door vacuum-cleaner
salesman ('Feel the suction, madam, go on, feel it'). I shovelled
coke in a coking plant – it can't have been more than a few days
I lasted at that job. We were like miners above ground, stripped
to the waist and plastered black with coal dust, shovelling the
anthracitic rubble until I felt my backbone would snap. Eventually I got a job with Houseman and Sons, a large gentleman's
outfitter on Shaftesbury Avenue, a vast warehouse of cheap
jackets, trousers, waistcoats and shirts, as well as underclothes,
handkerchiefs, belts, braces, umbrellas, walking sticks, canes,
shoes, boots and hats. Houseman's was staffed by elderly men
whose outlook upon life had changed little since the days of
the *fin de siècle*, and the shop was vast and labyrinthine. No one

knew how much stock we had. There were trousers in the shop that had been hanging there since the nineteenth century. Not surprisingly, the place reeked of mothballs.

It is a peculiar thought – the clothes that you wear during a lifetime. The items you outgrow, the ones that wear out. Imagine you could see them all at once, laid out on a bed. It would be like looking at all your past selves arrayed for inspection. The passing of clothes and the passing of selves seemed, to me, to be one and the same. Perhaps that was why, on being stripped of my life with April at Berryman's, I felt naked. Indeed, so strong was this feeling that I decided to confront it, and resumed my series of nude self-portraits. My life had been so different and busy since that earlier series I had almost forgotten them and wondered what had happened to them. Did Somarco still have them? Did he leer and enthuse over them in the privacy of his bedroom?

I bought a full-length mirror from a junk shop in Long Lane. The man there delivered it with a horse and cart, and helped me up the four flights of stairs with it. The self revealed in that mirror was not one that I had met before. I was shocked by its apparent undernourishment. There was nothing sublime about my pale form. I was as white as a snowman. As I looked closer there were other colours. A yellowness around the armpits and elbows, a faint flush of pink in the chest, the dirty orange of my nipples, then shadows, shading, and a sense of the underlying musculature and bone structure.

I was pleased with the paintings I did. I had rediscovered my talent. The colour no longer drained from my paintbrush; I felt life returning to my body, from the feet up. I became ambitious, and my paintings increased in scale and density. I began to wonder about showing them to the world.

*

In the shop, I became fascinated by the fitting rooms. Little booths with stage curtains into which grown men would place themselves, just like the pretty assistant in a magician's cabinet, and draw the curtain sharply and emphatically across. Then the curious and clumsy transformation, the curtain buffeted from behind, the grunts and groans of a portly man struggling into a new pair of trousers, to be revealed some time later as a different man – hot and red in the face, hair askew, glasses misplaced, the new trousers fitting awkwardly.

I was sometimes charged with the task of assisting people during these metamorphic episodes. Through chinks in the curtains I could sometimes see an ugly pair of thighs quiver with the effort of dressing, a truss or a sock suspender come into unwelcome view. I felt a reassuring bondedness with my own clothes at those times, patrolling the little range of curtained booths, carrying clothes on hangers like a valet, or a dresser in a theatre.

And they were a very theatrical environment, the fitting rooms at Houseman's, the ideal place to make a theatrical entrance. It did give me a shock, not to say a chill, when a booth had its curtain snappily drawn back from within to reveal not the portly gent I was sure I had seen enter but the dapper young half-Italian, half-Spaniard Somarco, wearing a sports jacket and a pair of plus-fours, with beige shirt and green tie, the knot of which – as plump as a toad – he was adjusting as he emerged.

I couldn't help but express delight to see him. All thoughts of the awkwardness and outrage of our last encounter were forgotten.

'Why, Kenneth, what a coincidence. Are you buying something for the outdoors too?'

'Don't pretend you don't know that I work here, Somarco.'

'But I can assure you I just happened to be looking for some outdoor gear and heard this was the best place in London. How do you think I look? Ready to climb a rock face? Have you been away? I didn't realize. I've been away myself for so long now. I could have done with you, Kenneth. I had to get someone else to feed my plants and they let all my orchids die.'

It is astonishing how time can transform one's perception of people – meeting Somarco again was like meeting my oldest and dearest friend. In the long months since my expulsion from Berryman's I had felt utterly friendless, so coming across someone who not only knew me from the old days but who greeted me with such warmth and familiarity was an experience to be treasured. It was in this state of mind that I accepted his invitation to dinner that very night. He was insistent. He said he had the most wonderful proposition to put to me. 'And I promise you, Kenneth, I promise you I will do nothing to embarrass you again.'

And so I was back at the *grande maisonette* that had been my home for so many weeks. Somarco cooked a wonderful meal of mussels in white wine – I had never tried shellfish before. 'They are an aphrodisiac,' said Somarco, 'but don't worry. The wine is an antidote.'

He asked me about my painting, and I was able to tell him that it was going well. He told me about our circle – Learmouth and Knell were the outstanding students of their year. That was hardly a surprise. They had staged their own exhibition, along with some other students, that had attracted the attention of the press. 'I contributed a couple of little prints, but they looked very out of place. Learmouth has become the most depressing sort of realist. They invited random members of the public to the private view – Learmouth picked names out of a telephone directory and sent off invitations. I suggested he picked people with the same names as famous artists – wouldn't it be wonderful to have a private view full of people called Mr Whistler and Mr Turner? But Learmouth said I was being too clever. I told him he'd lost his sense of humour since he joined the Communist Party. Did you know he is now officially Comrade Learmouth of the Order of the Red Star?'

'No, I didn't.'

'He believes that art should be for the common people, that it should raise class-consciousness and promote the class struggle. So now he paints nothing but bus stops and factory gates, labour exchanges and tramps. You said you were a tramp for a while – perhaps he painted you.'

'I doubt it.'

I asked Somarco where he had been travelling.

'Oh, everywhere, but mainly in Germany.'

He said this so casually, so offhandedly, as if everyone made trips to Germany every day.

'But Germany, Somarco. Why Germany?'

'Visiting friends.'

'Didn't know you had friends out there.'

'I didn't. I have now, though. And, apart from that, I was collecting specimens. Listen, Kenneth. I have a little project I would like you to help me with.'

He took me into the conservatory, and showed me a suitcase that was lying on its side. He opened the catches and lifted the lid. There was a strong, musty smell. Somarco lifted out a large parcel, a pillow-sized bundle wrapped in canvas. He brought it up to a table and laid it carefully down.

'What have you got there?'

'I'll show you.'

He began unfolding the damp, dirty sections of canvas. I could smell the earth strongly. For a moment I thought he had stolen something from a farm – or perhaps he had truffles, or some other exotic, expensive thing. But, no, what he unwrapped and placed on the table was simply a square of turf. Quite good-quality grass and a couple of inches of dark soil. Regular grass, as though it had come from a well-kept lawn. Dark green grass, thickly planted, though yellowing a little at the tips. The blades were flattened from their journey.

'Looks like a lump of grass,' I said. Somarco carefully tended the blades, lifting them up, untangling them, a bit like a hair-dresser examining a lacklustre bouffant.

'This will need to be transplanted very quickly – in the next few days, or it will be too late.'

'Transplanted where? You haven't got a garden.'

'This is very special grass, Kenneth.'

'Is it?'

'Yes. Very special.' Somarco was now wearing an expression of deep earnestness, and his lips were contracted in a way I hadn't noticed before, as though he was getting ready to play the trumpet.

'Where did you get it? Did you steal it?'

'It's German grass, Kenneth. I dug it up from a lawn in Germany. In fact, I dug it up from the grounds of the German Chancellery. The Reichstag.'

'What?'

'Yes. The feet of Hitler himself have probably flattened these blades.'

'But weren't there guards?'

'Yes. It was a very dangerous operation. If I'd been caught – well, I would probably have been imprisoned. Or worse. I have risked a great deal to bring this grass to England.'

'But why?'

'Just a little experiment, really.'

'In what way?'

'Well, you must know, Kenneth, that England's days are numbered. Adolf Hitler is quite certain to either invade, or persuade us to become part of a German Empire some time in the next few years.'

'Somarco, you promised me before that you were not in favour of Hitler.'

'Of course I'm not – but we have to recognize that he is a force in Europe that cannot be stopped. His will to succeed is insurmountable. There is nothing that can stop him. Apart from this grass.'

'Somarco, you are insane.'

'So what if I am? This grass is German rye grass. It is one of the most virulent, hardy grasses in the world. It grows from the base, not the tip, unlike most other grasses. It is the most durable, the most resilient. You can scythe it and scythe it and scythe it, it will just keep growing back. Kenneth, I have this plan. I brought this grass here for a reason. Do you realize that the English and the German people belong essentially to the same race, and that that race is directly descended from the ancient Greeks? That our royal family is really a German royal family, descended directly from the kings of Bavaria?'

'What are you getting at?'

'I brought this square of turf home from Germany, with the intention of transplanting it in England. German rye grass is one of the most robust and vigorous grasses. Once it has been planted, it will overpower the surrounding grasses and spread. Just one square foot of grass, like this, will, in time, spread across the whole of the English landscape.'

'Monstrous.' I laughed. 'You mean a sort of grass invasion, so that when the Germans invade for real, they will have the familiar smell of grass beneath their feet.'

'No, don't you see? There will be no need for invasion, once the grass does its work. All flesh is grass, Kenneth. Soon our cows will be eating German grass and giving us German milk. The pollens will cross-fertilize with agricultural wheat, and we will be eating German bread. From the bottom up, Kenneth, we will become German once again. There will be no need for an invasion. We will instead become partners. Brothers. Sisters.'

'Better than going to war, I suppose.' I was still thinking that Somarco was joking, or being overly poetic, as was his wont. 'Why doesn't Hitler do this with all those other countries he's invaded?'

'It's a question of time, Kenneth. Plant time and human time. Politics needs to adapt to plant time. Hitler recognizes a kinship with England, and this may give us the time for the grass to do its work. But I need you to help me, Kenneth. I can't do it on my own.'

'Can't do what on your own?'

'My transplantation project. It'll be a two-man operation.'

'Two man? Why?'

'The site I have chosen is one that is rather heavily fortified.'

'Oh, Somarco – what are you thinking of? Where have you chosen?'

'Kenneth, you have spoken many times about your gardening past. How your father is now the lord of a manor . . .'

'Yes. Why don't we just plant it at Heathrow? The soil there is the richest in the land, your German grass will have spread as far as Windsor in no time.'

Somarco chuckled in his lisping way, and sipped his deadly sherry.

'Why do you chuckle so, madman?'

'Listen to me, Kenneth. I am more serious than I have ever been in my life. I feel as though the future of Europe, of the whole world, rests on my shoulders. If you were to begin the project of replacing England's grass with its ancestral cousin, where would you start but in the most sacred stretch of lawn in the land?'

I put down my drink and looked at Somarco with as much

mock earnestness as I could manage. 'Good heavens, Somarco – you don't mean Lord's Cricket Ground?'

'No!' Somarco snapped, a brief and rare flame of anger burning in his eyes. 'Why should anyone care about a cricket pitch? No, I am suggesting we plant this grass in the King's own lawn. The gardens of the royal residence – Buckingham Palace.'

'But, Somarco, there's no grass there, just a parade ground where soldiers march up and down. You don't know England very well, do you?'

Somarco regained his patience and explained to me that at the back of the palace, hidden from public view, there was an enormous garden, with a lake, woods and a wide, sweeping lawn. 'It is well known that the King takes a constitutional every morning, walks about the grounds in his bare feet, the Queen by his side, also barefoot. How sweet, Kenneth, if they tread German grass, that they gather a sheen of German dew on their toes . . .'

'Well, the dew would still be English, wouldn't it? And wouldn't the spread of your grass be rather hampered by the isolation of this garden? How will it get over the wall?'

'Oh, don't worry, Kenneth. German rye grass, once established, has a seed dispersal range of over a hundred feet. Once Buckingham Palace has fallen, Green Park will shortly follow, along with St James's Park. Then it is but a little leap across to the immense greenery of Hyde Park, and all the little squares of Mayfair and Belgravia will fall like dominoes, Grosvenor Square, Berkeley Square, Vincent Square and, yes, Lord's Cricket Ground before very long, and then Regent's Park, all the grassy territories falling one by one, then the gardens of the suburbs, bang bang bang, all gone, back to their Germanic origins. And once London is taken, there can only be a surge outwards in every direction through the Home Counties, blade upon blade falling to the superior grasses. They will unroll their proud verdure up to the brim of the white cliffs themselves, then, at the other end, northwards into the toughest English grasses – Yorkshire will put up some resistance with their hardy marrams and sedges, and the Scots, well, we shall have to see about Scottish grass . . .'

You would need to see Somarco deliver this masterplan to appreciate how beguilingly funny he was in such moods, how sweetly witty he was being, holding his sherry aloft and winking so devilishly (not that I think the devil ever winked at anyone). This invasion from within by gardening seemed, in our moments of drunken enthusiasm, to be a worthy contribution to the peace movement that was simmering beneath the surface of everyday life. The Peace Pledge Union, Somarco assured me, was already overrun by Fascists.

*

We went on night-time reconnoitres along Constitution Hill and Grosvenor Place. We marvelled at the wall that surrounded the grounds of the Palace. I had never noticed it before. Not such a high wall, when one considered it. Certainly scaleable if one man acted as support for the other. Was that all Somarco was after, a leg-up? No. He wanted someone to come with him into the garden as well. Someone to help him with his equipment. Somarco had real climbing in mind, with ropes and a grappling hook. The deadly array of iron spikes on the wall made it too risky a venture, except for one spot Somarco had found on the south stretch of the wall, where it skirted an enormous plane tree. Here there were no spikes, but the wall was higher to compensate. Somarco estimated it was nine feet high at this point.

He was an experienced climber. He had scaled crags in the Pyrenees in search of rare orchids, had dangled from ropes in the Gorges du Tarn to get a better look at some lesser spotted saxifrage.

'I don't know, Somarco,' I said, during our more sober

moments, 'it seems rather risky. Surely there are dangers attached to an operation like this.'

But we had seen how empty the city was at night. I had rarely been out in the streets much beyond midnight, but an early hours stroll through the centre of London was like walking in a city of the dead. Not a thing stirred. No traffic in the streets, no people, no noise. If we should get stopped by a policeman, we were simply mountaineers heading for Victoria and an early train to the wilderness. I had not considered that Victoria would take you to nowhere higher than the South Downs. And on the other side of the wall? Somarco was quite sure there would be no guards except those close to the house. There would be no patrols in the grounds – why should there be? Had there ever, in the whole history of the royal residence, been an incursion over the wall? I could not think of one, I had to admit.

*

I'm not sure, now I come to think of it, that I ever formally agreed to be Somarco's partner in this absurd gardening adventure, but nevertheless, one moonless night in April, we were walking through London together in the small hours of the morning. Piccadilly Circus was a little theatre of stillness and silence. Piccadilly itself was the same, an empty street in which the only movement came from drifting newspapers caught in a breeze. How I loved the city in such a sempiternal state, with the machinery of power dozing. We only once glimpsed another living soul, and that happened to be a policeman emerging from a side-street. We ducked into St James's and were not troubled again before we reached the spot in the wall we had chosen for our assault.

Somarco had insisted that we dress correctly, which meant thick clothes, scarves, woolly hats, anoraks and climbing boots. We each had a canvas knapsack: Somarco was carrying ropes and grappling hooks and the turf; I was carrying a small spade, flash-lights, binoculars. I had a flask of hot tomato soup and a pack of sandwiches in case things went wrong and we had to hide in the grounds for a while.

'Are you sure there won't be any trip wires?' I said to Somarco, as we began unpacking our equipment. 'What about mantraps? I've heard they use mantraps up on the grouse moors, so why not here?'

Somarco put a firm hand on my shoulder as we crouched by the wall. 'Leave it, Kenneth. I have told you, there will be no such devices, because they will never expect a break-in. If you don't want to go through with this, Kenneth, I will quite under-stand. There would be severe consequences if we are caught. We could be charged with high treason and hanged.'

I told Somarco not to be silly.

Somarco approached the wall first, and was at the top in sec-onds. It took me a little longer, and I was surprised by how much effort was needed. I'd had no idea of my own body weight. By the time I was at the top, Somarco had lowered the rope down the other side and was invisible in the darkness at the foot of the wall. I lifted the rope on the street side, so as to leave no visible clue to our invasion, then lowered myself into the darkness.

We found ourselves immersed in dense, shrubby under-growth. Beneath our feet, a deep litter of leaf mould, and all around us thin, brittle, knotty branches that we had to push aside, with occasional backlashes of foliage striking us full in the face (the leathery touch, I thought, of rhododendron leaves) before we emerged into open space. Black grass seemed to stretch into infinity, though in the distance the curved smooth-ness of a lake was visible. Immense lone trees stood like towering candelabra. Then, just visible as a square, balustraded immens-ity, a wing of the Palace, so far away I could scarcely believe we occupied the same space. And it wasn't until now that we were over that I realized there had been noise outside, that London, in the small hours, did make a sort of collective hum, because that was now very noticeable by its absence. We were in a realm of exquisite silence, as though we had stepped out of the city in a single leap to enter a remote Arcadian paradise. And so we stepped out onto the lawns of England's sacred heart, and became giggly and childish. Having breached the perimeter of this fortress, we now capered and romped in our trespass, chasing each other across the grass, doing tumbles and handstands. To dance in the gardens of the monarch was such a glorious titillation. But before long we got down to the serious business of gardening.

We selected a spot in the middle of the vast grassed area, not too close to the house, yet boldly placed to represent a definite stake in a territory. The grass was very well maintained, beautifully clipped to a bowling-green smoothness. What an army of mowers they must have to keep it so well trimmed. This did present difficulties that we hadn't foreseen. A lawn as well maintained as this would bear its wounds very openly. It would be hard to insert some alien grass without it becoming noticed, not least because the German grass we had on us – stout, sturdy stuff as it was – had continued growing throughout its travels, and was now looking quite shaggy. Luckily, Somarco had brought a fishing knife with him. We saved the task of trimming for after we had completed the transplant, however. Our initial task was to prepare the German grass's new home. We knew the fit had to be as tight as possible, so using the German turf as a template, I made incisions all around the edge with the flat blade of my little spade. We had used a child's seaside spade for the purpose, the only such instrument small enough to fit in a knapsack. We then realized we hadn't foreseen the associated problem – what to do with the removed rectangle of Palace turf? There was no alternative apart from taking it away with us. So that was what we did. The digging was difficult, however, much more difficult than I'd anticipated. The ground was hard and the child's spade didn't provide much in the way of leverage; I was afraid that the thin wooden shaft would snap. It seemed to take an hour of careful probing and pulling before the desired section was finally lifted, and we were able to substitute our strong German grass, which slotted in perfectly. Then Somarco took his knife, sawed the grass to an acceptable shortness, and we trampled the ground to even it out a little. In the dim light our handiwork looked pretty good.

And then the dog arrived.

Out of nowhere it seemed to come, as black and as silent as its surroundings, yet with a thousand times the energy. It went for Somarco first, knocking him to the ground. He rolled about but managed to stand up and begin running, the dog tearing at his coat. We saw torches in the distance bobbing towards us, heard voices. Other dogs became visible, bounding out of the darkness. Suddenly I was running without thinking, my body moving of its own volition, while my mind tried to determine the best thing to do. Only after a while did I notice that Somarco and I had run in different directions and that the dogs had decided to follow him rather than me, as had most of the men who came after the dogs. I dared to think I might have been the lucky one.

After the initial burst of running I took a moment to look over my shoulder. Torches were still bobbing and swinging around, there were voices, but they were very distant. It seemed they had lost their quarry, and were pondering their next move. Perhaps they were inspecting the area of our digging, and the equipment we had left behind. But I felt far from safe. In my panic I seemed to have run blindly towards the Palace. I was within a few feet of its rear elevation. The only way out of the grounds was back over the wall via the rope we had left dangling, but the dogs and the bobbing torches cut off that route.

Looking back I could see that my hunters were spreading out, that very soon every escape route would be blocked and I would be unable to do anything but wait for the dogs to sniff me out. I was being forced closer and closer to the building itself. I climbed some steps, scaled a low balustrade wall, and found myself up against the back wall of the Palace.

Crouching beneath the tall, plainly regal architecture, I heard the sound of marching feet on stone. I was expecting to see Grenadier Guards in red coats and bearskins emerge from round the corner of the building. I put my back to the wall and crept silently past magnificent windows. Then, feeling I had no alternative, I tried one.

To my utter disbelief and amazement, the first window opened without any difficulty. An undignified moment of tummy-leverage over the sill delivered me head first into the Palace. I closed the window behind me.

My first glimpse of the interior of the royal residence revealed a space that was surprisingly functional, for I was among the pipe runs and painted brickwork of a service corridor. In a panic I ran up a set of stairs, then through another door, this time to find myself in a corridor of the Palace proper: a lush patterned carpet, walls adorned with pictures in gilt frames, tables with ornate legs supporting ornaments of extravagant, intricate craftsmanship, chandeliers like rain showers held apart from time, faceted and refractory, twinkling delightfully in the moonlight from tall windows. The carpet was so thick my footfalls were soaked up instantly, and I found it easy to move silently among the opulence of the monarchy. I turned several corners, found myself in a great gallery with paintings, vast and intimidating, of mounted personages or knee-breeched and periwigged folk standing proudly in landscapes. I felt like Alice must have felt at the bottom of the rabbit hole, for there were doors everywhere, but none that seemed meant for me. Suddenly at the far end I heard soft footsteps and froze, to see a figure in livery carrying an oil lamp stride quickly past, thankfully not taking the turning that would have brought us face to face, instead disappearing down the adjoining passage.

That he should be up at such an hour made me wonder if the interior of the Palace was being searched as well. I trod carefully. The silence was intense, but the darkness of the halls gave me a sense of safety. When I heard a door slam it seemed to echo from many miles away.

I quickly became lost in fascination with my surroundings. In the grandiose warren of gilded portraiture, pendentive chandeliers and luscious ornamentation, there were unspeakably gorgeous things. I would find myself exclaiming aloud, 'Is that a real Canaletto?' and pause before the controlled frenzy of that artist's masterly vision of Venice, only to find it was London-depicted. And then, just a few steps further on, a monstrous Tintoretto, flesh pouring across the towering canvas, some classical scene of fraught mortals as playthings of the gods. I couldn't help but wonder at the riches our monarch so casually possesses for his own private viewing – one of the finest collections of art in London yet it was invisible to its population. That in itself was grounds enough for revolution. I came upon a Donatello, a sweetly buttocked David, a prim-cocked treasure that I couldn't resist fondling, and other statues, one of a brilliantly appended Hercules, with club and lion pelt. I couldn't resist caressing with my fingertips the modest little marble cock with which the sculptor had endowed him. I tickled his cold, hard balls, giggling to myself.

And then a light came on.

VI

Dearest Angelica,

> *At times I could believe that a place like
this was my home. Glancing out of my window, watching a
woman tending her rooftop garden – she has chickens in little
wire enclosures, she has vines and creepers on trellises – what
are they, kumquats? Lemons? Too far away to tell. The woman
has her head uncovered, unaware that she is observed. Of all
the tall windows round about, she hasn't noticed mine. And
then I hear children in the kindergarten in the other block,
a kindergarten for Jewish children. How odd, in a place like
this, to find a remnant of my own childhood in those sweet
little boys and girls speaking the language I never learnt.*

> *I can walk down the street and people will nod at me.
They tell me how much they hate the British, but in such a
friendly, pleasant way that it is impossible to be offended, and
they smile when I agree with them, when they tell me stories
about how cruel the British were to their parents, who manned
the barricades in the first revolution, just after the Great War.
Impossible not to like these elegant, dapper people, even though
they spend most of their energies in trying to sell you something
or other.*

> *I have surprised myself by how readily I have adapted to
the army life, and sometimes think I have found my true home
here in this regimented existence. There are no difficult decisions
to make: everything is about strategy and a military purpose.
No one worries about what anything means. I might even stay
on, when this war is over, and make it my permanent career.*

I will end my days as an ancient general up to my eyes in brandy and cigars.

Angelica, I had a message from Mother, just a short one, to tell me of your terrible news. I know I have been a very neglectful and inconsiderate brother over the years, but this news made me feel all the worse for not coming to your wedding. It was not that I had declined your invitation, as I believe you thought, through some sort of disapproval of your husband – I had never met him so why should I judge? The reason I could not attend was that I have been incapacitated by nervous collapse brought on by the variety of stresses and shocks that befell me once I had been expelled from the Slade. You will have heard, I expect, about the tribulations I underwent in the period immediately afterwards – I took a job in which I was very happy, but lost it through no fault of my own. I went to prison as a result of another misunderstanding. I have been betrayed by those I love so many times that I am constantly on the edge of losing my trust in human beings altogether. But then I hear the Jewish children in the playground below, and some faith, a little, is restored. You have my deepest sympathy over your loss. There is no comfort or compensation in those words, I'm sure, and if there is any way I can do more in that respect, then please let me know.

There are those I have betrayed, of course. Do you remember that little boy who used to come to our house? The little boy with ginger hair and a bragging tendency? Well, he is here in Egypt with me. I could hardly believe it when I saw his name on a transfer form. 'Major M. J. Boone'. It was as though he had been sent to me or I to him. It was a simple thing to track him down. I found his headquarters and waited for him to emerge, then followed him through the streets of Cairo to his favoured drinking hole, one of the better hotels. What was I to do – follow him in there, go straight up to him, announce my presence? At first I did nothing but observe from afar, to confirm his identity, for it is not easy to be accurate when trying to identify someone you haven't seen since childhood, and out here, in the desert, childhood seems a very remote place. But it was he. The same in every way but for an increase in scale, a thickening of frame, a lengthening of the noble nose. I've never seen anyone so naturally suited to the officer's desert uniform. He was sitting at a table in the lounge bar of the hotel, beneath the rotating fans and half obscured by spindly fronds. He held forth with all the braggadocio I remembered of old. This was the man who, as a child, convinced me his father had a private army, who threw pennies into the air for his classmates to scramble over, with whom I had pistol duels and convoluted games of chess, sword fights with dinner knives instead of swords. He was still doing all of these things, with words and demeanour in place of instrumentation: I could see that from my vantage point. He was scattering words that his companions fought over, conducting silver-tongued persiflage carefully rigged in his favour – and his companions loved him for it.

You may never have been told, Angelica, about the terrible crime I committed against Marcus Boone. I don't mean the wounding with the knife, which I expect you remember, I mean the thing I did that got me expelled from St Saviour's. Have you ever been told? Well, it pains me and confuses me to describe it, and I will not do so here, but I will just try to put into your mind an image of a young boy, barely ten years old, stripped of all his clothes and huddling on the floor of a school lavatory cubicle whose roof is open to the sky. His clothes have been stolen, he has no way of covering himself. He is trapped by his own nakedness: he cannot leave the cubicle for the pain of indignity is too great. He tries to crawl along narrow gaps between buildings and walls so that he won't be seen, but there is no way out. He scratches and grazes himself in the process.

In the end he has no alternative but to present himself to the world, to walk naked into it, to his great shame. Angelica, I was the boy who stole his clothes. And I see now that a great deal of my suffering since has happened as a result of my failure to acknowledge this. The problem was that Marcus disappeared from my life the day that that happened, and I had not seen him since, until now. In my imagination he has remained the naked child in the school lavatory. He has been naked all these years.

I spoke to him, Angelica. I struck up a conversation. I had to wait until the end of the evening, when he left the hotel and parted from his companions. There in the boulevard I caught up with him as he headed home.

'Excuse me, hello.' I made so bold as to catch him by the shoulder, which caused him to stop in alarm. He gave me a scolding look, suspecting a breach of etiquette, before he noticed that I was also an officer. 'It's Major Boone, isn't it?'

As simple as that. Over this great chasm of childhood to adulthood I called out to him in the dark of a Cairo street.

'Yes,' he replied.

I hadn't introduced myself, hoping he would recognize me. Then, a little disappointed, I said, 'It's Kenneth. Kenny. Kenny Brill.'

The name elicited not a single spark of recognition, though I could see he was trying hard. The light was dim. We moved to a doorway where there was a porch lamp.

'I'm so sorry,' he said. 'Have we met?'

'Of course we have, Marcus.' I laughed. I was a little light-headed after a string of martinis in the hotel bar. 'Surely you remember? The Heath. St Saviour's. Sipson.'

Suddenly I thought of the danger I might be in. I had wholly neglected the fact that I was the cause of his exodus from the Heath: I had put him through that hell of exposure in the lavatories of St Saviour's. How would he respond to the awakening of that memory?

But there was no response. Not at first. Then a flicker of recognition.

'Sipson? Rings a bell. St Saviour's – was that a school or a church?'

'Both. We were at school together, you and I. Though you were a year above me.'

'I'm sorry, I have such a terrible memory for faces, and names for that matter.' He went on to explain how much he was moved around as a child – how he went from military town to military town; he was never in one school for very long. St Saviour's, the Heath, Sipson: the places that had filled the whole of my childhood had been only a fraction of his, a fleeting moment in a transient, itinerant life conducted in the wake of an important father. Even so, his lack of recollection shocked me, sickened me. I felt ill to be so forgotten. I felt as though part of me was missing. I felt half eviscerated, then I felt shame for harbouring such feelings towards the major, for feeling the need to be remembered at all by him, yet it was such an insulting thing to be forgotten. Have you ever been forgotten, Angelica? I so very much doubt it. I have remembered you in every detail, just like I remember everyone I have ever met. I think it is the highest compliment you can pay someone, the utmost tribute of respect, to remember them, and to remember them fully.

We strolled side by side along the quiet street. Marcus had given up trying to remember me and we talked instead about the war. Of course he was eager to impress me with his achievements. He had already been decorated for bravery during Dunkirk. In the desert he had commanded tank regiments and had won several decisive battles. There was something of the childhood bragging in what he said, but it

416

*was tempered now with a more considered outlook on life, and
a new awareness of those around him. No longer did his gaze
seem to pass right through me and back to himself. It stopped
at my face. He saw me, for the first time.*

*We have agreed to meet, Marcus and I, to talk over old
times, to help him remember (he is keen to remember, he told
me) – I will let you know what happens.*

I will never post this letter, of course.

Yours affectionately

Kenneth (your brother)

VII

What should I say about my time in prison? Perhaps it is best
passed over without comment. Fourteen days. I don't suppose
that sounds much to you. A fortnight. An Easter break. Two
weekends. But in prison time moves slowly. It hangs in the air
of your cell like a fog; you have to push against it just to breathe.
By the end of a day you find you have filled your pockets with the
stuff and can do nothing but lie down under its weight.

I managed things poorly. My fellow inmates spoke a language
I didn't understand. I was either shunned or the object of a
nudging curiosity. People laughed at my accent. I was sometimes
prodded or elbowed. At mealtimes I was given a child's portion,
dribbled on. In my second week my fortunes changed a little.
By then it became known what I had done, and this earned me a
modicum of respect. Two Irish pickpockets, men of influence on
my landing, thought my Palace invasion a bold act of republican
defiance. A Marxist fraudster thought I had done something of

revolutionary significance. The Irishmen even began taking me aside and asking me what I thought about the possibility of 'throwing a few surprises' in the direction of the royal carriage as it processed down the Mall.

On my release I felt as though I had been sent back into the world naked. I walked alone down Du Cane Road with the feeling that I should duck for cover. I had no idea where I should go or what I should do. At home I found the door barred against me. My landlady, when roused, gave me a long lecture on the breaking of contracts, claimed to have removed all my belongings, including my paintings – my life's work to date – and sent them to the dump. She also gave me her opinion on my artistic output, saying she had never been so disgusted in her life, that my paintings were so obscene she had had to get someone else to handle them as she couldn't bear even to touch them. Anything of value had been sold in lieu of rent. As for the state of my apartment, I was 'worse than a Parisian'. When I demanded compensation she laughed in my face. I suspected she was a keen royalist. 'My nephew said you should be hanged for what you did to our king, and it says that in the contract as well, "No TRAITORS"!'

And she slammed the door. It seemed that I had disgraced myself in every possible way in my landlady's eyes – aesthetically, morally, hygienically and politically.

My employers at Houseman's were no more sympathetic. They, too, seemed to regard me as some sort of Communist or anarchist, and eyed me with disdain from behind the racks of gentlemen's clothes. Only with great persistence was I able to secure a small amount of owed wages, which the manager gave me personally from a box in his office, then told me to be on my way.

I spent the greater part of the money on drink. I felt I could only straighten my thoughts and formulate plans with the aid of some bottles of strong milk stout, for which I had developed a liking during my earlier spell of vagrancy. I began spending nights under the bridges again. It was like returning home. People remembered me from my previous residency. Once, I found myself in Covent Garden as the dawn was breaking. I had slept there without knowing it and was woken by the sound of the first horses to arrive. It astonished me, even with my hungover brain, that this place existed in the heart of London, and that I had never visited it. My mother had been right: its smell permeated the whole city – the earthiness of countless good soils mixed together, and the produce of those soils, the scent of succulent green leaves wafting on the breeze. I was terrified for a moment, and dragged myself upright to hide behind one of the great pillars of St Paul's Church, in case anyone from the gardens of Heathrow should arrive – my father had his own stall there now, or at least some of his stuff was sold there. And what about the Joys? Did they have their own stall? The thought of seeing the landscape of my childhood transferred to this central acre of London seemed too heartrending to bear, and I left the Garden as discreetly as I could.

VIII

I had been in Egypt for nearly two years. In that time the pendulum of power in North Africa had swung back and forth so frequently I was beginning to lose track. One side would push against the other until both had run out of steam; then there were lulls in action while both regrouped and replenished themselves. Most recently the initiative had been with Rommel, and he had made a fearsome surge into Egyptian territory, after a ferocious tank battle in a region known as the Cauldron. But again he had stretched himself so far that the Afrika Korps ground to a halt just west of El Alamein. We estimated we had about a month to prepare a counter-offensive to push him back west. It was made clear to us that the coming conflict could be decisive. If we were to lose El Alamein, Egypt would quickly fall to the Nazis – Alexandria, the Delta, Cairo, Port Said, the sprawling depots, workshops, factories, Suez and the canal itself. The Red Sea and the Arabian oil fields, Persia, India and onward to a meeting with the Japanese. And this at a time when the tide was beginning to turn against the Fascists on the other fronts – in Russia and in the Pacific. To lose El Alamein would be to give a lifeline to those vile tyrannies. The nut would be cracked, and the Fascist powers would rule half the world.

I spent much of this time attempting to seduce Major Marcus Boone.

By now Boone claimed to have remembered me, though he had still not made any reference to our childhood games, and nothing in his manner suggested that this was a pretence. On the few occasions he did reminisce, he would talk of our cycling and fishing together. We had never done that, as far as I recalled. I didn't even have a bike until after our friendship had finished. 'Do you remember that whopping great trout we caught, Kenny? At least we thought it was a trout. Must have weighed three pounds.'

He liked to talk about his wife in England – 'She has such a silly little face' and sometimes chatted about his children. He had a boy and a girl, still very young. The girl liked lions and tigers; the boy wanted to be a sailor. We saw each other regularly, whenever Boone was in Cairo. He would leave a note at the office, a scribbled memo – 'How about a quick one at the Bally Turk?'

'I do like talking to you about the past,' he said on one occasion. 'One gets so few opportunities, especially when you have lived a life like mine, and have never stayed in one place for very long. Continuity is a very important thing, wouldn't you say? Forgive me if I start blubbing, but we mustn't forget where we come from. Out here it is very easy to forget there is such a thing as grass, isn't it?'

But still he failed to remember anything accurately about our childhoods. I tried prompting him as much as I could. 'Do you remember our sword-fights, Marcus?'

'Oh, yes, with our wooden swords. I did so love mine. I called it Excalibur. Not much use for our future career as soldiers, was it? If we waged war with swords, I think we would have won by now.'

Sometimes we would discuss the progress of the war. Marcus was stoical about the approaching offensive. There had been some fierce fighting in the desert. He had lost large numbers of his men, and was expecting to lose many more in the coming weeks. 'What sort of world are we living in, Brill, when we can describe an operation as a success because we lost only a hundred men? At the beginning of the war that would have been described as a bloody disaster. Now it's a reasonable price to pay. The value of human life is diminishing by the day. If this war goes on much longer – well, where will it all end?'

I don't know if he gave much thought to his own death. I sometimes felt awkward when I talked about my work. The sawing and nailing and painting of a camouflage artisan were puny activities compared to the actions of Marcus and his men, astride their iron horses, like the chivalrous knights of old. Yet I saw no sign of condescension in his manner whenever camouflage came into the conversation, though I wished at times I could bring a bit of swagger to my talk, I who had yet to fire a bullet.

*

Learmouth had been up to Army HQ and had been in conference with Montgomery himself. Camouflage was to play an
essential role in the forthcoming operation. He outlined the plan
to all of us in our office at Grey Pillars. Our purposes were
twofold: to conceal the true line of attack, and to suggest a false
one. The true line of attack was to be in the north, parallel to
the coast. Our job was to suggest a build-up of armour in the
south. Learmouth's plan for this deception was ingenious. The
real armour would amass at an assembly point in the south.
Then, by night, they would travel north, and we would put
dummy replicas in their place. The tanks that had travelled
north would be disguised as trucks and other non-combatant
vehicles. Operations were already under way to suggest a build-
up far bigger than the reality, in order to delay any attack by
Rommel for as long as possible. Learmouth put great emphasis
on the importance of the coming battle. He claimed that it was a
near certainty that whoever won would win Egypt, and if Egypt
were to fall to the Germans, half the world might fall also.

The *flamboyant* was in full bloom, the flame trees that had so
surprised me when I had first seen them, lining the road between
Helwan and Garden City, along the banks of the Nile, which I
now travelled frequently, an avenue of vaulted blood whose seeping crimson seemed to hang in the mind long after it was out of
sight. I was coming to know the seasons of Egypt. It was the time
of year when melons filled the markets, and seemed to pour into
the city like a sweet invasion of colour and fragrance, from boats,
from donkey-hauled carts and from overheating motor-trucks.
The Nile was in flood, the dry fields beside the road were now
brown lakes, and the fellahin huddled closer and closer together
as the waters rose, watching their world shrink to a narrow strip

as the river unloaded its Abyssinian silt onto their fields, as it did every year.

My mind was filled with the tasks ahead of us: the twin objects of concealment in the north, and display in the south. For the build-up in the north we had to find ways of concealing two thousand tons of petrol, countless tons of food, ammunition, tyres, ordnance, as well as four hundred 25-pounder field guns, which were to open the offensive with a barrage of shell-fire. We contrived structures of wood and netting that could be raised over these weapons to make them look, from the air, like three-ton trucks and other thin-skinned vehicles. The same was done with the dumps: we arranged the stored materials in stacked formations that roughly imitated the shape of a lorry and appeared from the air to be no different from the many hundreds of such vehicles that littered the desert. The petrol we concealed in the slit trenches that had already been dug and were well-established features of the landscape. Thus the enormous build-up made no perceptible difference to the terrain. In the south we did the opposite, constructing large, uncovered supply dumps that consisted of nothing but empty boxes and cans. We constructed a dummy water pipeline running south from the coast and, to go with it, dummy pump-houses and even a dummy reservoir.

The great deception was choreographed around the staging areas where the real armour was gradually assembled. We had built an expectation in the enemy that the armour would move from this staging post to an attack point in the south, when in fact it would move north. To make this effective, the real armour moved at night, along well-established tracks in the desert, and was instantly replaced by dummies, to make it appear it was still in position. In all we had to provide four hundred dummy tanks, a hundred dummy guns and nearly two thousand other dummy vehicles. There began the immense task of obtaining sufficient quantities of local materials and transporting them between Cairo and a construction camp that was set up south of the staging area. This desert workshop was filled with soldiers from three different companies, and every camouflage-trained soldier who could be spared. All leave was cancelled. A factory production line was established, with one company cutting and binding the split palm into the desired shapes, another to cut and stitch the hessian, and a third to paint and finish off details. We worked furiously. I hardly knew what I was doing from one day to the next, overseeing as much as I could of the operation, flitting between Helwan, Cairo and the new desert workshop, trying all the while to make sure the operation ran smoothly.

It was only a few days before the offensive was due to begin that I passed through Grey Pillars and saw a note that had been left for me. Boone was in town and wondered if I wanted to have a quick drink with him. I made my way to our usual bar, where I found him in a despondent mood. He had been in the desert for two weeks and was due on the front line the next day. I told him I was going up there too, that I was going to the staging area to make sure everything was ready for the great deception.

'But you'll be coming back, won't you, Brill? Once we're all safely despatched to Martello, you'll be on your jolly way back here, leaving the difficult stuff to us.'

It was the first time I had detected any bitterness or sarcasm or resentment of any kind in Boone's manner, though he quickly apologized. 'I'm sorry. I don't know why I'm talking like this. Well, it's the eve of battle. I should be up there, talking to my men, instilling them with the spirit of victory. But we all know this is going to be a bloody battle, Brill. A hell of a battle. We thought we had seen the worst of it in the Cauldron, but that was nothing compared to what's coming.'

'Don't be so sure,' I said. 'Rommel has been seriously weakened. The Afrika Korps has had the stuffing knocked out of it.'

Boone laughed politely, as if acknowledging my pitiful attempt to revive his mood.

'I do like talking to you, Brill. You have such stupid thoughts that they're quite refreshing. Kenneth, I'm not an easy man to like. I know it. But I sense there is something between us – a spirit of true, deep friendship.'

An idea suddenly occurred to me. 'Marcus – do you like dancing?'

'Dancing? Yes, when I get the chance.'

'There's a dance hall near here. It was set up by the Australians. I think they're having a last dance tonight. Would you like to go? I don't suppose there will be many women there but you never know.'

And so I went dancing with Marcus Boone.

PART FOUR

I woke up to the sound of bells. Not big, clanging church bells, but little bells, like sleigh bells, little fairy or goblin bells like those that are tinkled in green dells and fox holes in children's stories. They rang with a methodically solemn beat, as though in time to a march, close to my window at different times of day. I had known about the bells for some time, as a ringing presence at the back of my mind. I had had dreams in which the bells had summoned me to queer little fairy weddings among the tree roots of a forest floor. And then I had woken to find the bells were real.

My room was pleasant but filthy. It smelt of malt and there were husks of wheat and barley scattered on the floor. It had been, I later learnt, a grain store until just a little while before my arrival, and the transformation had been rather hurriedly undertaken. The ceiling was high and scarfed with cobwebs from which spiders would lower themselves cautiously. There was a marble-topped side table on which stood a basin and ewer, of plain design. On some rough shelves next to the door was a set of ancient scales – a big copper dish on one side and a pyramid of weights on the other, the weightiest of which was ten pounds. My bed was relatively new, iron-framed and sturdily sprung. A small casement window gave onto a view of farmland and trees, the tower of a village church tiny in the distance and, beyond that, some hazy downland. The most astonishing and delightful thing about the room, however, was the pretty young girl who visited it several times a day to bring me nourishment. This she delivered on a silver tray. In the morning, bacon and eggs and a pot of tea. At lunchtime, or thereabouts, a plate of sandwiches and a glass of milk. At teatime, some scones and jam, and another pot of tea. Then, in the evening, a main meal, chops, peas and potatoes, or a dish of beef stew. I didn't eat a great deal of it at first. The girl made no comment but only smiled, and we were both too embarrassed to say anything much to each other, apart from good morning, good afternoon, that sort of thing. I had to ask her where the lavatory was, and she took me out of the building and showed me across to an outhouse on the other side of what looked like a disused farmyard – low, whitewashed buildings that might once have been stables or cowsheds, rough cobbles underfoot, one or two people in peasant dress, as though borrowed from a picture book on English rural life, clumping along with pitchforks in hand. In the outhouse I found a white porcelain lavatory, and a tap at which I doused myself with cold water. Then, seeing no reason to be anywhere else, I would return to my room, there to fall back into sleep or a dazed type of half-dreaming, where I ruminated on the events of my life, those I could remember, which seemed fewer and fewer.

I was in a state of total exhaustion, I now realize. I had subjected my body to such deprivations that my mind had begun to disengage itself – not as part of a process of spiritual transcendence, more a tactic of self-preservation. I had almost no concern for my bodily predicament. My spatial whereabouts seemed trivial to me. I didn't have a care for where in the world I was. Instead my mind travelled through time, to my childhood, to the Heath and Three Cylinders, or Mr Joy with his profound lectures on the circularity of things. In these semi-hallucinations I was an adult, and would engage Mr Joy, my step-uncle, in long philosophical discussions, which always came back to statements about the efficacy of certain types of manure.

And I might have remained indefinitely in that netherworld of memories, if it hadn't been for those little bells.

The girl and I had exchanged a few words. I had asked where I was and she had replied with a single word: 'Hillmead.' As if that might be answer enough.

On the next occasion I said, 'And what sort of place is Hillmead?' wondering, for the first time, if I might not be in some sort of lunatic asylum after all, or perhaps a resort in which I might be unwittingly ringing up a large bill for food and accommodation.

She replied, 'Oh, it's just a place.' Stupidly I took this for a full answer, and didn't question her again for another day.

I have often wondered about madness. The most frightening thing about the whole business is that the madman doesn't think he's mad. He thinks the world around him is behaving strangely. This means it is impossible to grasp that one is mad. In a desperate way I clung to that straw of reasoning as I observed the goings-on of Hillmead. To doubt one's sanity is proof of sanity.

It was during one of my expeditions to the lavatory that I discovered the provenance of the bells. I emerged from my ablutions into the bright throughway that was part farmyard and part quadrangle, and they were suddenly right on top of me, a troop of men of varying ages, their faces blackened, their bodies attired in the most anachronistic fashions – tasselled knickerbockers, clogs, frilled shirts with highwayman's cuffs, stovepipe hats stuck with pheasant plumage. They marched through the farmyard like a military unit from a bygone age of romance, carrying with them articles I thought at first were rifles, then clubs, but which were long sticks with bells on the end. Yes, these were the bells I had heard. There were bells all about this little regiment, round their knees, on their hats and on their wrists, bangles of bells that chimed as they marched along.

I followed them cautiously as they disappeared around the corner of the buildings. They were marching towards a paddock at the far end of a driveway. There was a man with a piano accordion who provided music, and the dancers, for that was what they were, began their odd movements, hopping from leg to leg, jigging, with arms linked at the elbow, round in circles with partners one after the other. They formed arches for others to process beneath, and they banged their sticks together in a rhythmic clatter.

As I was contemplating the spectacle in a rather mesmerized way, I was greeted from behind by the mellifluous and sagacious tones of someone aged.

'What you are watching hasn't been seen in the English countryside for well over a hundred years. If you had been alive in the early part of the nineteenth century, such a spectacle would have been commonplace in the fields. And even in the towns there were morris dancers.'

'Is that what it is? Morris dancing?'

'Yes – have you heard of it?'

'Vaguely, I think.'

The man who'd spoken was a tall, weathered figure, wrinkled with kindliness and lost, almost, within clouds of white hair. He was wearing a smock that seemed empty on his thin frame, the open collar revealing a deep redness, and more white hair.

'After the barbarity of the Industrial Revolution it all but died out. That lady over there – you see her? Sitting on the tree stump, instructing the others? That dear old thing has spent her life researching the subject, and has devoted herself to its revival.'

I could see an elderly lady, dishevelled and pleasingly un-kempt, her regalia not quite fitting properly.

The man appeared eager to change the subject. 'Well, Mr Brill, isn't it? I'm very pleased to see that you are up and about. How are you feeling?'

'As if I'm in a dream,' I replied.

The kindly eyes of the elderly one smiled at me. 'We have a mutual friend, I think – Mr Somarco. He brought you here in a most distressed state. Do you recall?'

I told him I could not remember anything of the last few days or weeks. I was lying, because fragments of the recent past were beginning to emerge, a fluctuating mosaic of recollections that I was just starting to piece together. A sudden memory of being slapped across the jaws by the salty hands of the half-Italian, of being told to pull myself together. Me collapsing from the cold and from semi-starvation. I have a memory of the blow being returned by my frail fists, a failed attempt to strike Somarco on the nose. We had not met since our night on the royal lawns, and he was now, once again, indebted to my silence. I was aware that the last scrap of power I retained as a human being resided in my ability to incriminate him, not only as my co-conspirator in the theft of royal grass, but as a traitor. No one in authority yet knew the racial provenance of the grass we had transplanted, and that it constituted the first step in a biological invasion. I had murmured something like this to the madman.

'They will laugh at you. They will think you are as mad as you look.'

But there was no conviction behind the voice. Somarco was frightened.

'You must understand, Kenneth, my actions were those of a peacemaker. I am acting to dilute difference, to homogenize. That is the only hope for mankind.'

Paying his debt to me, he spirited me out of London. I have no memory of the journey.

'Mr Somarco told me about how you first came to be

friends.' He took a moment to see if I would return his smile. I didn't. 'We have a quite unconventional approach to the matter of the naked human body. We believe it is the perfect expression of form and harmony. You are no doubt an admirer, like us, of Pheidias, Praxiteles and Canova. Modern art has done so much to destroy and distort the harmoniousness of the human form. Our friend Anthony, who will be arriving soon, has a lot to say about that. *The deification of ugliness.* Art should always aspire to the immortal, wouldn't you agree?'

I had hardly had time to consider what he had just said before he went on, introducing himself, somewhat belatedly, as Rufus Quayle, then giving me a detailed description of the community of Hillmead, of which I had become an unwitting resident. He had founded the place just a few years before, on inheriting his father's estate. 'We have very simple aims: to return to a more harmonious existence, such as was in place long before machinery and science cut us off from nature. We believe in a revival of the ancient hierarchies, based on working the land in the old-fashioned way, and an economy that values craftsmanship rather than commerce.'

It sounded rather sweet.

Just then there was a commotion over by the morris dancers. A sleek black car had pulled into the drive and halted just by the gate to the field where they were practising. A man emerged from the vehicle, wearing a very stylish pinstriped double-breasted lounge suit with a yellow silk tie and matching handkerchief in his breast pocket. His hair was black and slicked back so smoothly it shone like a snooker ball, and his eyes were in dark shadow, which made them seem like black circles. Overall I had the impression of a man with the head of a housefly. He marched swiftly over to the dancers and started manhandling them, shoving and pushing some, grabbing others by the wrists and tugging them roughly to the edge of the arena. There were yelps and little feminine screams. I couldn't hear what was being said but the man in the suit was bellowing at the group he had extracted from the main body of the dancers, and also at the elderly lady, the instructor, whom Mr Quayle had pointed out to me. He gestured to the buildings, as if ordering the party to leave, and as they did so, he gave them a violently encouraging shove, and even kicked a few in their rumps, including the elderly lady.

I looked to Mr Quayle to see what he made of it. He was watching with a blank expression of exaggerated unconcern, almost as if he hadn't seen it. After giving the remaining dancers a stern talking-to, the man in the suit returned to his car and continued up the drive towards us, stopping when he reached us. He wound down the window and called out to Mr Quayle, 'I'm shocked that you allowed it, Rufus.' Up close the housefly head became human and very handsome. He spoke with a strong Italian accent. 'We cannot have women dancing the morris . . .'

'I agree, Antonio, but poor old Mary, she does have a rather significant role . . .'

'I don't give a damn about her so-called scholarship. It is absolutely wrong and immoral to allow women to dance the morris. It is well known that they never were allowed, and were forbidden. Rufus, you must not allow women to do this thing.'

The older gentleman smiled, as if to reassure me that everything was not quite as insane as it seemed. 'Antonio does have this bee in his bonnet about the role of women in the new European order. We agree to differ on many occasions. Antonio, let me introduce you, this is Mr Brill, an artist.'

Leaning out of the black window frame of his vehicle the Italian regarded me for the first time. His face folded itself into the most beautiful piece of fleshly origami I had seen: an utterly radiant smile. 'I have heard about this man,' he said, extending a soft hand to be shaken. 'I expect something great from him. You will come to my talk this evening?'

I looked at Mr Quayle for explanation.

'We have a series of evening talks for members of the community. Antonio is giving a talk on modern art this evening. He is an expert.'

Antonio left us, and I continued to talk with Rufus, who outlined what he had planned for me.

'Mr Brill, I would like you to be our resident artist. Mr Somarco recommended you in very strong terms when he brought you here. Well, see how you feel about it. Perhaps you hate it here and would like to leave at the first opportunity, but if not, we can provide you with living accommodation, a studio, the finest food grown on the finest soil in England, and all your practical needs. We cannot provide you with such twentieth-century luxuries as radio or even electric light, but we hope that you will come to see those things as modern vulgarities, as we do.'

And so I became an artist-in-residence at Hillmead. I loved the place, at first, even if I didn't agree with many of the principles it promoted. There seemed to be a true spirit of harmoniousness in operation: people went about their work in a state of contentment, and smiled even as the sweat broke out on their brows. Apart from Antonio's outburst over the morris dancers, I saw no sign of discord or anxiety. When I went to Antonio's talk, held in the large drawing room of the main house, I saw the same people, dressed in their countryman's Sunday-best clothes, sitting attentive and alert, as hungry for intellectual stimulation as they had been for the fulfilment of physical labour.

Antonio began his lecture by saying there were essentially two types of artist. 'The first kind is the one who transfigures nature and man, who paints the world as we see it but exalts it to a higher plane. He sees things fuller, grander, stronger and simpler than his fellows. When he speaks of life he speaks as a lover extolling his bride. This is the Dionysian artist, who rhapsodizes life and, in so doing, exalts humanity itself. Ordinary people benefit extremely from looking at the world through this artist's eyes: he makes life desirable for them.

'The other kind of artist is the sober realist, who sees sensory experience as preceding anything in the intellect, who walks towards life to order and value her, who believes every man is his own priest, who declares that we are all equal, that there is one truth for all, if only it can be found, who kills all gods and demi-gods with his mediocritizing. He operates as a sort of Midas in reverse, under whose touch all gold turns to tinsel, all pearls to beads, and all things of beauty are cast upon the dung heap. He sees life as smaller, thinner, weaker, greyer than it is, even to the ordinary people themselves. But, then, he comes from the people themselves, or from an even lower stratum than they. He is a field labourer among field labourers, a housewife among housewives. How could he point to any beauty or desire that field labourers and housewives have not already seen or felt? When they are drawn to his side they find he has made the world drabber, colder, uglier and stranger than it was to them before. He wishes to take man back to the world before creation, to the formless void. This man of science without art is reducing us to a state of utter ignorance. He takes from us what we already know about things and gives us nothing in return.'

After the lecture I spoke with Antonio, who coldly regarded me. 'And what sort of artist are you, Mr Brill? Do you show us what we can already see, or does your view extend to the higher levels?'

I stumbled for a reply, and attempted some humour, saying that although I was a realist, I was rarely sober, which he seemed to find amusing.

*

I set to my work as resident artist almost immediately. I was given a splendid room in the main house, whose window looked out across the estate, while the guest room I'd previously occupied became my studio. I began an extended project of recording everything I saw, and my studio rapidly filled with preparatory sketches depicting the daily life of Hillmead.

For the most part I was left alone to work as I pleased, but occasionally Rufus would visit unexpectedly, and seemed happy with the work I was doing.

'Although I would like to give you a small piece of advice, Mr Brill. Paint what you see, and paint it in such a way that other people can see it as you did. These shapes and textures are all very interesting, but what are they meant to be? You should think about art in the same way that I think about soil. It must have an untainted purity that connects it with its remote past. Modern pesticides contaminate food, just as modern ideas contaminate art. There is no need for new ideas. Look at the cave paintings if you want an idea of what the purity of art is about. Ever since those times, there has been no need to change the way we make paintings. You and I share the same bodies and brains as our ancient ancestors. If you want to have a role as an artist in our society, Mr Brill, you should be concentrating on producing paintings that enable people to appreciate the beauty of their surroundings.'

'Doesn't that put you rather at odds with Antonio's view of art? You want me to paint what people can already see?'

Rufus smiled. 'I think Antonio would say that it all depends on the subject matter. What you will find in Hillmead is beauty all around you, in the landscape and in the people. Hillmead itself is an exaltation of humanity, and so will your paintings be.'

With a dull, relieved sort of obedience, I compliantly did what Rufus bade me, and started doing careful, studied drawings of various craftspeople at work.

I found the blandness very soothing. My work was appreciated. In the farmyard or elsewhere, whenever I worked I was surrounded by interested spectators, many of them children. My subjects were excited at the prospect of being recorded in paint.

So here, ladies and gentlemen, is my exhibition of paintings executed at Hillmead, in the realist style encouraged by Mr Rufus Quayle and others. Exhibit number one (unsold) is a woman spinning flax from a heap of flax plants beside her, using a spinning wheel crafted by the subject of exhibit number five (unsold). Note the light falling on the soft cones of flax, an untroubled, cautious light, you might say, as if the sun was peeping into a room through a half-closed door, afraid of disturbing anyone. Note also that it is a light that doesn't bounce, but stays just where it is. And look at the woman, the wool-like stuff drawn in a string from her fingertips, and the motion of the wheel itself, how still it seems, yet it is spinning faster than you can actually see, but in my painting, oh, it is a universe of frozen mud. But very clean mud. Here, exhibit number two (unsold), a blacksmith at his forge, hammering at a red-hot piece of metal. But is it red-hot, or is it just red? And that smoke, so real and visible you feel you could wind it up and put it in your pocket. And every whisker on the blacksmith's chin is visible, like telegraph poles in a desert. And the fire of the forge, no hotter than a bowl of red apples. And his grubby shirt with sleeves rolled up to the elbow, and that glistening stalk of a cigarette in his lips, all so wonderfully dead. Yet is this not a real man? A living soul in the Utopia of Hillmead? Like these girls bringing in the harvest, sheaves of golden corn on their shoulders: they are hugging them like trophies, like lovers, like babies, and they are laughing, their mouths are wide open with laughing, but you can't hear a sound, can you? There is the laughter of silence in this painting. The laughter comes out as solid vibration in the wooden air. And what about these folk dancers, each with bells strapped to their calves? That one is even in mid-air, both feet off the ground, handkerchiefs fluttering in both hands (how does he ever hope to take flight with such paltry wings?). But the truth is, in my painting he has taken flight, because there is nothing in it that will bring him back to earth, for there is no gravity in this painting is there, no sense of a planet pulling these people down, of their counteracting jumping force breaking them free?

And here is a wider view, a panorama, you could call it. This is the community of Hillmead seen from the surrounding hills. Here, the view is from the north, looking down on the settlement, but including the bosomy hills beyond, and the tiny sliver of sea I managed to fit in, even though we are ten miles from the coast. Is there anything more English in the history of English painting? This could be a Samuel Palmer, could it not? Nothing in this painting gives evidence of the age of machines, of automation; here we see men and women bending in the fields – and, yes, that is a wild deer you see prancing happily in the meadow, and yes, they are wearing clothes akin to the dress of medieval peasants. You say it is a romanticized view of the English rural way of life? But it is a faithful rendition of what is happening now in our countryside. And if you are wondering why they are painted in such a traditional style I will have to refer you to Mr Quayle and Mr Ludovici, who are both experts on art, and you will find their views are not so far removed from those of people like Norman Learmouth, and I am thankful to them for enabling me to free myself of those beastly European influences, to go back to the boldness, the sincerity, the realism of cave paintings. Now, if you will excuse me, I must attend to my new paintings, which are waiting patiently to be painted, just over there, in the corner they are. Goodbye.

*

April wrote to me. It had been over a year since we had met, yet I hadn't stopped writing to her, although there had been big gaps recently between my letters. She wrote to tell me that she had rescued my paintings, or some of them at least, from Mrs Beech. She had called at my rooms while, unknown to her, I was in prison, just as that 'awful woman' was getting ready to dispose of my life's work. She didn't say much else. But I wrote back, saying that she should come down and visit me at Hillmead.

This place is the most beautiful place on earth. They are trying to re-create a golden age when man was at one with nature and his surroundings, where art was valued as much as food, where science was reduced to the subservient role of providing food and shelter and not becoming our master or generating wealth. Please see if you can arrange it. I have asked Mr Quayle, and he would welcome you most wholeheartedly.

This last sentence was a lie. April replied with caution.

Kenneth, who are these people you are living with? What do you know about them? Are they in any way connected with certain movements on the continent of Europe that have emerged recently? Do you read newspapers, Kenneth? Do you have any idea what is happening abroad?

Dearest April,

Let me put your mind at rest immediately – Mr Quayle and others here hold Mr Hitler in no esteem whatsoever. They believe in reviving the ancient lines of European nobility, and have respect for the monarchy and for the various aristocratic structures it supports because they contain the essence of traditional Englishness, which has been

*lost since the Industrial Revolution. Hitler is just a jumped-up
corporal, in their eyes. A trivial little fellow. 'Common,' is how
one of them put it. Now I don't entirely agree with them on
the aristocracy point – they believe in a return to a feudal
society and the revival of craftsmen's guilds – but they have
the highest regard for the world of nature and of beauty.
In the light of what is happening in Europe, I think that is
a rather worthwhile thing . . .*

*Dear Kenneth – Nothing you have said in your letter
convinces me that these people are not Fascists, in all but name.
Who is this Mr Quayle – is he of noble descent? No doubt in
this feudal society he would be the lord and the rest of us serfs.
Do you know how the serfs were treated in the Middle Ages?
It is not the kind of society anyone should think of reviving.
And what of the benefits of science? Do they despise those,
along with all other forms of rational thought? The Nazis, too,
despise the rational and the reasoned. How else could a society
like that exist but with the suppression of reasoned thought, and
the elevation of mythology? No doubt your Mr Quayle prefers
to believe in King Arthur and the knights of the romantic ages
rather than the philosophers of the enlightenment. You should
leave that place, Kenneth, before it is too late.*

Dearest April,
            *You are misunderstanding the people here.
How can I explain? You would have to see it for yourself.
They do not reject science, only those parts of it that have
become corrupted by commerce. Rufus cites the examples of
pesticides, which are used to increase profit for farmers but
ultimately poison the soil. In the society they seek to build,
the land will be worked by individuals to feed themselves,
not for profit. I don't see how that can be called Fascist.*

Corresponding with April, being in touch with her again after so long, affected me profoundly. I longed for her letters to arrive, and would trot hopefully to the little room at the end of the dairy where all the post for the site was held. If there was nothing for me I would drag my feet back to my room and agonize at how long I would have to wait for the next delivery. The post came only once a day to Hillmead. When there were letters from April I read them so intently I could recite them from memory by lunchtime. She was a good letter-writer, using all the usual protocols yet somehow investing them with warmth and intimacy. She moved seamlessly from sardonic chattiness to intellectual scorn to political concern. It was these parts of her letters that caused me most anxiety. She could not bring herself to think anything good of Rufus Quayle or the community he was building at Hillmead. I repeated my suggestion that she should come down and see for herself what was happening here. Eventually she rather surprised me by accepting, and told me that she had booked a train ticket for a Friday in May.

When I told Rufus and Antonio that I was expecting a visitor they didn't seem terribly pleased, and indicated that I should have consulted them first. I apologized.

'Not to worry, young man. Now, tell us about this gentleman. Who is he? What is his job?'

'It's not a gentleman, it is a lady.'

The two men looked at each other. Antonio seemed particularly displeased, in an almost visceral way, as though he had tasted something unpleasant.

'Who is this lady, Kenneth? A relation?'

'No, she is a friend. A rather good friend.'

'I see. Well, she must be a very good friend if she is coming all this way to see you. Does she have an occupation?'

Here Antonio spluttered. 'An occupation? Mr Brill just said she was a lady!'

'Well, unfortunately we are living in the modern age, Antonio. It is not uncommon for women, these days – as you yourself have written about.' He turned to address me. 'Antonio does have particularly strong views on the role of women in our society. Of course, in the world we are building we imagine women taking the role for which they are clearly adapted by evolution, that of home-making and child-rearing. Prior to marriage the only sensible role for a woman is in some sort of domestic service where she can learn these skills. But I doubt that your "friend" is likely to think such an occupation suitable.'

'No. She has been to university. She studied mathematics. She currently works as a secretary to a scientific publisher.' From the corner of my eye I could see waves of pain passing across Antonio's face. He was staring at the ground, concentrating all his fury, it seemed, on the innocent gravel and weeds by his feet.

*

I met April at the station and was impressed, even a little shocked, by her fashionable attire. Emerging from the boiling carriages with their steam-leaky couplings, she seemed to have been steam-cleaned, and was defiantly new and confidently spruce. She was wearing trousers. The flannel hose turned the heads of many Dorset locals, and I was myself almost frightened by the boldness of her appearance. More so by the boots that the trousers were tucked into – tall, calf-high black leather boots, highly polished, glossy as treacle. Aware of the attention these clothes had drawn, the first thing she said to me was an explanation.

'After a year of living in London I have very quickly forgotten the correct attire for the countryside.'

She kissed my cheek, in a sisterly way, and told me I was looking well. I told her I was feeling well. Weller than I had ever felt before.

'You have lost weight,' she said.

'That was the prison. I lost my appetite in there, and haven't regained it. Here, everything is fresh and raised on the local soil.'

We travelled back in a taxi, and April became uncharacteristically silent.

'It's so good of you to come all this way. I can't tell you how much I've missed you.'

She gave me a tired look, before glancing out of the window. 'Don't flatter yourself too much. I only came here to get a glimpse of the people we will soon be at war with.'

I laughed incredulously, gasped at her cynicism. 'You cannot mean that. Didn't you read my letters?'

'Kenneth, just because they've put a roof over your head and been kind to you, it doesn't make them good people. Try and learn to stop seeing the world from the narrow viewpoint of your own needs and desires. I will form my own opinion of these people.'

'Haven't you come to see me at all, then?'

After a long pause she turned to me, smiled and patted my hand. Then she returned to gazing out of the window.

*

April and I were not allowed, and would not have thought, to share sleeping quarters. A special part of the complex was reserved for single females, and she was accommodated there. We spent all day together. By now I was a quite well-established figure in the commune, and was able to give my guest a definitive guided tour. I showed her the orchard, the cider press, the grain store, the paddocks, the fields where crops were growing, some harvesting, and so on. She seemed unimpressed.

'It's just a farm, where you grow most of your own food.'

'But we don't use any pesticides or other chemicals. Everything is pure and natural. We have to pull up the weeds by hand, like they used to do in the old days. And if there are slugs or snails, we have to pick those off, too, by hand.'

'Quite an advocate for this little Utopia, aren't you? What are those plants? I've never seen them before.'

'They're just saplings. This area will be a little forest in a few years' time.'

'And these sheep – they're the cleanest sheep I've ever seen.'

'Southdowns,' I said, 'one of the original English breeds. I've learnt so much since I've been here. These little animals can actually fertilize the poor soil you get in chalk uplands all by themselves.'

'How very impressive. Don't you think it's odd the way everything's arranged here? There seems no sense to it. You have a field of crops running through the middle of a field of sheep, dividing them into two halves for no reason. Must make it all the more complicated when you have to gather them up.'

'You're quite determined to find fault with this place, aren't you? I'm sure Mr Quayle's got it all planned for a good efficient reason.'

*

In the evening, rather to my surprise, April and I were invited to dinner at the manor house with Rufus and Antonio. Antonio was all gushing charm and chivalry at first. We sat down at a table laden with ornate silverware, branching candelabra, napkins in big silver rings, lamb cutlets arranged around a mound of peas, perched on a stemmed silver server, trout mayonnaise, decorated with hard-boiled eggs and capers. All the food was from the farm, or had been caught nearby.

April did her best not to be impressed with the opulence. She made me feel ashamed of the sensations I was experiencing, of being so attracted to the magnificence of the spread. 'The rest of this community seem to live like cloistered monks, yet here you have all the imaginable luxuries.'

'I believe you have mistaken us for Communists,' said Antonio, pouring a glass of wine.

'No, I certainly didn't take you for those. Quite the opposite, actually.'

'You might think we enjoy privileges here,' said Antonio, 'but you'll notice that we have no servants. No butlers. There is a cook, who provided us with these magnificent dishes, but otherwise we do everything for ourselves.'

'My dear,' said Rufus, anxious to steer the conversation away from any contentious topics, 'our friend Kenneth tells us that you are a mathematician.'

'I have been trained as such.'

'Unusual for a lady.' Antonio sent out this comment before realizing that it had no obvious reply.

'Do you have any Jewish members of your community?' April asked, with a simple clarity of tone that seemed to pass like a knife through the air. I had expected a direct answer from either of the two men, but instead they behaved as if they had simply not heard the question. April looked at Rufus and Antonio, then at me.

Eventually Rufus spoke, but as if to no one in particular: 'I have always felt there is something profoundly embarrassing about the notion of the Crucifixion. It seems astonishing that we have built a civilization around an instance of terrible bad manners.'

When this produced another awkward silence, I blurted out, 'April is very good at chess.'

'Oh, really?' said Rufus. 'Antonio here is a grand master. Perhaps you would like a game after dinner.'

'No, I'm afraid Kenneth has exaggerated my abilities in that field.'

The rest of the evening passed in a quiet, terribly tense atmosphere, in which Antonio and Rufus conducted their conversation just as if April wasn't there.

*

After our evening with Rufus and Antonio, April wanted to leave. I pleaded with her to stay a little longer. In the end she agreed, so long as we could spend some time away from the farm. She found it too oppressive, she said, too stifling. So we agreed to pass a day in walking in the hills. Perhaps she would feel better about Hillmead, I thought, if she could view it from afar, and see it as I had seen it many times, as part of an exquisite, complicated landscape.

So, we packed a lunch and set off to the east, crossing the farmland beyond the estate, towards the chalk escarpment. April changed almost as soon as we were beyond the gates. She emerged from the silence she had fallen into, but she had lost none of her antagonism and suspicion towards Hillmead.

'You must be a fool, Kenneth, if you can't see what's going on there. If there is a war this place will be closed down and everyone interned. They're all Nazi sympathizers, even those nice old couples with warm, welcoming smiles. There was one who said all the Jews should be sent to work down coal mines.'

'You keep forgetting how beneficial this place is to me,' I said, as we crossed a stile. 'I have a role here as artist-in-residence. People are interested in what I do. I am allowed the freedom to do what I love doing – painting. This place is very good for me.'

'Yet again you're putting your personal happiness above everything else. Anyway, how can a place like this be beneficial, when the so-called leader walks around with a pair of antlers on his head?'

'He is harmlessly indulging in the regeneration of some

pagan deities. He thinks the modern world has severed us from our kinship with the earth, and I think he has a point.'

I tried to steer April away from such subjects, as I could see her anger was rising with our altitude. Eventually I managed to get her to talk about her work, something she'd said very little about so far. She told me how relieved she was to have left Berryman's and how wonderful it was working for a publisher. She described a slow, gentlemanly environment of book-lined rooms and sherry-laced lunches ('for the men – I can't drink during the day') and the silent perusal of handwritten manuscripts. She had recently been involved with editing an introductory work on Einstein's theories, and as we ascended the chalk slopes, she tried to explain the theory of relativity to me. It lasted for perhaps half a mile, and by then I was glad when we returned to politics. We rounded a small beech wood, then strode out along a ploughed stretch of upland, such a vast field, the sort that Rufus hated, because it could be worked only by mechanical traction. We discussed the possibility of a coming war.

'Don't you think our best strategy would be to play on our similarities with the Germans, and thus reach some sort of alliance with them, rather than going into another war?'

'Don't be a fool. Hitler has no interest in an alliance with us. He is determined to conquer the whole of Europe. Living space – what a ridiculous notion. There are over a hundred million people of Aryan descent in Europe, and he's going to fit them all into Austria? I know what your friends thought of Hitler – they thought of him as some semi-mystical mythical being . . .'

'Not true. Most of them think he is just a common, ordinary man, like I said in my letters. They despise him for that reason.'

'Well, then, that's almost as bad as the other thing.'

'And, besides, you can't blame Germany for doing what we were doing only a century ago. Versailles has taken away what little empire they had. Why shouldn't they try to rebuild it?'

It was perfectly right of April to call me an utter fool. Perhaps a dangerous fool.

'And what of Herr Hitler's racial theories? Are those to be blameless as well? If Germany is so interested in empire-building, they should look to the Roman example. The right of citizenship was extended to everyone, no matter what race or religion. You'd think they would understand that, now they have Mussolini as an ally.'

'Antonio says that Herr Hitler believes in a long period of peace. We are in danger of drifting into a new European war by misinterpreting Germany's actions.'

'I would pity you, Kenneth, if I thought you really believed that. You should see what is happening in London. They're digging trenches in Hyde Park. And every day there are new refugees arriving in the country. Respectable Jewish families, stripped of every penny so they have nothing to rebuild their lives with.'

Just then we came to another scarp, on what must have been the opposite side of the down to Hillmead. On the hill on the other side of the valley our attention was immediately drawn to a large chalk hill figure, of a man wielding a club and displaying a brazenly erect phallus. I had vaguely heard of the existence of this gleaming figure, but had not known precisely where it was.

'Well,' said April who, after a moment's pause, seemed quite unabashed, 'there's a fine figure of a chap.'

'I've heard of this. They call him the giant, I think . . .'

'I'm not surprised.'

Now I began to feel that I had encountered the god of nudity. A sheep, little bigger than a maggot from our perspective, seemed at that moment to be nibbling the giant's balls.

'I'm surprised this wasn't tampered with by the Victorians,' I said. 'You'd think they'd have given him a chalk fig leaf or a pair of breeches. Yet they left him alone. They let him rampage about the country in the nude.'

We began to make our way back to the other side of the Downs, so that we could get a good view of Hillmead. It was half an hour of walking through woods until we finally came to it. The hillside suddenly gave way, just as if the great green band of hills had collapsed, and there, below us, was the settlement, adorably cosy in its nook of the Dorset Downs, protected, sheltered. In the wide, empty expanses it seemed a clustered concentration of activity. In the fields there were people tilling, reaping, weeding. Horses were hauling things, vehicles were arriving, unloading or being loaded, and leaving again. What a busy place it seemed. We could see people dancing in the paddock again. I unfastened my sketchbook and began setting up my materials. April opened her book – a work of Bertrand Russell, if I remember – and began reading. She leant against me, using me like a pillow, as she read. The warmth of her contact stirred something deep in me, and we were soon kissing and caressing. And then it happened, up there on the hillside, though we moved a little away from the scarp and out of sight of the farm, just in case we could be discernible (although we must have been tiny white dots from there): we entered the woodland and made love. It was a repetition of our liaisons at Berryman's, but this time with a quite different out-come. Through some great effort of release, of relaxation of the will, or by some semi-conscious manipulation of my deeper internal divisions, I managed to find arousal in April's body. The unbuttoned and unlaced core that was exposed, from the deep dark well of her navel to the twin tumuli of her nipples, seemed suddenly and urgently beautiful. And the lower prospects of her body had gathered a luscious power. No longer was I horrified by an absence down there. Instead I was drawn to the warmth of a roseate pout, a nether-mouth nestled in a forest of curls that wanted to be kissed. And as I looked I realized to what school of painting April belonged – she was the nude Maja and I, somewhat to my surprise, was a Goya man.

What joy it was to experience that moment. What release. What demolition of walls. April cried out – we both did. Only now, when I think back to it, do I have the rather mean thought that my arousal was due to that earlier viewing of the chalk giant and his magnificent turfy balls. To be in the neighbourhood of a phallus as big as a London bus might have exercised the muscles of my loins in a way I hadn't hitherto experienced. I can't say now if it was the beauty of April's body that stirred those feelings or whether I was seeing that body reworked by the echo of the hill figure. Nevertheless my outpouring was like a herd of sheep seen from a hillside, shepherded by April's fleshly encompassments, stalled in her secret red pound.

*

It was shortly after this, when we returned, adjusting our clothing, to the spot where I had decided to do my painting, that we had what I can only call our great revelation. I had just set myself up with an easel and board, and April had, with some discomfort (I think our lovemaking had left her feeling clammy), settled herself on a tuffet to read, when she suddenly called out. A shriek of terror. I wasn't sure what her vocalization prefigured – I wondered if she had sat on an ants' nest, or been stung by a wasp. She stood up, shaking.

'Kenneth,' she said, a tremor in her voice I had never heard before, 'we have to go. We have to leave this place at once.'

'What are you talking about? I've only just started my painting.'

'You call yourself an artist? You can't even see what's right in front of you. Look down there, tell me what you can see.' Her emotion had transformed into one of barely controlled rage.

'I can see the farm. The people . . .' I looked back at April to see if I was on the right lines, I wasn't. 'Some animals, trees, fences . . .'

'Look at the fields, and the outlines of the orchard, and the paddock, and the farmyard. Look at them carefully. Follow the lines made by all the edges. What can you see?'

It was another few minutes of concentrated looking before it suddenly fell into place. There was no mistake about it, and I was ashamed that I hadn't seen it before. The farmed and managed land of Hillmead, all 120 acres of it, had been carefully arranged, after all. The reason for the odd juxtaposition of fields and orchards, for instance, where one might cut through the other, now made perfect sense. A vast swastika had been laid down on the English landscape, perfectly proportioned, no kinks or twists or unexpected curves but the straight parallel lines of the hooked cross of Nazi Germany, yet so subtly rendered, when the defining feature might be a lane, a hedge, the edge of a field, whose lines ran seamlessly into the surrounding landscape, that it could be so easily missed.

It was a quite appalling moment, to see something so loved, so comforting and homely as a pastoral landscape like this, to have had the ugly, wicked distortion of a swastika superimposed upon it, as though the mirror of reality had been broken to reveal an evil substructure. The familiar clothing of the landscape had been stripped, and this was the cruel nudity that lay beneath. For one moment I considered the possibility that it was some sort of extraordinary coincidence, an accidental configuration of random patterns; that we were seeing faces in curtains, or hearing words in birdsong; that we were like Pythagoras, who had seen an unintended mathematical truth laid down by the tilers of a bathhouse floor. But, no, there could be nothing accidental about such a perfect depiction.

'I'm so sorry,' I said. 'I don't understand . . .'

'Oh, no, of course you don't, Kenneth. You don't understand anything.'

*

It was as though the materials of my artistic vocation had dissolved into nothing. I thought of all the sketches, drawings and paintings I had done of Hillmead over the months, many from on high, all of which must have included that hidden symbolism. Rufus Quayle had been particularly fond of those panoramic views, Antonio as well. In fact, the more I thought back to it, wasn't it Rufus or Antonio who had first encouraged me to walk up into the hills and paint Hillmead from above? And now I thought they must have assumed I'd discerned the cross in the landscape – I was an artist, after all, and was good at discerning patterns. Everything I'd said to them in the course of my stay had been said with the implicit approval of their political allegiance. They assumed I approved of them. That I was one of them.

I wanted to go back there and retrieve my paintings, take them all and leave immediately, but April didn't want to return to the farm. She said we should just walk to the station, leave everything behind, go home in the clothes we were wearing. I couldn't do that, I said. 'I've got to get my sketchbooks, my . . .' My sketchbooks full of drawings exalting the men of Hillmead, my paintings of the hero farmers, the angelic dancers, the demi-god fence-builders.

For April, from that moment on the spur overlooking the valley, Hillmead had become a site of extreme toxicity; to set foot within the perimeter of that hidden symbol would be to risk exposure to some form of contamination. I began to feel the same, and I'm proud of myself for experiencing that sensation at least. Hillmead had unmasked itself, and what lay beneath was a vista of corrosive ugliness. But I was torn between immediate flight to the nearest railway station and a confrontation with Rufus and his followers. Surely there were others in the farm who had been as much deceived as I, and who still thought there was a simple, innocent purity about their project. They deserved to have their eyes opened to the truth.

But April was right: we should leave without even setting foot in the compound again. I left what I'd drawn so far on the hill where I'd sat, along with the rest of my sketches in that sketchbook. I threw down my palette and my paints on the shorn top of that nibbled little hill and declared an end to my career as an artist.

PART FIVE

I

I had never thought that I would want to fight. I had thought I would take the option of self-preservation so common among my kind, and would follow the stream of artists and poets who'd fled across the Atlantic to the haven of Hollywood or the speakeasies of the Lower East Side. But now I looked with contempt upon those who had abandoned everything for the sake of their muse. Learmouth's friend, so I heard, had long since divorced his Jewish wife, and they had both caught a boat to New York, living as divorcees and sharing a cabin in steerage. Just a few months ago I would have envied them and seen something heroic in their struggle to preserve their gift for the benefit of Western civilization. We don't destroy a culture by bombing its buildings, Learmouth's friend had said, but by exterminating its poets. Now I was beginning to feel that a culture could be destroyed from within by bad poetry.

War was declared at just the right time for me. I had nowhere else to go and had come to the end of a phase of my life. Having abandoned Hillmead, I thought I might step straight into the ranks of the army, if only for a roof over my head. I stayed for a short while with April, but she shared a flat with another girl, and her landlady lived downstairs. I spent two nights on the sitting-room floor, then went to a recruiting office in the centre of London and presented myself for service. The sergeant in there said, 'You're quick off the mark, aren't you?' Then, when it transpired I had no fixed address and no recent employment records, I was told to go home and await further instructions.

I then realized that home could only mean my parents in Heathrow. Contact with my family had been sporadic since I had left the Heath – I had only been back a small number of times for brief visits, and it must have been more than a year since the last. At first it seemed that nothing had changed. The fields were still full of crops, and people still laboured in them, looking perhaps a little wearier than before. The shit-heaps still smouldered; the stacks of sludgecake still sprouted their flowers. We were in the height of tomato season – they were everywhere, little red lights shining in the hedgerows, in the field margins, even in the corners of our driveway, where some seeds must have fallen from a passing cart.

Things were different. My mother's greeting was both tearful and scolding – how could you have left it so long, how could you have been so thoughtless, you beautiful beautiful boy?

My father was overflowing with sarcasm, 'Oh, so the great artist has decided, now that the Hun is at the door, to come scampering back to his mater and pater . . .' They wanted news, but I could tell them nothing. They wondered why I had left my promising job at Berryman's. They looked puzzled when I said I had been making my living as an artist. I confessed that this had not been successful, and that I had been working in a shop. My time in Wormwood Scrubs was not mentioned. I don't know if they knew about it or not. I told them I had returned for the simple reason that I was awaiting my call-up papers. My father, visibly older, though rather more relaxed and jovial than I had seen him for a long time, expressed surprise. 'An artist going off to fight for his country? What will you do – throw a painting at them?'

'I'm no longer an artist, Father. If it wasn't for the war, I would happily take up a spade and work on the fields here.'

In fact, the digging season was past and the fields were full of pickers and harvesters. The gypsies had set up camp on Tucker's Field and the lanes were busy with heavily laden carts. The new prosperity of my father's business was evident in ways I hadn't noticed at first. A new car, blacker and shinier than the old, now reclined on the gravel. My mother wore dresses that shone with newness and an elegant modernity.

'Your father has people working for him now,' said my mother, still shocked from my declaration. 'He and Tiberius manage the land between them. It is a very good arrangement.'

My father chuckled. 'We have equal shares in the sludge-cake business. We supply farms as far away as Maidenhead now. And we've taken on land from Longford to Hatton. It was all happening while you were away, my son.' He grinned like the comedian of old. He showed no concern for the demise of my artistic career, though my mother, whose face had dropped when I'd broken the news, did seek more explanation, when we were alone together.

'I've been such a bloody idiot, Mother. I've spent my life looking at things so closely I can't see what's going on in the wider world. I thought that if you were an artist, that was the same thing as being a good person. Because to be a good artist you have to have access to a sense of common humanity – but, no, all it means is that you have a good sense of proportion and colour. That's all it means. And human beings can go to Hell.'

'I'm sure that's not true, Kenny. Only the bad artist sees nothing beyond form and colour. The good artist sees beneath that to the essence of the thing within.'

But she could not talk me out of my disillusion.

I spent as much time as I could in the fields.

Three Cylinders was downcast, because he had been hoping that he was in a reserved occupation. 'Farmers,' he said. 'How's the country going to feed itself without farmers? That's what

I said to the recruiting officer. You know what he said? He said they're going to bring in kids and old men to work the land while the proper farmers go off to fight. I said, "How many kids know when's the best time to plant sea kale?"' Then some upstart sergeant had laughed at him, telling him he wasn't a proper farmer, and that the country didn't need to keep the likes of him in reserved occupations. 'Said I was just a gardener growing fruit and veg. Said a proper farmer grows wheat and corn or raises livestock. "The world won't end just because we haven't got enough blackcurrants." He laughed. Oh, how I would have loved to give that chap a punch up the bracket.'

I had no longing for such excuses. I presented myself at the recruitment centre, which was housed, as I recall, in a disused theatre somewhere in Wembley. I had in mind to say something like, *Put me in your most dangerous regiment. I want to go directly to the front of the front line.* In fact, I turned up at that office in a sort of dream, or daze, feeling that I was watching myself from the outside, as though in a film.

I filled in several buff slips, then was shown to a room that had been hurriedly decked out for medical examinations. Most of the equipment was, through my father's work, grindingly familiar to me. I recognized the sphygmomanometer model that had been in use since the 1900s, the one my father used to scoff at. My arm was put into the cuff and the bulb pumped by a cross-looking nurse. Then I stood before a doctor, who didn't even look up from the files on his desk when he told me to take my clothes off.

I could feel a dim-witted smile grow on my face as I followed the first command of my army career, unbuttoning my clothes and letting them fall to the floor. The doctor looked up. 'Behind that, man,' he barked, nodding to a screen in a corner of the room, 'and take your clothes with you. Don't just throw them on my floor.'

The examination consisted of a brief visual appraisal (a quick look up and down), a test of my reflexes (I wondered if my father had sold him that hammer), an inspection of the soles of my feet, my scrotum and the backs of my eyeballs.

Then he gave me a form, told me to get my clothes back on and return to the recruiting sergeant.

I found myself, after a long couple of hours of queuing, in a room where three uniformed officers were sitting behind desks. In the middle a senior-looking one with military whiskers and a gruff, indifferent manner was flanked by two fresher-faced, more interested captains. I was aware of men in lounge suits and felt hats leaning casually against walls.

I was asked my occupation.

'I don't have one,' I said.

The elder soldier in the middle appeared to confer with his colleagues either side, muttering something like 'What did he say?'

Eventually the left-hand captain spoke. 'There seems to be some confusion. You have put "failed artist" on your form. Would you care to clarify?'

I couldn't find a way of answering.

'How does one fail at being an artist?' said the captain on the right.

'By not being able to draw, I suppose,' said the other.

'Well, then, one wouldn't have become an artist in the first place. I don't see how, once you can draw, you can fail. Surely it's like riding a bike. Once you know how to ride one, you can't fail to be a bike rider.'

'What if you crash into a wall?'

'Perhaps what Mr Brill means is that he was unable to make a living from his art. Is that what you mean, Mr Brill?' The senior officer in the centre said this, and looked rather pleased with himself for having found what he thought was the answer to the riddle.

'No,' I replied. 'That is not what I mean.'

The senior officer seemed crestfallen. 'Oh. Well, then, what on earth do you mean?'

'I mean that I have lost my powers of observation. I no longer know how to look at the world.'

'I see. Well, that could certainly be a problem in the army. But Dr Welsh, who examined you earlier today, reports that you have perfect eyesight.'

Again, I could make no reply. The trio gazed at me with surprisingly tender expressions.

'Well, it doesn't make much difference. The army has no use for artists, even if they can see. I'm damned if I know what to do with you. What has happened to this country in the last twenty years? It seems to have lost its backbone.'

Eventually, after some rather disgruntled discussion, I was issued with a form that told me to report to another recruiting station in a week's time. I was to join the Corps of Royal Engineers.

*

The recruiting officers would have been as surprised as I was by how much demand there was in the army for the skills of a trained artist. From the day I joined the regiment I was rarely without a paintbrush in my hand, usually a horrible, coarse, stiff, bristly weapon, and painting something or other. My first task was to paint pandas, the regimental mascot, on the sides of all our vehicles. I rather enjoyed this job. It took only one tin of white paint and one tin of black paint. I painted huge pandas on the sides of transport vehicles, little pandas on the bonnets of DMVs. But also in the army there seemed to be an inexhaustible demand for signs. I spent a lot of time painting arrows in corridors, on the sides of buildings, not always sure whom I was supposed to be directing or to where. The major was so smitten with my calligraphic skills that he ordered me to paint a name sign for his door. He managed to procure from somewhere a nicely planed and seasoned piece of cherrywood on which I lettered, in white, serrifed capitals, *Major Derek Osbourne LLD.*

My life was now a blur of railway warrants and postings to various parts of the country – I did my basic training near York, then spent a month on the Northumbrian coast erecting sea defences. With the Germans now in Norway, it seemed an invasion across the North Sea was increasingly likely. I spent some cold weeks unwinding huge spools of barbed wire across the lonely sands.

With the fall of the Low Countries I was moved south again, to work on the sea defences there. By now things were happening so fast in the war we could hardly keep up with the news. Before the spring was over the Germans were on the other side of the Channel. There was some optimistic talk about clever manoeuvring and surprise counterattacks, but it soon became clear that the British Expeditionary Force was being overwhelmed. On the road above the beach we saw small parties of sappers, commanded by youthful subalterns, coming and going all day long with boxes of explosives, detonators and cables. We later learnt that they were laying demolition charges to destroy the harbour at Dover, and all the roads and railways thereabouts. If the Germans ever arrived in London, it would not be by train.

It was around this time that I married April at the St Pancras Register Office. I had obtained a weekend pass for the occasion. We had been seeing each other as frequently as I could manage. We were both pessimistic about the future of the war and felt that there wasn't much time left, that we had to compress what was left of our lives into a few months. Our ceremony was simple and brisk. We didn't inform our families or even our friends. Our witnesses were April's flatmate and two strangers we pulled in from the street. April wore a white trouser suit, but the effect was clinical and cold. She looked like a scientist. We had a reception in the saloon bar of a pub near Regent's Park, the two strangers coming with us. They turned out to be vinegary people who didn't mind expressing their sympathy for Hitler. This caused a row in the pub and there was nearly a fight. Our first married night was spent in a hotel near the British Museum. We made love painfully, and briefly.

Shortly after this, back at the barracks, I was called in to see the major. He said the following: 'I've had a request for your transfer, Private Brill. It seems someone somewhere in the higher echelons of command thinks you might have a use. The army is forming a Camouflage Corps, and they have specifically asked for you to be part of it. How does it feel to be loved, eh? Well, I suppose they're looking for anyone with artistic credentials. You used to be an art teacher, didn't you? Amazing, isn't it, how war finds use for anything, even artists? Here's your travel warrant. You'll be leaving tomorrow.'

At first I was quite horrified by the idea. 'Sir, am I able to refuse this request?'

'No, of course not. And why on earth would you want to?'

'Well, there must be some mistake. I'm not an artist. I used to be, but I lost the ability to see. I'm much happier with the kind of work I'm doing here. Barbed wire. Digging holes. Building walls. I've found my true vocation, I believe.'

'Well, that's very sweet to hear, but you are one of the worst wall-builders I've ever had the misfortune to command. You'll be leaving tomorrow, as I said.'

II

'Lieutenant Brill, the court requires that you take your clothes off so that the jury may see evidence of your injuries.'

The entire sum of all the eyes in the court, sixty-four balls of jelly, was turned in my direction. I looked at Davies. To my horror he was smirking. By facial expressions I asked him if I had to comply, and by facial expressions he said he supposed so. The judge advocate persisted.

'Lieutenant Brill, Captain Cunningham has made a most compelling case for the display of your body. If we had photographs, they would have sufficed, but we haven't, and there is very little point in wasting time taking and processing photographs for this purpose, when the scars may be viewed and the whole process done with in a matter of minutes. May I remind you that this is a military tribunal, and we are as pressed for time as any other branch of the armed forces.'

The eyes had not wavered from their fixed gaze.

'Here?' I said, in barely a whisper. 'At this moment?'

'If you would be so good. Come, come, this is a court of martial law, there are no ladies present. No need to be bashful.'

'Everything?'

'Well – Mr Cunningham, could you assist?'

'Yes, Your Honour. Lieutenant Brill, you just need to expose those parts of your body that show evidence of your injury. I suggest you lower your trousers and underwear, take off your jacket and shirt and lift your vest. That should suffice.'

I had never felt my clothes so stuck to my body. It was as though a layer of glue had been applied, and they were firmly affixed to my skin. Unbuttoning my trousers felt like pulling rivets out of the hull of a ship. I was in the centre of the courtroom, as usual, visible in three hundred and sixty degrees, encircled by watchful eyes, scrutinized from every possible angle. And, with a sense of piercing disbelief, I lowered my trousers slowly. What pants was I wearing? Army issue, from the stores of this very base, emergency pants, third or fourth hand, scrubbed to death, fraying in the crotch, and worn for three days. I lowered them quickly, before their soiling could be seen. There was pin-drop silence in the courtroom as I removed my jacket, then my shirt (turning awkwardly to hang them over the back of my chair), then, as instructed, lifted my vest.

The jury was invited to approach me, which they did with a rather tired shuffling motion. Twelve men in uniform, old men mostly, military men too old for active service, stooped and peered at my naked body. Oh, God, I could feel myself stiffening. Terror seemed to have that effect on me. The retired generals affected not to notice, even though by now I was fully extended and beyond any hope of restraining myself. They encircled me, muttering to each other and pointing at my scars. My lengthened cock was politely ignored, though I thought I heard a muttered 'Disgraceful,' from somewhere at the back of the court.

'The upper wounds are from a childhood injury, resulting from fooling around with a sword. The lower injury is a bullet wound, sustained during the battle of El Alamein. Correct me if I am wrong, Lieutenant Brill.'

I nodded.

We then went through the story I had told many times before, about how I was ambushed while travelling between the construction camp and Cairo.

'That is very interesting, Lieutenant Brill. Though we have

eyewitness evidence that you were shot by a colleague of yours during an argument. Can you tell us what that argument was about?'

III

You have never been shot, have you, Davies? You don't know the feel of a bullet passing through your loins. In fact, it is an event that happens so fast, you only ever experience it in retrospect. Fast is not the word. It seems to happen outside time altogether. A bullet travelling faster than the speed of sound hits you before news of its existence has reached your ears. In that way, it feels like an event with no dimensions at all. Like a religious experience, you could say.

*

It is perhaps a peculiar aspect of the camoufleur's life that by the time battle commences his work is done. The immense task of assembling the dummy regiments and putting them into position was eventually completed in the second half of October. I had been given, in strictest secrecy, the day and the hour of zero. There was nothing more for us to do. We had painted the scenery; now the play would start. It was a gorgeous golden day on which the sun seemed very reluctant to set. And out of the sun came Major Boone, his face awash with anguish, his whole frame shaking, a dazzled look in his eyes, tears streaming. He was ridiculous, like a clown.

'I wonder what makes you think you can take such liberties with a man.'

He said this in a low, tremulous growl, standing in the doorway of my tent.

'I don't know what you mean,' I said desperately. 'We both had a lot to drink that night.'

'You thought I wouldn't remember. You thought it would be forgotten for ever. But it's all come back to me, Brill. I can remember it as if it was an hour ago.'

His jowls were shaking with rage. The man hadn't shaved for two days. Ginger whiskers stood out like copper dust on his cheeks. The taste of his prick was still sharp in my mouth. The sight of his body, laid out on my bed, naked from head to toe, his skin flushed and glazed with the effort of a night of wonderful dancing, had filled my vision ever since. I couldn't help but feed. I had taken him in my hand, then my mouth. My lips had flown across the surface of his body, like a flounder over a seabed, exploring every golden outcrop and fleshy prominence. He had made noises that I took to be sounds of appreciation, gratitude, implorations to go further. I lay on top of him. Our bodies clamped together like scallop shells, we rolled across the bed, fell onto the floor. Just as we were about to conjoin, he seemed to wake up, to come to. Shock passed across his face. He pushed me away, scrambled for his clothes, stared at me, his cheeks trembling, as though I had beaten him about the face. I had never seen someone so frightened. His fear was so great he could produce no voice, but left the room backwards, as if to make sure I didn't attack him from behind.

I had wilfully misjudged the situation, just as Somarco had done with me all those years ago. I had been wondering, in the days since, what Major Boone might do by way of retribution.

'We have to keep our heads clear, Marcus. There's no time for any of this now.'

His eyes had lost all colour and become black.

'I'm sorry, Marcus. We drank too much, didn't we? Danced too much.'

He drew his pistol. It shook in his hand.

He was trying to find words, but they wouldn't come. Not at first, then he said, 'You – you're just a little painter and decorator.' He said it as though spitting out rotten food.

'I'm sorry, Marcus.'

He had taken a step forward, the gun still pointing at me, more steadily now.

'I was expelled from St Saviour's for brawling,' he said, puffing out his chest a little.

'Yes.'

'And I should have finished you off there and then.'

'Yes.'

'What makes you think you can take such liberties with a superior officer? Filth like you – you infest everything, like lice, you get in everywhere. You eat away the morals of good men.'

I don't even remember the shot. I was in the middle of saying something and the bullet didn't even make me stumble over my words.

IV

I pray, Davies, that you never fall ill in the desert. To be wounded by a bullet splicing one's nether parts like a knife through shit is bad enough, but then to have nothing but the lone and level sands in which to seek aid is little short of Hell. Thankfully my memory of those first few days is, like my abdomen, full of holes. I can remember surgery with little or no anaesthetic, I can remember a doctor talking openly about how I wasn't going to survive. I remember the feeling of flies walking around the precincts of my face, and being unable to lift a hand to brush them away, not even caring that I could not. At the dressing station I was patched up, then transported to the British Military Hospital in Alexandria, where I began to feel that I might recover. The building was a light and airy neo-classical structure, and was staffed mostly by female nurses, sweet things with red crosses on their white bosoms. The wards were high galleries, with chandeliers hanging from the vaulted ceilings and tall palms growing from pots. I suddenly fell into a swooning fever. My insides had become infected, my blood was poisoned, my whole body toxic. I endured more bouts of surgery and my life hung in the balance for many weeks. In all I spent nine months in Alexandria, and then, for some reason, I was moved to a hospital in Palestine. By now the Germans had more or less been driven out of North Africa. Allied soldiers were picking away at the soft underbelly of Europe, the Mediterranean was considered a safe route for shipping and so, with the shortened journey time, I was allowed to return to England.

I spent a further six months in a convalescent home in Oxfordshire, a dreamily beautiful place. Oh, you cannot think how sweet it was to smell cool English air after nearly three years in the desert, to hear English birdsong rather than the rasp of insects, the coarse cackling of ibis and other Egyptian birds.

About April I knew very little. I had not written to her since my injury, and I didn't know, at that time, if she had been informed by the authorities. I thought not, because the letters that came from her made no mention of the fact. I hadn't replied because I didn't know how. I didn't want to tell her that I was dying, when I had been, and then, after the event, I didn't want to tell her that I had been so close to death. And then I couldn't think how to account for my silence. But her letters continued to arrive, having followed a convoluted path across the world, arriving first at Cairo, then being forwarded to Alexandria, Palestine, then slowly back the way they had come, to arrive at last in Oxfordshire. She was still living in Derbyshire, with her parents. The little boy, Sebastian, whom I had never met, was now nearing his third birthday. What should I have done – picked up a pen and paper and written to the cement factory to tell her I was back in England?

As the months progressed the task became harder. I felt that I had betrayed her, and that Somarco was right: our marriage was a sham. My liaison with Marcus Boone had confirmed that for me. I did not belong with April. I did not deserve her.

My health gradually returned. The main disability – a severe pain in my groin area whenever I moved – was gradually subsiding, and my lower loins were returning to normal. The agony of urination and defecation was lessening, which meant that I could be put on a diet of gradually more solid foods. Like a baby, I had been feeding on possets and purées, soups and junkets, to the extent that I was beginning to think my teeth would soften, my jaws lose all their strength.

By the spring, the doctors told me I was ready to leave, but that I was unlikely to be fit for active service for another six months at the earliest. They would recommend that I be assigned to light, administrative duties for the foreseeable future. The only visitor I had in that time was Learmouth, who happened to be posted to Oxford. I was not very surprised to see him, as we had kept in touch during my hospitalization. He had told me about Somarco's disappearance. The half-Italian had left on a recceing mission to northern Palestine and had never returned. Officially he was missing in action, though there had been no reports of any fighting in the areas he was known to have visited. Knell was back in England, according to Learmouth, though he had no news of his precise whereabouts or activity.

Learmouth himself was now working in strategic operations alongside the intelligence service. His main work, he said, was in developing ways of spreading misinformation to the enemy. He had had the idea of writing fake letters to soldiers from their loved ones at home, with the intention that they would be found by the enemy. The letters would be full of misleading clues as to British plans for the war. 'Not an easy thing to do,' he said. 'The letter has to feel genuine, and the misinformation has to be subtly conveyed, but not so subtly that it's missed.' He wondered if it was work I might like to do. I said he must be mad if he thought I would be able to write a letter like that, but Learmouth seemed to think I had some sort of literary gift, from the letters I had been writing him, and the camouflage booklet had made an impression. 'Such a delightful little piece, all those case studies and imagined scenarios. You really do have a gift, Brill. I think you could write very convincing letters from a wife to her soldier husband.' I would have laughed all the louder had it not hurt so much.

In the meantime the doctors informed me that I was ready to leave. They assumed I had a family somewhere who could take care of me. A wife or mother? I had to say that my wife was not in a position to help me at the moment. Oh dear. Well, what about parents?

And so I returned to Heathrow.

*

I thought I had lost my desert eyes, Davies, when I returned to the Heath. By then I had become accustomed to greenery, to a leaden sky, to mist and rain. But when I arrived in the vicinities of Swan's Rest, I felt the desert perspectives return, and I had to struggle to see the English fields for what they were – arable land, starved, running to seed. It had been unusually hot. There had been a drought, I learnt. No rain of any significance had fallen for several weeks. The rivers were shrinking in their cracked beds, the ponds were evaporating – some had vanished altogether. I took a taxi from the station at West Drayton; the driver was a stranger to me, said he'd just moved out from Acton, bought one of the new houses they'd built in Hayes just before the war on one of the huge new estates that covered some old farmland.

When we crossed the Bath road into the land I had not seen for so long, I half feared it, too, would have been swamped by bricks and mortar, but I was delighted when we rounded the corner by the Three Magpies to find that we were in the lane itself, the one I'd trudged along to school so many times, whose hedges were thickening with bay and vetch, so tall they nearly touched over the road, and that scarcely anything had changed at all. I had to direct the driver, who'd never been to the Heath before, to take the right fork after we'd passed Old Hall, which I ducked to see as we went by – it seemed still to be empty.

But there was something wrong with the Heath, and it wasn't just due to the drought. There was much fallowness in the fields; many of the gardens were choked with weeds. The shit-heaps had gone, and there didn't seem to be many of the great stockpiles of sludgecake either. In short, the gardens were scrappy, untidy, overgrown, disused. There were fields where the crops had not been harvested the previous summer but had been left to rot – the beetroot had withered in its furrows; the thatch of the Morrises' was thick with vivid moss, the lanes were deep in weeds and becoming overgrown.

At Swan's Rest I was met by my mother in tears. They had been kept informed of developments, and I had replied politely to some of the letters they had sent me. But it was a shock for them to see me. 'We would have come to visit you, but travel now is so difficult, and your father – well, he's not as mobile as he was.'

My father seemed frail. The gloss had gone from his hair, which had turned a dark grey and was starting to thin on top. 'We thought of driving out to see you, son. But the car has packed up. Gearbox. But I'm finished with driving. You take the car out on the roads, these days, you're taking your life in your hands.'

'But the fields. What about the deal with Tiberius? How's the partnership going?'

My parents looked at each other.

'Why don't we have some dinner first? Mrs Rossiter has done one of her specials.'

'Wait,' I said. 'Tell me now if anything's wrong. Suspense is very bad for my health.'

My parents didn't seem to think I was joking, so my mother came straight to the point. 'There are going to be some changes on the Heath, Kenneth. It's all very secret, but the government has bought the land owned by the aerodrome, which they're going to expand.'

'The Fairey aerodrome? But that's good news, isn't it? Well, I know you don't like aeroplanes, Father, but it's better that it's properly developed, isn't it? It'll bring new trade into the area, perhaps.'

'You could look at it like that, Kenneth. On the other hand, the scale of the expansion took us all rather by surprise.'

'Will we lose some fields?'

'More than that.'

'How much more?' I suddenly noted the change of tone in the voice of my mother as she edged nearer to the truth of what lay afoot. Those looks I had taken for tiredness and surprise at my arrival had been looks of broken spirit, of deepest despair.

'I really think we should eat first, dear Kenneth.'

'How much?' I persisted. 'Surely you're not going to lose any of the Joys' land. Not after all the years it took you to acquire it.'

'Well, the government has special powers in wartime. It can take possession of any piece of land it wants.'

'Oh, God, no,' I said. 'So they're going to take those fields?'

'Yes, Kenneth. And not just those fields, but the old fields as well, the two by the road that were part of Larry's original inheritance.'

'But surely they can't build a new airport right up to the lane. It would be too near the houses.'

My parents exchanged glances again. This time my father spoke. He'd remained almost silent previously. 'Don't beat about the bush, Alicia. Let's tell the boy the truth. He's strong enough.' He turned to me. 'The whole lot's going. Not just the fields but the houses as well. The main runway will stretch from the back of Ferris's Farm, straight over Cain Lane, straight over the Plough and Harrow, all the way up to Perry Oaks. And that's just the main take-off and landing strip. They've got the taxiing runways, as they call them, running alongside, and eventually plans for a second runway that'll go from Hall Farm through the Ditch and over the Southlands estate, straight over the Heath to just south of the Fairey hangar. You've got no idea of the size of these things, son, the scale of what's planned . . .'

'But surely, I mean, what are they going to do – put Cain Lane under a tunnel?'

'He's saved the best bit for last,' said my mother.

'Yes. Well, where you and I and your mother are currently sitting, in this living room, will be situated between the two main runways.'

'What do you mean?'

'It's all going, son. The whole lot. Everything between the Bath road and the A30, everything from Barry's Farm up to the sludgeworks is being flattened. The fields will be dug up, the rivers and pools drained, everything covered with tarmac and cement. And this house, and all the houses in the whole of the Heath, every building, apart from the Fairey hangar, will be knocked down. This time next year, this living room will be under ten feet of cement.'

I was capable of nothing but silence as my father said those words, and for several minutes afterwards. I could see how hard he'd struggled to keep the tears back, but now they came, just one or two. He didn't seem to notice them.

I looked to my mother, as if for confirmation that my father was speaking the truth, that he wasn't reciting some horrible nightmare he'd had, but she was staring at the carpet, hiding her own tears.

Eventually I found something to say. 'But surely it can't all be settled. They must have to gain approval, get consent from the landowners . . .'

'Like your mother said, the government has special powers in wartime. They don't need planning consent, they don't need anything. They say there's a pressing need for a large air base with long runways in the south of England, so that they can carry on the fight in the Far East, and this is the ideal spot for one.'

Another long silence, which mother tried to deal with by changing the subject and talking about my sisters. Prudence and Angelica were doing very well. She hesitated a little before telling me that Angelica had become a land girl, and was working on a huge farm in the Midlands. 'She's been doing it for years, long before we heard about the plans for this area.' She was coping very well with her bereavement. 'A terrible thing to be a widow at such a young age. You never even met her husband, did you?' Prudence had joined the WRNS and was working as a telegraphist. Although it was astonishing to think of the girls in such unlikely roles, and though I was shocked to realize how little I'd kept in touch with them since leaving home, the news could do nothing more than chip away at the monolith of the other news.

'There must be a way of stopping it,' I said. 'In this day and age, you can't just bulldoze whole villages . . .'

My parents nodded slowly and emptily. They had thought the same, but were now resigned to the destruction of Swan's Rest.

Before I went to bed that night I had a moment alone with my mother.

'You'll be getting a decent payment from the government, at least,' I said. When she didn't answer, I pressed her on the subject.

'We will be given the market value for the house, yes.'

'And for the land?'

'I don't know, Kenneth. Your father isn't saying anything. It's best not to bring the subject up with him.'

She showed me the letter from the Air Ministry. '*Sir – I am instructed to inform you that the airfield at Heath Row is to be enlarged in the near future and it will be necessary for this purpose to take over your property . . .*'

'They have said nothing about where we are to go, what we should do. It is as though we've been invaded by a foreign power. There is no alternative but to comply and await our fate. Surely this is no different from the sort of letter the Jews of Berlin or Warsaw received when Hitler came in. What do you think?'

*

Over the next few days I found out more. My bicycle, the one I had been given by Roddy Joy, was still in the garage. I rode around the lanes, tentatively at first, fearful of the fragility of my loins. There were horrors around every corner. Demolition had already begun on Old Hall, which I hadn't noticed in the glimpse I'd had from the taxi. Curiously, the dismantling process seemed to be working from the inside out: the interior had been gutted, the plaster chipped away from the walls and the glass taken from the windows. Now, as I observed, there were men on the roof shearing the tiles off with pickaxes. They conducted this work in a slow, methodical, unhurried way. They paid me no attention even as I wheeled my bike up close to the front, which gaped doorless. I could see that the floors – boards and joists – had been removed.

I felt the pressure of tears. This was the fate that awaited Swan's Rest in as little as two months. That was the date given on the letter from the Air Ministry. Two months to vacate a house that had been in my father's family for generations. As I cycled further along the lanes I met more such instances of slow vanishing. I found Mr Morris and his son carrying a wardrobe out of their front door. It was an ancient thing that hadn't been exposed to sunlight for a hundred years. In the open air its flaked varnish and scuff marks glared horribly.

I stopped to talk to Mr Morris.

'This is madness. They expect you to leave with so little notice? Where can you go?'

To my surprise, Mr Morris was rather approving of the scheme to build a new air base. He seemed to see it as an opportunity to contribute to the war effort. A new base was essential, he said, to fight the war in the Far East. How well everyone had been drilled with that piece of information. 'They need long runways for the big aircraft that will carry troops and supplies to the other side of the world.' Apart from that, his son Jonas had got a job as one of the labourers. He'd been helping them with locating the drainage channels. All the water on the land would have to be pumped out. One of the surveyors had told him it would take several months just to do that, there were so many ponds and pools.

I didn't ask Mr Morris where he was going, or if he was getting properly compensated. I cycled on, feeling that I was travelling through a world that was being taken apart all around me. Fields of dead crops were being anxiously watered by farmers who'd learnt that they would be compensated only for live crops.

The Plough and Harrow was still open. My father said the landlord had promised to carry on pulling pints until the walls were falling about his ears. I cycled all the way to the Joys' farmhouse. As I arrived I chanced upon a family occasion: the whole clan were gathered on the front lawn for a photograph. I had never been so close to the house before – like Old Hall, it was a place that had governed my life from afar, and as I arrived I felt a sudden desire not to be seen by any of the Joys. There was Mr Joy, some of the daughters I remembered from the restoration of the carriage, a grandfather, some elders, and a parish priest I didn't recognize. They were arranged on various wooden chairs that had been brought out from the house, and a photographer with a large camera on a tripod was marshalling them into position. There was an air of funereal gloom about the gathering that was at odds with the brightness of the weather. Mr Joy saw me, and signalled for me to approach.

Mrs Joy, a woman I had never met before, greeted me as though I was a long-lost son. She came across the grass and hugged me, then led me by both hands to the others. I asked after Three Cylinders. He was abroad, of course, fighting.

'We heard so much about your heroic actions in Egypt, Kenneth. We are all really proud of you.'

And so I had my photograph taken with the Joys outside their magnificent old farmhouse, a few weeks before it was destroyed.

Perhaps it was that experience of record-making that gave me the idea of making my own record of the disappearing landscape. I returned to Swan's Rest and found what drawing materials I could in my old bedroom. Everything had been left as it was – my boxes of toys and my boyhood art things, but there wasn't much. I had to make a trip to the big art shop in Richmond to stock up on equipment, and then I spent every hour I could out in the landscape, recording as much detail as possible.

It astonished me to think that I had not done anything like that before. I was behaving like the great masters of landscape painting, setting off with my materials strapped to my back and seeking to immerse myself in the environment. I was lucky that the weather held good for long stretches at a time. I worked with an energy I'd never experienced before. I could paint and draw for three or four hours without a break, standing up. I began close to home, with a view of Swan's Rest and the cottages down the lane – my ancestral home looked finer than I had ever seen it, the walnut tree coming into leaf, the lawns and shrubberies lush and burgeoning, the fabric of the buildings seeming smooth and sweetly aged.

When I moved out beyond my home boundaries I became an object of interest, fascination even. I was constantly engaged in conversation; I had spectators, an audience. I talked to many people about the new air base and the destruction of the Heath. Many were appalled by what was happening. I heard many stories of hardship and unfairness, of people with nowhere to go. Some suspected they would be billeted with other families, like evacuees, or sent to emergency settlements, like prisoners of war. Many feared their families would be split up, that friends and loved ones would be scattered across wide areas. A few, like the Morrises, were stoically accepting of the new situation, even welcoming the work opportunities and the chance of a new life. But they were very few. Over all there was a sense of desolation, fear and lament.

I painted the lane from the gates. Then I painted the Morrises' house and its neighbouring cottages, by now empty. The Morrises had already gone. They'd loaded everything onto two high-siders pulled by the drays. They were the first in our part of the Heath to vacate their premises. I saw them go past our house, Mr Morris with a look of stern resolve on his face, refusing to glance to either side as he drove the horses, concentrating on the road ahead.

I soon felt there was too much to paint, too much to record. Even if I painted all day long every day it would have taken me years to record every building and every field. I concentrated at first, then, on the widest vistas, the broadest views, to get in as much of the disappearing landscape as I could, before dealing with more detailed scenes. I painted the Morrises' fields, with their silver poplars, the rows of shrivelled cabbages in the fields off Cain Lane, the leeks that had stood two seasons in Tucker's Field and were as hard as thorns. I thought about painting ripe crops in their place, but it was the deadness of the fields I wanted to record. I wanted Heathrow with all its wounds displayed, its abandoned crops and fallen fences, so that the future should know what had been lost here, and what agony there had been in taking it away. More painful to me were the little spots I came across that held a childhood significance. I made a tearful watercolour of Shepherd's Pool, where my sisters and I had made rafts with the other children and drifted among the water irises. Then the dark patches where Mr Joy's shit-heaps had been, and which I had thought to be mountains that would last for ever.

There were officials in the fields sometimes. Men in bowler hats with surveying equipment – theodolites, yardsticks, measuring wheels. I sometimes struck up a conversation with them, in a friendly manner, encouraging them to talk. Some were guarded and cautious; others were downright rude and told me to mind my own business. A few were more forthcoming, especially when they saw some of my work and were impressed by my skills. One in particular gave me a detailed outline of the plans, pointing, with his arms outstretched, to where the main runways would be, where the terminal buildings would eventually be raised and, most crucially from my viewpoint, where the perimeters of the whole area would be laid. I tried to conceal my shock as this gentleman outlined the dimensions of what was planned, my heart reeling at the vast areas that had been assigned for transformation. He described the processes that were required – how the land had to be thoroughly pumped dry of 'those blessed ponds' before any heavy machinery could be brought in, then how the top layer of soil would be removed to a level of ten feet in places. It wasn't until I had spoken to this man that I realized the new airport would have runways of cement – I had assumed they would be the same treated lawns as the Fairey aerodrome had but on a larger scale. But, no, the new runways were for the take-off and landing of giant aircraft, and would be huge deserts of stone, and beneath them, new systems of underground pipes for drainage and cabling. The Heath was not simply being built upon, it was being lifted out of the earth and removed. We were being dug out, down to a depth of ten feet. The man described all this with great enthusiasm and excitement. He said it was one of the biggest engineering projects ever undertaken and would result in the biggest aerodrome in the world. He said this, somehow, as though I should have been proud of the fact. The past was being swept away, and a glorious future would be delivered in its place. Where we were standing, not very far from Swan's Rest, would be near the centre of the whole complex. From this point, he said, the new aerodrome would stretch almost to the horizon in every direction.

I still managed to be polite to that man. He had imparted a wealth of information, and I finally grasped the reality of what was to come. I suffered with a vision, and have done so since then, of my mother and father standing on the lawn before Swan's Rest, in the shade of the walnut tree. But it is not the house that crumbles. It is them. They fall apart slowly before my eyes, as if they are made of sandstone. Small cracks appear across their bodies, which widen until large fissures open up, then pieces fall away, and there is nothing left of husband and wife but a little heap of dust.

V

'Do you recognize this picture, Lieutenant Brill?'

Captain Cunningham had called for the exhibit, and a little time had been spent arranging it on an easel so that the whole courtroom had a clear view. A large, blown-up aerial photograph, probably taken from around ten thousand feet. I was amazed that someone had taken the trouble to mount this image in a rather ornate wooden frame.

'Not immediately, no.'

'What do you surmise it to be?'

A big loop of track, several sidings, a length of platform and a series of what might have been loading ramps. So small it was hard to tell, but those were probably trucks on the line, and on the other side, a long row of vehicles, lorries probably, ready to transport people and equipment delivered by the trains. 'I would say it looks like a railway depot.'

'Excellent,' said the captain. 'And if I tell you that this photograph was taken by a British reconnaissance aircraft on the twenty-fifth of November 1941, would that help you?'

I knew already that the photograph was purportedly of the dummy railhead Somarco and I had built in the desert west of Fort Capuzzo, but by now I was in such a turmoil of thought, such a maelstrom of confusion about what was right and what was wrong, that I couldn't decide whether it would be wise or unwise to admit knowledge of this image. I remained silent.

'Are you having trouble remembering where you were on that date?' said the captain.

I realized it would be foolish to deny all knowledge of the photograph, and could see no reason why I should. 'No – it's just that I've never seen an air picture of it before. But, if I remember my facts correctly, then this must be the Capuzzo Dummy.'

'And perhaps you would care to explain to the court what the Capuzzo Dummy was.'

I jumped at the chance. Here was concrete evidence of my industriousness and ingenuity as a camoufleur. 'Well, it was part of a push against Rommel. We were preparing for a very heavy offensive against the Afrika Korps and the Eighth Army needed to move as much armour west as quickly as possible. So a railway was built with a railhead near Fort Capuzzo. I and my colleague were asked to do what we could to camouflage this railhead from the air. Well, we knew it would be nearly impossible to camouflage the real railhead, but what we could do was to build a dummy railhead a few miles further west, so that the real railhead would look like an insignificant halt on the way to the dummy railhead. We would thus lure the bombs away from the true railhead.'

'Ah, yes. What a clever plan. With all this back and forth between the fake and the real, it's no wonder you got confused.'

'Confused?'

'And this dummy railhead. When I first heard about it I must confess I was quite amazed that such a thing could have been possible. Again, perhaps you could explain to the court how such an operation would have been carried out.'

'Of course. We had long since understood how relatively simple it was to deceive the eye at ten thousand feet. At such a distance you cannot tell the difference between muslin and steel, between concrete and canvas. You can construct a tank, for instance, using any form of cheap fabric, pinned to a wooden frame. From ten thousand feet a tank is just a white oblong with a nose sticking out. A plane is just a cross shape. As long as it can cast a shadow, the eye will be fooled. The same goes, of course, for railway lines, locomotives and trucks. The rails were a problem because they had to have a metallic appearance, but we found that empty jerry cans could be quickly opened up and hammered into something that looked just like shiny steel rails from above. Of course, it took a lot of jerry cans to cover six miles, but the scale of operations in the desert meant that there was no shortage of such scrap materials. The trains and the trucks could be built just as we were later to build the dummy tanks at El Alamein – canvas, hessian, calico – whatever materials we had to hand, pinned to wooden frames, painted. It would take a couple of men an hour or so to build a lorry, or a tank, or a locomotive, once they'd got used to it. It was simple work. There were two of us in charge and we had a team of perhaps thirty assistants working for us. Including the tracks, it was a week's work to build the whole installation.'

'And very impressive it is too, I think the court will agree. You would not think for a moment, looking at this photograph, that this train was not a real train. If you look carefully you can see little puffs of smoke coming from the funnel.'

'Yes, that was Somarco's idea. It was a simple thing, just a question of burning some stuff and letting the smoke out through the funnel.'

'Excellent. And, I suppose, one other thing that would be necessary would be some movement in the depot. I mean, if the enemy took two photographs, even just a few hours apart, and saw everything in exactly the same position, that might arouse their suspicions, might it not?'

'That's right. And that is why we moved everything every

few hours. We would change the position of the trucks. We would move the locomotive onto a different track. Rearrange the sidings. Make it look as though it was a very busy depot.'

'And, of course, since everything was made of light wood and fabric, this could be done quite easily?'

'Yes. All the constructions had handles to make them easy to lift and carry. I once saw a rather brawny Scotsman pick up a tank on his own.'

There was some polite laughter. I was quite sure I was winning the approval of the court by now. They were clearly very impressed with the display of ingenuity and skill in my testimony.

'I think we can see evidence of this rearrangement if I reveal two other photographs. These were taken on the twenty-sixth and the twenty-seventh of June.' An usher brought out the two other photographs that had been stacked behind the original. 'And, if you look, the court will see how all the vehicles are in a different configuration – some trucks have gone, or are off down the track, others have been repositioned. Excellent. So tell me, Lieutenant, how do you assess the effectiveness of an installation like this?'

'Well, to put it quite simply, we can't be sure it has worked until it has been destroyed by the enemy.'

'I see. That's an odd thing, isn't it, when the success of something is only recognized when it is destroyed?'

'Yes. Every night we were praying for the bombs to fall.'

'And I understand you'd rigged the whole area with explosives, is that right?'

'Yes. If bombs had fallen on a real depot, there would be huge explosions as fuel tanks and weapons caches were hit and fires would have burnt for many days. We had to replicate such destruction with dynamite and oil tanks.'

'And were you successful, Lieutenant Brill?'

'Yes. It took two very anxious days, but on the third day there was an exceptionally heavy bombing raid on the depot. The Germans had dropped hundreds of tons of TNT on what was essentially empty desert. Moreover, they completely ignored the real railhead, six miles away.'

There was more laughter, even a little applause.

'And, of course, your dummy explosions went off and your pools of oil gave off black smoke for several days?'

'Yes, that's correct.'

'And how did that make you feel?'

'It made us feel elated. After a few aborted attempts it was the first time we had managed so convincingly to fool the enemy. It made everyone in command sit up and take notice, and realize that camouflage could be a vital tool in the war.'

'I see. It didn't make you feel disappointed at all?'

'Why on earth would I feel disappointed?'

'Well, all that work you put into it – and then it was destroyed.'

'But that was the point.'

'No, I don't mean all the work you put into the construction. I mean all the work you did in trying to warn the enemy that the installation was a dummy.'

There were some gasps around the courtroom.

'I'm sorry, Captain Cunningham, but I find what you have just said utterly incomprehensible.'

'Oh, I'm so sorry, Lieutenant Brill. I thought you understood. Well, let us take another look at these images of the dummy railhead. And the jury, please do look very closely, particularly at these.' He pointed with a stick to a part of the photograph. 'These are the trucks lined up by the platform ready to be loaded with whatever the train is carrying – troops, mostly, but also weapons, ammunition, food, goodness knows what else. And these are the tanks, APCs, DMVs that have just been rolled off the transport. Do you notice anything unusual about them?'

'No, not really.'

'Wouldn't you say they were parked in a rather odd formation?'

'How do you mean?'

'Well, normally you would expect troop carriers to be lined up in a row, one beside the other. The army likes everything arranged like that, don't they? In straight rows, serried ranks, et cetera.'

'Yes, I suppose so.'

'But these trucks, they're oddly spaced. There are gaps. Some are at right angles to their neighbours or parked halfway behind. It's very strange.'

'Well, like we discussed earlier, the idea was to create an impression of movement, of vehicles coming and going. Such a place isn't as orderly as you might think – there is movement and a certain amount of confusion.'

'Yes, I can see that. And at first I thought that explained the oddness of the positioning of these vehicles. Let's take an example. You see those trucks at the end?' He pointed with his stick again. 'One truck parked at right angles halfway behind the other. What shape does that make you think of? What sort of shape does it make?'

'I'm not sure what you mean.'

'Well, what I mean is that, to me and to other people who've seen it, it quite obviously looks like the letter T.' And then everything fell into place, about the officer's interest in the arrangement of the trucks. 'If I turn the picture the other way up, you see. There is no reason why the enemy should have any preconceived ideas about which is the right way up to view this scene, except that the railway line serves as a sort of line on which the words can be read. A line of writing. It's very clever, isn't it? You see, this group of trucks now forms the letter U, this one N and so on, in square block capitals.'

I looked hard. It was true: just as if I spilt a box of matches onto the floor, some would form letters (a lot of *x*s and *n*s, I should think), so these trucks did seem to form similar shapes, but then again many didn't, and in any case, no word was formed.

'It's just a random pattern,' I said. 'The trucks were meant to look as though they were moving around, to make it look busy, like I've said.'

'Yes, you have said that. But you accept that these first trucks could be a U and the second could be an N?'

'Yes, I suppose so.'

'Well, this next group of trucks is quite clearly an E. And so on. Of course, the sizes are mixed and uneven, the spacing irregular, which all helps to disguise the message.'

'Message? You think these trucks were spelling out a message?'

I looked at Davies, then around the court, desperate for some recognition that Cunningham had gone mad. There was none. Everyone was staring at the photographs with mouths agape.

'Look next – the letter C is a little clumsily formed, and we have a very untidy lower-case *h*. Then there is a large gap – then another lower-case letter, this time a *t*.'

And there we have it. Put them all together and what do they spell? He was quite right. Looked at in that special way, down there, ten thousand feet below, as plain as anything for anyone who was looking for a message, out of the ribbed and strafed expanses of sand, the word 'UNECh t' appeared before my eyes.

'And how's your German, Lieutenant Brill?'

'My German is not very good, sir.'

'Well, in that case let me help you. The German word *Unecht* generally translates as "unreal" or "false". It is the word

Nietzsche uses to cast doubt on the existence of God. When Werther laments his lost love, Maria, or describes the evanescence of Wertenberg, Goethe chooses that particular word to express his feelings of impermanence. It is a word that echoes down the halls of German romantic philosophy. Have you read the works of Mr Nietzsche, Lieutenant Brill?'

VI

I was back in the desert, watching Somarco directing things, marvelling at the effort he was putting into building a realistic installation, the way he took charge of the men, wouldn't rest, not for a minute. Sometimes we looked up to see if we could discern the enemy spy planes. Occasionally they were visible as little bubbles of silver drifting in the deeper blue of the zenith, but they were quickly lost in the vastness of the sky. What had they seen from up there? And back in their photographic labs, what did they make of what they had seen? The analysts poring over the aerial photographs, discussing and conferring with each other. Pointing things out to each other with the tip of a pencil.

'Movement, Kenneth, we have to keep things moving. If everything stays where it is, the game will be given away.'

Another spy plane circling, seven hours after the last. Another set of photographs. The analysts pore over them again, comparing and contrasting. See these trucks? They haven't moved in seven hours. That train still billowing smoke from its funnel hasn't moved a centimetre. We had to keep changing everything. Move the loco onto a siding. Change the number of carriages. Put some carriages onto a siding. Put some trucks onto the front of the loco. Somarco was out all day with a team of men shifting the components of our railhead from one place to another. Restlessly.

I played very little part in this endless reconfiguring. I thought it unnecessary. Change things once every few hours, if at all. Not this constant shuffling of the deck. But, then, I wasn't trying to spell things out to the readers in the sky, and in such a way no one on the ground would have had a second thought about it. Why park one truck at right angles to another? Because it's doing a three-point turn. Don't have everything in orderly rows: it will look false, too static. No, Somarco, not even you could have spelt out that word, could have thought of it, could have directed everything on the ground so that our men were unwittingly writing a letter to the spies. But, then, why did you take such a hand in the arrangement? You didn't just tell the boys to get out and rearrange the trucks and leave them to it. You walked up and down the rows of sham lorries making sure there wasn't one that was out of place. It would take only one misplaced truck, after all, to ruin the giant typeface you had constructed. And then an hour later you would do it all again, but further down the row, so that no one would suspect you were keeping the same pattern intact. You chose the shortest word you could think of to convey that message. Just six letters.

So there was real care taken in that shuffling. Not chaos, but order. You had it all planned out, and when, after three days, nothing happened, what triumph you must have felt, how relieved that your message had got through to those tiny bubbles in the sky. Still the rearranging went on. Perhaps you let the word disappear now, so that no one would start wondering why you wanted three trucks at right angles to two others every time, to spell the letter E. Let the word dissolve and so acknowledge to those distant readers that they had understood. Because you did become less controlling in the process of rearrangement, after three days. You thought you had done your job, that the word had been read.

But no bombs fell on the real railhead either. That should have given you pause. But I didn't see anything in your eyes. You looked at the sky with the same laden curiosity as I. We were like two astronomers of the old school, watching the heavens unaided, trying to discern the movements of wandering stars, but in daylight. The raids only came in daylight, when there was something to see. Night-time bombers would always have dropped their bombs into a vast lake of darkness. And then the bombers came. With horrific suddenness they ploughed the sky, crenellated, cruciform. We ran for our shelter, and the charges that had been primed. A direct hit would have killed both of us but the bombs fell all about us – we were like bees caught in a shower that, by chance, are not touched by a single drop and remain dry. I thought we embraced at that point, do I misremember? I thought we embraced as the bombs landed. I thought we kissed at the moment the charges went off, and we were amid chrysanthemums of flame, a firestorm that we had conjured and orchestrated, immune and unassailable at its centre.

*

Davies came to my cell again. Alone.

'Am I to be hanged?' I said.

He smiled.

'You know the result. Why do you have to ask?'

He pulled the chair out from under the table, and sat on it, crossing his legs, leaning back, hands folded in his lap, contemplating me like a father might his wayward son.

'Did they consider hanging me?'

'Don't flatter yourself, Brill. I'm afraid they regard you as nothing more than a nuisance who must be kept out of the way, like someone's mad aunt, until the war is over.'

'And then?'

Davies shrugged. 'Who knows? The world will be a new one, by then. Perhaps if they ever find that Italian friend of yours, he will be hanged. Your friend Learmouth said he never came back from the Middle East.'

'I know. I hope he never does.'

'I doubt he will, even if he could.'

We were silent for a moment.

'And will I be kept here, in this particular cell, for however long the war lasts?'

'Of that I have no idea. Does it matter?'

We were silent again. Like two actors in a rather grim mime, it seemed we suddenly remembered our roles, which were to say everything without use of words. Davies stood up, gave me a nod, then held out his hand. We shook. Then, turning smartly and suddenly, he strode towards the door. He was about to call the guard to let him out, when he turned again.

'Almost forgot. The whole reason for my visit. That man Learmouth – he has a little job for you.'

'A job?'

'Yes. Seems to think you'd be good at it. Something about writing fake letters to divert the enemy. Useful war work you could do without leaving your cell. Wants you to write letters in the voice of a wife writing to her serving husband. I wondered if that wasn't a job better suited to a female, and he just smiled. What do you make of it?'

*

My parents have not visited, though they write, now and again. They are still in Swan's Rest, though they are nearly the last residents left on the Heath. The Joys have gone already, and have found a nice house north of Sipson. They have offered to put my parents up, if they can't find anywhere else. My mother writes of the suggestion with undisguised scorn. The Heath is already crowded with navvies and bulldozers, she tells me. The heavy work will begin soon.

18 Ash Tree Lane
Nr Woodbridge
Suffolk

Dearest Kenneth,

I hope you are well. I am well, and so are the children. They miss you very much and they are very proud of you. Sebastian and Alexandra. And Hugh. Who would have thought someone like you could produce such healthy offspring? Or such pretty ones?

I find it hard to remember what you look like. The other day I realized I don't have a single photograph of you. Not even a wedding photograph. We should really have organized that, shouldn't we? Are you handsome? I suppose you must be, otherwise I wouldn't have married you, would I? Does it matter what you or I look like to each other?

Where are you? These days I simply send these letters care of your regiment, and they could send them anywhere in the world. Why do you never write back? What secret are you hiding from me? Are you alive? How could you answer that?

I have gone mad. It is the lack of sleep. The noise, it just doesn't stop. The marching soldiers – they march right past the window, all through the day and all through the night. Then there are the vehicles churning, growling, barking. It seems the entire military might of the British Empire is assembling outside my bedroom window. Well, it is all for the good. Bernadette next door said they are massing an invasion force – the long-awaited second front. I went down to the seafront on my bike yesterday and I have never seen so many ships in my life; they were all hidden, filling every channel and inlet, anywhere where the water was deep enough, and all along the coast, hidden beneath huge camouflage nets, and thousands of soldiers – Americans, Australians – it was as though they were building a new country at the edge of our own. They are going to cross the North Sea from the Suffolk coast to land in Belgium – quelle surprise!! Not sure when but it must be soon – pray for its success, Kenneth, and before long the Germans will have been defeated.

And what a strange world will then emerge, eh, Kenneth? Can't imagine what peace would be like. If I think about it, I imagine a row of suburban gardens in which the fences have been knocked down by a tornado, so all the gardens have merged into one, and all the people come out of the houses and cross over into each other's gardens, because they can't tell which is which – where one ends and another begins. And if I think about it long enough they start embracing each other, and kissing each other, and before long they are all making love on the lawns with the splintered fences flat on the ground around them, a bit like an orgy, but more decorous and English.

And then the dream ends when I see someone with a hammer and nails, putting a new fence post in the ground. The new world will have boundaries as well, won't it? And as long as there are boundaries, there can be wars. How will we stop it happening again?

Do you think, when you have come back to life and have stopped being a little character in a story that I tell myself, that we can love one another?

Whatever else I can think of to say I will leave till the next time I write a letter.

Meanwhile I am waiting for you, waiting waiting waiting
With love
April

ACKNOWLEDGEMENTS

During the research for this novel I came across many wonderful books and authors, far too many to acknowledge individually, though two were particularly important. In Africa, Kenneth Brill follows closely in the footsteps of Geoffrey Barkas, whose delightful memoir *The Camouflage Story* provided much useful detail. Otherwise Brill and Barkas bear little similarity. In Heathrow the local historian Philip Sherwood has done much to illuminate the past of this neglected corner of England, and his books have been invaluable. The librarians of Uxbridge library shed some further light on forgotten corners. The barmaid and locals at the Three Magpies, which stands on the A4 and marks what was once the turning for Heathrow, are thanked for their help and interest. Bath Spa University provided me with some spells of research leave, without which this novel would have been first published in 2016. At Picador Paul Baggaley's insights helped me make this a better novel, and thanks, as always, to my wonderful agent Zoe Waldie. The Authors' Foundation also helped me through a difficult patch. Part of this novel was written in Chicago while I was writer in residence at Columbia College. I am very grateful to students and staff there for their friendship and hospitality, and especially to Patty McNair, for initiating the whole thing. There is nothing like having an office overlooking a frozen Lake Michigan for concentrating the mind on writing about rural England. Thanks to Terry Gifford and Gill Round for the use of their cool house when mine got too hot. If there is anyone else who has helped me along the way and I have forgotten about you, I'm sorry. To any others whose lives and worlds I've borrowed and messed about with – I apologize. The hamlet of Heathrow was destroyed by a disgraceful misuse of wartime powers by the British government; that it was allowed to happen shames us all.

picador.com

blog
videos
interviews
extracts